THE WHISTLE BLOWER

LIBRARIES NI
WITHDRAWN FROM STOCK

LIBRARIES NI
WITHDRAWN FROM STOCK

Robert Peston is ITV's political editor, presenter of the politics show 'Peston', founder of the education charity, Speakers for Schools (www.speakers4schools.org), and vice president of Hospice UK. He has written four critically acclaimed non-fiction books, *How Do We Fix This Mess?*, *Who Runs Britain?*, *Brown's Britain* and his latest, *WTF?*, which was described by the *Financial Times* as 'mandatory reading' for anyone seeking to understand Brexit, Trump and the collapse of confidence in western liberalism.

For a decade until the end of 2015, he was at the BBC, as economics editor and business editor, and in the 1990s he was at the *Financial Times*, as political editor, financial editor and head of investigations. At the BBC he played a prominent role in exposing the causes and consequences of the credit crunch, banking crisis and Great Recession. Peston has won more than 30 awards for his journalism, including Journalist of the Year and Scoop of the Year (twice) from the Royal Television Society. *The Whistleblower* is his first novel.

Find him on his blog at itv.com/robertpeston, on Facebook at facebook.com/pestonITV, and on Twitter @peston.

ROBERT PESTON

THE WHISTLE BLOWER

ZAFFRE

First published in the UK in 2021
This edition published in 2022 by
ZAFFRE
An imprint of Bonnier Books UK
4th Floor, Victoria House, Bloomsbury Square,
London WC1B 4DA
Owned by Bonnier Books
Sveavägen 56, Stockholm, Sweden

Copyright © Robert Peston, 2021

All rights reserved.
No part of this publication may be reproduced,
stored or transmitted in any form by any means, electronic,
mechanical, photocopying or otherwise, without the
prior written permission of the publisher.

The right of Robert Peston to be identified as Author of this
work has been asserted by him in accordance with the
Copyright, Designs and Patents Act, 1988.

This is a work of fiction. Names, places, events and
incidents are either the products of the author's
imagination or used fictitiously. Any resemblance to
actual persons, living or dead, or actual
events is purely coincidental.

A CIP catalogue record for this book is
available from the British Library.

ISBN: 978–1–83877–526–1

Also available as an ebook and an audiobook

1 3 5 7 9 10 8 6 4 2

Typeset by IDSUK (Data Connection) Ltd
Printed and bound in Great Britain by Clays Ltd, Elcograf S.p.A.

Zaffre is an imprint of Bonnier Books UK
www.bonnierbooks.co.uk

To my darling sister Juliet

Chapter 1

ALL THAT INTERESTS ME IS the narrative, the story, and who controls it. As a glory-seeking journalist, I sometimes reveal scandals. But more often I try to find out what the powerful in politics and business are planning, so that I can reveal it before they have the opportunity to impose their interpretation, their spin. In my more pretentious moments, I justify what I do as empowering 'the people' to make up their own minds about how they are governed. Most of the time I am just having fun, pissing off ministers, chief executives, their minders, putting their secret schemes on the *FC*'s front page. If London is a collection of villages, I am the pedlar who wanders between the communities of politicians, financiers and businessmen, trading nuggets of information until I have enough to tell a tale that you'll pay to read. Britain's capital is vast *and* claustrophobically small. Everyone who matters knows everyone else who matters. My job is to eavesdrop, then share it with you.

Tonight, I have an appointment that I hope will furnish me with a grade B scoop. Not something wholly unexpected, but in this time of general-election fever, a nugget that will sizzle at

1

the top of the front page of the influential newspaper that pays me to make mischief. So on this windy wet evening in early March, I am pedalling south-west down Shaftesbury Avenue, past Formica-furnished Chinese restaurants and all-night super-markets, rainwater cascading down my cycle helmet, blurring my contact lenses. The English winter is blowing itself out with a cathartic storm that is sweeping the pavements clean. Commuters struggle with umbrellas, black cabs' headlights are the mournful eyes of the hounds of Andersen's Tinder Box.

I swerve left to avoid the mirrored surface of a water-filled pothole, right around the stationary 38 bus. Fiennes and Scott Thomas are snogging on the side for *The English Patient*. I catch the driver's eye. It's a superstitious thing I do, giving thanks that he didn't swing out and flatten me. He stares, just for a second. He's wondering why on earth I would be out here under these curtains of water. I only half notice the rain because I am plot-ting how to land my mackerel; a story about the new darling of British politics, the prince of hope, Labour's immaculately groomed and smooth young leader, Johnny Todd.

I know something is up, that Todd is planning one of his trademark policy coups, because my calls to his advisers are not being returned. My hunch is that they'll want to announce whatever it is on Thursday morning, to set the agenda for one of the last Prime Minister's questions before the looming election. Which means they'll place it on Wednesday night in friendly newspapers – via the political hacks who take their dictation – to set the agenda for the *Today* programme the following morning. It will be a wheeze to woo the right-wing press, to reinforce Todd's big claim that his party of the left won't punish success and the successful. Or maybe Todd will wrap himself in the Union flag.

One Nation, that's the conceit he wants to steal from the Tories, I mutter, as I glance left at the oncoming traffic, weigh the odds, and swerve right into Dean Street. It's only when I am heading to the junction with Old Compton Street that I curse my risk assessment: I could have skidded under the wheels of the approaching Mondeo.

My obsession is blowing up all politicians' best-laid plans, regardless of party or ideological allegiance; to nick the information first, interpret it in my own way and blitz it on the *FC*'s front page. My reward? The knowledge that when the *FC* first edition drops, my scoop will prompt night editors to ring up my rivals, pissed or asleep, to bollock them for missing the story. To earn this joyous *Schadenfreude*, I have to deploy shameless skills of persuasion, to persuade one of Johnny Todd's colleagues that I know more than I do and that I'm doing him a favour by listening to him. It's a spiel, but it usually gets me there.

I shoot across Old Compton Street, checking traffic in both directions. The revolving door of The Groucho Club is on my right. Even in the pissing rain, the vagrant who always asks for neither more nor less than 50p is in his spot next to the entrance with his right hand outstretched; no anorak, sodden in a fraying brown polyester jacket, flowery shirt and purple-stained flared trousers, new when Bolan was God. 'Gimme 50p,' he says. 'Fifty pence for a cup of tea.'

I blank him as I slide the U-bend of the steel lock around the stanchion of a street sign and then guide it between the spokes of my front wheel and around the bike frame. I attach the top bar of the lock, turn the key, and give it a close inspection to make sure the bike is secure. I wiggle the top bar to check it really is set properly. Even when done, I panic that I haven't locked it properly. So I wiggle it again. And again. And once more. Definitely done.

I walk to the door.

'Gimme 50p.'

My loose change is in my trouser pocket, underneath my silver Gore-Tex waterproof trousers. I wriggle my fingers inside the elastic waist. The first coin I feel is – 50p! An omen. I drop it into his palm, careful my fingers don't brush his.

The storm is hushed as I go through the spinning door into the club's low-ceilinged vestibule. I remove my helmet, peel off the protective outerwear and check myself in the mirror. The wide-lapelled, oversize-cut jacket and matching grey trousers – Dries Van Noten – have kept dry, though there's a bit of annoying damp around the collar. My top two shirt buttons are undone, and my round-toed shoes from Trickers are scuffed. I'm unkempt, by design, just messy enough so that not everyone can spy my vanity.

'Hi, Gil,' says Petra, the jolly guardian of the signing-in book. She gingerly takes my wet outer coat and trousers, holds them in thumb and forefinger as far from herself as possible, and drapes them on a hanger to drip in the cloakroom behind her.

'I'm expecting a guest,' I say. 'I'll be in the downstairs bar.'

As I push open double doors into the long drinking room, the chatter crashes over me. It's 8.15 p.m., still too early for Jools Holland to be at the upright piano that stands between the bar and the club restaurant. I grab one of the fat sofas by the front window and while I wait, I check my pockets: two Nokia 2110 mobile phones, one for normal, one for special contacts; and my pager. I am obsessive about always being reachable. It's not uncommon for me to have three conversations on the go: one on each of the mobiles and another on the office landline. My editor dines out on tales of me ringing him and then putting him on hold. I should be embarrassed, but no, I am flattered.

Silver Nokia in the left pocket, blue Nokia in the right. And in my right trouser pocket ...

Nothing. I should feel the familiar bulge of the pager pressing against thigh, instead there is just a crumpled handkerchief. I pat myself all over, left pocket too. It's not there.

Could it have fallen out when I was cycling? That seems unlikely, given all my clothes were sealed by the Gore-Tex outerwear. Could it be in the pocket of the wet-weather overtrousers, or the back pouch of the waterproof jacket? I wouldn't have risked it. I check every pocket again, and a third time. I know I look mad. And then I remember. The 50p. The pager must have spilled out then when I was handing it over. It was raining so I wouldn't have noticed when it hit the ground. I run for the door. It's still pissing down and there's nothing on the wet pavement. The beggar has vanished.

I can get another pager, but that's not the point. I hate it when things aren't where they should be, it's an itch to scratch. To calm myself, I chant one of my spells. It has to be short, and repeated a specific number of times (three and seven are normally good; five works sometimes too, as does saying 'times infinity'). Under my breath, I say, *'If it's gone forever, that's OK.'* Then I mutter it twice more. Relief steals over me.

I've been using these rituals to cope since I was in my teens. I never trusted my parents to have locked the front door or turned off the gas. I would press the knob on the hob seven times, making an indentation in my finger, and then stare at it. I would do this at two in the morning, when everyone else was asleep. Mum and Dad never noticed. But my sister Clare would come down to find her anxious little brother and steer me back to bed. It was Clare, when we were both at university, who gave my rituals a name; she asked me how I was coping with my 'obsessive compulsive disorder'. Clare usually knew more about me than I did.

In The Groucho's vestibule, I have one more thing to do. I descend the narrow staircase to the men's room. In the cubicle, I take a pinch of lumpy white powder from the cling film I've repackaged it in and begin a little ceremony with a Barclaycard on the top of the cistern. I am an unusual user; when strung out and unable to focus, this stuff calms me.

Two and a half snorts later, I'm myself. It is a wonder drug. Back upstairs, Petra tells me my guest has arrived; she shooed him to the bar. Tony Cannon, the Labour MP for Preston, is sitting by the window on the sofa I nabbed. He's my age, mid-thirties, though I carry it better. His skin is rough, the colour and texture of cottage cheese, eyes deep in his greying sockets. His suit is a size too big. Unlike mine, it's not a fashion statement. My grandmother would have told him he needs a good meal. Actually, what he needs to do is cut down the substance abuse. His red eyes dart like a cornered rabbit, obviously a line or two ahead of me.

'What do you fancy to drink?'

'Champagne?'

'Flippin' 'eck Tony. You have become the living embodiment of Todd's Modern Labour.' I catch the eye of the waitress.

If Todd is an abrupt rupture from Labour's past, Tony Cannon is an evolutionary link. Perhaps the last authentic working man at the top of Modern Labour, complete with never-pressed C&A suit, he left school to become a train mechanic, then an organiser with the Transport and General Workers' Union.

The champagne arrives and I swap it for my gold card.

'Here's to Keir Hardie,' I toast.

'Keir isn't testing well in focus groups,' he says grimly.

'How's Johnny?' I ask, aware that I am treating Tony Cannon like the boy at school who was interesting only because his sister was hot.

'The supreme leader is in the peak of health.'

Johnny Todd is the closest thing to Hollywood that British politics has seen since, well, ever. Cannon is Johnny's ambassador with the trade unions, trying to allay their fears that Todd's programme to make them electable is a despicable attempt to turn Labour into a red-tinged Tory party. Some of my colleagues in the Lobby see Cannon as Todd's *useful idiot*. More fool them. Cannon has acute political nous and he is part of the Labour movement in a way that Todd never could be. Theirs is a relationship based on mutual need.

What matters most about Cannon is that he knows pretty much everything that is happening inside his party. He is one of a small clique on this island at the fulcrum of knowledge. Some are bankers and corporate brokers, others are in the despised industry of PR; a handful are in politics. I've found and cultivated them. The innate snobbery of my journalistic colleagues – and indeed in the group that surrounds Todd – mean few take him seriously. When he leaks, no one suspects him. Perfect.

I grab a fistful of The Groucho's stale Twiglets from the small bowl on the table and stuff them in my mouth, brushing my fingers together to remove the stickiness. 'Much going on, Tony?'

He lowers his voice and leans across the table. 'I've got a big scoop for you, Gil: there's a bloody election coming. So yes, there's a great deal going on.'

The election date hasn't been announced. But the maximum five-year term for Parliament is almost up. Everyone who cares knows that the Prime Minister, Sir Peter Ramsey, will go to the country at the beginning of May.

'Have you seen today's *Mail*?' he asks. Course. I read it at quarter to seven this morning, along with every other paper. Cannon pulls a battered copy out of his bag and spreads it open.

WHO'S IN CHARGE? says the headline. Below it, there's a photograph of two men standing outside an office building. One is Todd. To his left, in a brown corduroy suit, is Dennis Kenilworth. Kenilworth has his muscular arm around Todd's waist, like a wrestler's clinch. Johnny is wearing his trademark grin, but here it is the forced smile of a prisoner in a hostage video.

Cannon turns to the *Mail*'s leader column. *Johnny Todd may promise a break from the past,* it reads. *But yesterday the Labour leader was photographed arm in arm with the most militant socialist in Britain, Mr 'Strike first, negotiate later'. If this is the company he keeps, how can we be confident that Labour in power won't yet again revert to its true colours of crushing the enterprise that pays all our bills and taxing all of us till the pips squeak?*

'Johnny almost blew the roof off HQ when he saw that,' Cannon says. He closes the paper and puts his drink on Kenilworth's face, ringing it like a target.

'What do you expect from the *Mail*?'

'The truth would be a good start. Feels like the last election all over again, tabloids killing us with vicious scaremongering about our income tax plans.'

'Don't be so neurotic. Your lead is huge.'

8

'Don't let Johnny hear you say that.' He actually scans the room. 'He's convinced the Tories will turn it around – with the help of your lot.'

'What do you mean, my lot? The *FC* said it was time for a change.'

'I mean Breitner. The *Globe*.'

He's winding me up, deliberately. The *Globe* is a tabloid, a megaphone for the views of its owner, the South African-born billionaire Jimmy Breitner. My paper, the *FC* – the *Financial Chronicle* – is one of the most respected business papers on the planet. Breitner owns us too, but our editorial independence is sacrosanct. Or at least, that's how I persuade myself it's OK to work for him.

'*Tax nightmare if Labour wins*. We never recovered from that.' He takes a slug of champagne. The glass looks small in his hand. Five years ago, the Conservatives snatched a win in injury time. Of course Todd is paranoid. Only losers aren't.

But my thoughts are focusing. *Tax nightmare?* That's the second time he's mentioned tax.

'When are you announcing that you won't increase the basic rate of tax?' I bluff, as if it's a widely known fact.

'Fuck off.'

Classic Cannon: a non-denial denial. Time for my first educated fib.

'Thursday, I'm told.'

'How the fuck do you know that?'

Bingo.

'But what really interests me is what you'll do on the top rate of tax.'

'Now you can really fuck yourself.'

9

I smirk. 'OK. But there is another story I am working on that would be of interest to you.'

Cannon takes the bait. 'What?'

'I've got a recording of a senior T&G official telling me that Johnny promised to put your friend Kenilworth in the House of Lords.' I don't have such a recording. But there are rumours Kenilworth is in line for a peerage if Labour wins the election. 'BROTHERS IN ERMINE – not a bad headline.'

'You're not really going to write that?'

'Why not?'

'It's not true.'

'I have the recording.'

He stares at the picture of Kenilworth.

'But obviously I am more interested in your tax plans ...'

'We haven't made any announcements.' He snaps a Twiglet in half and crumbles it into splinters and dust.

'Todd can't leave himself vulnerable on this.'

'Correct.'

'So he'll say he's not putting up the basic rate. Right?'

'I am not confirming that.' But he's also not denying it.

'If I run that, will I look stupid?'

Cannon looks at his empty glass. Even with coke and champagne in his system, spilling party secrets is not second nature. He sighs.

'You won't look stupid.'

And there's the story. BASIC RATE WON'T RISE UNDER LABOUR GOVERNMENT. Not too shabby. Admittedly I prefer finding out when a cabinet minister has fiddled his taxes, or a civil servant has been entertained in a lap-dancing club by a private-sector contractor. But this is real news. Probably the splash.

I knock back the rest of the fizz, and my hand's already halfway in the air to attract the attention of the young waiter whose manner suggests she is doing me a favour by taking an order. But I am also thinking I should get to the office to write this up.

Cannon is folding his copy of the *Mail*. That story really got to Todd. He'll want to make a big noise, something that'll force the *Globe* and the *Mail* to re-evaluate their assumption that he's a socialist wolf in a Hugo Boss suit.

I turn to Cannon. 'What about the top rate of tax?'

He lifts his hollow eyes. 'What about the top rate?'

'What will Todd say about that?'

'You're a piece of work. You've got a story with the basic rate.'

A Labour party promising that taxes won't go up for nurses and teachers is important, but neither brave or all that surprising. But a pledge not to go after the incomes of bankers and stock-brokers? That would be sensational. It would be Todd sticking two fingers up to those Labour members and trade unionists for whom it is a moral duty to at least put the rich on warning that Labour is out to get them.

'In terms of symbolism, tax on higher incomes, that's more important for Labour. Todd is desperate to have business on side so he'll promise not to increase the top rate. Now I think of it, it's obvious.'

Cannon says nothing.

'You've gone quiet,' I say. 'Let's be clear, Tony, if you tell me now that it's not true, I won't run it.'

'I am not saying anything.'

'So you're not denying it?'

He stays silent.

11

'Look. This conversation is not happening. We both know that. But to repeat, if I write that on Thursday Todd will set out that the party's manifesto will include promises not to increase either the basic or top rate of taxes, is that my career over?'

I am beginning to get the telltale adrenaline surge from landing a big exclusive.

'I wish it was. But not this time.'

'OK. Wow. Thank you.'

'Do me a favour, Gil.' He leans forward. 'No fingerprints. And be a bit vague on the timing.'

'No problem.' I have the story. I can be magnanimous.

It is 9 p.m. I need a polite way to end the conversation so I can ring my news editor and see if there is any way to shoehorn the story on to the front page for the second and third editions. I hate sitting on a scoop – there is always a danger that someone else will get the story.

But Cannon is already getting up. 'I think I'll make a move,' he says. 'Back to the barricades.' He looks as dejected as ever, despite the booze and drugs, and heads for the exit.

I start composing the story in my head. But it's interrupted by the habitual nagging voice of self-protection. How do I know I haven't been played by Cannon? Maybe he always planned to give me the story for reasons I can't quite fathom. Maybe he wants to damage me by telling me a pack of lies – again for reasons I can't quite see right now. The problem with being scoop-obsessed is that there are risks – risks of being manipulated, or just getting stuff wrong. I play the percentages. There are no guarantees I'll be right.

But mostly I am, I remind myself.

I leave the bar to ring Mary Nichols, the *FC*'s news editor, in the underlit hall by the reception desk. Just then, the Nokia screen lights up, accompanied by the distinctive plinkety-plink ringtone. I register the digits. It is a phone number I know as well as my own, but I haven't seen for months. I hadn't expected to see it for a few more.

My thumb hovers over the keypad, moving between the green button and the red. I don't want to take this call. Even if I wanted to speak to her, I need to phone in the story. I can't waste time.

But then again, she never rings at this time. Maybe it is something important. Fuck. I'll give her five minutes. I press the green button.

'Hello, Mum.'

Chapter 2

I T'S 4 A.M. AND I'M in a windowless, airless room next to intensive care in St Thomas's Hospital; the 'Friends and Relatives Room'. The pale hospital green is supposed to soothe, but has become an annoying visual muzak behind my gnawing anxiety. I've been here for six hours, the heating is giving me brain fug and the brown vinyl armchair, which squeaks each time I try to find a position of minimal comfort, has made my back ache. This is supposed to be a sterile environment but I feel as if I am in a Petri dish. I've already washed my hands three times and have spent the last half hour resisting the urge to do so again. The champagne and coke in my system have been metabolising and the whirring in my head is returning. The idea that my sister's life is in danger is a vice around my chest. Deep breaths are impossible, just shallow inhales into the top of my diaphragm. I chant 'God, let me die first' five times, to ward off the growing panic.

The moment I saw Mum's number on the Nokia's screen I knew something was up. She never rings my mobile. If I don't call her (and I rarely do), we don't speak. My first thought was something must have happened to Dad.

15

'Hi, Mum.' Before she even speaks I yawn. It's a reflex.

'Clare has had an accident.' *Eccident*. My mother's a grammar-school girl from the East End, but when stressed her accent is Buckingham Palace. 'She's in St Thomas's ICU. It's bad, Gilbert.'

'*What*? What's happened?'

I tried to turn away from the noise in The Groucho's reception. I was in the corner by the slatted blinds of the tinted window and facing a YBA line drawing of a crack pipe. I must have misheard. 'Tell me again, I don't understand!'

'Clare is hurt. You need to help.'

At this admission of powerlessness, I felt sick with dread. The blurry lights from the street fused with the alcohol, the din.

'We had a call from Jeremy. He said —'

'Who's Jeremy?'

'Jeremy is Clare's PA.' Her anxiety has made her cross with me. 'He phoned to tell us she'd been knocked off her bike, turning on to the Embankment. It's her head.'

'Where's she now?'

'In St Thomas's, in intensive care. I thought I said that. It's across from where she was knocked off.'

'I know that, Mum. Are you OK?'

'Gilbert, your father and I are so worried.' She always uses my full name when she is under pressure. 'Can you get to the hospital and let us know what's happening?'

I felt conflicted. A part of my brain would not let go of the story. I hate myself for it.

'But don't you want to be there?' I said. 'And what about Charles? Surely he's there already.' Charles is Clare's pompous American banker husband. Everything my parents should

16

despise, but he charms them with his claim to be the only man in the City who supports Labour, and by regaling them with stories of bankers' excesses. The way he tells it, he's waging a one-man war on the system from the inside. Luckily he's on the losing side, or his humungous bonus might shrink.

'Charlie's in New York,' my mother said. 'No one's been able to get hold of him yet. Your father's not coping.'

There's nothing wrong with my dad, but their relationship is based on the conceit that he's a frail genius who could drop dead at any minute and it's her duty to look after him.

Fuck. Mum and Dad are actually paralysed. 'OK. I'll go. I'll keep you updated.'

The senior ward sister is talking to me. She has wavy blonde hair and her watch pinned upside-down on her bosom. 'How are you doing, hon?' she asks. 'Can I get you a cup of tea?'

I shake my head. 'How's my sister?'

A small smile, looking me in the eye. It's meant to reassure, but it makes me squirm. I don't want sympathy. I want my sister to be OK.

'She's a battler isn't she. She's not giving up.'

Of course she's not giving up. Clare's the most tenacious person I've known. But the nurse hasn't answered my question. 'Is she going to be OK?'

She glances over her shoulder as if she's afraid of being overheard. 'The doctor will talk to you.'

'When?'

'As soon as he can.'

'Can you tell me anything? Anything at all?' I add a little helplessly. 'Please.' It sounds pathetic. I spend my life prising secrets out of powerful people and yet I've been here seven hours and I can't get the prognosis for my sister.

That smile again, the unsettling eye contact. 'The doctor will fill you in.'

I sigh.

She pauses. 'I'll see what I can do.'

The moment she's gone I spring from my chair and rush to the bathroom to wash my hands. Staring into the square little mirror above the sink, I wince. Looking back are the hollow eye sockets in grey skin of my father. It is a resemblance I deny, but that's impossible tonight.

This is your fault, the reflection says to me.

'Not true.' I say it out loud. How can it be my fault? We've barely spoken for years.

I hold a paper towel while turning the bathroom door handle (*minimise contact with germs at all times*) and return to the relatives' room. My mind is at war. I feel guilty at all the missed opportunities to reconcile with Clare, but I can't quite relinquish the idea that the fault was hers. She was self-righteous. But then, what if I'd been less precious, had rung her up for a chat as if nothing had happened, maybe about our beloved Spurs and nerve-wracking rumours that Teddy Sheringham would be leaving at the end of the season? *What if I'd called her yesterday afternoon, asked after her boys? Could we have met for a cup of tea?* She'd have left her teabag in the mug of course. Only a small dash of milk. We could have chatted for an hour. Half an hour. Even a few seconds would have been long enough to stop her from turning on to the Embankment at that moment. But I am fooling myself, even now. The most senior woman at the Treasury. Tipped for even greater things. If she saw my number, she'd assume I was simply ringing to confirm a story. And she'd have been right. She would have refused to take my call.

I twist in the chair. There's no comfort. It is my fault. Everything that's gone wrong with my family always has been my fault.

The silence of the room is amplifying the unbearable noise of my thoughts. I try to drown them out. I hum. And then, when the humming is not enough, I start to sing. Mark Morrison's 'Return of the Mack'. I obsessively repeat the refrain about lying, and crying, and dying. It's what I do. Slowly, I lullaby myself into a fitful doze, where Clare and I are ten and eight, holding hands outside the school gate. There's snow everywhere, too deep to allow cars to move. No sign of Mum or Dad. We're shivering, more out of anxiety at being lost and forgotten than from the cold. 'They'll be here in a minute,' Clare says. I can tell she doesn't believe it. But I feel safer, knowing that my big sister will look after me.

When I wake, my eyes are blurry because my contact lenses have been in too long and I can't read the clock. But I can hear a voice – a man's voice – in the corridor.

There have been noises all night, but this feels significant. They are the tones of someone feigning classlessness, like a BBC presenter. 'How is Clare Peck?' he asks. The nurse replies in a whisper, as if she doesn't want to be heard. She talks at length, providing more information than she gave to me. Why would she do that? It's not Charlie or Dad. Maybe it's the doctor.

But when the man speaks again, she says, 'You're welcome to wait in the relatives' room.' I hear the sound of shoes clacking towards the waiting-room door and I sit up, blinking at its beige nothingness. The back of the door opens towards me.

'Mrs Prince's brother is already there,' the nurse is saying.

The door stops moving. The handle – depressed, half down – springs back, and the man says he needs to be getting home.

I spring from my chair to see who it is, but by the time I am in the corridor, the lift doors are closing, the visitor has escaped. I return to the nurses' station.

'Who was that?' I ask the nurse. My hands are on the edge of her desk.

She does not lift her eyes from the paperwork she is filling in. 'Someone from your sister's work.'

'Who? Did he give a name?'

'He did.' She frowns. Before I can press her, a set of swing doors to the ward burst open, and a silver-haired man in surgeon's scrubs bursts through, followed by a pair of orderlies.

The nurse says, 'This is Mr Lloyd. He specialises in cranial fractures and brain injuries. He's here to assess your sister.'

I follow the surgeon into the ward. In an abstract sense, I know what to expect, but I feel sick – all the tubes and sensors, the beeping screens, have turned my unconscious sister into some kind of captive of a merciless machine. I think of Gulliver, tied down on Lilliput. I try to understand what the beeps, moving electronic cursor and flickering numbers are saying about Clare's condition.

'Hello, Mr Lloyd. I am Clare's brother, Gil Peck. Is there anything you can tell me?'

'Good to meet you,' he says. *Please save her, please save her, please save her.* 'Your sister has suffered a traumatic brain injury.

It is a concern to us that she's been more or less unconscious since the accident. We are going to take her downstairs now for a scan, to assess where she stands on the Glasgow coma scale.' He talks drily, as if relating the details of the weather forecast. 'Depending on what that shows, I may have to take her pretty rapidly into theatre.'

I hear but I don't understand. The noise in my head is growing louder and all I can do is stare stupidly at my sister. The nurse nudges me. 'Speak to her. Even though she is unconscious, she'll be able to sense you are here. Just feeling someone who loves her will help, so hold her hand, if you like.'

Someone who loves her. If only the nurse knew. I go round the side of the bed and gently squeeze her limp fingers, and then hold her hand as she held mine. I bend down and murmur, 'Clare, it's Gil. I am so sorry. Really I am. And you're going to be fine. You're going to be more than fine. I'll make sure of that.'

I am screaming inside but the nurse gently urges me on. 'Just chat about anything. It'll help.'

I lean in. A memory is triggered. Something about the warmth of her hand takes me to the woods behind our childhood house, aged seven and five. Holding on to each other, we are running as fast as we can from a bearded man who had something in his hand and we've decided it's a gun. Out of breath. Panting. Clare shouting 'Gil, run run run!'

Now I'm thinking, 'This time I'll save you.'

'I'm here sis,' I whisper. 'You'll be OK. I won't leave you.'

But Mr Lloyd cuts in. 'I am sorry, Mr Peck, but I am afraid I have to ask you to return to the waiting room.' They start to pull the curtains around her bed.

'I'll see you in couple of hours, sis.' I am sure she squeezes my hand. Just faintly. I am certain.

I stand. At the door, I realise what I didn't say, and it's too late. But I can still help to rescue her. I murmur, 'I love you, Clare', seven times. Seven is a good number. That'll work.

Chapter 3

THERE IS AN ICY GREY dawn as I cycle over Westminster Bridge. The air carries a hint of the Essex marshes. After Clare was taken to the operating theatre, the ward sister instructed me to go home. I should call Mum and Dad, but I tell myself it's too early, they'll be asleep. That is a convenient fiction. They will be at the kitchen table, trying to think and talk about anything but their worst fears.

There is almost no one on the streets, just weary immigrants traipsing from a night of underpaid cleaning to the bus stop. My face is numb with cold, but not my brain. It's in anxious overdrive. I am close to where Clare had her accident. The orange shard of a broken indicator light gleams in the gutter: could it be from the van? I am momentarily shaken out of my rhythm. My foot slips on the pedal; the bike careers towards the kerb. I jerk back to true and depress the silver gear lever. As the chain clicks to a more comfortable gear, I wonder whether I've got time to file my 'no-tax-rises-under-Labour' scoop, and whether that would be the right thing to do.

I'm on Victoria Embankment, head down, hands gripping the drop handlebars, legs pumping. Despite everything my brain returns to my work. The *Daily Mail*, on the right, and the

Sentinel, on the left, will be furious to be scooped on a story that will probably lead *News at Ten* on both channels. Why can't I switch off? An ex-girlfriend once described me as a shark. I thought she meant a remorseless and unpredictable killer, metaphorically speaking, and I took offence. It turned out she was talking about my obsession with work. *You are always swimming, always chasing the next story. You're terrified that if you stop swimming, you will die.*

For the past half mile I've barely registered any cars. But as I pass the Savoy Hotel's riverside entrance, I hear a rattling engine. A glance back reveals a filthy white van – a Ford Transit – about a hundred yards away. I instinctively touch my bike helmet and move to the left of the road to give the van room. Instead of thanks, I get a long beep on the horn.

The van comes up behind, keeping pace with my furious peddling, so close I can almost feel its heat. Why doesn't it overtake? *Beep beep.* I slow to let it past. But before the brakes have done their job, the van accelerates, overtaking inches to my right. I swerve, clip the kerb, put my left foot down on the ground. I stay upright. Just.

The van roars away. I hear the sound of raucous laughter from the front seat. *Cunts.* I don't move for perhaps a minute.

I'm alone and shaking. Nothing happened, I tell myself, I'm fine. But I need a minute to compose myself before cycling on. There is a way to distract myself.

Leaning the bike against a street sign, I sit on the kerb and punch a memorised number into the Nokia.

'*FC.* How can I direct your call?'

'Copy, please.'

'Who shall I say is calling.'

'It's Gil. Gil Peck.'

'Hi, Gil. Putting you through now.'

Then: 'Copydesk.'

'Gil Peck here.'

'Hello, Gil, it's Sheila. Bit early in the day for you. All OK?'

She doesn't really expect a response, but my disingenuous reaction is automatic. 'Never been better.'

'Good to hear. Give me a moment while I create a new file ... OK, go.'

Although I have only had a few fitful moments of dozing in the waiting room, the adrenaline and cortisol has pumped me up. My voice does not stumble or hesitate as I dictate.

'Labour leader Johnny Todd is poised to announce that the party would not increase income tax if it forms the next government. Stop. Sources close to Labour's apostrophe 's' leader have revealed to the *FC* that a new Labour government would freeze income tax rates, comma, including for high earners. Stop. New paragraph. The symbolic announcement is designed to show how determined Todd is to tackle Labour's image as a high hyphen tax party. Stop. But the pledge will outrage Labour traditionalists, both in Parliament and among trade union bosses. Stop. New paragraph.'

And so I go on, as relentlessly as the fingers on the keyboard that I hear clacking down the line: 40-odd words per paragraph, 16 paragraphs, 4 columns, leaving enough space for a picture in what I assume will be an above-the-fold splash. The subeditors will go through it later, but the *FC* could run it straight as I delivered it.

By the time I've finished I'm almost myself again. No longer shaking.

Time to get home, clean up and maybe grab an hour or two of sleep before Clare comes out of surgery.

And then the Nokia trills. It must be the copydesk, wanting to double check something. No. It's Mum again. Except it isn't.

'Gil?'

Something's not right. 'Hi, Dad.'

'The hospital rang. It's bad news.'

'What do you mean?'

Stupidest question I've ever asked. The answer is in the silence. The ground disappears and I start to fall.

'Clare died.'

I walk in a daze back to the hospital, pushing my bike, to meet my parents. Charles has still not landed. So it is down to me, Mum and Dad to hear the meaningless explanations from the doctors and start the numbing administration of formalising a death. I don't feel present. I am a ghostly observer, not taking anything in. By two o'clock Clare has been processed and we can leave.

'Come to the house at four,' says Mum. An order, not a suggestion. 'We need to talk things through.'

It's actually gone five by the time I'm in Mecklenburgh Square, banging the knocker on their glossy black front door. Thomas Carlyle, Virginia Woolf, R. H. Tawney and Emanuel Litvinoff all lived round here, so obviously it's where my mum and dad would feel at home.

My father answers the door. Bernard Peck, world-renowned Professor of Sociology and Politics at the London School of Economics, fellow of the British Academy, adviser to successive (and now dead) Labour leaders, and Nobel prizewinner in the category reserved for arrested emotional development. His face is creased, like a semi-deflated balloon. His broad shoulders seem shrunken, hunched inside a white cable-knit jumper that looks two sizes too big. His eyes are puffy. From tears? That would be remarkable. I've never seen him cry, not even when his mum, my grandma, died.

'Gilbert. I thought you'd come sooner.'

'Sorry.'

'Well, you're here now.'

A chasm of a pause. 'Dad. Clare ... She ...' It is impossible to know what to say. 'How are you getting on?'

'We've all had a bit of a cry.'

I wonder if, after all these years, this is the moment to hug him. No. He wouldn't know how to respond. I follow him over the dark kilim rugs in the hall, past the grandfather clock and bold screen prints of iconic London buildings – my mum's creations – and up the stairs to the sitting room, from where I can hear the low hum of family and friends paying their respects. This is not a small affair. My parents have summoned the clan, and more. They are perched on sofa-arms, leaning against door frames, others are downstairs in the kitchen. Voices are low, which only serves to make the clatter of Royal Copenhagen teacups placed on saucers seem deafening. Beigels – pronounced the British way in our family, 'byegul' – and onion platzels, heaped with smoked salmon and chopped egg, are stacked in pyramids on white porcelain platters, largely untouched. My surviving grandmother, Esther – almost blind, a ninety-year-old *bubbe*, our last direct link with the *shtetl* – is in a corner armchair, Clare's two boys at her feet. They are nine and seven, and both look bewildered, lost in the undergrowth of grown-ups' misery. Their dad, Charlie, will be landing soon at Heathrow. The bank is flying him home on Concorde.

We've gathered to remember Clare, and it would be hard to forget her in this room. Young Clare, student Clare, bride Clare, mother Clare. Framed photos on bookshelves, coffee tables, mantelpiece. Eight year-old Clare on a pony with a red rosette pinned on her vest. Clare in a mortarboard collecting her double first from Cambridge. Clare and Charlie in a vintage open-top Daimler on their wedding day. A diptych of Clare cradling each of her babies.

She was pronounced dead just after seven o'clock this morning. The surgeon said that her heart stopped during the operation. There was an implication that she would have been appallingly incapacitated if she had lived. Whether or not they said that to suggest death wasn't the worst thing that could have happened, that's not how it feels.

I have spoken to the police and pieced together some of what happened. Around seven last night, a Polish builder named Henryk Deyna turned right in his white van on to the Embankment. Clare was in his blind spot. The first he knew about her was a thud against the side panel. *A white van.* Like the one that ran me off the road. Not pure coincidence. It is an acknowledged law that white-van drivers are unable to see cyclists.

Though Deyna seems not to have been irresponsible. According to witnesses, he hadn't been speeding or driving dangerously and the police say there was no alcohol in his blood. He stopped as soon as he realised what had happened. He had a mobile phone and called 999. A nurse who had just finished her shift was walking past: she and Deyna put Clare in the recovery position while they waited for the ambulance. Her head had been knocked into the kerbstone and bashed hard.

'Why wasn't Mummy wearing her helmet?' says a small voice from the floor. While I have been talking to my father about what happened, I haven't noticed the nine year-old at our feet. He's been absorbing every word. 'Mummy always wears a helmet.'

This doesn't seem the right time to tell him that even seemingly infallible beings like his mum are capable of mistakes. 'I don't know Sam,' I say. 'These things happen.' I'm not entirely sure he knows who I am. To him, 'Uncle Gil' is probably less significant than Father Christmas – and doesn't deliver presents.

'No they don't!' he shouts. 'She *never* forgets the helmet. Luke and I aren't ever allowed on our bikes without one.' He's inherited his mother's furious logic.

'We all forget things sometimes.'

'Mummy *never* does.' He shakes his head, determined. The person who kept him and his brother safe is not here to explain and make things right. Everything is confusing. The helmet is the key to everything, Sam knows.

'He's young,' Uncle Jake soothes. 'He can't really grasp it.'

'Do you think we can?' We're all out of our depth.

'We should be sitting shiva,' Jake nags. For him there is comfort in tradition, the low stools and muttered prayers of a ritual that half the family practice and the other half – my half – despise.

'For Clare?' Dad says scornfully. 'She didn't believe in any of that . . .' The words 'mumbo jumbo' are unspoken.

He's right. Clare got that from him: remorseless rationality, a kind of religion of its own, everything explicable through the scientific method. No mysteries, just problems waiting to be solved.

'But the burial, Bernard.' Jake will not let an argument go either. 'It should be tomorrow. We can't wait.'

'There has to be an inquest,' Dad insists. 'Because . . .' He trails off, sighs, then starts again. He is not a man to shy away from difficult facts. 'Because of the accident. We can't get a death certificate until after a post-mortem examination.'

Jake shakes his head. 'You can't wait so long.' He takes a beigel and bites into it. A piece of egg drops down his shirt front. 'There must be something you can do. With your connections?'

'Maybe . . .' Dad says uncertainly. I detect a crack in the atheist's fortress, an atavistic desire to expedite the burial. 'But my connections are not exactly current.'

'I've got a friend in the Home Office who may be able to help,' I say, my hand already pulling the Nokia from my pocket. The strain of suppressed grief in this room is suffocating me and I'm desperate for something to do. 'A senior official and adviser to the Home Secretary. I could give her a call and see if she can think of a way to get us the death certificate faster.'

My father fixes me with the stare that so terrified generations of his students. I find it absurd. 'Please. Don't trouble yourself.'

'It's no trouble.'

'It will complicate things, Gilbert.'

I clench my jaw. When I'm seventy and he's one hundred, he'll still make me feel a disappointment. I feel the sting of the old wound. 'You'd say yes if it was Clare offering.'

Dad shakes his head. *The weariness of a long-suffering parent.* 'Clare was . . .' *better than me at everything?* Mum has spotted the danger. 'For goodness' sake you two, today of all days?'

30

I smile weakly at her. 'Sorry,' I mouth.

Everywhere I look, this room reinforces the idea that the wrong child was killed. Everyone here knows that she and I were barely speaking, because of the way I abused her trust for the sake of my career. I grab my coat, head down the stairs, and yank open the door so fast I don't notice the young man on the other side until I'm almost in his face.

He backs off the doormat. 'Sorry. Clumsy of me,' I say. 'Who are you?' I size up his tortoiseshell glasses, North Face anorak and mousey hair.

'Jeremy. Jeremy MacDonald.'

Clare's PA. 'You're Jeremy.'

'That's right.'

'You called Mum about the accident.'

He nods. I feel bad about my hostility.

'I'm Gil.'

He already knows. 'Clare's brother. I've seen you at briefings with the Chancellor.' I don't pretend to remember. 'You wouldn't have noticed me. I was always offstage. I used to be in the press office.'

I'm blocking his way. Jeremy was probably the last person to see Clare alive and I need to keep him here for a bit longer. 'What was your job with Clare?'

'I was her bagman. Fetching, carrying, did a bit of everything. She was amazing, actually. It was hard to keep up with her. But you know that better than me.'

'I was out of touch.' To put it mildly, though this surprises him.

'Clare was so devoted to you. Every morning, she'd be looking for your byline.'

That can't be true. I know what Clare thought of my work, that I am a 'scavenger on the scrapheap of better men's efforts', to use my father's memorable phrase. Before I correct him, I hear my mother's voice at the bottom of the stairs.

'Who is that, Gilbert?' Using her voice for visitors, my regression to adolescence all forgotten. If MPs could bury their awkward truths half as well as my mother, I'd be out of a job. And because I am more her son than I care to admit, I call back, 'It's Jeremy, Mum. From Clare's work.'

'Jeremy.' You would think *he* was her long-lost son. She bustles towards us, her wide mouth almost forming a smile. 'So good of you to come.'

He pushes his glasses up his nose. 'I'm sorry for your loss. I think I am supposed to say "long life".'

'Thank you, Jeremy. So kind of you. Gilbert didn't offer you tea, I suppose.' Of course he didn't. *She supposed right. A misdemeanour to add to the crimes.* 'The kettle is on. Or perhaps a proper drink? Gil, could you show Jeremy upstairs?'

I stifle a 'but Mum' as she moves to the kitchen.

He looks troubled. 'Are you OK?' I ask as we head for the sitting room.

He lowers his voice: 'Well, yes. But I need to ask … Do you know if there was anything going on with Clare?'

'What do you mean?'

'Her behaviour had been unusual in the last few weeks. She kept popping out of the office, nothing in the diary. She even missed scheduled meetings. I had to cover up for her. It was out of character. I wondered if something was, you know, troubling her?'

I'd have been the last to know. But I find it hard to believe anything got on top of my perfect sister.

'Like the cycle helmet thing,' he continues. 'It was weird. She looked everywhere for it yesterday evening before she went out.

32

She couldn't find it. But when I went into her room this morning it was where she always kept it, on the shelf behind her desk.' He bites his lip. 'It's not like her to be so distracted.'

I nod. 'If there's one thing I know – knew – about my sister, she made sure everything was in the right place.'

We are by the sitting room door when there is a crash of crockery breaking, and the wail of a child. Luke had walked over to a coffee table, covered in plates of beigels, and pushed it over. 'I want Mummy, I want Mummy,' he cries. The room is in turmoil as everyone tries to mop spilled drinks and retrieve pieces of egg. Uncle Jake rushes over to scoop up the small, weeping boy.

It is my cue to run.

Chapter 4

Monday, 10 March

I F YOU WALKED PAST GOLDERS Green Crematorium without knowing its purpose, you would see redbrick Victorian chapels built in the Italian style and probably think births, marriages and hymns. The rolling gardens behind, and the slender-columned colonnade, are a well-intentioned deceit, an attempt to lighten the burden of the grim industrial-scale processing that takes place inside. The business of saying fond farewells and then disposing of the evidence never stops. The only sign of what really goes on in this factory is a chimney, though one hidden inside a bell tower. This is traditional British squeamishness about death made manifest in bricks and mortar.

As we wait to be let into the larger of the two non-denominational chapels, the car park outside is a flower bed of brightly coloured coats and jackets. There are Marks & Spencer and Jaeger overcoats, and furs worn only for high holidays or funerals; greens and navy blues, oranges and reds, browns, greys and charcoals. We're wrapped up against a biting March wind. I'm in my Jean-Paul Gaultier three-quarter length deep blue coat, grey narrow-legged Paul Smith suit, and electric-blue wide Kenzo tie. Jews – atheist, agnostic, religious – don't wear black to funerals. Or at least it's not compulsory.

The hearse arrives and the ushers herd us in. Over the speaker system, I can hear Mahler's *Das Lied von der Erde*, 'The Song of the Earth'. Whether Clare would really have wanted Mahler, I doubt. The last time we talked music, years ago, she joked she would take the Ramones to her desert island, and I said I would take Funkadelic. Mahler – one of Dad's pantheon of geniuses who were born to our faith though like him not professing it – is my father's notion of what Clare wanted.

The chapel, if that's what we are supposed to call it, is a cavern of Victorian dark wood. The light oak of the coffin under an avalanche of lilies can't be missed. I don't want to think about who is inside and what happens next. I am praying softly, 'Never leave me, Clare, never leave me, Clare; Clare, never . . .' to still my panic, fifteen times, to the power of infinity.

'It should be a burial,' sighs Uncle Jake, behind me. Technically, he's right: Judaism frowns on cremation. But this is where North London Jews who no longer practice the faith – agnostics, atheists, Arsenal and Spurs supporters – have their funerals. I can't tell you how many times I've been here in my life. I take my place in the front pew, third along from the aisle next to Mum and Dad. Mum is weeping as quietly as she can. I've never seen her cry either, except possibly in exasperation, and I am not precisely sure what is expected of me. My father – sitting bolt upright, skin stretched over his skull – will not notice. I put my arm around her and give her a gentle squeeze.

'Thank you, Gilbert' she says. 'I'll pull myself together in a minute.'

There are no religious icons in the chapel, but two poster-size pictures of Clare are on stands at the front. One is a headshot of her looking indomitable in a long mauve dress, declaiming at a Cambridge Union debate; the other is her, Charles, Samuel and Luke, all beaming proudly at an ornate sandcastle they've meticulously constructed on the beach at Broadstairs. The boys and Charles are in the front row, though across the aisle from us. Sam's hand has disappeared into Charles's. They are both staring straight ahead, trying to fight back the tears. On their right is a wriggly Luke. Charles's mum, next to Luke – and immaculate in a grey tailored suit and blow-dried swept-back hair of similar hue – is sensibly trying to shoosh him rather than insist he become catatonic with grief like the rest of us.

One of Clare's friends from Cambridge, Tim, a famous actor, is the secular vicar of our eccentric service. As the Mahler fades, he tells us that it is the saddest and greatest honour of his life to be the master of this tragic ceremony. It was always his assumption that if he ever had to stand in front of an audience and discuss Clare, it would be because she had just been elected prime minister, or been made head of the civil service or Secretary General of the United Nations. There was, he says, something obviously prophetic in how he and Clare first properly met, in Footlights, as writers and performers of a sketch about a young female civil servant being patronised by a stuffy male mandarin. In the sketch, she explained the intricacies of quantum physics to the permanent secretary, who then asked her to be a 'love' and make him a cup of tea, 'two lumps'. 'I always thought she would turn those tables and end up running the country,' Tim intones. 'That is what should have happened. She was the best of us.' His voice is a melodic tenor with a faint Welsh accent.

It's like listening to a song. Much of what he says is to me calming noise, devoid of meaning.

Soon he calls us up one by one for our tributes. Dad, who has lost not only his daughter but his protégée, insisted on delivering the first and longest eulogy. It is mostly an account of Clare's academic and professional achievements: prizes won, distinctions earned, every job a springboard to the next dizzying height. It is all factual and true, but it is mostly about how she presented herself to the world; it hides what was inside her and what today is inside Dad. He can't break the habits of a lifetime and go anywhere near his real feelings. I've always thought he would explode and then collapse if he ever let his emotions out. The nearest he comes to something meaningful is the family myth – well, family fact – that Clare was better than me at football, and how she once humiliated me in front of my friends by tackling the ball off me on Hampstead Heath and haring the length of the field to score. She teased me about it for years.

Charlie's face is as grey as ash. He is fluent while battling tears. He may be a buttoned-up preppy boy from Boston, Mass. – Harvard and King's College, Cambridge – but the gaping wound of Clare's death is unmissable. He starts by recounting how they met, shortly after university. They'd gone to a soul night organised by a mutual friend. It was the top floor of a Soho strip club, and as both of them arrived early the stripper was still in the middle of her routine, entertaining the middle-aged male customers. They were both so embarrassed, the only thing they could do was talk to each other.

'I didn't dare take my eyes off her,' says Charlie. 'I had nowhere else to look. By the end, there wasn't anywhere else I wanted to look.'

He is sweet, and natural. Not what I expected. I'm praying he never ends. I'm hunched over, hands tightly clasped, agonising. It's my turn next.

When he's finished, I squeeze out of the pew, past Mum and Dad. The backs of my trouser legs feel as if they are clinging to my thighs and calves and I want to fidget with them. The five paces to the lectern are the most exhausting of my life.

I cough nervously and briefly look up from the A4 sheet I am clutching. There are more than two hundred people in the congregation (I know this because I heard my parents talking about catering numbers for the reception afterwards), standing room only. And although I don't think of myself as suffering from stage fright, I start to hyperventilate and think I may faint. *Breathe Gil, breathe.* I surprise myself that I am still on my feet. *Start talking, Gil; talk, Gil. What's the worst that can happen? That I will make a fool of myself? But everyone knows that it is the better of the two Pecks who has gone.*

I cough to clear my throat. 'I tried to write something,' I say. My voice sounds dry and hoarse. 'But I couldn't get it right.'

Approving nods, murmurs of sympathy. Perhaps this is poignant, the brother who writes for a living but today can't find the words. I avoid the gaze of those who've known me longest and best. I don't have to look at my father to feel his disappointment. 'What on earth is the boy going to do now?' his voice says in my head.

'Instead I thought about what she would have wanted me to read.' I look at the A4, which is now creased from the pressure of my damp and anxious clutch. 'It should really be a classic by Joey Ramone.' Tim on my right gives an approving nod and smile. Phew.

'But on reflection this is more suitable.' I tamp the paper down on the lectern. 'It's by Thomas Hardy.'

Not a line of her writing have I
Not a thread of her hair,
No mark of her late time as dame in her dwelling, whereby
I may picture her there;
And in vain do I urge my unsight
To conceive my lost prize
At her close, whom I knew when her dreams were upbrimming
with light
And with laughter her eyes.

The poem is called *Thoughts of Phena, at News of Her Death*, written by him to mourn the death of his cousin. Clare loved Hardy, having been introduced to him by our favourite English schoolteacher. Hardy is lamenting how he was estranged from Phena, wishing he could find her again. It's too late.

Halfway through I almost break down, but somehow get through it. By the time I'm finished, Dad is rigid, Mum is crumpled, in tears. When I return to my seat, I give her my fresh handkerchief from my pocket, though resist her offer to swap it for her sodden one. 'Sorry' she mutters. She puts it in her handbag.

It's Luke's and Sam's turn. Helped by Dad, their memories are simple and unaffected: how they miss Mummy getting them up in the morning, making sure they eat their Crunchy Nut Cornflakes (she wanted them to eat something healthy, they refused, she surrendered), Mummy doing funny impersonations of cross Dad, reading them *Where the Wild Things Are* in their

'Max' sleepsuits, singing them to sleep with 'Sweet dreams till sunbeams find you'. It's too much to bear, but I want them to keep going because as long as they speak, Clare is alive and I am catching up on so much of her life that I missed.

The chapel is still after they finish, except for muted sobs. Tim tells us there will be drinks and a bite to eat at Charles and Clare's family home in Primrose Hill. We are all welcome. He asks most of the congregation to stay where they are until the family has left the chapel.

We file past the coffin and I turn and whisper 'Goodbye, I love you,' to the box, and again seven more times in my head. And then I am outside in the colonnade behind the chapel, with a view over a huge rolling green field. Floral tributes lean against the walls, though none of them are for Clare. In my family's utilitarian way, my parents requested donations to Oxfam instead.

The mourners gather in threes and fours. Except for one older man with immaculately swept-back grey hair in a tan Daks raincoat, on his own at a distance from the other guests. He looks around with the awkward air of someone normally the centre of attention. One of us has to thank the Chancellor of the Exchequer for coming. I know my duty.

'I didn't know the Hardy,' Keith Kendall says. 'It was a good choice. These things are tricky.'

'Thank you. I agonised over it. Some would say it wasn't suitable, because there's a theory that although Phena was Hardy's cousin he may have had an affair with her. As you know, he had affairs with almost everyone.'

To my surprise, the Chancellor turns bright red and coughs. Have I committed a *faux pas*? It wouldn't be the first time.

41

'I don't suppose there were too many Hardy scholars here today,' he manages. *Because we're Jews?* No, he can't mean that.

'It was good of you to come,' I say, changing the subject. If I look in any direction, I can see my parents' network: disappointed former Labour ministers, ageing trade union leaders, once-feted sociologists refusing to let go of the glamour of 1968, all disenfranchised by the Thatcher hegemony. 'Not your normal social circle, I would imagine.'

'It was important to be here. Clare was a superstar. What's happened, it's just . . .'

There is no possible reply. But at that moment, and to my alarm, I see my father scything through the crowd. I remember with a shudder that Bernard Peck and Keith Kendall were contemporaries at the LSE in the mid-1950s. I've lost count of the number of times I've heard my dad refer to Kendall as 'that blithering idiot' – or worse.

Dad judders to a stop. 'Good of you to come, Kendall.'

A nod. 'Don't mention it. Clare was remarkable. The work she did for me was outstanding.'

'You didn't really deserve her.'

Kendall is more decorous than I expected. 'She kept me honest.'

Dad's chest swells. His head goes up. For a moment, I think he is about to launch into a broadside on the subject of the honesty of Tory governments. How can I stop the inevitable scene?

He remembers where he is and who he is: a dad whose worst nightmare has come true.

'I am sure she tried,' he says softly. He moves away.

Kendall watches him go. 'After all these years,' he murmurs to himself. 'Peck's daughter . . .' He checks himself. 'I'd better make a move. It's all pretty hectic.'

'I imagine so,' I say. 'I don't suppose you have a sense of when the PM will announce the election date?' The question is out before I even know what I'm saying. I can tell how it sounds from Kendall's expression.

'You know you should switch off from time to time.'

I scramble to recover. 'Sorry. What I meant is that I am probably going to take a few days leave. For obvious reasons. And I just wanted to work out when I need to be back.'

As it happens, I am scared of what I'll do if I stop work, even temporarily. Probably drink myself into oblivion at The Groucho.

Kendall relents. 'Absolutely not for reporting, but think about being back on Monday.' He glances down, and I realise with some embarrassment that my hand is gripping the Nokia in my pocket. A reflex. Perhaps I will call this in. Another scoop for Gilbert Peck, the pro who is always on, even at his sister's funeral. Nah. Clare would expect me to be that disrespectful, and for once I'll let her down.

'Thank you for coming,' I say. 'It means a lot to the family, even Dad.' Kendall gives a politician's practised handshake and turns away, almost knocking over Jeremy, Clare's assistant, who has been hovering to one side.

'Goodness!' Kendall barks angrily – and both of us can hear him muttering under his breath, 'Idiot.' Jeremy is shaken. Maybe he is too lowly at the Treasury to be known to Kendall, who trudges back to the official car that is waiting for him round the front.

Jeremy's face is puffy. 'I must look a mess,' he says. 'I couldn't keep it together. What the boys said was so beautiful.'

'Yes. They were wonderful.'

He moves closer. I recoil and feel embarrassed. All he wants is to bond over a shared loss. But I want to hold on jealously to mine.

'Gil . . . Would it be OK to tell you something, in private?' he asks. *Hell. There is something a bit creepy about this bloke.* I fight my instinct to ward him off, and steer him a few paces away from the mourners, through the colonnade, towards the floral tributes and terms of endearment for another beloved and departed mum. 'Of course. How can I help?'

'I'm being ridiculous,' he begins, glancing over at me. I give him an encouraging smile and he continues, 'There's something not right about how Clare died.'

'What do you mean?' What he's saying is clearly the voice of grief. In that freezing colonnade, next to countless marble plaques, it is my duty to listen.

'The bicycle helmet. It's the bloody bicycle helmet. It literally makes no sense that she wasn't wearing it.'

Not this again. My mum, young Luke, now Jeremy, all fixating on the missing helmet, because Clare was perfect. For once in her life she made a mistake.

'Look, Jeremy. People misplace keys, lose wallets – even their pagers. People drink too much, and they smoke, and they make bad choices or they just forget.' I'm wound up. It comes out loudly enough to draw a glance from a cousin whose name I momentarily cannot recall. *Why can't anyone accept Clare was human and fallible?*

'Clare wasn't scatty. She wasn't reckless,' he persists. 'You know that. And it wasn't that she forgot her helmet. It vanished. She was looking for it before she left the office.'

'Jeremy . . . You told me yourself it was on the shelf all along. She must have been in a hurry and not noticed it. These things happen. We all do it.' I am making a great effort to hide my

44

impatience. I turn, to start heading towards the car park. The mourners have begun to drift off to the wake and if I am late it will be another black mark against me.

'I didn't say that!' he calls after me. 'I said it was back there when I looked the next morning. I don't know whether it was there all along. And there's another thing.' I turn round. 'She was behaving strangely in the last few weeks.'

'Is this the thing about her missing meetings? You already told me.'

'Yes. And other things.' He won't let me go. 'I shouldn't tell you this, but she had a blistering row with the Chancellor in front of his private office staff. It was extraordinary.'

Now I am interested. Clare avoided conflict. Except with me, when we were children and I deliberately tormented her. 'She blew up with the Chancellor? Really? Why?'

'You may think this is strange, but it was over some work we had been doing on the tax breaks available to pension funds.'

A furious argument about the tax status of pension funds? Seriously, I would laugh if it weren't my sister's funeral.

'We were just a couple of days away from putting out a white paper on it when the policy was canned.' Yes, that would be frustrating: a white paper is a government document setting out an intention to legislate. Once published, it means the reform is more or less set in stone. 'Kendall went into Clare's office and I could hear them shouting. When he left, she followed him out. She said he was a coward, that she had lost all respect for him. In front of everyone. It was painful.'

'Wait. Let me get this straight. You think my sister's death is in some way connected to the tax status of pension funds?' *Jesus. This guy's losing it.*

'No, you're right. I'm not thinking straight.' He bows his head and puts his hands in his pockets. 'Kendall is a decent man,' he says, a propos of nothing. 'It is just that Clare had not been herself. I felt I had to tell someone.'

I put on a reassuring voice. 'Look, all of us who knew Clare are feeling confused and upset.' I finding myself trotting out a familiar line. 'I'll make some calls, have a dig around.'

He looks grateful, making me feel guilty. His expression suddenly changes.

'Obviously this is all off the record?'

'Obviously,' I sigh. If this were any other setting, I would educate him that when talking to a journalist, invoke the confidentiality clause *before* the conversation, not after.

His naivete is touching. One day I will share with him Peck's First Law of Scandal Dynamics: the British way of catastrophe is born of cockup, not conspiracy. Nine times out of ten – ninety-nine times out of a hundred, even – a tragic accident is simply that.

'Let's keep in touch,' I say.

He takes a cotton handkerchief from his pocket and blows his nose. 'See you at the wake.'

Before he can suggest we travel together, I say, 'I'm on my bike.' I walk fast, without looking back, to the railing where it's attached. As I reach into my jacket pocket for my cycle clips, I can't resist checking my phones. Nothing on the blue Nokia, but on the silver phone – select contacts only – there are three missed calls from a familiar number.

I know it is a terrible idea, but I cannot resist. I press the green button to dial the number back.

'It's me.'

'Sorry, I know I shouldn't have rung you.' *I'm relieved you did.*

'I only worked out afterwards you must be at the funeral. Are you OK?'

'Not really. There wasn't a dry eye in the house after Clare's kids told us how much they miss Mummy.'

She gives a short laugh. 'God, Gil, are you jealous? Did the little nephews upstage you?'

'Be nice.'

'You really ought to spend more time with human beings.'

'Do you know any?'

'Ha ha, very funny.' Her voice is deep, the St Paul's drawl still discernible under the practised Mockney. 'Why don't you come over to mine?'

I think – briefly – about how deeply pissed off my entire family will be if I miss the wake. Even by my standards, that would be a new low.

'I'll be there in half an hour.'

Chapter 5

AN HOUR AND A QUARTER later I am on my back. Marilyn Krol is naked beside me, smoking. The room is a tip: underwear and clothes everywhere, an unemptied ashtray on a broken chair. Worse than a student room.

'Thank you,' I say.

'What for? I wasn't doing you a favour.' Somewhere in the tangle of sheets she finds a greying white T-shirt, with a fading Labour red rose on the front, and pulls it on.

'I only meant it was nice.'

'You are a bad distraction. I should be focused on the election.'

Marilyn sits up. She has a boyish face, hair that is long in front, short at the back. Her gamine look disguises the political instincts of a veteran. She has few inhibitions. Or at least with me. She lies down again, arches her back and wriggles into her silk culotte knickers.

'Are you sure the plaster isn't going to fall on our heads?' I ask, staring up at the unnerving bulges in the ceiling. 'It looks dodgy.'

'It's been like that since I moved in.'

'Looks to me like it could come crashing down at any moment. I wouldn't want to sleep under that.'

'Well, you're not. So stop being such an old woman.'

It's a relief to escape from the claustrophobic family sadness if only for a couple of hours. Marilyn is incapable of being maudlin. She is thirty-one and has one objective, to install Johnny Todd in Number 10. A couple of years ago he plucked her as a policy adviser from a left-of-centre think tank, where she acquired a reputation for understanding the UK's Byzantine welfare system better than paunchy men twice her age. She quickly established herself as one of his most important aides, part policy adviser, part gatekeeper. She is competitive, tough, funny, cynical. And I've never been with anyone who shouts louder at orgasm.

'Do you think anyone knows about us?' I ask.

'There *is* no "us".'

'Stop it. You know what I mean.'

'I haven't told anyone. Are you getting worried someone will find out about your deep-throat source?'

'Not funny. A leak about us would be a pain. Do you really think Johnny would think you should be closer to the *FC* than to the *Globe*?'

She leans over and makes her eyes wide as if full of innocence. 'You mean you haven't told your boss? I thought it was compulsory on the *FC* for all conflicts of interest to be disclosed.'

I laugh. 'Jesus. Can you imagine that conversation with Lorimer? Even if he knew, he'd probably die of embarrassment before he said anything.' I roll over. 'Do you think Johnny suspects?'

She shrugs. 'It's my job to make sure Johnny only knows what's useful.'

'It's not as if we're doing anything that doesn't go on all the time,' I say, mostly to reassure myself. *I don't want to jeopardise work.* 'Being boring for a second, isn't it better that we aren't being talked about?'

She ignores me, swings her legs out of bed, reaches down and grabs her jeans off the floor. I am pretty sure she was wearing something else when I arrived. 'Get dressed,' she says. 'I've got a meeting with Johnny in half an hour.'

Marilyn and I have been seeing each other for almost three months, since we snogged in the back of a taxi after a drunken night in The Groucho. Marilyn's idea of pillow talk is to grill me for intelligence on the Tories, hint at some great secret about her party that she only wishes she could share, then abruptly decide she needs to get back to the office. Even though I can't get enough of her, I never stay the night.

Right now, I don't want her to leave. I try a bribe.

'I've heard something you'll find interesting.'

'What's that?'

'Ramsey will announce the election on Monday.'

'Are you sure? We thought Wednesday.'

'No. Definitely Monday.'

'How do you know?'

'I can't say. Just trust me.'

'When did you hear?'

'This afternoon.'

'Jesus, Gil. Were you working the room at your sister's funeral? Actually, don't tell me. I really don't want to know.' She laughs. 'You are such a piece of work.'

'I'm on compassionate leave. I needed to know how long I could afford to be off.'

'You're right. I'm sorry.' She turns serious. 'I can't imagine what it must feel like to lose a sister. From what I read in the papers, she must have been amazing.'

Clare's death has attracted a surprising amount of coverage. The tabloids focused on the tragedy of a young mum killed on her bike, while the broadsheets went with the rising civil service star cut off in her prime. I don't know who briefed them. My parents, obviously, assume it was me.

'It turns out I met her,' Marilyn says. 'She came in to see Johnny.'

'*What*? Why didn't you tell me? When was that?'

'Couple of months ago? Her name was in the diary as Clare Prince. I didn't make the connection until I saw her photo in the paper.'

'Wait,' I say. 'Clare *Prince*? She always used her maiden name.'

'It said "Prince" in the diary. I would have joined up the dots otherwise.'

In protecting Todd, Marilyn is scrupulous. She vets everyone. It seems odd that Clare would use her married name. Another thing I didn't know about her.

'Why did she see Todd? Was it a transition meeting?'

That would make sense. When an election is nearing, senior mandarins have 'transition' meetings with Opposition leaders, so that the civil service can do preparatory work in case there's a change of government. It is all proper, part of how Whitehall tries to provide continuity in the run up to and aftermath of an election.

'I wasn't in the room.' There's an edge in her voice. Marilyn does not like to be kept out of anything. 'No one was.'

This seems odder still. All her life Clare was a stickler. Private meetings between senior civil servants and Opposition MPs are not the norm, and in some circumstances would be a serious breach of propriety. 'So did Johnny say what it was about?'

'He was evasive. I thought maybe she wanted to get in with him. Chances are we'll appoint a new Permanent Secretary at the Treasury after the election.' She adds, as a superstitious rejoinder, 'If we win.'

It's true Clare was ambitious: she definitely wanted to be the first ever woman boss at HM Treasury. But she would also know that if it leaked she was cosying up to the leader of the Opposition, all bets would be off; she might even be sacked. Clare wasn't that kind of risk-taker.

'None of this sounds like Clare.' I scratch the back of my neck. 'But what do I know?'

Marilyn goes to her dresser. Behind bottles of Chanel and Lancôme, beads and hair clips, is a bottle of red wine, half-empty, cork wedged in. God knows how long it has been there. I am wondering whether she was sharing it with someone else in her bedroom. I banish the thought: I have no claim on Marilyn. *There is no us.*

She opens the bottle. 'Drink?'

'How long has it been there?'

'A day. Two days, maybe.' She takes a small swig. 'It's fine. Wait here.' She disappears to the kitchen and comes back with two tumblers that don't look quite clean.

I'm desperate for a drink, but I don't trust the glasses. 'Thanks. I'll do without.'

Marilyn fills her own glass to the top, and sits on the hard-backed chair by the dresser. I sit up in the bed. 'How come you never told me you had a high-flying sister at the Treasury?'

'We sort of fell out.'

She takes a swig and grimaces. 'How did you piss her off?'

'What makes you think it was my fault?'

She raises an eyebrow. 'Erm, an educated guess.'

I stare at the wall. I have never talked about this, but since Clare died I've been haunted by guilt. I'm only here to escape it.

'Don't you have to be at work?'

'I've got a few minutes,' she says, without checking her watch.

'I'll have that drink, then.'

She pours the wine. It burns, but I sink it.

'Fuck. It was about three years ago now. A family lunch.' For years we had a routine – Mum, Dad, Clare and me – of gathering at my dad's favourite Chinese restaurant at 1.30 on Sundays. Crispy duck with plum sauce and pancakes. Singapore Rice Noodles. Shredded crispy beef. Always the same dishes.

'At the time I was the *FC*'s business correspondent and Clare was soaring up through Whitehall: she had been seconded from the Treasury to the Prime Minister's office in Downing Street.' Clare regaled us with a story that had us in stitches – the PM had asked to have a meeting with Daniel Williamson, the Noble Prize-winning economist, but somehow the private office misunderstood and invited Dan Williamson the rugby player. Who actually turned up. Ramsey, being such a decent sort, sat through twenty excruciating minutes with him, pretending to be interested in the fortunes of the England team, when actually he hates rugby. 'I'd never heard anything quite so funny,' I say.

Marilyn peers at me over the rim of her glass. 'I remember. It was all over the tabloids. The columnists went to town on it being the perfect metaphor for a chaotic government.' Then her eyes widen. 'Oh my God! You didn't?'

I hang my head. 'Bottom of the front page, in the "Fancy That" slot.'

'Jesus. You turned over your sister for a byline? What an arsehole.'

'It wasn't a state secret or anything.'

'My God, are you still trying to justify it? You treated family lunch like a press briefing.'

I sigh.

'So why didn't you just apologise and promise not to do it again?'

I don't feel like explaining there's more to it than that. 'It wasn't that simple.'

'You never apologised? Christ, you really are a wanker.'

I can't look at her. This confession isn't really helping me feel better about myself.

'God, Gil, I thought I had a complicated relationship with *my* family.'

'Look. I was the perennial fuck-up. She was always the golden child. That's how it was. Now it's too late to sort out.'

I feel the threat of tears. Marilyn strokes my hand. 'Sorry. I don't want to make you feel bad,' she says. 'If it's any consolation, it's no easier being the golden child.'

Without meaning too, she's made me feel even worse about Clare, always being the one who had to meet our parents' expectations, get the best exam results, be perfect, achieve all the things they never did.

I look at Marilyn. And for the first time since Clare died, I can't hold back. The tears flow until I'm gasping for air.

Marilyn sits next to me on the bed and holds me, I don't know for how long.

As the tears stop, I realise I haven't dressed. I suddenly feel vulnerable. I release Marilyn, reach down for my Calvins and my trousers. They've got hooked onto one of Marilyn's shirts, poking out from under the bed. When I retrieve it, I notice some kind of buzzing coming from further back.

'What's that?'

'What's what?'

'Under your bed?'

'Radiator pipes?' She shakes her head. 'I'm used to it.' She sees the look I'm giving her. 'What?'

Marilyn's processing power is awesome when it comes to calculating the implicit withdrawal rates in the social security system, identifying which marginal seats are winnable in a general election, or evaluating which newspaper serves which important electoral demographic best. And she knows, better than any witchfinder, which MPs are the true believers and which the apostates. But when it comes to her home, she doesn't give a fuck.

'That's not a radiator.' I get down on my knees and pull out knickers, newspapers, unwashed plates with unidentifiable food hardened on. With trepidation I stick my hand all the way under, because I recognise that sound. Bingo. I fish out an oblong piece of black plastic. I wave it triumphantly.

'My pager!'

Eww. It's sticky. I wish I could wash it – and my hands – immediately. But the pager is buzzing angrily, its tiny black-and-white screen glowing as it displays numbers that have been chasing me. The latest is an outer London 181 telephone number, followed by the digits '999.'

It must have slipped out of my pocket the last time I was here and I somehow kicked it under the bed when I was getting dressed in a hurry. It was pissing with rain; I'd spent longer with Marilyn than I had intended and was late for my meeting with Tony Cannon at The Groucho.

Marilyn peers over my shoulder and sees the '999' code. She knows what it means: *call urgently.*

'Someone's angry husband after you?'

'Ha, ha,' I reply.

'Sorry. Not appropriate.'

I find the Nokia in my jacket, which is on the back of the chair where Marilyn had been sitting. I punch in the number from the pager. Not a number I call often, but I know whose it is.

The phone rings and rings, as if daring me to hang up. *You've made the effort*, says the voice in my head. *It's not your fault if he doesn't answer.*

Abruptly, I hear the American accent of my brother-in-law. 'Charles Prince.'

Deep breath. 'Look, I'm so, so sorry I didn't make it.'

'Your own sister's wake! For Christ's sake.' His voice is tight with rage, and I guess the only reason he's not shouting at me is because he's surrounded by mourners, whom I hear murmuring in the background. 'Everyone is here – except you.'

'Something came up.'

He's not listening.

'The boys could have done with the support. *I* could have done with the support.'

'I'm sorry.'

'Ginger thinks something terrible must have happened to you. How selfish can you be? It's the worst day of her life, it's the worst day of my life, how could something have come up for you?'

'Sorry.' I don't know what else to say.

'Not good enough. On top of everything else, there was a break-in while we were at the funeral.'

Too slowly, I process what he's said. 'What do you mean?'

It's not just anger in his voice. He's overwhelmed. 'Someone broke in while we were out. Put a brick or something through the glass back door. Mess everywhere.'

'Fuck. That's awful. What did they take?'

'Jewellery, that sort of thing.' Intake of breath. 'Some candlesticks your mum gave us. They left the Nintendo.'

'I am so sorry, Charles.'

'Her office looked ransacked. The police think they were looking for cash.' He pauses. 'Hold on ...' Someone is talking to him in the background. 'I have to go.'

'I'll be there as soon as I can.'

He hangs up. All my dealings with my family leave me feeling useless.

Marilyn stands over me and gives me a maternal hug. It's the most intimate gesture she's ever made. I tell myself not to cry again.

'You can still sort this out, you know,' she says. 'I'm here if you want to talk.'

For a moment I think she means it. But then I remember she's saying what everyone says.

I am in a black cab, stucco-fronted Nash terraces on my right, Regent's Park on my left. I can no longer separate the emotional battering from the way I feel physically: the burning wine I drank in Marilyn's flat weighs heavily, and I feel crushed, like my bones have all been broken.

58

'Everything all right in the back, sir?' asks the driver. 'You look like you've seen a ghost.'

'Difficult day,' I say, skirting the truth. The choice to be with Marilyn, the choice to have sex, was an escape from the agony I would feel at the wake. I have always been terrible at confronting pain. But even an arsehole – as Marilyn had called me – should know better than to think you can outrun pain as big as this.

My anxiety is at defcon five. The idea of a heart-to-heart with Charles fills me with dread. I didn't have the guts to tell Marilyn that the biggest cause of my rupture from Clare was over him. I humiliated him, because I hated him, her darling husband.

What word could Marilyn come up with to describe what I had actually done? *Arsehole* is too tame. I'd written a story about a disgraced American insider trader, Ronnie Piskin, and I could not help pointing out that his son is a partner in the London office of Schon. Yup. I actually did that. Clare was completely right that it was gratuitous of me to show off my own 'insider' knowledge. There was no editorial justification. On the most generous interpretation – my one – I was insensitive. Clare was in no doubt I had been wilfully malicious, having told me when she first met Charles about how his mother and he had rebuilt their lives after his parents' messy divorce. Charles even changed his name from 'Piskin' to 'Prince', because he no longer wanted anything to do with his father. No one at Schon where he works, or in his friendship circle, was aware of the connection. But within hours of me mentioning his name in the *FC* splash, journalists from the *Globe*, *Daily Mail* and other papers were banging on their Primrose Hill door and hanging around outside Schon's HQ hoping to get a comment from him on how he felt to be the son of the world's most notorious financial crook.

Charles was devastated. I later discovered that he quite reasonably feared that Schon – as one of Wall Street's elite 'white-shoe' firms – would find a way to sack him. Clare was angrier with me even than when she was fourteen and I stole her diary to repeat choice extracts over breakfast about her agonies over the changes in her body ('Ooh, my breasts are sore, I think I've started my period, there's blood in my knickers'). She was blunt on the phone: 'You betrayed Charles. You betrayed me. I don't wish to speak to you ever again.'

'Don't be silly Clare,' I whined. 'It was just a story.' She hung up. That was just over two years ago: she kept her word. And even at family gatherings she skirted around me and refused to engage.

As the yellow brick of their Victorian home comes into view on the right, I try to calm myself by muttering under my breath a safe number of times, 'Let me die, save Charles and the boys,' I whisper, once, twice, thrice. Having offered myself up as a sacrifice, I feel calmer.

'Something you needed, sir?' asks the driver.

'No. Everything's fine.'

As I draw up, my parents are about to leave. It's eleven and everyone else has. 'Don't talk to me Gilbert,' says Mum, from the cab. Her lips are rigid. 'Help Charles with the washing-up. The teacups and crystal glasses are not to go in the dishwasher.' She winds up the window and they drive off.

I walk into the hall and everything returns in an instant of familiarity: the tessellated tiles, the grandfather clock, the pile of unopened junk mail, Clare's gloves, waiting on the side table for her to slip on. I want to make a new start with Charles, but the first thing I do is lie. 'The editor called me in for an impromptu

60

meeting at work. He panicked that we hadn't properly planned our general election coverage.' Even as I say it out loud, it sounds phoney, and Charles seems to know.

I follow him into the kitchen. 'I'll wash, you dry,' he instructs.

The windows are open to air the house of cigarette smoke. He fills me in on his afternoon. Having discovered the burglary, he had every right to call off the gathering. There is no way I would have gone ahead. But he has an American never-shall-evil-triumph attitude to life. He told the guests it was an important lesson for his boys that life goes on, even if the mourners' recollections of Clare would be shared over the percussion of a local builder nailing planks of wood across the jemmied back door to make it secure.

Only after guests started to drift away did two officers turn up, one uniformed, one plain-clothes. They complained the crime scene had been contaminated by the builder and by my drinking, weeping relatives and that there was no possibility of obtaining a clean set of fingerprints. Charles apologised but said there was a bigger priority.

'Then one of the officers told me there was no chance of them finding the thieves in any case. There were just too many break-ins to investigate.' Charles chuckles sardonically. 'Can you believe it? He admitted that all they are doing by turning up is rubber-stamping my insurance claim.'

He seems to want to share with me. 'Do you think any of this will change after the election?' he asks.

I grunt something about how tackling crime will, as usual, figure in the campaigns, but it always seems to be an argument about how long to lock up criminals rather than actually catching them. 'If you think the prosecution rate is rubbish for burglary, it's almost non-existent for corporate and financial crime. Not like in the US.' I wince at my thoughtlessness. Perhaps he didn't notice.

We concentrate on the washing-up. We have a system. He puts a piece of crockery or glass on the draining board, I pick it up, run the cloth over it and then monosyllabically ask where it lives. 'For the third time, Gil, those go in the glasses' cupboard in the dining room, the one your parents gave us when they moved back from Oxford.'

'Sorry.' I take it to the cupboard. I remember fighting with Clare in front of it when we were little. I had Clare in a wrestling hold and was pushing her too close to the glass front. *'Gil. You're too close. You could go right through it. Be careful of her head.'*

I put down the tea towel, turn and try to make eye contact with Charles. 'I'm really sorry, Charles.'

He is wrist deep in suds. 'It's just a bit annoying you keep forgetting where things go.'

'I didn't mean that. I meant I'm sorry for being such an arsehole brother-in-law. And more than anything I am really sorry for putting that stuff in the paper about you. I was a piece of work. I should have had the guts to straighten things out years ago.'

Charles lifts a large white rustic bowl, decorated with pink flowers, from the sink, places it on the draining board, and sighs. 'To be honest, it was never really about you and me. It was about you and Clare.' I am not sure what he means. And he seems to sense that. 'Look, I've thought about this and it was naïve of me to think I could pretend forever I'm not that man's son. I can't say it wasn't painful when it came out. But I learned that real friends judge you on who you are, not who your dad is. I stopped cursing you quite a long time ago. But for Clare you crossed a line. She could just about forgive you writing up that funny story about the PM and the rugby guy. But this was different. She thought you were deliberately trying to wound us. That was unforgiveable.'

I pick up the bowl and start to wipe it; neither of us say anything for a minute or two. I've rarely thought about any of this since we fell out and, as if for the first time, I realise it wasn't an accident – I was *trying* to hurt. This wasn't just me blurring the line between family and work, friends' confidences and a story, the private and the professional. It was an attack on Charles and, more particularly, on Clare.

'Charles, this is a funny thing to say, but I was jealous of you. I think. The thing is, it was always me and Clare. We were the double act. We looked after each other. Actually, that's not right. She looked after me. Did Clare ever speak to you about our childhood?'

'A bit. But it would be good to hear about it from you.'

'When we reached our teens we told each other our parents never really wanted children. I know they are charming, and I have no doubt they are fond of you, and you of them. But they didn't do the hard parenting stuff, like asking us what we wanted. They just expected us to come top of the class, win prizes, to honour them.'

While other kids were reading the *Beano* and DC comics, we were presented with *The Little Red Schoolbook*, Simone de Beauvoir and books on Marxist theory too numerous to mention. I rebelled. I hated it. From about the age of twelve or thirteen I nicked money from them to buy porn mags. I would sleep over at friends without telling them. I smoked, drank, took drugs. This was Bohemian North London in the seventies. Everything

63

was available. And the thing is, our parents didn't even seem to notice. They had their own important lives, especially after they moved part of the time to Oxford. We were supposed to amuse and impress them over the breakfast and dinner table but otherwise look after ourselves. This didn't seem to be a problem for Clare who worked hard. But I was intent on failing. And it was Clare, when I was fifteen, and she was seventeen, who saved me.

I explain to Charles that in my circle of school friends we progressed pretty quickly from cannabis, to speed and then to LSD. 'One night, I was at my mate Dave's and we'd all dropped a tab. I had a really bad trip. I was shouting and screaming, terrified. I could see devils and demons and I was freaking my friends out. Apparently I was doing that clichéd thing of saying I could fly and that I would show them.

'Dave panicked, rang the house and Clare picked up. She came straightaway and told my idiot friends she would take over. She calmed me down, took me outside, held my hand. And we just walked for hours until the stuff was out of my system.' I look hard at Charles. 'Clare sort of saved my life. Or at least, that is how I always thought about it.'

I become self-conscious. 'This must be boring for you. Sorry. We should be talking about you, not me.' And for the second time that day, the walls of my throat close in. But this time I control myself; it may be the chore of drying dishes that I've continued to do on automatic.

'I did know something about that,' he says.

'The point,' I say, 'is that I never did acid again. And, with Clare's support, I even knuckled down and passed my exams. I've never really spoken about this to anyone. Clare wasn't just a sister. She looked out for me. And in a way she took the place of Mum and Dad by looking after me. She was the most important person in my life. When you turned up, it was hard. I was no longer the most important person in *her* life … I felt betrayed.'

Charles takes his hands out of the sink. They are red from hot water. 'You should have spoken to her about all of this,' he says. 'You never had any reason to be jealous of me. I knew almost from the first time I met her that her relationship with you was special. Nothing like mine with my sister. Honest truth: I was jealous of you.'

And then we're both crying and looking at each other helplessly.

'Fuck the dishes,' says Charles. 'We need a drink.'

In the sitting room, the surface of the piano is covered with family photographs. It was always like that, but now it feels like a shrine to Clare.

'Give me a minute,' he says, 'I am just going to check on the boys.'

I plonk myself down on the tan leather sofa and check the rest of the messages on my pager. There is a week of them and I scroll through. Mostly they're stale breadcrumbs left by PR flacks, MPs and City contacts: none look enticing or important. Then I reach the last – oldest – message. Monday, 3 March, 5.45 p.m., from a number I recognise as coming from inside Whitehall.

I need your help.

The little screen only shows the first four words. I have to twiddle and the blocky letters jerk sideways to the sender's name.

Clare.

Chapter 6

THE BURMA ROAD IS SEVEN hundred miles of hard road, built at tremendous human cost, through the mountains of southern China. It is also what Lobby hacks call the corridor of journalists' offices on the top floor of the Palace of Westminster. How the two became twinned is lost to memory, though it might have been the invention of a legendary Press Gallery secretary who had a habit of attributing military ranks to all of us.

Here I am, back on the long march to freedom. Without bothering to consult my editor, I have unilaterally ended my leave; it was not helping. On each side of the Burma Road are rooms filled with reporters, mostly men, whose ostensible role is to be the public's eyes and ears on those we choose to rule us. The rooms are high-ceilinged and the windows ogival and majestic, with views over slate roofs and courtyards. It smells of dust toasting on radiators, wet outer garments, tea, and the sweet, woody smell of old newspapers. This place is everything that is right and wrong with Britain's great institutions. The neo-Gothic structure is sturdy and built to last. The fixtures are cheap and decaying: frayed grubby green carpet, walls a grimy shade of cream, large wooden tables covered in papers and battered personal computers, even the odd typewriter and Tippex bottle. Most mornings we're greeted by dead mice in the traps. In the afternoons, their cousins scuttle past.

We are on the cusp between technological and cultural ages. The older gents are the gallery reporters, a dying breed of deferential journalistic herbivore, who sit in the gods of the Lords and Commons chambers, chronicling the speeches and interventions and votes. Off duty, they regale anyone who'll listen with the legends of Churchill and Atlee mesmerising the House, in debates that were a matter of life and death. They witnessed giants, before this age of pygmies.

Soon they will have been pensioned off, or will have drunk and smoked themselves to death, leaving these attic rooms to disrespectful predators like me. My obsession, our obsession, is with the deeds of ministers and MPs – their secret plans and their often grubby extra-curricular activities – rather than their words. We want to find out if the secretary of state for health is selling off the NHS, and whether he is asking his 28-year-old secretary to put on a nurse's uniform and give him an enema.

Collectively, we are known as the Lobby. We work for rival publications, are ostensibly in competition with each other. But the weight of history in the physical space where we work has turned us into a sort of guild. There is naked collusion between us against the common enemy, the Prime Minister and his Downing Street machine. A few Lobby hacks are agents provocateurs for either Labour or the Tories. Most are anarchists, just trying to cause trouble for anyone with a big job and sense of entitlement.

I exit the juddering wood-panelled lift on to a tiny landing, next to a cafeteria that has been selling the same plain cheese sandwiches on white bread for forty years. Now, at 10.30 a.m. the place is half-empty. Parliament doesn't really get going until nearer lunchtime. The few hacks who are at their desks already aren't engaging in the day job. They're mostly writing tedious 'lineage' pieces, freelance work paid per line, for trade publications – on likely new building regulations for *Housebuilding Weekly*, or rail privatisation for *Railway News* – to help with the mortgage. Some glance up as I wander past, offering the obligatory words of sympathy.

I acknowledge the condolences, but am distracted. For a day and a half almost all I have been able to think about is the message on the pager.

I need your help. Clare.

Five words, seen too late. I rage at her for not calling me directly, or not paging me earlier. But of course she couldn't ring me, because I never gave her either of the Nokia numbers, and she was probably too embarrassed to ask Mum and Dad for them. I rage at my own pig-headed failure to mend with her, and the obsessive thought that everything is my fault. If I hadn't been with Marilyn, if I hadn't lost the pager, if I had called Clare back, she would have been on the phone to me rather than on her bicycle.

What did she need? Why, after being estranged so long, did she decide to contact me? In the last day I've rung everyone to see if they have the faintest idea what she might have wanted. Mum and Dad were coldly dismissive of the idea that my sister would share anything important with me. Charles was in America and didn't have a clue; he used their short chats on the phone to receive news about the boys. Jeremy, her assistant, said he'd already told me everything. I am out of ideas.

Before I turn left into the *FC*'s room, I nod at Alan Scott, political correspondent of the *Sentinel*, who is at his desk on the Burma Road's right bank. I brace myself for the platitudinous condolences. He and I have a grudging mutual respect. Actually, I may be flattering myself. I see him as a diligent and effective political reporter, though tediously worthy. He probably despises me as a glory boy and a chancer. Which is fair enough. I play the odds when writing an exclusive and there is always an element of controlled risk that I might have got it wrong. I am addicted to the adrenaline rush of never being quite certain whether the latest scoop will be the career-ending one that is comprehensively trashed. Until now, at least, and whether by luck or judgement, I've never screwed up – or at least, not disastrously.

I am halfway past his door, when I see he has jumped up from his desk and is rushing towards me.

'So terrible about your sister.' He peers through unfashionable steel-rimmed spectacles, under a mop of reddish hair, his paunch struggling out of a faded stripy brown-and-white Viyella shirt. Just a few years older than me, he would be at home in a polytechnic common room. He typically prefaces everything he says with 'Erm', which weights his words with deliberateness. 'Erm, I'm so sorry.'

'Thank you,' I say.

'Erm, it must be hard for you.'

'It's OK. I'm bearing up.'

This is excruciating. Alan Scott is a legend at exposing financial scandal and complex public-sector corruption, his forensic invest-igative powers second to none. But although well meaning, he is shy. In Parliament's bars, while the rest of us are deploying our papers' expense accounts to buy round after round for the mob of biddable MPs, he'll be persuading a junior civil servant to photocopy a valuable road-widening contract that proves a couple of million quid of public sector money is lining the pocket of a mate of the secretary of state. He's like a terrier chasing a rat. Once he has the scent, he won't stop until the scandal is exposed. Right now, I have a feeling his solicitude isn't quite what it seems, because he is blocking my way and showing no signs of moving.

'Alan, is there something on your mind?'

'Erm ...' He hesitates, furrowing his brow. 'Well, actually ...' Another pause. And then he blurts, 'You don't happen to know if she left anything for me?'

'*She* ... Who?'

'Clare. Some papers, or maybe a floppy disk?'

'I haven't a clue, Alan. What on earth do you mean?' This feels inappropriate. I know he's gauche, but ...

He already backing away. 'Sorry, I shouldn't have said anything. Dim of me. It's not something you should be bothering yourself about now. Let's have a chat in a few days.'

This is annoying. He can't say that he has been in contact with my sister and then expect me to back off without knowing more. If Clare needed help from a journalist, why from him? Why not me?

I need your help.

Did she turn to him because she couldn't get hold of me?

'When did you speak to her?'

The urgency in my question stops his retreat. He sucks in his cheeks.

Too many painful thoughts are colliding. Nothing makes sense: neither that Clare broke the principled habits of a lifetime and ignored Civil Service rules against unauthorised contact with the press, nor that she chose to do so with this holier-than-thou prick.

'Spit it out,' I say. 'Why was she in touch with you?'

He glances around, looking for an escape. 'Gil. I don't know what ...'

'Who do you think you are protecting?' I interrupt. 'Your source is in no position to complain.'

'If our roles were reversed, would you tell me?'

I am only half aware that I'm raving. Along the corridor, heads poke from doors to watch, just in case one of us throws a punch (which has happened in this over-testosteroned place).

'Can you calm down, Gil? It was wrong of me to bring it up.' I want him to feed my fury, instead he is conciliatory. 'Forgive me. It was a terrible thing you've been through and ...'

'Just fuck off.'

'I'm in the wrong, but maybe it's a mistake for you to be at work.' I walk round him and into the *FC*'s room.

'Sanctimonious prick,' I mutter, just loud enough for him and everyone to hear.

What could Clare have wanted to tell Scott, with his stamp collector's brain and his obsession with proving that every Tory MP is on the take? I am tormented by the feeling that he's stolen something my sister wanted to give me. Jeremy's ramblings at the funeral come back to me, something about: *A piece of work we had been doing for months on the tax breaks available to pension funds. We were just a couple of days away from putting out a white paper on it when the whole thing was canned. She had a blistering row with the Chancellor.*

Would she have been angry enough to leak to a journalist, to Scott? I turn back to him. 'Don't be such a dick,' I shout. 'Literally no one is interested in pensions.' His gaze shifts down to my shoes. Ah, nailed him.

The *FC*'s office is on the courtyard side of the Burma Road, roughly in the middle. As political editor, I have a separate desk by the window, while the rest of the team are squashed on a scuffed table. At full strength there are six of us, and by five o'clock the room will be a cacophony of keyboards clattering away like a typing pool, interspersed with the chirruping of mobile phones. I am the second to turn up. Predictably, Jessica Neeskens has her nose buried in a five-hundred-page parliamentary select committee report with its characteristic powder-blue cover.

'Do you actually have a life?' I ask.

'That's rich from someone supposed to be on compassionate leave.'

Jess has shoulder-length brown hair. Her face is 'round and pointy', as I once heard her tell her best friend on the phone when they were discussing whether she should go for a bob. She's pretty, but I've never tried on any funny stuff with her. Even I am not so dumb as to want to complicate the most important professional relationship in my life. She is the yin to my yang, detail to my broad brush, caution to my recklessness, Lisa to my Bart. I brought her into the Lobby from the accountancy team eighteen months ago, and for the first time in my life I've gone from being a lone wolf to hunting in a pack – of two. Her superficial qualifications are a first-class degree in mathematics and a doctorate in monetary economics. More important, she likes a drink, a laugh and nicking the secrets of the powerful, rich and pompous almost as much as I do. When I hired her, my conceit was that I was her Sensei and she was Grasshopper. These days, too often I am the student. She'll end up my boss. Bet on it.

She runs a disapproving eye over me.

'What on earth was all that about with Scott? Have you gone mad?'

'Crossed wires. About a story.'

'Gil. You were seconds from decking him. You are too overwrought to be at work.'

'Don't exaggerate.'

'I'm not. You are not yourself. Please go home.'

'I hate being there. You know that.'

'Then you should be with your family.'

'That's worse than being on my own.' I drop into my chair and swivel it towards her. 'I need to pick your brains. About pensions ...'

She decides to humour me, a habitual reaction. 'OK. What exactly?' She takes her pen and starts tapping it nervously on the desk.

'Is there talk about the government doing something about how they're taxed?'

She snorts in exasperation. 'You mean something like what I wrote about a month ago?'

'Ah. Probably.'

'You didn't read it.' No point me arguing. I shrug in half apology. 'I wrote that Kendall was planning to raise billions from pension funds. It was quite a big deal.'

'Sorry.'

'I am assuming you haven't looked at the Treasury Select Committee's report, either?' She sighs. 'It catalogues the huge tax incentives given by the government to encourage saving for a pension.'

I try to suppress a yawn.

'You are pathetic. This stuff *matters*. The report says that much of the subsidy for pensions is poor value for money. It looks to me as if the MPs on the committee were front-running for the Treasury, conditioning opinion for a big reform.'

'So why hasn't anything been announced?'

'Dunno. It's been nagging at me. I've been meaning to follow it up.'

I tell Jess what I know, that it was my sister who devised the scheme she wrote about, that the Chancellor dropped it and she was livid. She stops tapping her pen.

'Wow. I wonder if my piece spooked them.'

'I'm not sure.' I close my eyes and press my fingers to my temples. Jeremy's voice plays in my head.

There's something not right about how Clare died.

This is mad. One pager message has made me as loopy as Jeremy.

I open my eyes to see Jess's concerned face staring at me. 'Are you OK, boss?'

It's embarrassing to say it out loud, but perhaps that's the best way to exorcise the demon. 'Clare's PA is convinced there's something funny about . . . about the accident. He thinks – at least, I think he thinks – it's connected to the policy she'd been working on.' I laugh. 'That's mad, right? No one dies because of pensions tax. Unless they lose the will to live from boredom.'

I'm waiting for Jess's scorn. Instead she tilts her head and starts rhythmically clicking her ballpoint. Christ, she's thinking.

'The pensions industry is worth about a trillion quid. It's the backbone of the stock market. If the government does something that affects the money going into those funds, that *is* a big deal.'

I feel confused – which may have something to do with the seven glasses of white Burgundy I glugged in The Groucho last night.

'Are you saying it is plausible Clare was killed to stop pension funds losing money?'

'No, of course not. That's mad. I am just saying when you change the regulation or taxation of pension funds, there are winners and losers. The sums involved can be massive. Someone would have wanted it stopped.'

I drum my fingers on the edge of the computer keyboard. 'It would be helpful to know precisely what it was Clare was working on.' We might even get a decent story out of it. I wince. I should not be thinking about a byline.

'How do we find out?'

'Scott knows, I reckon. She was going to send him a document or something about it. But that sanctimonious wanker won't tell us.'

'So that was why you were being such a prat with him. I honestly don't think *you'd* have handed over the story, if the roles were reversed?'

She's right. 'Who do we ask?'

I'm still contemplating this when the door bangs open and a bald man with a bristle of moustache sticks his head in. 'Ah, Peck. Surprised to see you back.'

'Couldn't keep away. You know what it's like. The drug of news, and all that.'

He raises his eyebrows, but Kevin Wilkinson is also an addict. He is the Political Editor of the *Globe*, the best-selling British tabloid, notorious for its bare-breasted 'Page 5 Globes'. The *Globe* is the antithesis of the *FC* in its culture and values – but we are blood relatives. Both papers belong to the same worldwide television and newspaper empire, Media Corp. And there's another thing we have in common: in an election, every party leader wants the endorsement of both papers, because mine speaks directly to business leaders and his to pretty much everyone else.

'Huddle in half an hour, OK?'

'Where?'

'The *Globe* room.'

And with that, he retreats.

'I'm going to make a call,' I tell Jess.

Around the back of the Burma Road is a line of telephone booths, dark wood cubbyholes, like the phone booths in posh hotels you see in 1940s British movies. I enter one and take out the blue Nokia.

'Metropolitan Police,' says a male voice.

'Kim Jansen, please.'

Kim is a contemporary of mine from Chicheley College, Oxford who did something eccentric after graduation. When everyone else in our year was applying for the BBC trainee scheme, or taking the exams for the Foreign Office or the Treasury, Kim joined the police. This was, to put it mildly, unusual, although it has turned out useful for me. She's risen to become Deputy Chief something-or-other, and I hope one day she'll become Commissioner of the London Metropolitan Police. Though the notion of a woman becoming the most powerful police officer in the land is probably fanciful.

'I'm so sorry about Clare,' she says.

I'm well-rehearsed in my grunt of acknowledgement. 'That's what I'm calling about, actually.'

There's a slow intake of breath. 'I'm not on the case, Gil.'

'But you know about it.'

'It's in my section.'

'I'm not asking you to break confidences. It will all come out at the inquest in any case. It's just … it would give me some reassurance.'

A long pause. 'What do you want to know?'

'Just … whatever you can find out.'

'I'll call you back in five minutes.'

Her efficiency has always been legendary. Five minutes later, almost to the second, the Nokia rings.

'I've spoken with the investigating officer,' she says without preamble. 'The driver of the van was a Polish builder, Henryk Deyna. Not in this country long, but perfectly legal. Breathalysed, nothing. Ditto drugs. Clare was in his blind spot and that's the whole story.'

'Nothing suspicious?'

This time she sighs. 'It was a traffic accident, Gil. We get about 20,000 of those a year. Most people survive, some don't. She wasn't wearing a helmet.'

'I know. I just thought …'

'This is hard for you, for any brother. If you're trying to give your tragedy a reason, give up now.'

'I guess you are right.'

'I get this every day from grieving families. People want to believe that death isn't random. But usually it is, just one of those terrible and shocking things.' She pauses. In the background I hear the hubbub of a large open-plan office. 'You know there's no shame in getting help, speaking to a therapist or someone who understands what you are going through?'

She says she can recommend someone who specialises in grief. I'm non-committal as I say goodbye.

Kim Jansen is right. It was a calamitous accident. My fantasy of homicidal pension fund managers who hide bike helmets was a distraction from my guilt, desperation, sadness. I do need help. I will look for it in a couple of hours in a bottle of flinty white wine.

Jess can see I'm fed up. 'Not the conversation you wanted?'

'I've been an idiot.'

'You've had a tough time.'

'All that stuff about pensions. Forget I said it.'

'Right,' she sighs. 'Let's pick it up later. First, you need to set off now if you're going to make the huddle?'

'Christ.' I glance at my watch.

At least once a day, the political editors of the leading newspapers gather in a group to swap information and – more cancerously for the government – to agree a common line on what the story of the day should be. This pack mentality has been a disaster for the Tories, since the consensus for about three years is that the Prime Minister is comically inept, unable to maintain discipline over a chaotic party in the grip of a civil war. Generally, the serious plotting is disguised by very male joshing. I can't really face it today, but it's better than being left to my own thoughts.

In the corridor, the Commons postman is weaving from room to room, leaving parcels and letters in each newspaper's basket. He is coming towards me, which means he has already deposited letters in the *Sentinel*'s room. Scott is their Whitehall correspondent, not a political editor, but his boss is away so it is possible he'll be deputising in the Pol Eds' huddle.

I wander innocently into the *Sentinel*'s room on the other side of the corridor. The office is empty. And at the top of the wire post tray is a battered A4 manilla envelope that catches my eye. Or rather, it's not the envelope, but the handwriting. It's an elegant italic script, written in fountain pen, learned by a scrupulous seven-year-old who was always impatient to grow up. Even though I haven't seen it in years, I recognise it instantly. Every ascender in black Quink ink is perfectly vertical, every loop geometrically exact.

I look around for witnesses. None. Without pausing, I scoop up the envelope and return to my desk. From the creases in the paper, it looks as though it has been stuck in the system for a while. Parliament's post room was shut down for a couple of days the previous week, following accusations from a couple of Tory MPs – denied by the posties – of pilfering and petty theft. The postmen walked out in high dudgeon. And this letter has probably been in limbo since then.

Jess sees it, and me.

'What's that?'

I check no one is in earshot. 'It's something my sister sent to our friend from the *Sentinel*.'

'Am I right to assume he doesn't know you've got it?'

'I think that would be reasonable.'

'Gil!'

'Let's open it, shall we?'

Chapter 7

J ESS SLITS THE ENVELOPE WITH the office scissors and
pulls out the papers. On the top sheet, the first words are
the ones that are irresistible to us: *Highly confidential.*

She pulls the lot out. My pulse quickens, the familiar excitement of a scoop in the making. It is the sensation of trowel
chinking against treasure in an archaeological dig. This habitual
thrill that never wanes is why I am still a journalist, when so
many of my contemporaries have quit for the bigger bucks of
public relations. I'll never tire of revealing what a powerful person
wants hidden, depriving them of the control over whether they
disclose their secrets and their proprietary information. It is how
hacks like Jess and me level the playing field between the rulers
and the ruled, the bosses and the bossed.

Even by my amoral standards, stealing a letter that was sent
to a rival journalist by a whistleblower is – well – unorthodox.
Not amoral. Immoral, despite the whistleblower being my dead
sister.

Jess reads the full title.

'Options for Reforming or Abolishing the Dividend Tax Credit.'

I take it out of her hands and flick through it. It's a forty-odd
page photocopied document and, at first glance, the cover does

not lie. It seems to be all about tax credits for pension funds. I don't understand.

'What the hell is this?' My blast of excitement has faded. And I'm late for the Political Editors' chinwag.

'Leave it with me. I'll look it over while you're in the huddle.'

I slip in late to the *Globe*'s room. A half dozen other editors or their deputies are already there. With Wilkinson are the *Mirror*, *The Times*, the *Telegraph*, the *Mail* and the *Sentinel*, represented by Scott. He gives me an embarrassed look, but both of us pretend our contretemps never happened.

'Glad you could honour us with your presence,' says Wilkinson.

'Sorry, Kevin.'

'Don't sweat. We've just been organising a little sweepstake on when Ramsey will announce the election.'

'I'll take Monday,' I say, too quickly, drawing a quizzical look from Wilkinson.

'Is there something you want to share?'

I flash him my best fuck-off smile. 'Just a feeling,' I say, cursing my instinct always to show off when I know something.

We are twitchy. Elections are our World Cup finals. The individual games we report on can be dull, defensive affairs, but the prize at the end still lends every word and deed of the party leaders – every speech, press conference, broadcast and constituency visit – with life-or-death potential.

Of course, the idea that elections change anything in a fundamental structural way is only occasionally true. Usually Britain plods along in its smug mediocrity, regardless of who forms the government. Every now and then, though, a politician turns up who tantalisingly offers something different, something that persuades us that we can again be united, or great, or both. Such hope and promise usually ends in humiliation, bitterness and recriminations. Margaret Thatcher's prime ministerial arc – from heartless sower of strife and mass unemployment, to heroine of the Falklands and economic renaissance, to the victim of a party coup – was the classic.

This time, the object of our excitement is the new Labour leader. All of us in the Lobby know our role is to write and create the first part of the myth of Johnny Todd. What we can't know is whether his is a star that will rise and fall over a decade, or a flashy meteor that will have crashed and burned by the time the exit polls are announced at 10 p.m. on election day. Hero or zero, the story of the election will be his story.

'A friend of mine in Downing Street says the PM is thinking of keeping out journos he doesn't like from his press conferences,' says the chap from the *Mirror*. It's a plausible threat: the Prime Minister is famously thin-skinned. We agree it would be an outrageous assault on the freedom of the press, and that if anyone is kept out then none of us will turn up. A fine sentiment. If push comes to shove, the professional advantage of being a scab is bound to triumph.

'So, gents,' says Wilkinson, 'what's the real story about Labour and tax?'

This is a predictable topic, given that the Tories brought to a grinding halt Labour's momentum in the polls at the last election with the charge they'd put up taxes for everyone. 'Specifically,' Wilkinson continues, 'we need a line on what the government has up its sleeve to neutralise Labour's pledge not to raise income tax.'

That triggers a smug smile which I try to hide. The story I got out of Tony Cannon – Labour's commitment not to increase either the basic or top rate of tax – has had a lot of play since it was splashed on the front page of the *FC*. Every other paper had to follow it up and for a couple of days it dominated the TV and radio news agenda. It is the sort of coup which does not go unbegrudged.

'I can't remember where I first read that tale,' says Wilkinson. 'Probably in one of the Labour rags'.

'Ha ha, Trevor,' I say.

'I can't see Ramsey pledging a reduction in taxes,' says the man from the *Telegraph*. 'They're running a deficit. If they promise to slash a penny or two off the basic rate, Labour will say the Tories can't make their sums add up.'

'Well, if they are *not* going into an election on a promise to cut taxes, that's a story.'

The scheming intensifies, though I'm only half paying attention. I'm distracted by the thought of what was in the envelope. My distinguished colleagues agree the line: fury with Ramsey from Tory MPs and candidates for his refusal to pledge tax cuts, a fury we'll cynically foment. Deal done, I rush back to the office.

The rest of my team has drifted in, filling up the space around the central table and depriving Jess and me of privacy. I trust them, but this is not a conversation I can have in front of others. Jess gives me a meaningful look.

'Shall we go for a coffee?'

We are in Strangers cafeteria, on the Thames side of Parliament. It is a relic of the 1950s, with its dark-brown wood tables and strip lighting. Strangers is the only place in Parliament where there is little conspicuous hierarchy: on the other tables are policemen, clerks, cleaners and caterers. Even the odd MP. We grab a table by the window, from where we can see the river and on the other side, fringed by trees, the white cubes of St Thomas's Hospital. Too raw. I angle my chair so that I don't have to look at it.

I clasp my hands around my mug of stewed black coffee, taking comfort from the warmth.

'What have you learned?'

Jess lays out the papers on the table. 'This is a fascinating document. But there is bad news.'

'You'd better start with that, then.'

'I can't for the life of me see anything that would give any clue to what happened to Clare.'

I am unsurprised. Treasury policy papers aren't normally a trail to unexplained death.

'Did you say there was good news?'

'Well, only to confirm something you know. Your sister was brilliant.'

My pavlovian response is a proud smile. 'Well?'

Jess settles back in her chair. 'How much do you know about pensions?'

'I know that maybe 6 per cent of my salary is deducted each month to go into the Media Corp pension fund, and that Media Corp puts in more than that.'

'Correct.' She nods, eager to show off. 'And in twenty-five years' time, that money's going to come back to you as a pension, as a proportion of your salary just before retirement – probably two-thirds of it, if you keep up the payments. But what happens to your savings in the meantime?'

'Please don't patronise me.'

'But it's irresistible,' she flashes back with a grin. 'Anyway you presumably know that they invest the money in assorted assets, mostly in shares and bonds.'

'Yup. I sort of knew that.'

'And, twice a year, the shares they buy pay income to them, in the form of dividends.'

'I'm still with you.'

Jess explains that the dividends are reinvested by the pension funds, to buy even more shares, which earn more dividends, so that the funds grow in value and the promised pensions can eventually be paid. She leans forward. 'This is where it gets counter-intuitive and weird – almost as if the system was designed by Lewis Carroll.'

'Like so much that comes out of the Treasury.'

'True.' She gives me a lesson on the subtle but important link between superannuation and fiscal policy. 'When companies pay dividends, those dividends are taken from profits on which corporation tax is levied. But pension funds don't have to pay tax. They are what is known as tax-exempt institutions, as are charities. And when a pension fund receives a dividend, the government tops up the payment by giving back to the pension fund the tax that the company has paid on it. To put it another way, each dividend comes with an associated tax credit, which the pension fund can turn into cash. I know this is complicated, but are you still with me?' she asks.

'To be honest, I am starting to lose the will to live.'

'Sorry. But in the end all you really need to know is this: those tax credits are worth at least five billion pounds a year to pension schemes, probably more, in fact. And Clare seems to have come up with a plan to abolish those tax credits. Which would increase the revenues of the government by the corresponding amount. So at least five billion pounds a year.'

I am no longer bored. 'You're telling me Clare found a way to raise five billion pounds every single year?' That, I can see, would be a big deal.

'Yes. But that's not all.' She points out that most pension schemes are in surplus, sometimes to a huge extent. In other words, the value of the income they expect to receive from the investments they own is significantly more than what they're committed to paying out as pensions in future. 'So abolishing tax credits is almost the perfect tax rise because it brings in a colossal sum of money while seemingly hurting no one.'

I am not convinced. 'What do you mean pension funds have a stonking surplus? Surely not all of them. What about the Maxwell schemes, for example?' Robert Maxwell was a media baron whose pension funds had collapsed about five years ago, causing untold harm to thousands of pensioners who worked for his newspapers and print works.

'First of all, Maxwell was a crook. His pension schemes collapsed because he plundered their assets to prop up his failing businesses. But of course, you're right: the Treasury's not saying there are no pension schemes in deficit, just that on average most schemes have a big surplus. And they won't miss all those billions of tax refunds.'

I slurp the bitter instant coffee, now lukewarm. I am confused by why Kendall backed off doing this. 'I've just been talking with our esteemed colleagues about how desperate the Tories are for money. This seems perfect for them.'

'Totally right. This would have financed a five billion pound cut in the basic rate of income tax – a massive electoral bribe.'

'So why not do it?'

'I don't know. All I can think is that maybe Ramsey was worried he would alienate the votes of pensioners and older people. Taking money out of their savings just before an election might not be a good look – and remember, the Tories are more dependent than Labour on the support of older people.'

'Maybe. Though if my sister was right that there'd be no actual harm to pensioners, it would be a risk worth taking.'

Jess narrows her eyes and points two fingers at me, like a pistol. 'Totally right.'

A thought gnaws at me, something Lorimer my editor told me when appointing me political editor. *'There's no such thing as a tax that hurts no one. The money always comes from someone.'*

The coffee has gone cold. 'If the Chancellor has killed Clare's scheme, that in itself would be a decent story, wouldn't it?'

She nods. 'A big story. *Government backtracks on pensions raid.* But we have to stand it up.'

For a moment, I have a pang of conscience. Is this what Clare would have wanted? Am I just using her to write another ego-boosting scoop?

We need to talk. This *is* what she wanted *me* to write. Maybe. She definitely wanted it out there – why else send it to Scott? – and presumably she wanted people to know the Tories had dumped it. Even so, the idea of my sister as a whistleblower is extraordinary, shocking. Something made her desperate.

'Could you ring the Treasury for a statement of some sort? You'll probably get a "we never comment on leaks", but we have to go through the motions. And perhaps start writing it up.'

A sharp look. 'Whose byline?'

'Yours.'

'You sure?' She's surprised.

'You were on to this first. I'll just sprinkle my magic dust on it when you've done the initial draft.'

She gathers up the papers and stuffs them back in the envelope. She has the energised eyes of a hack on the hunt. When we leave the café, I swing left.

'Where are you going?' she asks, then realises the answer. 'Oh, yes. It's afternoon Lobby.'

I glance at my watch. Quarter to four, bang on time. 'I'll call Mary to tell her we've got a decent tale for her.' Mary Nichols is the news editor, who has a mystical understanding of what the *FC*'s crusty male readers want to see on the paper's front page. She'd be the next editor, except that she went to the wrong college – well, no college at all – and is the wrong sex.

'Don't forget to ring the Treasury'.

I head to the Lobby briefing feeling almost buoyant. The news editor loved the story – 'It sounds like a splash. Can you do me 650 words?' – and I am back in the saddle. With this I can belatedly make it up to Clare, in my own way.

I speed-walk along the corridor parallel to the river, up broad majestic stairs, down a capacious corridor whose dark wooden doors are all firmly closed and guarded by attendants. This is the committee room corridor. I swing a left, and then a right, to another richly carpeted staircase; and then up three floors to a narrow corridor of glass-fronted offices that are always empty. I follow the green carpet to a stone staircase wide enough for just a single person, at the top of which is a closed and unlabelled dark door.

I push through it into a cavernous bare-raftered room at the top of one of Parliament's neo-Gothic towers – a place where absurd rituals are enacted and secrets are shared. It is satirically appropriate that this hidden chamber is shared with a masonic lodge. As usual, my Lobby colleagues are turning chairs to face the front, because they were the other way round for the just-finished meeting of the Press Gallery's freemasons. No one has ever invited me to join the chapter, probably because I am conspicuously an Oxbridge-educated, know-it-all Jew. Fuck 'em.

The other mystical ceremony here is the afternoon briefing of journalists by the Prime Minister's press secretary. Under the rules of the Lobby, we are not supposed to reveal that these briefings take place. We listen to what the PM's representative has to say, statements he has prepared in advance or elliptical answers he improvises to our questions. When we write them up, we are not allowed to attribute the quotes, or make any reference to a source. We report them either as simple facts, or the authentic view of the PM. It turns us, the members of the Lobby, into all-knowing oracles. And it allows the PM and the government to disseminate whatever is in their interest, but with no strings, no possible comeback. We are the soothsayers, they are the gods. Or, to put it another way, it is a shabby and inces-tuous system, a stain on our democracy.

Around forty of us are nattering as the PM's press secretary arrives, out of breath, flanked by two note-taking younger officials. Sebastian Mendes is a high-flyer at the Treasury who has been seconded to the post. Bright red socks are his bold defiance of convention, and he is more irreverent than most in this post – arching his right eyebrow when he wants to distance himself from one of the less persuasive views of his boss, Sir Peter

Ramsey. 'Afternoon, afternoon,' he says. 'Sorry I'm late. Shall I start by giving you a run-through of the Prime Minister's day?'

Wilkinson nods. He is the elected chairman of the Lobby, and chairs the meetings when they take place in the Palace of Westminster, our home turf. There is a morning Lobby as well, in Downing Street, and because it is on government property it is run by Mendes himself.

He runs through a few of the meetings the Prime Minister has had today or is scheduled to have: no useful detail of what's been said or agreed with ministers or foreign counterparts or business supplicants, a briefing shaped to hide more than it reveals.

Mendes wraps up. 'I haven't got much else to share with you today. Government seems strangely quiet at the moment.'

Polite laughter. Everyone knows the government is focused on the coming election.

'Maybe if we go to questions . . .'

Wilkinson calls on the man from the *Mirror*, who wants to know the PM's view on an MP who has left his wife and moved in with his children's nanny. 'The Prime Minister would take the view that these are private matters, though he prides himself on his own strong family values.'

More laughter, less polite.

I catch Wilkinson's eye. 'Gil,' he calls.

I have been doing this for years, often twice a day, yet today I feel a churn in my stomach as if it was my first time.

'Can you confirm that the Treasury has abandoned plans to force pension funds to pay tax on the dividends they receive?'

Three seats down I can feel Alan Scott staring at me with a mixture of puzzlement and frustration. I ignore him: all my

91

attention is on Mendes, who squints, then turns his eyes up to the ceiling as if he is trying to remember. This is his tell: I've seen it before. Playing for time.

'You're referring to the article your colleague wrote last month.' Christ, he has a good memory. 'As I recall, that was speculative. And as you know, there is a time-honoured tradition that we never comment on taxation, which are matters for the budget.'

I won't let it drop. 'Just to be clear, you are neither confirming or denying that the Treasury was planning a raid on pension fund tax credits, and that you've backed off.'

I've now got the attention of the room. My colleagues spot I have a story, though for most of them the tax status of pension funds is inhospitable territory.

'Again, I can't comment on speculation. But –' A dramatic pause. Mendes loves this pantomime. 'What I can say is that the Prime Minister and the Chancellor are united in their view that the duty of government is to protect people's hard-earned pensions, and they would never do anything to put that at risk.'

Bingo. That's not a denial, or even a non-denial denial. And if he hasn't denied it, then I have my story.

Mendes takes a few other questions but there isn't much more to say. As soon as we're done, I rush back to the office before Scott can collar me.

'He as good as confirmed it,' I tell Jess, who is tapping away at her keyboard. 'Any word from the Chancellor's office?'

'They said they'll get back to us.'

'Fine.' I stand behind her and read over her shoulder. In the time I've been at the Lobby briefing, she's already written most of the story.

The government has abandoned a £5bn tax raid on pension funds.

As first reported in the *FC*, the government had been devising plans for what was described as a 'painless' reform to the pension tax credit system. The policy would have raised over £5bn per year. However, government sources say the tax reform has been dropped.

The government had been widely expected to seek new revenue raising measures to pay for tax cuts. It is not clear why the abolition of the so-called dividend tax credit has been shelved.

A Treasury spokesman said *blah blah blah* . . .

'I'll drop in the quote when we get it.'

Bang on cue, the phone in my pocket starts to ring. I recognise the number. 'It's the Treasury.'

'Why are they calling you?' says Jess, annoyed. Even on the cusp of the twenty-first century, political journalism is still a boys' game.

I answer. 'Gil Peck.'

'Glad I caught you,' says a familiar and unexpected voice. 'What's this I hear about a pensions story you've got hold of?'

I cover the microphone with my hand. 'It's Kendall,' I mouth.

Jess acts out a silent theatrical scream. Why on earth has the Chancellor rung me rather than instructing a flunky to do so?

'The story will be in tomorrow's papers,' I say matter-of-factly. 'Would you like to give me some background?'

I'm expecting the usual flim-flam, another variant on the 'we don't comment on speculation' line. But instead he says, 'What is the point of a story about something that's not happening?'

Even on the tinny phone line, I can hear the frustration in his voice.

I am unsure how to respond. 'What do you mean?'

'This policy you've been asking questions about – it's not going to happen. Something that didn't happen isn't news. So why would you write about it?'

'Because it *was* going to happen and it is a sensible reform, but you backed off. Care to tell me why?'

My attitude only seems to infuriate him. 'How did you find out about it? Did Clare leave confidential papers at home? If you are using them, that would be a breach of the Official Secrets Act.'

This raising of the stakes knocks me back.

'I – I have no idea what you are talking about,' I stutter.

'There were documents missing from her desk. If you've got hold of something you shouldn't –'

'What are you suggesting?' I ask, forcefully now. I am annoyed.

'Think of your sister's reputation. Why would you want her dragged into this?'

He really ought to know – every politician ought to know – that if you want to kill a story, never intimidate the journalist. Nothing gets my back up more than being told what to do.

'I'm going to run this story,' I say firmly, my jaw tightening as I struggle to keep my composure. 'It'll be on the front page of the *FC* in the morning. And if you try to pin this in any way on Clare, or imply she did anything inappropriate . . .' A significant pause. 'Well, maybe there are some things she *did* tell me that I would write about.'

That last line is an entirely empty threat. I've only said it to warn him off. But it lands harder than I expected. Kendall goes silent. I hear a thud in the background, the sound of a desk or a filing cabinet taking a kicking.

'Now,' I say, a model professional again, 'do you want to give me a quote?'

Silence. Then, with a terse 'No comment', he hangs up.

I press the red button. Only then do I realise I'm shaking.

'What was that about?' Jess looks almost as stunned as I feel.

'Honestly? I'm not altogether sure.' Was he threatening me? 'He doesn't want us to put this story out.' I puff out my cheeks.

'All the more reason we should.'

'I guess so.' I'm puzzled why Kendall is so keen to kill a story that would probably make him a hero among his backbench colleagues, who are terrified of losing their seats in the election and would welcome any initiative that would allow them to flourish an income tax cut at their constituents. It doesn't make sense.

Jess goes back to the keyboard and finishes typing it up. I read it over, adorn it with hyperbole and then put it in the subeditors' electronic basket for editing and polishing.

'Happy?' asks Jess.

Happy isn't the word. I thought the papers might help to explain Clare's death, but they've simply yielded a classic *FC* splash, a difficult chat with the Chancellor, and funny looks from Scott.

'It's a decent story, Jess. Good work.'

My phone is still on the desk where I left it after Kendall's call when the screen lights up. As the Nokia trills, I read another number I know.

'Lorimer,' I say. The editor. I smile. 'He does love a pensions story.' I pick it up, anticipating a herogram. 'Peck here.'

'We're not running the story,' he says without preamble. *Shit.* 'You can't have read it.'

'Mary ran me through it. All you've got is something that was never announced, that isn't going ahead. Something that didn't happen isn't a story.'

It's the second time this evening I've heard that phrase. For now, I'm too stunned to process it properly.

'We ran Jess's story that something like it was in the works. This is the follow-up.'

'I'm sorry, Gil. Your judgement's off on this one.' A change of tone, now, his arm-around-the-shoulder voice. 'Not surprising, really, given all you've been through. You should have taken some proper downtime. We'll need you in fighting fettle when the campaign starts.'

I want to tell him it's bullshit. I want to argue, make him see that this is an important story that deserves to run. But the decision to spike it has stunned and deflated me.

'John, this is a mistake,' I say.

'That's my prerogative.'

I end the call, and only then start swearing.

'What happened?'

'They spiked the story,' I say, redundantly. Jess read the gist of the conversation from the pain written on my face. 'And Lorimer told me my judgement was shot.'

'Wow. That's mad. What now?'

'I think you know.'

Chapter 8

I T'S 1 A.M. IN THE Groucho and I am still seething. Not only did Lorimer spike my story, but the news desk rang me three hours ago with what felt like gratuitous provocation. The first edition of the *Globe* had dropped. Wilkinson splashed with the disclosure that Ramsey will announce the election on Monday. I reckon what put him on to it was my swaggering claim in the Pol Eds' huddle. It's irritating. Why do I have to show off?

'That was my story,' I say to Jess, for the fifth time. Why on earth didn't I write it? A story is a story, even if acquired at a family funeral.

'For God's sake, stop it,' she says. 'So you let one go. So what?'

'Sorry,' I say, sinking the rest of the Chablis in my glass. 'It's not even a real scoop. Everyone knew the timetable. Wilkinson just tarted it up with a couple of quotes.'

This is ungenerous. The game is the game. Scoops aren't just about revealing something that no one has thought of. They're partly about show business, about taking something that may already be in the ether and then writing about it with certainty and with a context that gives it authority and oomph. Wilkinson put the ball in the net. I'm off my game.

'What a flippin' awful day.' I look wistfully at the empty bottle. 'Our pensions story is spiked, and Wilkinson gets the front page with reheated gossip.'

'Stop feeling sorry for yourself.' I notice, not for the first time, that her attention is focused somewhere to my right.

'Found a better offer?'

'A different kind of tosser. Alex Elliott's over there.'

I turn round as discreetly as I can, which is to say drunkenly and clumsily. Alex Elliott is the public relations head at Media Corp, an Old Etonian with ruddy, fleshy cheeks and dark brown hair too long at the front, like an extra from *Four Weddings and a Funeral*. His manner is hail-fellow-well-met, a disguise for his ruthless calculation.

'Let's go over,' says Jess.

'It's come to this? You prefer Elliott's company to mine.'

She sighs. 'Strictly business. There's a tip off I want to put to him. Also, he's buying a proper drink.'

I clock the two-hundred-quid-a-bottle Krug Champagne in an ice bucket on his table, which we'll be happy to guzzle all night if a PR prick is paying. Jess and I are members of a dwindling band of hacks who resist the temptation to go through the looking glass into public relations. We prefer our mission of embarrassing the rich and powerful to manipulating the media and public opinion on their behalf. Even so, it's hard not to have expense account envy.

We saunter over. 'Wotcha, Elliott.'

Elliott gives an offhand wave, *noblesse oblige*. Jess and I squeeze our chairs around the table. He proffers the Krug. 'You know Patrick and Frankie, of course,' says Elliott, nodding to his companions. Patrick is Patrick Munis, the young *Times* leader writer. He's feted as the brightest young journalist of his generation – pass the sick bag. Frankie is Frankie Crowther, City Editor of the *Daily Telegraph*. My stamina for champagne and the white powder is highly developed, but I am an amateur compared with Crowther.

'Sorry about Clare,' says Munis. He's bellowing, because at this time of the night the club is packed and everyone is shouting to be heard. I'm aware Munis's sister was at Cambridge with Clare. If voters only knew the close social, educational and familial connections between politicians, media and the City, there'd be riots on the street. The people who end up in positions of power or influence come from the same schools, universities, and postcodes. Class and education trump ideology. The young Tory and Labour apparatchiks drink together across party lines, swap gossip about their bosses together, and sleep together. And because journalists, hacks, policy wonks and civil servants all know each other, usually from university – Oxford mostly, with diversity provided by Cambridge, occasionally Edinburgh – the ideological and sexual promiscuity runs across the establishment. Sleeping with the putative enemy is fine – almost a cliché – so long as it's discreet.

'I read about her in the *Tel*,' Crowther joins in. 'Hope you're OK, mate.' His accent is nasal estuary, a classic disguise assumed by alumni of the more expensive London fee-paying schools. He was one of the hacks who wrote up the story of Clare's death and it rankles that he did.

'I wish you hadn't done the story,' I say. 'The publicity makes it harder for her husband to shield the boys. And the story must have tipped off some toerag thieves, because their home in Primrose Hill was burgled during the funeral.'

Crowther looks sheepish. 'Fuck. Sorry. For what it's worth, I didn't put anything about the funeral in the copy.'

I am being a hypocrite, in that I've put my byline on too many stories that breach the line between the public and private. Even so, I ask, 'Why did you write it?'

'Mother of two tipped to be head of the Treasury dies in tragic bicycle accident? You know the form, Gil. That was always a story.'

'Yes, I know that'. I am tetchy. 'I mean where did the story come from? We didn't tell anyone and the Treasury told me they were surprised when they started getting calls about it.'

Crowther frowns. He has the build of a rugby front row gone to seed, an ageing bull with a stone or two of too-many-lunches flab. After a glass or six, his face is red and swollen. 'Fisher. I was talking to him about arranging a briefing on Labour's economic plans and he told me. I passed it to the Lobby guys. And they stood it up.'

Cameron Fisher was not the name I anticipated. He is Todd's press secretary, an abrasive former tabloid hack whose self-appointed mission is to search out, humiliate and destroy any journalist who somehow fails to acclaim Todd as the messiah. 'Cameron Fisher? How on earth did he know about Clare?'

'Search me.' Crowther has not given it a moment's thought. He is the sort of journalist who City PRs adore, men whose self-love is so complete that they can't be arsed to ask fairly basic questions such as 'Why am I being told this?' They take dictation from an Elliott or Fisher, and so long as what they are being told is a splash or even a page lead, they'll write it up and not bother to think about the source's ulterior motive.

'You didn't think it was odd that Labour's flack-in-chief told you about the death of a Treasury director?'

'He mentioned her dad – sorry, *your* dad – was some kind of grandee from Labour's past. Jurassic Labour, as Todd and his gang put it.' Crowther works out that even by his standards he is being insensitive. 'Sorry. No offence intended. I assume Fisher knew because you're all part of the Labour family. Aren't you?'

Crowther is not the first or last posh boy to accuse me of being incestuously close to Labour. It offends against my sense of who I am. I pride myself that everything I've achieved has been despite Dad, not because of him. So the idea that I might have better relations with Labour because the great Bernard Peck was an adviser to an ancient Labour government horrifies and upsets me. In fact, I've spent quite a lot of my working life trying to dig up dirt on Labour, just to prove how impartial I am.

More relevantly, it's impossible that my proud dad would have said anything about Clare to anyone close to the party's current leadership team. Dad regards Todd as an untrustworthy right-wing entryist who has hijacked the party he thinks he owns.

If I want to find out how Fisher knew, Frankie Crowther is probably not the man with the answer. I change tack. 'You were a cunt for not telling me you were running it.'

'I wasn't sure you would want me to bother you at a difficult time.'

'Hang on. You knew it was a difficult time, but you still ran the story? Jesus. It's shit Frankie, you hurt my family.'

Crowther looks resentful. Apparently he's blaming me for making him feel bad. His narcissism is in a league of its own.

Munis, whose eyes are glued to Jess's breasts in a tight blue top, won't validate my annoyance either.

'It's grief,' he says to me, with the kind of gravity reserved for statements that are supposed to be profound. 'Your anger, it's normal, natural. Part of the seven stages.'

'Oh my God, Patrick, this is my life – not some fucking feature you've written for the lifestyle pages of *The Times*. If you really wanted to be new age, you'd look at Jess's face, not her tits.'

Elliott guffaws. 'Boys, boys!' he says. 'Time for another drink.' He calls over the young student waitress and orders more Krug.

'I see it's 1.45. I must be at the "bargaining" stage by now,' I say. 'Let's hope I can get through all five grief stages by the time I leave.'

Elliott is relieved I have switched from fury to sarcasm. Jess squeezes my arm. And then she pounces on Alex. 'So,' she says, 'What's all this about Media Corp and Capital Television?'

'I've already heard Elliott's bullshit on this,' says Crowther. 'I'll be back in a minute.' He heads for the downstairs men's room, presumably to fortify himself with a line or three. Munis also excuses himself, as he's spotted his paper's deputy editor walking past. Alex tops up Jess's glass.

'I am not sure what you mean,' he says glibly.

'Really? It's the talk of EC2,' she replies. 'The arbs are betting huge that you are about to launch a bid. Literally no one is short of the stock. It's seen as a one-way bet.'

'It's bollocks.'

'Is that "bollocks" as in "it's categorically not true", or "bollocks" as in "maybe the little girl won't notice I haven't denied it"?'

Elliott's eyes widen. He's close to lashing out. Jess continues, 'Capital is a match made in heaven for you. Breitner understands TV. It's mature. Capital may not have growth but it spews out cash. And the one thing you need is cash.' She points out that much of Media Corp is in satellite TV and the buzzwords of the moment that no one understands, 'the information super-highway', are high growth and massively cash negative. 'This is the kind of deal Breitner orgasms over. It might even give Breitner the financial platform to do what we all know he really wants to do, which is buy AOL.'

Elliott puts down his glass. 'You are very intelligent and very persuasive. But listen to me, sweetie. I will say this slowly. The arbs are wrong. The City boys are wrong. We're not interested.'

Jess is undeterred. 'Everyone knows Capital needs a buyer. Its shareholders have lost patience with management. And if you buy it, Media Corp becomes incomparably the most powerful media business in the UK. No one could touch you. I just don't get why you wouldn't buy it.'

'Jimmy is interested in owning the businesses of the future, not some fucking franchise that was created in the 1950s to offer a fig leaf of competition to the BBC,' he snaps.

'For fuck's sake, the *Globe* wasn't exactly the white heat of technology when Breitner bought it.' Jess leans forward, the fabric stretching tighter. It's one of her kill moves, but I've never had the guts to ask whether she is consciously flaunting. 'What Breitner is mostly about is power,' she continues with admirable fluency given how much we've drunk. 'Businesses of any vintage can deliver that to him. Why does he own all those newspapers, including ours, if all that excites him is some nebulous high-tech future?'

'It's not happening. Forget it.' Elliott's easy charm is fraying.

'Pull the other one. The power Breitner would wield! There wouldn't be a politician he couldn't own.'

'Not our style, sweetie.' His self-righteous pose is nauseating. Jess changes tack. 'I've got two impeccable sources who say you are a liar. Media Corp is going to bid for it.'

Elliott sniffs and shoots his shirt cuffs. 'If you had two impeccable sources, we wouldn't be having this conversation. You would have written it.'

Jess is pushing her luck. But Elliott is not sure how far she is bluffing. She doubles down. 'I know for a fact that Breitner has lined up Schon for this. And I am going to write it, unless you give me a categorical denial. None of the "it's bollocks" stuff.'

Elliott's nerve has been touched. Schon Partners is the world's most powerful and profitable investment bank. Having them on side in a takeover or a merger is the City equivalent of having Mossad and the Israeli Defence Force on the team. You would not bet against them.

Elliott takes a breath, smiles and says, 'You are 100 per cent wrong. It's a lie, it is false. If you print that, you'll look like an idiot.'

'A hundred quid says you'll announce next week.'

'Jesus,' says Elliott, 'you're so annoying, I don't know whether to hit you or fuck you.'

Jess bursts out laughing. I interject, 'All that money on an expensive education and that's the best you can come up with?'

No need for my chivalry. Jess has it covered. 'If you want to get fucked, Elliott, just bend over. I'm writing the story.'

She glances at me, I thank Elliott for his hospitality and we saunter to the cloakroom to collect our coats. I can feel Elliott's eyes following us.

'You need to take care,' I say, as we stand on the corner of Dean Street and Old Compton Street, hoping to spot a black cab. 'Don't forget we all work for the same company.'

'He's such a fucking liar.' Jess is trembling with righteous anger. 'I couldn't do what he does, for all the money in the world.'

Elliott has an incentive worth billions to lie to us: if the story gets out before Breitner has strong-armed Capital's board into agreeing the takeover and locking it in, Capital's share price will skyrocket, other potential bidders may enter the fray and it could get very messy. It could make the purchase prohibitively expensive for Breitner.

'He's a snake whose only interest is in protecting his boss's fortune,' I say. 'Have we got enough to write the story?'

'Of course not. Breitner has definitely been talking to Schon. But I can't prove it's for this deal. And Elliott gave me a categorical denial.'

'He was fibbing. You have him bang to rights. He wouldn't have been so on edge if not.'

But it doesn't matter that we know we're right. My most basic rule is that the deniability of a story is far more important than whether or not it's actually true. I've lost count of the number of amazing stories I've never published, even though I knew they were accurate. If there is a risk that the target or subject of a story will deny it, and there is an associated risk that no one else will come forward to prove the denial is a lie, then there is no point in publishing. Goodness only knows how many nefarious activities of the great and the good of this country have been withheld from public view, because the likes of Elliott are prepared to tell egregious untruths.

There are no taxis to be found on Dean Street, so we walk back up towards Oxford Street. Elliott has also left the club and is on the pavement a few yards away, presumably waiting for his driver to bring his car around. He is facing away and can't see us.

I'm about to steer Jess across the street – she's capable of continuing the argument if we get too close – when I see Elliott has his Motorola handset pressed to his ear and is talking rapidly and loudly. I put my fingers to my lips and we quietly move closer.

'Whether or not she actually knows, it's all round the City.' Elliott says. 'The lanky poof simply can't keep his mouth shut. You'd better instruct him to zip it, or the whole thing will fall apart.'

I glance at Jess, and we share a knowing look. Among our captains of industry, you can count the number who are openly gay on the fingers of one hand. One of the few is Sean Lanchester, who happens to be tall and thin, and is the chief executive of Capital Television.

'Gotcha,' I think.

A black Range Rover with tinted windows swings around the corner and pulls up on the kerb. Elliott gets in the back, not bothering to glance behind him.

'I knew it was true,' says Jess. 'I bloody knew it.'

'He's a cock,' I observe, with all the insight lent by what I've been drinking and sniffing. 'And Crowther. And Munis. They're all cocks.'

On Oxford Street, we flag down a cab with its orange light on. 'You go first,' I tell Jess, 'I'll get the next one.' But she's in charge. She pushes me in, guiding my head under the door frame, and instructs the driver to take me to Highbury.

'See you, Gil.'

*

Thirty minutes later I am turning the key in the door of my North London flat. It's the ground floor of a grand late-Victorian house that implies an income I don't earn. I bought it for a bargain in the housing slump of five years ago, from the keyboard player of a two-hit-wonder synthesiser pop trio of the 1980s. I was lucky. It has high ceilings, white walls, and windows the size of church doors, which in daylight look on to a communal garden at the back, and the expansive green of Highbury Fields at the front.

I perform my little ritual, laying out the two Nokias, the pager, my notebook and pens on a battered white Scandinavian side table that's next to my bed. Then I pour myself a glass of white wine from the fridge, flop on to the sofa and switch on Sky News. I don't pay it much attention, but it's nice to have something to ignore. I'm physically shattered; but my brain refuses to quieten. I'm still angry and that drives my thoughts in circles.

I am resentful of Wilkinson for writing the scoop I should have had. I am furious with my editor, Lorimer, for spiking the story I did have. I am contemptuous of Alex Elliott for being a lying bastard. And don't get me started on Frankie Crowther.

Most of all I hate Clare for stupidly getting herself killed.

I fumble inside my rucksack. There's the envelope I stole from Alan Scott, forty-odd pages of a defunct pensions policy that no one cares about.

I flip through it, reading it again by the flickering light of the television. Not that there's any chance that in my current state I'll spot anything that Vulcan Jess missed. The page becomes spotted and damp. From out of nowhere, I am weeping.

For the Alex Elliotts of this world, the truth is what you put in a press release. It is what they want the world to think about their clients. For me, truth is what the proprietor, the editor and the lawyer will allow me to write. Clare lived by a simpler and higher standard. She believed the distinction between truth and lies – between right and wrong – mattered.

So what is the simple truth about her death? What am I missing? To coin a phrase, I know nothing. And I can't leave it alone. Lorimer implies it's the shock, that I need time offline to recharge. But sod him. I've investigated enough dodgy stories to know when something doesn't feel right.

He is always going to lie when there are hundreds of millions of pounds of his boss's cash at stake. The Capital Television deal will be worth a couple of billion pounds. For that sort of money, I saw Elliott make up nonsense without even blinking.

Those tax credits are worth at least five billion pounds a year. Five billion every year. That is an incentive to dissemble on an epic scale.

There's something not right about how Clare died.

What on earth am I thinking? The policy was dead, killed by the Chancellor.

Something that doesn't happen isn't news. And that is the point. Nobody would bump off someone over a tax plan that's been dropped, that would have caused no one any serious harm, even if it had happened. I've got to stop obsessing.

On the television is a repeat of the 10.30 lookahead to the morning's papers. Kay Burley holds up a copy of the *Globe*, with Wilkinson's story about the election announcement splashed all over it. Literally shoving it in my face. I reach for the remote control and I'm about to switch it off when something on the front page she's holding catches my eye.

It's the Cheltenham Gold Cup tomorrow, and the *Globe*'s editor has decided to spice up the election story with a horse racing metaphor. OFF TO THE RACES, says the big block headline. Underneath is a photo of two horses neck and neck, with Todd's and Ramsey's oversized photos superimposed on the jockeys' faces. Ramsey is grinning madly, a manic gleam in his eye, but it's the picture of Todd that's caught my attention. A surer smile, staring into the distance with the confidence of a man who knows his time has come.

He's probably going to win the election, unless he completely cocks it up. It's triggered me to go back to what Frankie Crowther said this evening, how he got the story of Clare's death from Todd's press secretary.

Why would Fisher know what happened to Clare?

Marilyn said Clare met with Todd, not long before she died. An unorthodox meeting that she attended under an alias.

What did they talk about? Maybe Clare hadn't given up on the tax plan. Would that give anyone reason to kill her?

In the depths of the night, with very expensive alcohol sloshing around my system, a lot of crazy ideas seem plausible. Suddenly I'm seized by an overwhelming and wholly irrational need to know.

Marilyn will know.

I take the phone off the table and dial the number before I have time for second thoughts. It rings for so long that I start to wonder whether she's spending the night somewhere else, with someone else.

Just as I'm about to ring off, she answers.

'What's happened?' She must have been fast asleep, but I can hear her rousing herself. In her world, a call at this hour is usually an MP pulled over for speeding with a woman who isn't his wife sitting next to him. Or a shadow cabinet minister photographed in the bushes on Clapham Common.

'Don't worry. It's just me.'

'Gil? For Christ's sake, it's four in the morning.'

'I know. Sorry.' Now that I have her, I'm not even sure what I want to ask. I burble. 'When Johnny met Clare, do you think they talked about pensions?'

An incredulous pause. 'How much have you had to drink?'

This was a bad idea. Saying it aloud, I realise how ridiculous it sounds. But I've started. 'You know, that meeting they had.'

'I told you, Johnny didn't tell me what they discussed. I also told you the meeting was a secret. I hope to fuck you haven't mentioned it to anyone.'

'I just wondered . . .' I'm losing confidence. 'If he mentioned anything afterwards, about pensions . . . or tax credits . . . or . . .' The silence from the other end of the phone is a wall. 'Never mind. Can you set up an interview for me with Johnny?'

Another pause. 'Is this for real?'

'Yeah. Look, I'm sorry. I'll call you in the morning. Wasn't thinking straight.'

'You can say that again.' She waits. 'Anything else?'

'Can I come over?'

A snort. 'I don't do sympathy fucks.'

'I just meant –'

'Get some sleep, Gil.'

She hangs up without saying goodbye. I turn the Nokia over and over in my hands. What was I thinking, calling Marilyn? All I did was embarrass myself.

I'm too tired to think. I turn on the phone and dial another number that I use more often than I should.

A woman picks up and pretends to be cross. 'Have you been a bad boy?'

'Erm ... Yes I have.'

'Yes what?'

'Yes, miss.'

This is a mistake. My phone bills are exorbitant.

'You need to be punished, don't you?'

Hard to disagree.

Chapter 9

Thursday, 20 March – 42 days until Election Day

THE PRIME MINISTER, SIR PETER Ramsey, has taken a short drive in his official Daimler: one mile from Downing Street to Buckingham Palace and back. On his return, he stood on a red carpet in front of the door of Number 10, where he sonorously announced that Her Majesty would be dissolving parliament and a General Election would be held on the first of May. That was three days ago. It would be an unusually long campaign, six weeks. Ramsey's hope is that the longer voters have to focus on the consequences of change, the more likely they'll be to stick with him. It is not a sophisticated strategy but it's all he's got.

The dam has burst: everywhere you look, on TV, in the press, on billboards, there'll be non-stop politics for a month and a half. For Labour, perhaps more than the Tories, the stakes are incalculably high. If the party loses yet again, after nearly two decades in opposition, the game would probably be up for it as a credible party of government.

As for the journalists of the parliamentary Lobby, we're high on our brief moment of real power. In normal times, it is the ministers, MPs and civil servants who hold the precious information, and we ferret around for scraps. Now those same MPs are just candidates, desperate for our attention, hoping we will convey their words to the voters who'll decide whether to back them or sack them. We are the masters now. It won't last.

I am running down the Embankment from Parliament to Millbank Tower, an isolated 1960s skyscraper on the north bank of the Thames, an architectural giving of the finger to the London skyline. This is where Labour has moved its headquarters and where it will host a 9 a.m. general election press conference every day during the campaign. I am anxious. These events are recorded for television news and broadcast live on the BBC and on Sky's twenty-four hour news channel. America's rolling news culture has arrived to change and taint public life. Instead of my off-the-record conversations in the lobbies and corridors of the Palace of Westminster, my questions will be on screen. If I make a fool of myself, there will be an audience. A big one. Nowhere to hide.

The officials in the entrance hall recognise me and wave me through to the auditorium. There is a hum of excitement. Spin doctors are cracking jokes with hacks and TV presenters. At the back of the room is a raised platform crammed with television cameras. There are more at the sides for 'cutaway' shots. Down the front there is a mob of press photographers.

I am one of the last to arrive. There are almost no seats left at the front. Damn. The only one I can see is alongside Alan Scott. Shit. Needs must.

As soon as he sees me, he juts his jaw forward. 'Erm, rumour has it you had a decent story spiked last week,' he says, as I squeeze into the chair next to him.

'It happens.'

'Something to do with pension tax credits?'

I'm not surprised it's out. Someone in the Treasury press office has been gossiping. 'Yeah, maybe,' I say, trying to ignore his accusatory stare. 'Kendall was working up a policy to snatch five billion pounds of tax credits bunged at pension funds. But he dropped it.'

'Yes. I was aware.' Scott is being eaten up by the disappearance of the package he expected from Clare. I can't reassure him.

'So we've been working along similar lines,' I say, as if this is a revelation. 'Do you think we should ask a question about it this morning?'

Under that ragged haircut, his pale skin has flushed red. He's not sure if I am playing him.

'Erm ... Why?'

'Labour need to raise money somehow to pay for their campaign promises. They've ruled out raising income tax. The pensions wheeze would be perfect for them.'

Scott looks down at the doodles he's been making on his notepad. The idea of collaborating with me goes against his instincts.

'Look, we might neither of us get a question,' I say. 'But if one of us does, let's ask about the tax credit. Unless you've got a better line you want to put to them.'

He fidgets as though uncomfortable. He knows I am being rational. 'Fine.'

It's almost 9 a.m. A hush descends on the room as Todd and his *de facto* number two, the Shadow Chancellor, Neville Tudor, walk out of the wings and take their places behind the desk on the podium. The photographers surge to the front like hounds, all pushing as close as possible to get the best shot. The room is filled with shutter clicks, the whirring of automatic wind-on, and flashes. It's a feeding frenzy. Labour apparatchiks are forming a thin and fragile line of defence. One of the photographers – Joe Davidson, a crop-headed bulldog of a man known as 'the Bruiser' – won't be stopped from getting the money shot and elbows through.

'Just look at Todd,' I whisper to Scott. On stage, the Shadow Chancellor is scowling, but Todd is beaming in the strobes of the flash guns like an actor on the Oscars red carpet. 'He loves this.'

And then there's a crash. In the melee, one of the aides has knocked a camera lens. Obscenities are traded, and two officials haul the Bruiser towards the exit. He's jostling and threatening to file charges. This is not the slick start Johnny Todd expected and wanted.

But he turns even this to advantage. 'Wait!' Todd signals. 'Of course Joe can have his shot. Don't you know how important he is?'

'What a fucking operator,' I whisper to Scott.

The Bruiser is mollified. Todd waits while he screws in a new lens and takes instruction on the best pose to strike. 'Look towards the camera, Mr Todd. Give us a wink, please.' He obliges, then sits down. The snappers crouch, Tudor takes the lectern.

Neville Tudor is a whale, with a mop of black hair and the baritone of a Welsh male-voice chorister (his *Who's Who* hobby). His mission is to prove as heresy that only the Tories can be trusted to manage the economy. Like a Methodist preacher, his fire-and-brimstone sermons from the stump are on the virtues of what he calls – with a massive rolling 'r' – 'fiscal *rrrr*ectitude.' He and Todd are the double act at the heart of

116

the Party. Todd is in a long line of upper-middle class 'natural' leaders of this country. He would not look out of place among the Tories. Tudor is the son of schoolteachers and the grandson of miners, educated at Llandudno state schools and Cardiff University. He personifies the UK's post-war social mobility, and is rooted in the Labour movement in a way that public-school Todd is not. Tudor doesn't have to reach out to the brothers, he is one of them, like my tax-story source, Cannon. But there is a difference. Cannon is Todd's loyal servant; he will never publicly disagree with him. Tudor does not, and will not, accept that Todd is the boss.

'Welcome to the most important general election of our age,' Tudor booms. 'Eighteen years of Tory misrule coming to an end. The people of Britain deserve better. Better than a Conservative party that puts up VAT because they can't balance the books. Better than leaving schools to crrrrumble, and NHS waiting lists to rrrrise and rrrrise. Better than a prime minister and his crrrronies taking money from hardworking families to reward fat cat friends.' Tudor grips the lectern as if he's about to lift it up and slam it down.

'In less than six weeks from today we will wake up from this nightmare and Modern Labour will start the work of building the Modern Britain we all deserve.' The logo on the screen behind the stage now dissolves into a video clip. A nurse called June in a Manchester hospital talks about how funding cuts have devastated the National Health Service's ability to provide top-class free universal healthcare. She herself has suffered. After finding a lump in her breast, she waited months for a mammogram, and weeks more to see a specialist. By the time they discovered the cancer it had spread too far. The film finishes with a shot of her in the park with her eight- and nine-year-old girls and the implication they will soon be without a mother.

'That was filmed a month ago. June died just last week.' The room gulps. Tudor's voice is almost a whisper. But now it rises, becoming angry. 'That is why our first pledge for this election is that in every year of a Labour government, we will increase NHS funding by 4 per cent above the retail price index rate of inflation. This is our first promise, the most important promise, a real 4 per cent for the NHS.' And projected on the screen behind him is: 'Because June deserved better, a real 4 per cent for our NHS.'

For an instant, everything is still, silent. And then we're abuzz with murmurs about the drama we've witnessed and the massive spending commitment Tudor's just made. It feels like a big moment.

'Over to you for questions,' says Tudor. 'Roger Oaks from the BBC?'

There is a hierarchy to the questions that are called. The BBC always goes first, followed by ITV and then Sky, and then the BBC again for some reason. Print hacks are relegated to the undercard.

'If I may,' says the silver-haired Oaks, all old-school courtesy, 'Mr Todd, you've already said that Labour won't put up income taxes. How will you pay for this very expensive NHS commitment? Aren't you reinforcing the charge you can't be trusted with the nation's finances.'

Todd opens his mouth to reply – but Tudor beats him to it. 'This is for me,' he says briskly. 'We will be giving a detailed account of how each and every one of our spending promises will be funded, over the course of the campaign. I can reassure you that there will be fiscal *rrrr*ectitude in everything we do, unlike Ramsey's Big British Bankruptcy.'

Belatedly, he turns back to Todd. 'Do you want to add anything, Johnny?'

'I think you covered it,' he replies, with a flicker of irritation, so subtle it won't be caught by the cameras.

The press conference continues. Predictably, most of the questions are focused on whether Labour's spending promises are affordable. Scott and I have been waving our hands frenziedly in the air, hoping we'll be seen by Tudor. I'm starting to think it's not going to happen – there are only two or three minutes left, and the aides are looking at their watches – when I hear Tudor's unmistakeable voice calling my name.

'Mr Peck. What have you got to say for yourself?'

A Labour flack passes me a microphone. I panic at the thought of being on TV. Deep breath. 'You need to raise money,' I begin. 'What is your policy on the dividend tax credit system that gives pension funds five billion pounds each year? Would you abolish it?'

This is a technical question, obviously one for Tudor. He sucks in his cheeks. 'I'm afraid you'll have to wait for our manifesto for that. But what I will say –'

I never find out how he's going to fob me off, because Todd leans towards his microphone and says, with a sly grin, 'If I may, Neville, I think I'll take this.'

Tudor stares at him, astonished.

'I've been thinking about this,' says Todd, with a smirk. 'It's complicated. But there is a strong case for abolishing the tax credit and putting that money into the NHS. In fact, I can't understand why the government hasn't done it already.'

He ignores the daggers from Tudor.

'Does that answer your question, Gil?' Todd has that knack, when he speaks, of making you feel he's sharing an important confidence.

I nod. I'm wearing an embarrassed smile, not immune to his charm.

'Erm, that's a story,' says Scott, as the leaders leave the stage and the journalists file out. 'Labour stealing a Tory idea.'

'Is that how you'll play it?' Scott's paper, the *Sentinel*, is the only left-wing broadsheet and is in two minds about Todd's 'modernisation' of Labour. Its leader writers' conferences are a microcosm of the debate within the party about whether Todd is selling out too much.

'We prefer Labour governments to come up with their own ideas.'

'But what if an idea dreamed up by a Tory government is just a good idea?'

He scowls. I head out of the auditorium, musing whether Lorimer will let me write about the tax credit this time.

I look around in case Marilyn is near, so that I can double check the weight of what Todd just said. I haven't spoken to her since that embarrassing phone call in the early hours. Also I really want that interview with Todd and am worried my neediness may have pissed her off.

'Did Todd's people put you up to that?' someone hisses behind me. I've come out into the Millbank lobby, and a tall, athletic brunette blocks my exit. I'd have more chance getting past William 'The Refrigerator' Perry to score a touchdown.

'Hello, Jane.'

Jane Walters is the Shadow Chancellor's economic adviser and licensed destroyer. She's there to jealously guard Tudor's turf – economic and tax policy – and keep Todd well clear of it. Tudor and Todd have a relationship based on mutual advantage and chronic mistrust. He's the older by fifteen years, and when Todd became leader, three years earlier, he abandoned dreams of becoming PM. But Tudor will never be Todd's cipher, and he's surrounded by a clique of true believers, led by Jane, who still see him as the king across the water. For them, every interaction between Todd and Tudor has a winner and a loser.

She shepherds me to the side of the lobby, away from the throng, and backs me against the wall.

'What was that about?'

'What do –'

'Your clever little pensions question. Did your girlfriend put you up to it?'

'Sorry?'

'Todd was using you to bounce Neville into a tax change we haven't agreed and that hasn't gone to shadow cabinet.'

'Thanks for the tip. Makes the story stronger. *Todd overrules Shadow Chancellor.* Nice one.'

'Fuck off. Why did you ask the question?'

Her face is too close to mine. I'm inhaling lungfuls of Jo Malone's English Pear & Freesia.

'I've been looking at the whole dividend tax credit thing. You must have seen Jess's piece on it?' She's halfway buying it. 'It's free money, for God's sake. Why wouldn't you do it?'

She snorts.

'That's not a denial.'

'I'm not in the mood for silly buggers, Gil. We'll look at our options, and if the Shadow Chancellor thinks they're sound, then and only then will they become Labour policy.'

She steams back to the auditorium. I head for the street. I'm three paces beyond the door when the silver Nokia rings. I look at the number and sigh.

'Are you going to give me a bollocking as well?'

'And it's lovely to hear your voice, too,' says Marilyn. 'Are you in trouble again?'

'I've just been mugged by Jane.'

'Poor you. Did she crush you between her muscle-bound thighs?'

'Christ! Does your sexism ever worry you?'

'Not especially.'

I spy Walters and Tudor deep in conversation across the other side of the road.

'She accused me of being your lackey and trying to bounce Tudor into a pensions raid.'

'You couldn't have done it better if I had asked you. You were magnificent.'

I don't like the compliment. 'She also implied she knows about our extra-curricular activities.'

'That's standard Jane Walters mind games.'

I'm not reassured. 'Is there a risk people are talking about us?'

She clicks her tongue. 'I don't think so. But that's not why I rang. I've got you what you wanted.'

My mind is temporarily blank.

'The interview with Johnny? The one you woke me up for? Don't tell me you don't want it any more. I've got a queue of your panting competitors.'

The first big interview of the campaign with the leader of the Opposition? If I don't bugger it up, it'll drive the news agenda for days. 'That's amazing. When?'

'His house, Tufnell Park, 9.30 Monday morning.'

Chapter 10

ONE OF THE PERKS OF North London life is that the biggest story in British politics is happening on my doorstep. From my flat, it's a short bike ride down the Holloway Road and then left to the Victorian villas of Lady Margaret Road.

I push the old-fashioned white enamelled doorbell. In five weeks, if all goes according to Labour's plan, the owner of this house will pack up and move across town to Number 10. He will be the leader of the world's fourth largest economy, with a military capacity to match, including a sizeable arsenal of nuclear warheads. The journey from the bay-windowed family home to the wind tunnel of Downing Street will squeeze his private space and private life to almost nothing. He'll become our property – and by us I don't mean 'you the people,' I mean 'we the media'.

A blonde woman in an office suit and stockinged feet opens the door. She has her hair in a bun speared with a pencil, and a two-year-old girl on her hip. Superwoman, or rather Super PR Woman.

'Oh sugar, I thought you were the nanny,' she says. She looks back through the doorway – 'Johnny! Your guest is here' – and then back at me. 'You *are* here for Johnny, aren't you?'

'That's right. I –'

'Everybody is, these days. You'd think his job was more important than mine.' She gives a mannish snort. 'It'll only get worse when he wins. Shit.' She has stepped backwards on to a Lego brick.

From inside, I hear Todd's honeyed voice. 'Is that Gil?'

I nod.

'Then you'd better come in.'

I follow, picking my way through the Lego, Duplo and remote-controlled cars that have turned the parquet floor into a neo-expressionist canvas. 'Excuse the mess,' she says.

Johnny Todd is sitting at a large white oak table in the kitchen extension at the back. Sunshine floods in through the skylights above and the glass doors to a small garden. In his crisp white shirt and sage knitted silk tie, he looks like a management consultant. A Boss jacket hangs on the back of his straight-backed chair.

He rises and clasps my hand, the over-familiar two-handed squeeze of American politicians. He clamps his eyes on mine. Their green is startling.

'Gil, great to see you. Sit down, sit down. Coffee?' There's a large cafetière on the table. 'How do you take it? Black? Super.' His eyes drift over my shoulder, as if he's expecting someone else. 'When's your snapper arriving?'

'I asked him to come a bit later.' I take the chair he offers me opposite him. 'I prefer to talk for a bit without distractions, if that's OK?'

'If it's OK with him. I'm a bit tight for time.'

'I am sure it won't be a problem,' I say, disingenuously. The photographer will be furious I've shunted him to the last fifteen minutes, and the picture desk will be too. But I hate witnesses to my technique when I'm trying to persuade an interviewee to say something they'll live to regret.

Todd tilts his head back and drains his mug. Pushing it to one side, his hand drifts to his neck and checks the knot of his tie is centred.

'Shall we start?'

'OK if I turn on the recorder?' I take out my two Sonys – I always use a backup – and check the power and that the cassettes are at the start.

'Yuh. Before we begin though, if I want to go off the record at any point, you'll respect that, won't you?'

'Of course.' The machine's red light starts to flash. I open my notebook and scan an optimistic thirty questions. 'If we can begin with –'

'There's a lot of myth about Labour and business,' he interjects, before I can ask anything. He tips back his chair on two legs and gazes at a point on the wall behind my head. 'Did you know stock markets actually perform much better when there's a Labour government?'

I did. Most people in my line do. But it was a rhetorical question, so I don't reply.

'Yet everybody thinks that we're somehow against business. Why is that?'

This time he wants an answer. 'Pretty much every Labour government we've ever had has had to confront some kind of economic crisis. High inflation, excessive public borrowing, strikes, pressure on sterling – sooner or later the markets do you in. Denis Healey going cap in hand to the IMF for a bailout is the abiding image of incompetent Labour.'

The chair legs rap back on to the floor as he leans forward. 'I know! And that was 1976, for goodness' sake. Twenty years ago, and people still bring it up. They hold it against me!' He shakes his head, as if marvelling at the injustice of the world. 'This time it will be different. We will not bankrupt the country. As my friend Neville says – quite often, as you may have noticed – we are now the party of fiscal rectitude.' He flashes a smirk, invisible to the tape recorder. I make a note of it. 'We don't want businesses to see us as the enemy. We want to be their partner, their friend.'

It's a jarring moment. Here we are at his kitchen table, drinking coffee out of mismatched mugs. I can hear a child wailing upstairs and another one shouting something about a missing remote control. If it wasn't for the tape recorder between us, we would look like a couple of North London dads chatting about football or schools. Instead, I am chronicling the shifting tectonic plates of British politics.

He seems to be enjoying the incongruity. His smile broadens. 'We can achieve nothing unless business prospers and makes profits. Profits create jobs, jobs pay wages, and all that income generates taxes which pay for schools and hospitals. So here is something few, if any, Labour leaders have ever said: the bigger the profits made by business, the better.'

The tape is recording everything, but even so I feel compelled to write that down in my notebook. I visualise it as a large-font pull-quote in the centre of the long version of the published interview.

'Are you deliberately setting out to alienate your trade union supporters by moving closer to business?' *Alienate* is putting it mildly. Some union bosses – Denis Kenilworth comes to mind – will be apoplectic. 'Isn't there a risk they'll punish you by withholding funding from you, money you desperately need?'

'I don't think anyone's under any illusions about how I see that particular relationship. I have enormous respect for our trade unions, and their general secretaries. The work they do on behalf of their members is vital. But they aren't elected to run the Labour Party. *I* am. I take orders from the people of Britain, from no one else.'

From the hall Mrs Todd is shouting, 'Johnny, have you seen the bloody car keys?' He breaks off. 'Bear with me a second.' He fishes the keys out of his jacket pocket, walks to the kitchen door, and throws them to his wife. 'Sorry, Gil. Where was I?'

'You run the party, not the unions.'

'Oh yes. There's another point. If we can invest more in our vital public services – our schools and hospitals – thanks to the taxes that are levied on rising profits and wages, then everyone benefits. Including trade unionists. We have a collective shared interest in economic success, and my reading of the general secretaries is they recognise that.'

Clare would have had a few withering things to say to Johnny about the idea that there is no tension between the interests of bosses and workers. I am sure of that. She was a daddy's girl. But she's not here, I am, and this is a big story.

'On the subject of the public finances ... You'll remember I asked at your press conference the other morning about the dividend tax credit?' He nods. 'You seemed to be entertaining the idea of abolishing it. Can you confirm that if you become Prime Minister you will definitely do that?'

His hand actually reaches out and taps the wooden tabletop a couple of times. '*If* I become …' He can't bring himself to say it. '*If* we win. Yes. It's a sensible reform that will be in our manifesto.'

'That's the most honest answer I've had from a politician – at least for a while.'

'I'm a pretty honest guy.'

'Can I ask where the idea came from?'

I've tried to frame the question casually, just a point of detail, but Todd is no fool. He fixes me with those dazzling green eyes. In public, he can project a puppyish energy, a nice guy who accidentally found himself in charge of a major political party. But no one gets to the top in politics without being steeped in Machiavelli, and a dash of Sun Tzu.

'Does it matter?'

'Well, that policy was originally a government plan. The Treasury worked it up. There was a white paper all ready to go to the printers, and then at the last minute the Chancellor ditched it. So it's curious that a few weeks later it will be in a Labour manifesto.'

His eyes glance at the flashing red light on the tape recorders.

'Can we go off the record?'

I press the pause buttons on the recorders and put down my pen. 'The reason I'm interested in this policy – as I think you may know – is that my sister was working on it. Before she died, three weeks ago.'

Todd's brow furrows in sympathy. He reaches out across the table and grips my hand. My instinct is to recoil. With effort, I don't.

'I heard about that. I'm so sorry.'

'You met her?' I know he did, from Marilyn. But I don't want to reveal that connection – and I'm curious what he'll volunteer.

'She was in a few transition meetings. One of the most impressive civil servants I've met, actually. Such a commitment to public service, and a conspicuous sense of duty. Whoever forms the next government, we'll be poorer for not having her in Whitehall.'

Although I've heard all those things said about Clare for weeks and grown numb to them, when he says them it's as though they are credible only now. God he's good. To my embarrassment, there are tears pricking the corner of my eyes.

'Were those the only times you met her?'

Does my tone give it away? He tilts his head to the left and studies me. 'I think you know the answer to that.' A pause. 'You're sure this is off the record?'

'Completely.'

'The last thing I want is for her name to be brought into any kind of disrepute. After what you and your family have been through.'

'Then we want the same thing.' I hold his gaze.

Todd presses with his index finger on a knot in the shiny, yellowy wood of the kitchen table. 'It turns out she was at Cambridge with Harry, my PPS.' A PPS is a Parliamentary Private Secretary, an MP who is the eyes and ears of a minister or shadow minister in the House of Commons. 'Harry had been in the transition meetings too. He got chatting with her on one of the coffee breaks. And then a couple of days later she rang Harry and said there was something sensitive she wanted to discuss with me. All hush hush, secret squirrel.'

It chimes with what I'd guessed, but I am as puzzled as ever by why she was so fired up that she would drive a coach and horse through Whitehall's rules to have a secret meeting with the leader of the Opposition.

'I was intrigued. At first, I assumed she was angling for a job if we won the election. But it was something else. She came here – exactly where you're sitting, actually – and quite literally put five billion pounds on the table.'

'She gave you the tax credit policy.' I feel desperately sad she'd spoken to him not me. I try to hide it.

'She did. She had a whole economic rationale for it too. The gist was that the current system short-changes British workers and damages the economy. Her argument was that because the government effectively subsidises dividend payments with the tax credits, pension funds put pressure on companies to pay bigger dividends, rather than investing more of their profits in new machinery, or plant or other kit. And that means companies in Britain are less productive than they would otherwise be, which means wages are lower. In other words, she argued that wages would actually rise if we took all that money away from pension funds. She was pretty persuasive.'

It's an elegant analysis. Dad would be proud. Even so, I'm struggling to believe it was so compelling that it would motivate Clare to break every rule in the civil service book.

'Was that the only reason she came to you?'

Todd hesitates. 'There might have been more to it than that.'

'Tell me.'

'I didn't know her well, obviously. But she seemed, well, pretty upset.'

'Because the government dropped it?'

132

'Because of *how* they dropped it.'

Again, I remember what Jeremy said. *A blistering row with the Chancellor.* 'Did she explain?'

'I wish I'd asked. Looking back, it smells like another Tory scandal – and that would suit us down to the ground.' A cheeky half-smile. Is he goading me to find the truth behind Clare's estrangement from her boss? There is something he's holding back but I can't work out what and I'm uneasy. There *is* a scandal here. But how big? And is it connected to how she died? Or is that my grief talking? As Patrick Munis would no doubt have it: an invented conspiracy to distract me from feelings of unbearable pain.

A scandal. Todd wasn't the only person to whom Clare spoke about this tax raid. She also confided in Alan Scott. Who, for all his trainspotting tedium, is a wizard at rooting out complex public-sector corruption. Is that why she went to him?

I'm about to put this to Todd, when we're interrupted by the chime of the front-door bell.

'That'll be your snapper.' Todd jumps up and goes to put the kettle on, while I hear his wife running for the door again. 'I'm afraid we went a bit off topic, didn't we. Did you get enough? I'm going to have to run after this.'

I look down at my notebook. Thirty prepared questions and perhaps one and a half answered. But I got what I came for.

'That's plenty to be going on with. Thanks.'

Chapter 11

Tuesday, 25 March – 37 days until Election Day

I'M WOKEN BY A DRAUGHT and the sandpaper feeling of the cat licking my big toe. 'Morning,' I croak at him. He's about the only person who gives me affection at the moment, which is ironic, given that he is the least affectionate cat I've ever known. He's an enormous tabby – a killer, who models himself on Clint Eastwood in those Spaghetti Westerns – and this licking is his signal that it's time to eat. For him; *my* breakfast is never more than strong black coffee. I badly need it this morning. My mouth is dryer than as if I'd subsisted on sawdust for a week, and my head is in a vice. I push myself into a sitting position. Outside the window it's as if the volume knob for the world has been turned right up: a mum shouting at her children to get in the car and stop squabbling may as well be in the next room.

Cat sees he has my attention and starts to miaow loudly. When that doesn't work, he leaps back on the bed and bites my foot. A tussle ensues between man, cat and duvet, which ends with the cat on the floor and me swivelling off the bed.

I note the time on the alarm clock. Nine fifteen. *Shit.* I've missed the *Today* programme, and all the morning press conferences. *Shit shit shit*. Cat pads up to my side and purrs in expectation. 'I don't suppose you listened to the *Today* programme, did you?' I ask. The Chancellor was scheduled to do the headline 8.10 interview and I want to know if he said anything I need to know. Cat looks at me with a condescension that says: if I had the information, I wouldn't share it with you.

I reach for my Filofax on the bedside table and turn to the notes section at the back. Another memory jogged of Clare. Ever since secondary school, in the era before Filofax, her diary was her most precious possession – 'my memoir', she pretentiously called it. Between the woven brown covers of her Letts, her whole existence was scheduled, catalogued and recorded in colour-coded pen: homework, after-school clubs, music lessons, dates, first snog. When I was twelve, she took me to Smiths to buy my own. More surrogate parenting. She would always joke that she wished she could teach me to shave.

We were both early adopters of the Filofax in the 1980s. Buying the accessories was an easy stocking-filler present – though I never understood the point of the bendy ruler with punched holes for the ring binder clips. At the back I write long comprehensive lists of all the things I have to do. It's a way of assuaging my permanent anxiety that I've forgotten something important. Every night I cross off completed tasks and add anything new. The list regularly grows out of control; some reminders never get crossed off. But the act of writing it calms me.

There are various projects outstanding on the list this morning: stories I need to follow up, contacts to warm over, bills to pay. And in block letters, underscored three times. *WHAT'S THE REAL KENDALL STORY???* I added it after my meeting with Todd.

I turn to the diary section for today. *Bob Ringer, 1.15 Harry's Bar.*

Proper fun. Ringer is the best-connected PR man in London. Typically, I'll suggest we meet and he'll choose the venue – one which he knows neither I nor the *FC* can afford, so he'll end up putting the egregious bill through his business. We arranged this meeting before Clare died, but it is serendipitous. If there is someone who knows what might be in Kendall's dark closet, it will be Ringer. When I think of the champagne, al dente linguine, exquisite olive oil and scandalous gossip that awaits, the day ahead doesn't feel too bad.

Barefoot, I pad through the living room to the kitchen to give Cat his breakfast. There's a chilly draught blowing through the flat, and I register the loud burst of a motorbike passing. Did I leave a window open?

I'm still on morning autopilot. I wander into the kitchen, with its ATAG stainless steel hob and polished black granite worktops, and scoop a can of Whiskas into Cat's bowl. I wash my hands, fill the kettle, and retrace my steps across the living room to the front hall, to collect two bundles of newspaper first editions, which – if they haven't been nicked – should be in the building's communal corridor by the door to the street. It is only when I am in my front hall that I register why the street sound has been rising and falling all morning. The front door of my flat, which gives on to the communal corridor, is ajar. It's just a couple of inches, but open all the same.

Impossible. No matter how drunk or stoned I am, however late I come home, it is a religious ritual to make sure the door is shut, locked and bolted. I always triple check, then tug on the handle until there's a dent in my fingers. Even after that, if there's the tiniest trace of doubt in my head, I'll head back and check it again, before I am able to go to sleep.

How can it be open? The thought of someone else's hand on the knob makes me squirm. I am wearing a red sweatshirt and I pull the sleeve over my hand before touching anything. The door frame is intact, not splintered at all. There are no gouges or scratches around any of the locks. There is nothing to suggest it was forced in any way.

Could I have forgotten to lock it? Is that possible? I was a bit out of my head last night, but I am sure I went through my compulsive door-locking palaver. Could I have broken the habits of a lifetime? Did I sleep walk and unlock everything? The more I say this to myself, the less plausible it seems, especially since my keys are exactly where I always leave them, in the lower of the two deadlocks.

Cat rubs past my leg and sticks his nose out to scan the corridor in case someone will let him out to the Fields. We both plod down the corridor and I open the street door for him. Cat pauses for a moment, weighing up whether to embark on a hunt in the crisp air of a sunshiny morning or pad back to my armchair. He opts for the predatory life, as he typically does, except when the weather is foul.

I bend down to pick up the papers and I see it. The front page of the *FC* is ripped. It might have torn when it was pushed through the letterbox. But since I asked the wholesaler to divide the papers into rolls, that normally doesn't happen. When I look more closely, there is what looks like the indentation of the sole of a trainer next to the head of Peter Ramsey, who is pictured on the front page at a rally in Solihull. Has a neighbour trodden on it when leaving for work? My brain conjures a shadowy figure picking the Yale lock of the street door some time after 4 a.m., which is when the first editions are delivered, and whispering 'Oh shit' when he accidentally encounters my papers.

A flash of panic. Someone has been in my flat while I was asleep. He – in my mind it's a 'he' – has invaded my territory. He had access to all my stuff. He may even have come into my bedroom, perhaps stood over me while I was snoring.

How do I know he's not hiding in there somewhere right now? My hangover paranoia threatens to overwhelm me. *Everything's fine, everything's fine, everything's fine,* I tell myself.

I walk briskly to the pavement, scan both ways in the hope that there might be a police car cruising the street. Surely if there was anyone in the flat wanting to hurt me they would have done it while I was asleep? Also, unless they were in the spare bedroom or second bathroom, I would have noticed them. Only then do I become aware that I've gone out in nothing but the red sweatshirt and a pair of grey boxers.

I don't think of myself as a wuss, but I would prefer to wait for a friend before going back into the flat. The problem is I can't ring anyone, because my phones are by my bed. I sit on the wall at the bottom of the stone steps, paralysed by imaginings of who – or what – may be in the flat.

'Gil, are you OK?'

Not the voice I wanted to hear, when I'm on the street in my pants. It's my news editor, Mary Nichols, walking to Highbury and Islington underground station, presumably on the way to the office. She's in her smart Chloe trouser suit. She loves that suit. And she's found me looking like a nutter, staring at Highbury Fields.

'Gil?' she repeats.

'Fine, I'm fine.' I stand up, waving the morning edition at her. 'Just getting the papers in.'

She gives me a long, hard look. She's not a fool.

'You look terrible.'

'Late night.'

Another intense, studying look. She is only a few years older, but she has the urge to mother me. I can't face it.

'Are you sure . . .?'

'Absolutely,' I insist, in my boxers. 'All good.'

I'm trapped. She is plainly not going to move on while I am here. Should I tell her that I think I've had a break-in and ask her to come with me inside? A few minutes ago I was frantic, desperate for help. But now, with the morning sun delineating the Fields with such sharp clarity, and Mary's quizzical eyes on me, my fear seems ridiculous. If I tried to explain myself, I'd come across like a headcase.

'I'll see you at the office,' I say.

'Might be an idea to put on some trousers.'

I laugh, slightly too much. I know there isn't a cat's chance in hell she won't tell the entire newsroom she saw me in the street in my underwear. I fold the newspaper under my left arm, nod goodbye, and turn to go back in. It's not until after I've closed the door that I hear the clack of her heels walking on again.

I'm shaky. With trepidation, I search every room, look behind every door and round the back of the sofa, pull the curtains out, open every cupboard, check the shower cubicle.

Everything is as it should be. The windows are fastened shut and the garden door is deadbolted. If there was an intruder in my flat, he got out before I woke.

Once I am sure I'm alone, I carry out a stock check. The telly, the VCR, the Sky box, the Bang and Olufsen CD player, the Acoustics Research speakers, and my pride and joy, my Sansui belt turntable: nothing has been nicked. The work laptop is in its shoulder bag, my inherited gold cufflinks – possibly the only transportable items of any value – are in their little box on top of the chest of drawers. The two Nokias and my pagers are on the side table where they belong. I'd already noticed that my bike is where it should be in the hall. And the heavy silver art deco menorah, inherited from my great-great uncle, is on the mantelpiece in the living room. I can't think there was anything else worth stealing. Maybe I imagined the whole thing.

I pick up the Yellow Pages and agree to pay an exorbitant amount of money for a Banham locksmith to come straight-away. No chance of relaxing until he has replaced all the front door locks. After I've tested them once, twice, three times, and he's gone, I shower and put on a simple Paul Smith single-breasted suit, grey with the faintest of blue stripe. It's a Missoni day, and I knot the woven silk tie that's assorted threads of blue and pink. *I miss you Clare, I miss you Clare, I miss you Clare.* The *sotto voce* chant calms me.

The sound of padding feet startles me. It's only Cat, who has returned through the kitchen door flap. I shouldn't be so jumpy. According to the locksmith, my flat is now 'more secure than the Bank of England'.

I think about doing a line, just for my nerves. But it's too early. I put the phones and the pager in their requisite pockets, wheel out my bike, and put on my helmet. Finally, I go to grab my notebook. There isn't much point taking it: these are off-the-record lunches. And it is bad manners to write at the table. Apart from anything else, 90 per cent of what Ringer tells me will be libellous and almost impossible to corroborate. But as soon as lunch ends, I'll jot everything down anyway. Because that's the job and I'll feel uneasy if I don't make a record. If he tells me anything explosive, I'll excuse myself and nip to the loos to write it up, so that I don't lose any important nuance.

Like everything else, the notebook has its place. I leave it on the bedside table every night, under the Filofax, next to the novelty People's Republic of China coasters, each with its own iconic Mao image, to the right of the lamp. That's odd ... The notebook isn't there.

This is bad. I don't lose my notes, ever. I guard them with neurotic fastidious, obsessive care, and hoard them for years. At the *FC* there is an entire locked filing cabinet of these lined, A7-size notebooks that are filled with indecipherable shorthand scrawl, transcripts of conversations and jottings of off-the-record conversations.

The shadowy person standing over my bed returns to my imagination. He lurked while I was asleep, and pocketed the notebook from my bedside table. I feel sick. Maybe it's the residue of last night's alcohol. But the door, the notebook ... Should I ring the police? They would think I am raving mad. *I see sir. Someone broke into your house and all he took was a used notepad of the sort you can buy three for a pound from Woolworths. We'll put our best people on to the hunt for the master criminals, don't you worry.* No. There's no point alerting the authorities. To what would I be alerting them? To my emotional crisis?

Everything suddenly feels tainted, unclean. I walk fast to the kitchen, grab a roll of kitchen paper, fill a plastic tub with Dettol and water and then wipe handles and any surface that my real or imaginary adversary may have touched. Everything sterilised, I go to the bathroom, and scrub my hands with soap and water.

I try to reassure myself: maybe I left the notebook in my office on Burma Road; maybe I left the door open when I came in; maybe a neighbour stepped on the newspapers. *Everything's fine, everything's fine, everything's fine,* I mutter to myself. A lucky troika.

Time for lunch.

'You all right, Gil?' Bob Ringer's voice has the smoothness and underlying crackle of a lifetime smoking Silk Cut. It's Establishment suave, with an undertone of East End childhood. 'You look as though you've had a rough morning.'

We are on a corner table at Harry's in Mayfair, working our way through a bottle of Pol Roger. I try not to drink in daylight hours – my afternoon metabolism does not suit lunchtime boozing – but I definitely need a glass today. I must look drawn, but I'm beginning to feel myself again. The starched white linen, the exaggerated courtesy of waiters with Italian accents, is all so comfortingly dependable that I can almost forget the disconcerting start to the day. And London is still being dazzled by blinding sun from an almost cloudless sky.

'I'm fine.' I think about unburdening myself to Ringer about the possible break-in. No point. A distraction. 'Dunno whether I am unusual, but I'd never thought about what it would mean to lose someone. I was unprepared for . . .' And I tail off.

Ringer takes out a cigarette, offers me one – I decline, I gave up six months ago – and lights up. As he exhales, he says, 'I've been insensitive, Gil. Forgive me. I was sad to read about your

143

sister's accident, I meant to say so at once. Such a terrible thing.'
He coughs a smoker's rasping cough.

'Don't worry. In some ways, I quite like the pretence that life
just carries on.' Which is true. I am less and less tolerant of the
saccharin condolences from people who barely knew Clare.

I am saved by the waiter, who is desperate to unburden himself
of today's specials. I ignore his salesman's patter, because I want
what I always have: lobster with linguine, which I know from
experience will be simple, the sumptuous shellfish sautéed in
olive oil with garlic and parsley.

The restaurant is full and buzzing. On an adjacent table I spy
the one-time 1960s starlet, now intimidating, grande dame,
Jackie Elstree. Surgically rejuvenated and in her Chanel armour,
she must be thirty years older than the boy in his early twenties
sitting opposite her. Ringer confides he is not her son, and I
am not sure whether to admire or pity him.

'I'll just be a minute.'

Ringer leaves me to pay court to Elstree, theatrically kissing
her on each cheek, as she air kisses him back. He shakes the toy
boy's hand and then ambles to the table on the right, where he
whispers in the ear of a pin-stripe suited, tanned and white-
haired seventy-year-old, who guffaws in an exaggerated way. He
is Sir Alistair Jensen, the billionaire tycoon who, in the deal
frenzy of the 1980s, built the biggest conglomerate the UK had
ever seen, Jensen & Co. He's spent the last five years dismantling
it, after investors turned against him, but still has more money
than he could spend in several lifetimes. Ringer is, of course, on
bosom-buddy terms with him too.

If there is a thread that links these people (excluding the
anonymous toy boy), it is that they long for what they think of

as the simple certainties of Margaret Thatcher's Britain – where there was seemingly no higher calling than making as much money as possible and conscience was an anachronism. The 1980s changed everything, and from its dismantling of state industries and workers' rights the legend of Bob Ringer was born. He had spotted Thatcher's potential in the 1970s, long before Tory MPs had any inkling she would one day be their leader. He cultivated her, lobbied for her, and when his investment in her paid off, he made a fortune from his proximity to her, to power.

His winning streak didn't end with her downfall. She's gone, but he's almost as powerful as ever. The great and the good (and the bad) all share their secrets with him, because if anyone can manipulate the media and public opinion to save their reputations, it's Ringer. He has a direct line to the news desks of all the important papers. If one of his clients has been a naughty boy, shtupping a twenty-three year-old secretary, and the *Globe* has pictures of her leaving his London house at 5 a.m., Ringer will telephone the editor and offer up some other exclusive on another client. Voilá, the story vanishes. For Ringer, every conversation is a deal being negotiated, a bargain being struck. Often an unholy one.

He is one of a small number of London fixers always to be found in the shadows wherever there's a crisis to be quietly sorted, or power to be brokered. He is one of the elusive ten or so people who know everything there is to know about what is going on in business, the City, government.

I've never understood why he decided to cultivate me, or why he tells me so much of what is supposed to be in his vault. Maybe he's just showing off. That said, the risks of spilling the beans to me are not as great as you may think. A lot of what he gives me is of no interest to the *FC*, compelling though it may be, and much of the rest is unprintable. Ringer can offer up whatever salacious revelations he likes, because he knows there is only the remotest prospect of me finding a corroborating second source. I have tried, repeatedly, to persuade Ringer to give me documented evidence of what he says, but he normally fobs me off with flattery. 'Over to you. You're the brilliant journalist.'

So why do we have these lunches? I suppose they stem from my vanity, my need to know about the misdeeds of those who run this place, even when I can't report them. And there are usually a few crumbs of information that lay a trail to a printable story.

Ringer plonks himself back down and lights another Silk Cut. He'll have another packet with him, just in case. He beckons the waiter to refill the champagne. 'Enjoy it while you can,' he growls. 'The socialists will be back in a few weeks, won't they?'

I'm not sure whether it's a rhetorical question, but I answer anyway. 'It is not 100 per cent, but likely. By the way, Todd isn't really a socialist you know.'

He snorts. 'If he isn't, he's certainly surrounded by them. But I shouldn't complain. He's no worse than Ramsey.'

The uselessness of Sir Peter Ramsey, the beleaguered Prime Minster, is a recurring theme of these lunches. 'How did my party ever choose such a wanker? Poor Margaret is beside herself.'

'He's all right. It's just the party is ungovernable.' I am deliberately winding him up.

'You would say that. You're another bloody socialist. Everything Margaret did is being dismantled. Taxes up. Brussels in charge. It's appalling.'

'But Kendall ...' I say, knowing full well the reaction that will get.

'Worse still! So wet you could mop him off the floor.'

This is where I wanted to steer the conversation. 'You know my sister worked with him at the Treasury?'

'Poor girl.'

'She hatched a plan to raise several billion a year from pension funds, by abolishing the tax credit.'

'Never heard of it.' Did he say that a shade too quickly?

'It was never public. And just before they were going to announce, Kendall killed it.'

He peers at me over the top of his rectangular spectacles.

'What's your interest? If it's not happening, why does it matter?'

Not that again!

'I'd like to understand whose decision it was to drop the tax raid. Kendall's, or Ramsey's? And why did they choose not to go ahead? There's a funny smell around it.'

I let the silence play out. Ringer tips back his head and blows out a long stream of smoke. '*Cui bono?*'

'What?'

'*Cui bono?* Who benefits?'

'Well, pensioners might if the tax raid is dead. No?'

Ringer gives me a pitying look. 'What about the companies that stand behind the funds, which put money into them? Is the tax credit good or bad for them?'

He takes a breath of air, and then of Silk Cut. 'The dividend credit is worth billions to pension funds, right? There must be funds that can't afford to lose it.'

'The majority of pension funds are in surplus,' I say, parroting what Jess told me.

'Yes. But just because the average fund is in surplus, it doesn't mean they all are. I would have thought someone who works on the *FC* would know that. And someone who works on the *FC* might have picked up rumours about one or two funds in deep, dark, smelly doo-doo.'

He's trying to make me feel inadequate and it's working. I am desperate to make an educated guess but I have nothing to offer.

He blows his lips out, extinguishes the cigarette stub and lights another. 'Say, for the sake of argument, there's an important fund that has an enormous black hole. And say that hole got bigger because the tax credit was taken away. There'd be contagion to the company that sponsors the fund. Creditors to that sponsoring company would take a dim view – and if the company was already sitting on a ton of debt, that could be curtains.'

I can't tell if this is hypothesis, or whether he's directing me to something he knows. 'Are you saying that Kendall was leaned on by a powerful business to shelve the tax raid?'

'I'm not saying anything.'

His riddles are annoying, but par for the course. Ringer's loyalty to his clients is like that of a double or treble agent in a le Carré novel. It's never clear who he is working for, or why, and it amazes me his customers don't clock when he's playing them off against each other.

On this occasion, he won't name the company, if there is one. Time to move the conversation to Kendall. 'When I wanted to write a story about the tax credit fiasco, Kendall was desperate to block me. He tried to bully me, seemed upset. Why would such a technical tax change have got under his skin?'

Ringer tilts his glass from side to side, studying the bubbles in the champagne. His answer sounds like a *non sequitur*. 'You know his marriage is on the rocks?'

No, I didn't know. 'I thought he and Amanda were the perfect shire couple.' I read a recent profile in *Tatler*. Cotswold farmhouse, Range Rover, equestrian daughter. The Tory squire's idyll.

Ringer gives me a disappointed look. 'Keith Kendall is a naughty boy who can't keep his hands to himself.'

'Oh yes?'

Again, that 'I know everything' smirk. 'Talk to your sister paper. They know.'

'You're saying he's had an affair? *Having* an affair?'

'Did I say that?'

'You think the *Globe* has the story.'

'You'd have to ask them.'

'So why haven't they run it?'

'I couldn't say. But if I were you, I'd also have a look at who's funding Kendall's constituency office, who pays his bills. That might be interesting.'

My heart sinks. Pretty much the only way to get to the bottom of where the money comes from in politics is to hire one of the dodgy firms, normally set up by ex-coppers, who bribe bank staff to supply confidential details on customers' bank accounts. I occasionally use these services, though only *in extremis*, because doing so is contrary to all the rules of the *FC*. And it's a real bugger getting the fee back on expenses.

'I can't tell if you're saying Kendall was bribed, or blackmailed, or both.'

Ringer laughs. 'This is England, for God's sake, not Italy. We don't do bribery and blackmail.'

'Then ... what?'

'In Britain, all our leaders are expected to do their patriotic duty. Occasionally, it has to be pointed out to them what that duty may be.'

At that point, the intoxicating smell of garlic and seafood announces that the waiter has arrived with our main courses. Ringer tucks his napkin into his collar, spreads it carefully over his shirtfront like a child's bib, and plunges his fork into the linguine. With unexpected delicacy, he slowly winds the linguine around the fork.

'How old are you, Gil?' he asks.

An odd question, but I see no reason not to answer. 'Thirty-five.'

'Thought much about your own pension?'

'That's an odd question.'

'It's a relevant question. Go away and consider it.'

By that, I gather it's the end of this strand of this conversation. What is he trying to tell me? I'm left with the feeling that I'm missing something obvious, like a crossword clue I haven't cracked. Kendall, his marriage, sources of funding, pension schemes – how do they connect?

Too many puzzles. But he's made no attempt to put me off the scent that there was something funny about why Kendall dropped Clare's policy. In fact, he's deliberately stoked up my suspicions. Everything comes back to Kendall. And even though Ringer won't say more, I know someone who will.

I twirl the slippery linguine onto my fork, inhale the aroma, and wonder whether anticipation is better than gratification.

Chapter 12

I T's PISSING DOWN WHEN I leave the house. Usually, I trust my Gore-Tex outers to keep me dry enough on my bike, but since Clare's accident I am less relaxed about cycling. Also, there is something to be said for arriving at my meeting not looking like a mutt who's been locked out in a storm.

Outside my flat, on Highbury Fields, there's a blue Peugeot 205, which I use so little that it costs me more in insurance than petrol. It's filthy, the windscreen gummed with dirt and sap from the maple trees that fringe the street. I have to let the wipers run for five minutes before the windscreen's clear enough.

As I sit in the driver's seat, waiting, I look at the new notebook I have picked up from the *FC*'s stationery cupboard. The first few pages are already filled with scribbles about conversations I've had with contacts, some random, some specifically related to stories I'm chasing. A couple of pages from the back, I've created a separate section where I keep notes relating to Clare. It's overkill hiding it there, because all the notes are scrawled in

151

my peculiar variety of indecipherable shorthand that even GCHQ couldn't crack (I too struggle to understand my own script). In more lucid moments, I tell myself I have no proof anyone stole my other notebook.

Even so, I've disguised my subjects. The page I'm looking at now is headed, simply, 'Mole', for Adrian Mole, my too obvious code for Jeremy. Underneath is a list of questions about his boss, the Chancellor, based on Ringer's annoying hints.

Who did K speak to before dropping the policy?
Who is paying K's bills?
Is K having an affair???

It's a week since my lunch with Ringer and I have finally persuaded Jeremy to meet me. He kept putting me off with lame excuses about being too busy. Having been desperate to share his conspiracy theories with me, he's become hesitant and anxious. Eventually I lost my patience and questioned whether he really cared about Clare. Stung, he's agreed to meet me in St James's Park, on the other side of the road from the Treasury.

Fifteen minutes later I am driving down Shaftesbury Avenue. The blue Nokia rings. I look over to where it's lying on the passenger seat. Jess. I wedge the phone under my chin.

'Hiya, boss.'

'What's up?'

'Haven't you heard?'

'Heard what?'

'Media Corp announced an agreed bid for Capital TV this morning. Both boards recommended. Two and a half billion pounds, all in Media Corp shares, 40 per cent premium to yesterday's price.'

152

'Shit, shit, shit!' I think of Alex Elliott's cast-iron denial in The Groucho, two weeks ago. 'Elliott's a mendacious toerag. You must be fuming.'

'Yup'. I can hear the contained rage in her voice above the hiss of the mobile phone connection.

'We've got to find a way to fuck Elliott.'

'Thanks for the kind thought, boss.'

'He won't get away with it,' I insist, though not really believing myself. This world seems made for the Alex Elliotts. Their lies and dishonesty, even when found out, only serve to make them stronger. 'Anything else I need to know?'

Jess ticks off the important facts. 'Media Corp is being advised by Schon, so I was right about that too. Schon have underwritten the new shares that are being created and are offering a £7.20 per share cash alternative.'

'So they're massively on the hook.' That's important. If the market doesn't like the deal, and Media Corp's shares go down, Schon will lose a ton of money.

It is a remote risk. 'Investors think it's a steal,' she says. 'Both companies' share prices have soared.'

'They'll make out like bandits.'

'Like bankers.'

I am now on Charing Cross Road, heading towards Trafalgar Square. I admit to being an erratic driver at the best of times; spatial awareness is not my thing. Nor is my driving improved by the rain on a smeary windscreen and the effort of trying to keep the phone from falling. I stray into the centre of the road and swerve back just before a Jag almost clips my side. The irate driver thumps his horn.

'Shit, Jess. Can I call you back? When I'm not driving?'

'Course, boss.'

I park in my grace-and-favour parking place on the Mall, just outside the white Regency elegance of the Institute for Contemporary Arts, three hundred yards from the eyesore that is Buckingham Palace. The car-parking space is an amazing perk of the job, which I barely use, but which insidiously buys my loyalty to the institutions of Parliament and government.

By now, the rain has eased off. I fit the crook lock on the car's steering wheel, which I know is over the top: there must be more cops within a hundred yards than any other place in the country. And there's the other relevant point, made by Marilyn, cigarette in mouth: 'Do you actually think someone is going to steal that pile of junk?'

I walk across St James's Park to the east side of the lake. I'm a few minutes early, so I pass the time watching the pelicans. I've been obsessed with these monstrous birds, and a little afraid of them, ever since my grandparents would bring Clare and me here as children. Clare and I would be in between grandma and grandpa, each of us holding one of their hands. We would wear the matching powder-blue tailored woollen overcoats, run up by grandpa on his Singer sewing machine, that made us look as though we might have just walked out of the regal gaff down the road. I remember how we watched the park-keepers throw fish to the birds, which they swallowed whole, and the mixture of disgust and admiration I felt. Though mostly I would be fixating on the looming treat of a 99 cone from one of the ice cream vans.

Today I am wearing my navy blue three-quarter length Jean Paul Gaultier coat, perhaps my proudest sartorial possession, and an understated grey cashmere Dunhill scarf. The rain storm drove everyone out of the park and most are still sheltering indoors, so it isn't hard to spot Jeremy hurrying breathlessly towards me from my right. He has the hood up on his North Face anorak, which has fogged his glasses so much I'm surprised he can recognise me.

He stops slightly further away than is normal, as if I'm contagious.

'Would you mind if we walk and talk?' he says, conspicuously nervous about us being seen together.

'Surely there's nothing sinister about the two of us meeting? We might be making arrangements for me to collect Clare's personal effects,' I say.

'That's already in hand,' he tells me. 'I had to go through it all myself, sorting out what's confidential, what's personal, what's Treasury property.' He gives a twitchy glance over his shoulder and starts walking. I quicken my pace and fall in step beside him. 'It was horrible, brought home that she's never coming back. Silly things, like her calculator. When I picked it up, all I could think of was that look on her face, how hard she concentrated when she was working.' Inside the anorak hood, he looks despondent. 'You probably think I'm pathetic.'

'Don't be silly.' I might cringe at his naïvety, but we have a connection. When Clare bought her first scientific calculator at the start of her O levels, she showed the same kind of joy many boys have on owning their first old banger of a motor. I see her hunched over it at the table in her bedroom, acing pure maths. I know what Jeremy means. When Clare had a problem to solve, everything else was screened out.

'You loved Clare, didn't you,' I say, too bluntly. Jeremy flushes.

'She looked out for me. She took care of her team – especially those who were ... vulnerable.'

'That was Clare.' I'm back at a family dinner – spaghetti Bolognese and iceberg salad, my mum's speciality – with Dad lecturing me on how I will never do as well as my sister if I don't apply myself; how my study habits are a disgrace and how it's impossible to know whether my homework is an 'A' or a fail, because nobody could possibly read my scrawl. Clare interrupts that he shouldn't expect everyone to do things the way he used to, that everyone's different, that he should back off and give me a chance.

Jeremy breaks in. 'What was it you wanted? Have you found out anything?'

'Nothing solid.' Or rather only speculation that may see me joining him in the club of unhinged conspiracy theorists. 'I've been looking at the pensions policy you mentioned, the dividend tax credit raid. There are loose ends, about your boss, the Chancellor. Can you help?'

'I'll try.' I'm taking him seriously at last; fingers crossed, he will tell me what I need.

'When Clare had her row with Kendall, remind me what she said. Exactly, if possible.'

He nods. 'She said – these were pretty much her words – "You're all so bloody corrupt".'

'She said that? To the Chancellor of the Exchequer? Christ.'

'I'd never heard her like that with anyone, let *alone* the boss. And in front of everybody.'

I'm as stunned as he must have been. Clare did not like scenes. Usually she was the family diplomat, brokering uneasy truces between me and Mum and Dad – perhaps the best training for a future mandarin. So what could have triggered her to fire both barrels at the Chancellor?

I remember Ringer's hint. *We don't do bribery and blackmail. This is England, not Italy.*

'"Corrupt" is a very precise word,' I observe. I can't believe Clare used it thoughtlessly. '"Bloody corrupt". You're sure that's what she said?'

He pauses, blushing. 'Not exactly.'

'Well, what?'

'Actually it was "fucking corrupt".'

I laugh. Can't help it.

'Do you have any idea why she said that? Was it connected with the pensions thing?'

By now we're halfway around the lake, on the Blue Bridge. Beyond the budding trees, the towers and domes of Royal Horse Guards building on Whitehall frame a crystalline sky. Jeremy leans on the railing, takes off misted glasses and wipes them on the lapel of his jacket.

'Have you heard of a bank called Schon Partners?'

I bridle. 'That's a bit like asking a twelve-year-old girl if she's heard of the Spice Girls.'

He peers at me.

'Schon is not just any bank, it's *the* bank. The Man U of banks – and I say that as a Spurs supporter.' I patronisingly spell out to Jeremy that when there's a corporate mega-merger or takeover, or a government in financial difficulties, Schon will be there, counselling and scheming – for a humungous fee. And whatever side of the deal they're on, erstwhile Schon partners will occupy important positions at the relevant multinational company or state institution. Schon's network is everywhere, which is why it's known as the 'Brotherhood'. Who is the current American Treasury Secretary? A former Schon partner. Who is the finance director of Europe's biggest oil company? An ex Schon Partner. Who is governor of the Banque de France? No need to ask.

This is the second time Schon has come up this morning. As Jess mentioned, they're advising Media Corp. A coincidence? It's a piece of the jigsaw, but I can't see where it fits.

'You make them sound like the Freemasons,' says Jeremy.

'No. The Freemasons are amateurs. Schon *does* run the world.'

Jeremy can't tell whether I'm joking or not.

'Jeremy, what's Schon got to do with Clare?'

A seagull flaps down and lands on the lake about twenty yards in front of us.

'I am not entirely sure. But Kendall had met a senior bloke from Schon the day before he dropped the policy. All very last minute, arranged that morning. I remember the Diary Secretary in a flap because she had to delay a meeting with the Governor of the Bank of England which had been in the schedule for months.'

Kendall kept the Governor waiting? For Schon? We've started walking again, across the bridge, back towards Whitehall. Buckingham Palace is behind us, and St James's Palace to our left. To the right, the Home Office's brutalist 1970s Lubyanka, 50 Queen Anne's Gate, glowers from on high, unforgiving. Hundreds of years of imperial arrogance squatting in a few acres.

What is the connection between Schon and Clare's outburst? Schon would be on a short list of financial institutions whose business would be hurt if pension funds had less money for investment and trading. But that kind of a hit would be a normal business risk for Schon, not life or death. I am missing something.

'I don't suppose you remember the name of the banker who visited Kendall?'

'I asked the Diary Secretary this morning,' Jeremy says.

I am impressed. 'You are turning into quite the sleuth,' I compliment. He grins. I should have clocked how desperate he is for approbation.

'She told me it was someone called Robin Muller.' He glances at me. 'Does that name mean anything to you?'

Robin Muller. That's a blast from the past. Robin and I were at Oxford together, next door colleges. People talked about him in reverential tones as the genius of the year, though what I had in common with him was more recreational: we got our dope from the same source. The dealer was a mature student at St Antony's, and as neither of us much fancied the long schlep up the Woodstock Road, we took it in turns to collect. We had a friendship of convenience. Robin graduated with a First and the offer of a Fellowship at All Souls' – at which he stuck up two fingers. In the spirit of Thatcher's loads-a-money times, he opted for the City over ivory tower. He took a job in what was then called merchant banking, at one of the small advisory banks mostly founded by German Jews – which would soon be gobbled up by their American and Swiss rivals. We lost touch, but I'm not surprised to find out he's now something at Schon. It's where someone with his brains and lack of scruples would prosper. He'll be on course to trouser tens of millions of pounds. The success of the City and Wall Street is rooted in the piratical nineteenth century. They disguise their swashbuckling with wood-panelled solemnity. But when colossal sums are at stake, they do what's needed.

You're all so fucking corrupt. Who are the 'all' to whom Clare was referring? Kendall and who? Kendall and Schon? Kendall and Muller?

I think back to what Bob Ringer said about the Chancellor. *Who pays his bills? That might be interesting.*

'Did you ever have any sense that Kendall has money worries?'

'You mean the deficit?'

'No, not the fucking deficit,' I laugh. 'Does he personally seem short of money?'

Jeremy looks confused. 'He made a good living in law before entering politics. And everyone knows that his wife, Mandy, is a supermarket heiress.'

Oh yes. But fortunes can be lost. Is that vast Cotswold estate remortgaged up to the hilt and effectively owned by the banks? I try another tack. 'What about his campaign? There's an election coming. Who pays for his office?'

But even while asking the question, I know it's probably a red herring. British democracy runs on a shoestring. Last year in America, Bill Clinton spent a hundred and fifty million dollars to see off a Republican waxwork. If you add in all the congressional races as well, they spent over two billion dollars. In Britain, you can elect a whole Parliament for a few million pounds and change. This is not money to die for. Or to kill for.

'Never mind.' The mention of Kendall's wife has reminded me of the other half of Ringer's hints. *Keith Kendall is a naughty boy who can't keep his hands to himself.* 'What about his love life?'

'He's married to Mandy,' says Jeremy, stating the obvious.

'Come on, you know what I mean. Is Kendall the only Tory minister without a bit on the side?'

It's a joke – but Jeremy looks horrified. 'Well, if he has, he certainly wouldn't tell me.'

I'm struck by Jeremy's squeamishness. 'Obviously he would hide it from Lady Mandy,' I say. 'Though you'd be surprised how many of these posh people have "open" marriages. I imagine his secretary would know. A decent secretary knows everything.'

Jeremy sticks his hands in his pockets and stares at the ground. 'I don't think there's anything like that going on.'

'Are you sure. No telltale signs? Sudden departures from the office that aren't in the diary? A decision to walk somewhere rather than take the ministerial car? Has there been tittle-tattle from the official drivers about being parked outside a residential address for a couple of hours?'

Jeremy is now staring vacantly at the lake. I don't know what to make of it. Ringer is rarely wrong, but if Kendall indulged in extra-curricular bonking, surely there'd be rumours at the office?

But before I can press him, his head snaps to the right. 'What's that over there?'

'Where?'

'Behind the willow. Is that a camera lens?'

I scan the bank on the other side of the pond. About a hundred yards away I can make out a point of reflective light. It could be a telephoto lens, or binoculars.

'Probably a birdwatcher,' I say.

'You're right. I'm on edge. Meeting like this ...' The sun is now fully out, but Jeremy has kept his hood up the whole time. 'I'd better get back. Would you mind if we split up?'

'Of course not.' I too feel the strain. Being with him and his brain full of plots reinforces my anxiety. 'But about Kendall, and his love life ...'

'There's nothing. I am sure there's nothing there. Got to get back before they miss me.'

He digs his hands into his pockets and strides purposefully towards Horse Guards.

I cross the bridge again and turn left on the far side of the lake, towards the place where Jeremy thought he saw the snapper. Of course there's no one there, but I linger, trying to make sense of what I heard.

Kendall's finances feel like a blind alley. His private life is another matter, but if there's anything doing there, I won't find it from Jeremy. He's a choirboy. Kendall could have been shagging his secretary sideways on the dispatch box in the Commons and Jeremy wouldn't have noticed.

Which leaves Schon. I run the gut check. Is there something I don't know, that I need to know? Yes. No question. Time to renew acquaintances with Muller. It's been a long time since we've been in touch. I assume he'll take my call, but there's no point ringing him blind. He's too smart to yield anything if I go on a pure fishing exercise. I'll need to prepare. Jess can help. She'll have gone through every analyst's report on Schon and picked up whatever gossip there is. But I also need an inside source.

I'll have to do what I should have been doing every day since Clare died.

I'll ring my brother-in-law.

Chapter 13

THE SPRING WEATHER HAS CHANGED again, whistling up another mass of dark clouds that will unleash a pelting shower any minute. I buy myself a copy of the *Evening Standard* and shelter in the Red Lion on Derby Gate. This has the double benefit of keeping me out of the rain and giving me time to summon up the courage to ring Charles.

The barman fills my glass. 'For another five quid you can have the whole bottle,' he tempts me. It is impolite to decline, even though it's a sticky and heavy Australian Chardonnay that I would usually reject.

In a few hours, the pub – a fulcrum between Treasury, Foreign Office and department of Health – will be rammed with civil servants, special advisers and MPs. Now, just after the lunchtime crush, it contains only a few of us running away from our lives. I take a table in the corner where I can be alone with bottle and paper, comforted by the rhythmic rain pounding the pavement. Actually, it sounds more like hail, an April squall blown up out of nowhere. It will vanish fifteen minutes later into a sky so blue that I will forget it happened.

I sip my drink and flip through the *Standard*. Media Corp's bid for Capital Television is big enough to make the news section, page five. It's illustrated with a snap of Media Corp's founder, Jimmy Breitner, leaving HQ, protected by a posse of acolytes and advisors. The gaunt, buzz-cut man at his side is Jock Streatham, Breitner's fixer and consigliere, who for fifteen years was editor of the *Globe*. Just behind the boss is Alex Elliott, half visible at the edge of the frame. There is just enough of his poncy floppy hair and smirk in view to trigger my automatic response of jaw thrust forward and grinding teeth. I skim the article, but there's less in it than Jess briefed me.

The shower is easing off and I can't put off phoning Charles. I stand and mouth 'goodbye' to the barman. Despite my tearful reconciliation with Charles, I still feel that the Duke of Gloucester, he of the Princes in the Tower infamy, was a model uncle compared with me. Thankfully the wine has taken the edge off my guilt. The sky *is* a brilliant blue, trees are dripping, the air is reviving. *I'm sorry Charles, I'm sorry Charles, I'm sorry Charles*. His phone rings and rings as I walk up Whitehall towards Trafalgar Square. I half hope the mechanical clunk of an Ansafone tape will rescue me. But then:

'Charles.' His inflexion is flat, tired.

'Hi, it's Gil.'

'Gil.' Repeated back to me, mechanically.

I launch into the script I've prepared.

'How have you been?' No answer. 'Sorry again about everything. How are the boys? How are you? Is there anything you need.'

There's a sigh. 'What do you want, Gil?'

The resigned cynicism in his voice is a warning. I wanted to tell him there is something sinister about how Clare died, but not now. Better to obfuscate.

'Look, this is probably inappropriate. Sorry in advance. But I am doing a story that relates to your employer, so I wanted to pick your brains. Completely off the record.'

'As you say, it is completely inappropriate.'

But he doesn't hang up. I chance my arm. 'Do Schon manage much pension fund money?'

'That's a dumb question. Of course we do. A ton of it.'

'In the UK?'

'Among other places.'

'And do you know a partner called Robin Muller?'

A cautious pause. The wait is like opening a door to a house and not knowing if the alarm is switched on. 'What's Muller got to do with this?'

'Nothing. I don't know. He was someone I knew at Oxford, we lost touch, I heard he's at your shop.'

'I know him, a bit.'

'Does he work in asset management? Looking after pensions' investments?'

I'm expecting confirmation and am hurrying to my next question, so I almost don't notice when Charles says, 'No. Nowhere near. He works in corporate advisory. Mergers and acquisitions.'

Oh. Muller does deals for big companies. Why on earth would he go to a meeting with the Chancellor to lobby against the pensions policy if he had nothing to do with managing the money that goes into pension funds?

I stall to rearrange my thoughts. 'Is he doing well?'

'He's the boy wonder. The British rainmaker. Back at base they worship him.'

'Gosh,' I say stupidly, wondering what the Schon partners would think if they knew about his university habits. My creaking brain tries to join the dots: if Robin lobbied Kendall, maybe it was for one of his clients, rather than on behalf of Schon itself. 'I suppose he advises some pretty big companies?'

'You could say that.' Even with my brother-in-law I am banging up against the notorious Schon wall of silence. The bank is as secretive – and paranoid – as the Church of Scientology. And as controlling. They monitor everything about their employees, from their conversations to what they eat. But loyalty to the faith is not unrewarded. Schon partners' bonuses are 50 per cent bigger than bonuses paid by other banks. Anyone who becomes one of the firm's 250 partners is guaranteed to be able to retire at fifty, with enough capital to live in splendour till death and well beyond.

'So come on, tell me, who are Robin's clients?'

'If you were as good a journalist as you think you are, you'd have found that out. For goodness' sake, his name goes on press releases for takeovers and rights issues and other corporate transactions.'

'Sorry. You're right. It's just I am a bit short of time.'

I am about to give up. I'm not just up against his disappointment in me, but also his corporate loyalty.

'Do you not even read your own paper?'

'What do you mean?'

'Turn to the front page of the companies section. You might see a clue.'

'I haven't got it with me.'

'For fuck's sake! I am pretty sure the picture I'm talking about is in every paper.'

I yank the *Standard* out of my pocket, wedge the phone under my chin and unfold it. I have an idea what I'm looking for. I open on page five and look again at the picture of Breitner flanked by his minders.

Charles is right. I *am* having an off day. The link I needed was in front of my nose. I was so triggered by Elliott that I ignored the lanky, eagle-nosed man in a dark blue Savile Row suit to his left. The thick blond hair is immaculately cut, rather than long and unkempt. The eyes, half hidden behind professorial, horn-rimmed specs, seem more pocketed. But he is unmistakeable: my long-lost, dope-buying brother.

'Robin works on the Media Corp account?'

'Robin *is* the Media Corp account. Somehow he's charmed Breitner, who won't now work with anyone else at the firm. Why the interest in Muller?'

I don't want to tell him that I am poking around in the affairs of his late wife. But I have no choice. 'I am not sure if you knew, but Clare developed a clever way for the government to fill the hole in the public finances, by forcing pension funds to pay tax on the dividends they receive. Muller tried to block it. I want to know why.'

A pause. I hear a hiss on the line. I am not sure if that's some kind of electrical interference or a sudden intake of breath. 'I didn't know that.'

'Would she have told you?'

'We had to be careful about what we said to each other about our lives outside home.' There seems to be an edge in his voice.

'Obviously she was subject to the Official Secrets Act. And I guess you've got to be careful about all those rules against insider trading. Sis was a stickler for the rules.'

A hollow laugh. 'Yup. Clare never broke the rules.'

Charles sounds angry.

'Are you OK?'

'Never been better, as you can imagine, with the boys waking up at night calling for their mum, making it impossible for me to get enough sleep to do my job properly – and with you ringing me up as some kind of a source for a story, rather than doing what any other brother-in-law might do, which is to come round to see his nephews and offer to help. Yeah, everything is great.'

His anger hits me like a physical blow. 'Sorry. I've been a shit uncle. No excuse.'

I am at the junction of Whitehall and Trafalgar Square. On autopilot to return to the Palace of Westminster, via Horse Guards, I do a loop back towards the Mall. As I cross Whitehall, towards Drummonds Bank, a late middle-aged woman tut-tuts at the noise pollution I am generating with my conversation. I avoid catching her eye.

'Look, Gil. I understand. Sort of. You *have* been a shit uncle. And you were a shit brother. At least in recent years. But Clare loved you. She was always talking about you. I assume you loved her too.'

'I have been a prick. A total prick.'

'Yes.'

I think he's almost relaxing. It is as though a pressure valve has been released and some of the tension eased. 'I was actually going to ring you later today. Something has happened that I needed to tell someone about. And even though you are a world-class A-hole, there is no one else I can share this with.'

I am surprised, and pleased. 'Obviously I want to help if I can. What's happened?'

'We had the post-mortem back,' he says. 'I thought maybe you knew and that's why you were ringing.'

'I had no idea. But presumably there was nothing of interest in the pathologist's report. St Thomas's already told us she had a lethal blow to the head. The cause of death wasn't in doubt.'

'I'm not talking about the cause of death.'

'What else?'

'For a start, she had a bucketload of alcohol in her blood. Bottle and a half of wine.'

'That can't be right.'

'It's what the report says.'

'But Clare –'

' – hardly drank, no. It's odd. Especially for a woman who was six weeks pregnant.'

'She didn't drink in . . .' As so often, my mouth has started speaking before my brain has finished processing. I rewind in my head what Charles has just said.

'*Pregnant?*'

'First trimester.'

Oh my God. 'I'm so sorry, Charles. A third child. That is devastating.'

'Yes. I feel I am being punished, but don't know why.' He collapses into sobs. And sobs. For a minute. And then another minute. And another. I don't know what to do. He switches to deep, agonised inhaling.

I speak when he sounds calmer. 'You really had no idea you were about to have a third child.'

Between gulps of breath, he says 'I didn't. It wasn't something we discussed. This is why I needed to talk to you.'

'I understand.'

'You don't. You *can't* understand. I want to tell you something, but you have to swear you won't mention any of it to anyone, not even your mum and dad. Can you do that?'

Not tell my mum and dad something? Not usually a problem. 'Of course. You can say anything to me, in confidence.' There's a pause. He is struggling.

'The thing is . . . The thing is, I don't think it would have been our third child.'

'What do you mean? I thought you said she was pregnant?'

'Yes. She was. But I don't see how the child could have been mine.'

I don't know what to say. I can feel his anguish as if he's with me.

'It's almost impossible to talk about this. But equally the secret is killing me. I've played this over and over in my head and I am sure we hadn't had sex at the right time. If she was six weeks pregnant, the father must have been someone else.'

No, no, no. It's impossible.

'Are you sure?' is all I can manage. 'I'm sure you must be wrong. It's easy to forget these things.'

'It might be easy for you. Not for me. The truth is we hadn't had sex since before Christmas. We were worried about it. Well, *I* was worried about it.'

This makes no sense. I don't believe it. The pathologist made a mistake. Clare would never have blown up her family like this. Impossible.

'I am sorry things between you and Clare were tricky, but the baby *must* have been yours. Your memory is playing tricks on you. It happens.'

'It is kind of you to think that. And I want to believe it. I can't.'

'But if not you . . .?' I can't bring myself to say it

'Obviously, that's been haunting me. But I don't want to know.'

'Oh.'

I hear a muffled voice in the background and the sound of Charles covering the phone with his hand.

'I've got to go. You have to swear never to mention this to anyone, especially not to Bernie and Ginger.'

'I promise.'

'It's the boys. I can't have people sniggering behind their back. But I had to tell someone. Someone who wouldn't judge me. Or Clare. There was only you.'

Well, that's a bond. Of sorts. *Welcome to the North London fuck-ups club. Official membership, two.*

'I am grateful you told me. Seriously.' There's a rueful snort. Which is a relief. 'There's a lot for me to think about too,' I say.

A pause. 'I guessed you'd somehow end up making this about you.' He sighs. 'See you, Gil.'

I've been walking angry, unthinking strides. I clock my surroundings. I've reached the north-east corner of Parliament Square. The familiar silhouette of Big Ben's tower looms, solid and eternal. I can't face the Burma Road. I know who I need to see.

I am in my nothing box: my psychological state where there is nothing definable, nothing conscious, absolutely nothing happening in my head. This ability to blank my mind, to go into a sort of short-term hibernation, like a computer entering sleep mode, is what keeps me sane. Since Clare's death I've been more or less always on and if I keep it up much longer I'll overload. It's bliss to be back in this imaginary flotation tank.

It's 9 p.m. and I'm on my king-sized bed, with the senior policy adviser to the Leader of the Opposition lying naked beside me. Marilyn does not have a mind-blank mode. She's been cuddled against me for about five minutes and most of that was spent fiddling with a knot in her necklace chain. Now she sits up and pulls a packet of Marlboro Lights out of her battered brown leather rucksack.

I snap out of the trance. 'Do you really have to?'

'I thought you were asleep.'

'It'll stink up the bedroom.'

She just laughs. She knows she'll get her way. I sigh, and pass her the Spurs mug on my bedside table to use as an ashtray.

She lights up, takes a drag and blows out a long stream of smoke. 'Your sister. Jesus, Gil. And you've really no idea who the father could be?'

I wince. My promise to Charles has not survived more than a few hours. I kid myself there's no one Marilyn would possibly wish to tell, as if one woman in politics would never want to gossip about another who was a rising star in Whitehall.

'You've got to promise you'll keep this to yourself. I can barely imagine the humiliation my brother-in-law would feel. And I want to protect my nephews.' It's absurd that I am asking her to show a duty of care to the boys when I've so casually betrayed them by gushing to her.

'Not quite the memory of Mummy giving them their Weetabix.' She sees the look I'm giving her. 'Sorry. Inappropriate. It's just that when I met her she always seemed so – well – strait-laced.'

It's odd being reminded that Marilyn knew Clare, however briefly. It reminds me of something that's been nagging at me.

'Can I ask you something?'

'That sounds ominous.'

'Did you really not realise Clare was my sister when she came to see Johnny? I know she called herself "Prince", but you wouldn't just let your boss have private meetings with a random Treasury official. You'd have checked her out. Someone would have given you the family connection.'

Marilyn stubs out her cigarette in the mug. There's a small fizzle from the teabag that's been sitting in the bottom since breakfast. She looks me in the eye.

'Truthfully, I didn't know, at first. But Clare mentioned it to Johnny, and Johnny told me.'

'*Johnny* knew?' Did he mention that in our interview? I can't remember. I'm too stunned by this apparent habit Clare had of talking about me, rather than denying my existence – which is what I'd imagined she did. 'Do you know what she said about me?'

She shakes her head. 'Johnny mentioned it in passing. As I said before, and honestly this is true, he never discussed the detail of his conversations with Clare.'

'She was leaking the tax credit policy. She knew she'd be in big trouble if anyone found out.' I stare at the Rorschach blotches of the Expressionist print on the wall opposite. I am not sure what I see.

'I could tell he was impressed with her.'

'My sister had a knack of impressing powerful men. Something to do with learning to cope with our overbearing dad, I think.

But why didn't you tell me as soon as you knew the connection with me?'

There's heat in my voice. I've been so desperate to find out every scrap I can of Clare's life, and now it emerges Marilyn's been holding back.

Marilyn's reaction to emotion from me is to become icy. 'I always assumed that if Clare wanted you to know, she'd have told you. And it wasn't my place. I suppose I should have guessed you'd have fucked up your relationship with her.'

I wince and Marilyn thaws. 'Sorry. I shouldn't have said that.'

'It doesn't matter. But is there anything else you haven't told me? Anything Johnny mentioned that they'd talked about?'

'Nothing.' She's pissed off he seemingly had secrets with Clare he didn't share with her.

'Didn't you have any suspicions, any inklings?' Something flashes across her face. 'I know you. You always have a theory.'

She clicks on her yellow Bic to light another cigarette. She hunches her knees up against her chest and takes a long draw.

'Off the record?'

'Completely.'

'All right. Here's the thing. Just a few days ago, Cameron Fisher was in Johnny's office. He's in there all the time, so I didn't think anything of it, just walked in without knocking. Cameron had his back to me and he was blocking the door so Johnny didn't see me for a second. I heard Cameron say – at least, I *think* I heard him say – "When is Kendall coming across?" And then Johnny shooshed him.'

'"When. Is. Kendall. Coming. Across?"' I repeat. 'Blimey!'

'When Johnny saw me, he shouted, "Hello" to me, so loudly it shut Cameron up. Very obvious. Very deliberate.'

I ponder. Astonishing. I no longer mind her noxious cigarette smoke.

'You think the Chancellor of the Exchequer is crossing the floor to Labour? Can that be? You must have asked Johnny.'

'Of course I fucking did. Johnny gave me a look that meant I wasn't supposed to go there. Very annoying.'

'That would be a story. Right before an election. Unprecedented.'

'We're off the record,' she reminds me quickly. 'You are not to breathe this to a soul.'

'Listen I've just told you something that would kill me if it came out. Of course I am not going to turn you over.' *Though I am certainly going to make discreet enquiries.*

But even if Kendall was about to defect, why would Clare be the messenger? That would be an even more serious breach of Whitehall's strictures. I don't know what to make of this.

'Didn't you say Kendall was at university with your father?' Marilyn's animated. 'Kendall would have trusted Clare, and she would felt a connection with him. Wouldn't she?'

'My dad and Kendall were hardly buddies,' I say. But I've seen a different link. 'Frankie Crowther told me in The Groucho a few days ago that it was Cameron who briefed the papers about Clare dying.'

'Why on earth would he do that?'

'I don't know. But it suggests he may have been in regular contact with Kendall.' I shake my head in frustration. So many threads in one big tangle. 'Can you ask Cameron how he learned about Clare's death?'

'I'll try. I have what you might call a complicated relationship with Cameron.'

'Don't we all.'

175

We lapse into silence. One of the things I like about Marilyn is we can talk, or sit in comfortable silence. Which for me is unusual. There are some people who make me feel nervous when I have nothing to say or share, but not Marilyn. She tolerates my retreats into my own head. But what I'm thinking about now is the long finger of ash growing on the end of her cigarette. It's drooping and will make a mess of the white bedsheets. Just in time she taps it into the mug.

'You know that break-in I had here?' I say. The change of topic catches her by surprise.

'I thought there was no evidence it was a break-in? Weren't you too pissed to shut the door.'

'I don't think so. I'm not like that. Please humour me. Let's say it was a break-in. Who can do something like that? Who can break in noiselessly and leave without a trace?'

She shrugs. 'I'm an economics geek, remember? But I suppose you want me to say the security services?'

'Precisely. And which minister ran the security services until two years ago?'

'Hmmm. Kendall. He was Home Secretary before he became Chancellor.'

I don't say anything. A face is forming in the jigsaw puzzle. Wherever I look for clues for why Clare died, Kendall turns up.

Marilyn gives me a harsh look. 'I see where you're going with this. You're mad.'

Chapter 14

'SCHON PARTNERS,' SAYS A CLIPPED female voice. 'How can I direct your call?' Poised, cool: a voice that says immaculate hair and make-up, ineffable boredom, and a daily commute from comfortable Essex suburbia. She is the gatekeeper to a world of power and money, which she sees but can't enter.

'Robin Muller, please?'

'Please hold. I'll see if he's available. Who can I say is calling?'

'Gil. Gil Peck.'

'And where can I say you are calling from?'

'Don't worry about that. He knows me.'

I am projected into the no-man's land of being placed on hold. 'Winter' from Vivaldi's *Four Seasons* assaults my ears. I stare at the tiny winking light on the multi-channel phone that the *FC* has installed for all of us. Serendipitously, the light is blinking in time to the cresting violin. This is the fifth time I've heard it in the past two days. Its trills and acrobatics haunt my sleep.

The receptionist comes back. 'Mr Muller sends his apologies. He has back-to-back meetings. He says he got your earlier message and will ring you when he has a moment.'

'OK,' I sigh petulantly. And then, checking myself, add, 'Thank you so much for your help. Just in case I'm on the line when he calls, can I give you a second number?' Which I duly recite, though only out of habit rather than any expectation that he will actually ring. Pothead Muller is blanking me.

I put down the phone and stare out of the Burma Road's neo-Gothic mullioned windows, at an identical set of windows across the yard. A wave of exhaustion comes over me and slows my thoughts. Why is it so hard to do this one final thing for my sister? The two-day-old *Evening Standard* is open on my desk, with Muller's face – so much more knowing than when we ran our dope rota – taunting me. He's not looking at the camera: half-turned, it is as if someone out of shot has just said something to him.

Come on Robin, talk to me, for old times' sake. It is irksome that Muller has worked out that the best policy of dealing with the press is never to engage. Many people, who quite frankly should know better, get a thrill from talking to journalists like me and from the knowledge they've played a secret role in a story that causes a sensation. I don't pretend to understand the psychology of those who leak to me just for the hell of it, but I am grateful to them: I'd be out of a job without them. And thanks to years of learning how to persuade them to say more than they planned, I have a ruse to get Muller to spill. I will imply to him that others are talking and that he is damaging himself by keeping shtum. But first I have to somehow get him on the end of a phone.

It's 10.30 in the morning and the only other person in the cavernous room is the political correspondent of the *Western Mail*, who is pounding the keyboard with the fury of a young reporter terrified of missing the deadline. He won't pay any attention to me. I won't be overheard.

I take out my Nokia and dial.

'Boss,' she says brightly.

'You sound cheerful.'

'Well, I was. What's happening?'

'Are you still following the Capital deal?'

'Course.' It's the biggest story in the City right now, and the politics of Breitner becoming so powerful are seismic.

'Tell me about the role Schon is playing.'

'Nothing out of the ordinary. Breitner wants the deal so he's hired Schon. Schon are never on the losing side.'

'There's something else, I'm sure of it.'

'That's not a lot to work on.'

'I know. Sorry. The partner on the deal is Robin Muller?'

'Yes, Muller. Classic public school wanker. Though brighter than most.'

'I knew him at university.'

'You mean you knew him at Oxford. I hate it when people like you say "university".'

People like me. Ha.

'Muller won't take my calls. He's avoiding me. Which tells me there is something dodgy.'

'But what?' she asks.

'You remember that pensions story we looked at.'

'You're not still on it?' I hear concern in her voice. 'Gil, Lorimer told you to back off.'

179

I pretend not to hear. 'A source, someone I trust, tells me the Chancellor canned the tax raid after meeting Muller.'

She whistles down the phone. I can hear the cogs in her exquisitely engineered brain clicking into gear. 'You think Muller pressurised Kendall to dump the pensions tax?'

'My source is sure there is a connection.'

There's a clicking noise: Jess neurotically pressing the end of her retractable ballpoint pen.

'If Robin wanted to kill the pensions tax, what could be motivating him?' I ask her.

'There's a Chinese Wall at Schon between M&A, where he's a big wheel, and the fund managers who run money for pension funds. He'd have to be doing it on behalf of a client.'

'Media Corp?'

'Maybe. But he works for others too.'

'Can you check out whether any of them have a pensions problem.'

'I'll do what I can.'

One of my team saunters in and sits in the chair nearest me. I instinctively lower my voice. 'There's something going on with Kendall, too. He's covering up something.' I think of what Marilyn told me, the notion that Kendall could cross the floor to Labour. She told me to keep it to myself, knowing full well I wouldn't let it go.

'Is he happy in the Conservative party?'

Jess puffs down her nose, a half-laugh. 'I'm not sure what you mean. He's a natural Tory. It's in the blood, along with shooting, slagging off socialists and unthinking sexism.'

I stand up and walk into the corridor with my mobile. I don't want to be overheard.

'But the right of his party hate him. Wets like him are a dying breed.'

'Sure. He despises the Eurosceptics and the Thatcherite zealots. But what are you suggesting? That he might leave the party?'

'Maybe.'

'Doesn't feel right. For MPs like Kendall, the party is family. They live and die in it.'

It's not so unusual to fall out with your family, I mutter to myself.

Jess ignores me. 'Anyway, if he defects he'll screw up his chance of going to the Lords. He wouldn't take that risk.'

'Maybe not.'

Perhaps Marilyn got the wrong end of the stick, wishful thinking. Though what if Todd bribed Kendall to defect with the offer of a peerage? 'Kendall's hiding something. Clare knew what it was. Maybe Muller knows, too.'

'I'll talk with a few of the backbenchers who are close to him. I'll see what I can find out.'

'One thing. Don't be too explicit about the idea of him crossing the floor. I promised the person who told me I'd keep it to myself.'

'You and your promises. All right!'

After she hangs up, I return to my chair and stare at the white strip lighting that vandalises a white ceiling of moulded coving and cornices. Half a plan forms in my head. I bound down the steps two at a time to the ground floor and ask the morning-coated attendant in the wooden booth on Palace Yard to switch on the illuminating call sign to summon a black taxi.

The taxi takes me on a short journey across Westminster Bridge, past Waterloo, to the *FC*'s office in Blackfriars. Near lunchtime, the newsroom is warming up. There is a bank of clocks at the river end, showing the time in New York, Paris, Tokyo and Hong Kong. To its right is an electronic ticker tape feed from Reuters flashing up share prices and headlines. This is not the raucousness of a tabloid newsroom or a commodities trading pit. But around a hundred people are chatting on phones, or to each other, or munching overfilled sandwiches at their desks. At the centre of the hive is the queen, the news editor, Mary Nichols.

'Wotcha, Peck. Makes a change to see you with your clothes on.'

The news editors of the different sections – foreign, home, markets, companies – snigger.

'Can we have a word in private?' I ask.

'No problem. Boys, I'll be back in five,' she tells them.

I follow her to a row of glass boxes, each about twelve feet square, that run along the edge of the room like oversized fish tanks. She offers me a black leather and chrome Corbusier-inspired stool, while she leans back in the capacious swivel chair behind her desk. The hierarchy is clear.

'What's on your mind?'

'There's a story I want to write that's quite, ah, sensitive.'

'That sounds promising.'

'You remember the pensions raid we were talking about a couple of weeks ago? I've been looking at it some more, and I've reason to believe that there's more to why it was dropped than just a simple change of heart. I think Schon killed it.'

I have her attention. At the *FC*, we're obsessed with Schon, though not in a consistent way. Half the time we paint them as superheroes, the rest of the time as arch villains.

'Go on.'

182

The painful truth is I don't have much more. 'Schon got wind of the pensions tax change and leaned on the Chancellor to drop it.'

'Can you prove it?'

'I can prove they had a meeting.'

'Meetings happen all the time. So what?'

'The Chancellor dropped the policy moments afterwards.' And my sister called him *fucking corrupt*.

Her grey eyes bore into me. 'That's not enough. Why was Schon doing this? For itself or for a client?'

I'm running out of facts. Time to improvise. 'I am pretty sure it was for a client.'

Her eye goes to the glass door where one of her news editors is waving at her. She holds up five fingers at him. 'I haven't got long. Tell me what you *actually* know'.

'Schon advises the biggest companies in the country. They provide pensions to their employees through pension funds that are substantial liabilities for them. Like the Media Corp pension fund which will pay our pensions.'

'As and when the time comes.' She has no interest in retiring.

'All those clients would prefer the tax raid didn't happen.'

'We'd *all* prefer there were no taxes at all. None of that is a story. So what if Schon lobbied the Chancellor?'

'There is a difference between lobbying and blackmail.'

I've now strayed a distance beyond what I actually know. I'm not sure whether Mary sees through me.

Her eyebrows furrow. 'That's quite a claim. Are you saying they *threatened* Kendall?'

'That's what I think.'

'Think, or can prove?'

'*Will* prove.' I can see her deliberating. 'I know I haven't got enough. Yet. But what I'd like to do is write about the pressures on the government to drop the pensions tax, and mention the meeting with Schon. Not as cause and effect. But as raising questions that need to be answered. It just might flush someone out of the woodwork who can help with the bigger story. A sprat to catch a mackerel.'

She accepts the logic, warily. 'It would be stronger if you had more of a hunch about what was motivating Schon. If they were working for a big company, which one?' Mary's on it. 'It's got to be someone big,' she muses. 'Schon represent half the companies in the FTSE. Hell, they even represent us.' A pause. 'Are you still with me, Gil?'

Although I'm staring out of the glass cube, I'm hanging on her every word. I've remembered what Ringer said at lunch, something that puzzled me. *Think about your own pension.*

My own pension, courtesy of the *FC*, is the Media Corp pension scheme.

Robin Muller is working on the Capital deal for Media Corp. *Hell, they even represent us.*

I refocus and give an apologetic smile. 'Sorry. I was just thinking, what if the client was Media Corp? Would you run the story if the client who wanted the policy axed was Breitner?'

'You mean, would we run a potentially damaging news story about our own employer? Our owner?' She gazes in mock exasperation at the cream ceiling tiles. 'You know you've always been an absolute pain in the arse, Peck?'

'You sound like my mum.'

She takes this with a wry smile. 'We print what our readers need to know. We don't do favours for anyone, even the owner.'

She leans forward, studying me closely. 'It *was* Media Corp, wasn't it?'

'Yes, I think so.'

She glances again at the door, as though she's worried we're being watched.

'Just so we're clear, you want to write that the Chancellor backed off his pensions raid because of inappropriate pressure from Jimmy Breitner?'

I hadn't framed it quite so baldly. But the moment she says it, I know it's true.

Though truth is still a long way from being provable and not deniable. 'I can't write it yet. But I'm close.' Stretching a point. 'Just let me set some hares running and we'll see what we catch.'

'You're asking a lot.' She thinks in silence for a moment. 'You have my permission to make discreet enquiries, but I will need to run it past the editor.'

Shit. 'Look, I should have reminded you earlier. He warned me off the pensions story a few days ago. Remember?'

'You are a fucking piece of work, Gil.' She smiles. 'I'll handle the boss.'

It's a dilemma for Lorimer, but no one claims to set more store by the paper's reputation for independence than him. Nothing winds him up more than malicious whispers in our incestuous trade that after the *FC*'s 150 years of reporting without fear or favour he takes dictation from James Breitner. 'The day the proprietor tells me what to print, or not to print, is the day I am no longer the editor,' he once bellowed during a leader conference, after a catty piece in the satirical magazine *Private Eye* about how Breitner was allegedly interfering with the *FC*'s content.

Mary opens the door. 'Leave it with me.'

I stroll back to my desk, picking up a Diet Coke from the vending machine along the way. I hardly need the caffeine. I am exhilarated by my conviction that Media Corp was the client Muller was representing when he met the Chancellor.

I have to call Jess.

'You know I actually have a job to do?' is her faux-grumpy greeting.

'I've worked something out.' An audible sigh. 'No, really.' I spell out my hypothesis, though in my mind it's far more certain than that. 'If our pension fund took a hit during the Capital TV deal, that would spook the markets, wouldn't it?'

'For fuck's sake, boss! As I must have told you a thousand times, most pension funds are sitting on fat surpluses. That is why your sister was convinced they could afford to pay the tax. Why on earth should Media Corp be any different? Breitner doesn't like paying taxes. But there's no reason why this tax would be worse for him than any other. You haven't proved a motive for Breitner putting the squeeze on Kendall.'

I'm only half listening. My mind is driving at two hundred miles an hour and it's not noticing the signs along the motorway. For whatever reason, the Chancellor took orders from Breitner. Kendall became incensed when Clare called him out about it. He used his security service connections to silence Clare, and then to burgle my flat to see what was in my notebook.

The clicking of Jess's pen summons me back. I realise I'm accusing my employer of blackmailing the Chancellor and I'm on the point of articulating this on the office phone. If anyone were listening in, I'd be dismissed on the grounds of mental incapacity.

'Let's meet for a drink to talk it over. There's something else.'
I can tell Jess is anxious about my swerves, but I continue. 'I
need a favour.'

'The sort of favour that would get me fired?'

'You know the builder who knocked Clare off her bike? I
need to find out more about him.'

A long silence. 'I am not sure that's one of your better ideas.'

'I just want a quick once-over, to see if he is what he seems
to be.'

'What do you want me to do?'

'Would you mind going round to his house and banging on
his door?'

'Lorimer's right, boss. You're losing your grip.'

'Will you or won't you?' Her reluctance is annoying. 'It's not
that big a deal.'

'If it's not that big, then do it yourself.'

'Fine.'

She sighs. 'But if you're going to do it, you'd better have adult
supervision.'

A red light on my phone has started blinking. Someone's
trying to reach me. I ignore it. 'Shall we head there now?'

'Won't he be out at work?' She's right. Tiredness is clouding
my thinking.

'Oh yes.' The phone light is still blinking. 'What if I drive to
the Commons at 6.45 and pick you up.'

'It's a date,' she says, without enthusiasm.

'I've got a call coming in. Hold on.' I push the button to
switch to the other line. 'Yes?'

It's Lorimer's secretary. 'Can you go up to the tenth floor?'

The tenth floor is where the bosses live. 'Why?'

'I understand you've been chatting with Mary about a possible story. The editor thinks it would be sensible for you to talk it through with the lawyers.'

'Ah.'

'If you go to reception and ask for Nigel Sands, he'll be expecting you.' She hangs up, abruptly.

This is a first. I have never been to the tenth floor. I've never been ordered to chat with one of the company lawyers, just on the basis of a conversation with the news editor, before I've even filed anything. And I've never heard of Sands. He's presumably not just one of the young lawyers we pay to check copy for libel.

Another flashing light on the handset reminds me that Jess's still holding for me. I fill her in.

'So basically you made up a tale about Media Corp putting the squeeze on the Chancellor, and the fire alarm went off in the building?'

'I was trying to sell her a background analysis. Nothing sensational. Maybe I got a bit carried away.'

'You know Breitner has one of his London offices on the tenth floor?'

'If you want to reassure me, you can do better than that.'

'You'd better not keep them waiting. I'll see you at 6.45.'

'If I still have a job.'

Chapter 15

THE TENTH FLOOR HAS ITS own reception desk, guarded by a stern woman with cropped grey hair. She fixes me with a stare that implies she thinks I'm lost and have exited the lift on the wrong floor.

'Can I help?'

'Nigel Sands is expecting me.'

She changes her expression to one of sympathy. She murmurs my name into her headset. 'He'll be right down to collect you.'

A couple of minutes later a rhinoceros of a man, with a crooked nose that looks as if it was smashed in a rugby scrummage, comes stomping down the corridor.

'Gil, Gil, what a treat.' He is florid and beaming. 'Thanks so much for popping up. I'm such a fan of your work.'

I purr like a cat that's having its chin stroked. Maybe this won't be so bad.

'What can we get you?' he says, as he leads me back up the corridor. 'Tea? Coffee? Bit early for a beer – well, for me – but do say if you'd like one. I know what you journos are like.'

'Nothing, thanks. I'm fine.'

Sands ushers me into his corner office. South London is a vast patchwork quilt below us, through the floor-to-ceiling windows.

'On a good day you can see Croydon,' he says cheerfully, flinging himself into a dark blue sofa by the window. A matching sofa faces it. 'Take a pew, squire.'

Before I can sit down, there's a bang at the door. 'Come,' Sands barks, although the door is already opening. 'Ah, Jock. Just the man. I presume you two know each other.' He cocks an eyebrow at me. 'Gil Peck, Jock Streatham. Absolute legends, both of you.'

As Sands says, Streatham *is* a bona fide legend in my industry. Breitner installed him as editor of the *Globe* the moment he bought it and Streatham repaid the faith by turning it from a shrinking left-leaning broadsheet into the UK's biggest selling, no-holds-barred tabloid. He stepped down three years ago to become 'senior vice president' of Media Corp, a title that confers power though no precise responsibilities. When he's interviewed on TV, they caption him 'former tabloid editor', but that's not correct. A *fixer* or *mob consigliere* would be nearer the mark.

With his grizzled hair cut soldier-style short, he's lean – not a hint of fat – and wearing a blue blazer, grey slacks, pink shirt with top button undone. He'd be at home propping up the bar at a home counties golf club, where he'd eviscerate all and anyone he plays, even his mum. Energy crackles off him. You can't ignore him – and you can't relax.

I walk towards him with arm outstretched.

'Don't be a cock, Peck,' he says. 'We're not going to shake hands. Only poofs shake hands.'

I freeze. He's even more of a thug than I knew. And then he bursts out laughing. 'Of course I'll shake your hand. Just having a bit of fun. Sit down, sit down.'

We go back to the sofas. I find myself on the seat by the window, while Streatham occupies one nearer the door. Sands pulls up a hard-backed chair and takes out a notebook. The real meeting here is between me and Streatham.

'Now, laddie,' says Streatham. 'I understand someone has been whispering dangerous bollocks in your ear.'

'I don't know what you mean, Mr Streatham.'

'First names here, Gil. It's Jock to you. And don't kid a kidder. You know what I'm talking about.'

He waits expectantly, his gaze fixed on me. Offering me every opportunity to incriminate myself. We are in a well-appointed office and everyone is smiling. But the feeling I have is of being dangled by my ankles out of those tenth-storey windows.

'OK.' His smile doesn't flicker. 'Let me be more specific. That tosh about us leaning on the government over some pensions stuff. Who said that to you?'

'If it's not true, why does it matter?'

'We're in the middle of a significant corporate transaction and there's no shortage of dirty tricks going on. We don't need this kind of crap being talked about in polite society.'

When he says 'we' he means Jimmy Breitner. To pull off the Capital TV takeover, Breitner needs Media Corp's share price to rise, or at least stay stable. If the share price falls – say, because some irritating journo prints allegations about unethical behaviour – then there's a risk that Capital TV's shareholders will vote against the opportunity to exchange their gold-standard shares for Media Corp's lead tokens.

191

Except for one thing. As Jess stressed to me, Schon has underwritten a cash alternative offer for Capital shareholders. So if Media Corp shares were to tank, and Capital shareholders chose cash rather than Media Corp shares, Schon would be sitting on a massive underwriting loss. Schon and Breitner are both up to their necks in it.

'You've been in this game far longer than me, Jock. You know better than anyone that if I give up my sources to anyone, even you, I might as well start looking for a new career.'

I glance at Sands. He refuses to make eye contact. 'We're supposed to be on the same team, laddie,' says Streatham. 'And teammates work together and trust each other. If it's the fucking socialists feeding you this shite, you know they're all liars, don't you? Especially that cunt Fisher.'

Fisher, Labour's chief spin doctor, cut his teeth as political editor of the *Globe* ten years ago. He and Streatham go way back. There are Fleet Street stories of Fisher disappearing for benders that lasted days on end until Streatham caught up with him and delivered him to the rehab clinic at the Minster to dry him out.

'Where are you going with this?'

'I'm trying to protect you, laddie. Don't shit where you eat.'

Sands catches Streatham's eye. 'I'm sure you're perfectly aware of the delicacy of this situation. Everything Jock's said is strictly off the record, not for repetition. Obviously, Mr Breitner would never interfere in the editorial independence of the *FC*. All Jock is saying is that he expects the paper to only publish stories that are well-sourced and verifiable.'

He's emollience and reason. Their double act is a cliche. Jock gives me a Chinese burn, Sands strokes me. It isn't subtle. And it's pissing me off.

'Mr Streatham – Jock – we've never met before, and I assume you haven't read a lot of what I write. But you and Mr Sands should know that I never write unsourced or unverified hearsay. And you have my word that when I publish this story' – emphasis on the *when* – 'there will be multiple sources, and no one will be able to deny it.'

I'm shaking inside. I'm not sure if it's fear, or anger, or maybe it's both. I've been told that when I'm riled I shout without really knowing it, and it must have come out fiercely because even Streatham looks a bit taken aback. He and Sands exchange a glance.

'I think you understand us,' says Streatham, in a voice that says we're done.

I get up to go. 'Very nice to meet you both.'

'Mind how you go, laddie.' Streatham gives me a cold smile that conveys precisely the opposite sentiment.

As soon as I'm back on the first floor, I take out the Nokia and dial. 'Jeremy, it's Gil.'

'Ah.' I'm sensing he is as excited to hear from me as he would be if I were his dentist booking him in for root canal surgery.

'I need to ask something important.'

'Give me a minute. I'll ring you back from a private phone.'

Three minutes pass, during which I have ample time to reflect that Jeremy's paranoia no longer seems as absurd as it did. When the red light twinkles I snatch the handset before it starts ringing.

'I want to write a story about the Chancellor meeting Schon and dumping the pensions raid straight afterwards.'

'You're not going to mention me, are you?'

'I'll protect you completely,' I assure him. 'But' – I hear an intake of breath down the line – 'I need to know: in the event, the *unlikely* event, that someone sued us over it, would you be prepared to give evidence? If we subpoenaed you?'

'A subpoena?' His voice goes up almost an octave. 'Why would anyone sue?'

This is not the time to tutor him on how the rich can abuse British libel law to suppress the truth and keep their dirty secrets, or the distinction between a story that is true and one that is deniable.

'I really don't think it will come to that. But our lawyers are going to insist on knowing whether our sources would stand by us if – and it's only an "if" – it gets messy.'

I'm on tenterhooks and twiddle the phone cord with my index finger. If Jeremy won't promise to stand by us in court, I am stuffed.

'Please don't ask me to do that, Gil. It would kill my career.'

'But if Clare called out the Chancellor, shouldn't you?'

It's a low blow, bringing Clare into it. I feel cheapened, and then worse when I hear a whimper.

'I'm sorry. I shouldn't have asked. I know it's a lot to take in. Let's chat about it later.'

I hang up and my landline starts to ring. This is getting ridiculous, I think – and that's before I hear the editor's stentorian tones. It's amazing how everyone who matters wants to speak to me today.

'I heard you were in the building. Have you got a minute?'

In between being roughed up by Breitner's sidekicks and having my source wimp out on me? 'For you, John, always.'

'We haven't really spoken since you came back to work. How are you feeling?'

'Fine, thanks. It's good to be back.'

'Everyone's impressed by how you've got back on the bicycle. It can't be easy.'

A pause. I think I'm expected to say something, so I make a sort of non-specific grunt.

'You must be feeling pretty emotional about Clare.' This is not a question. 'We all understand. But I hear you're still working on that pensions story we discussed.'

'I had a feeling that might be why you called.'

'Now listen, Gil. Charging around trying to prove there's some kind of terrible conspiracy behind a routine government decision is a waste of your time. And a waste of the newspaper's time.'

'I'm just doing what I always do, which is following my instincts. There's an important story here, I'm sure of it.'

'Well, *I'm* sure you're wrong. You're barking up the wrong tree.'

'How do you know?'

'It's obvious. The government dropped the policy because it didn't want to be seen to be punishing pensioners ahead of a general election. Occam's razor. The simplest explanation is the truth.'

I reflexively stand up in exasperation. 'My dad used to say that Occam's razor is just an excuse for shallow thinking.'

I think I hear Lorimer grinding his teeth. 'Well, we're going to have to agree to disagree.'

'Does that mean you'll agree to let me pursue the story?' Of course it doesn't: I'm not obtuse. But I want to make him say it.

'It means I'm telling you to leave this story alone. Apart from anything else, there's an election on, you're the political editor, and that's the biggest story you'll have this year. You haven't got time for this nonsense.'

'You're the boss.'

'I'm afraid so.' He breathes outs heavily, as though relieved. 'Let's have a fun dinner as soon as the election is over.'

I hear the click as he hangs up.

My sensible sister died with the equivalent of eight glasses of wine in her system, carrying a child by an unknown father. She'd been working on a policy that could have cost some of the most powerful men in the country billions of pounds. And my employer is somehow up to his own neck in this.

'Fuck you, Lorimer,' I say to the ringtone of the handset. 'And if you're listening, fuck you, Jimmy Breitner.'

Chapter 16

'**Y**OU'RE TOO CLOSE TO THE kerb!' Jess shrieks. 'Please remind me never to get in a car with you again.'

She's not the first of my passengers to regret the offer of a ride. What they hate is that I drive the battered blue Peugeot hatchback like I ride my bike. I don't quite take it up on the pavement to get around traffic, or routinely run red lights, but I am impatient and can be aggressive when overtaking on the outside – or the inside.

'There's nothing wrong with my driving.'

'Er, more or less everything is wrong with your driving. How on earth did you pass your test?'

'A posh accent, and sexism. I simply persuaded the examiner I was the sort of man who ought to have a licence.' I am only half joking. My driving instructor was horrified I passed.

'Sexism and a posh accent' she repeats. 'Jesus. Welcome to how Britain works.'

We're crawling along the Embankment towards Blackfriars in rush-hour traffic. It's early evening, grey sky, lights gradually being switched on. Our destination is north east London, Wood Green.

'You never slow down, do you?'

'I'm going about ten miles an hour.'

'I'm talking about the way you work. The editor has told you to back off. Streatham has said the same. And you just keep going.'

'And you wouldn't?'

'Dunno.'

'Jess, you know there is a bloody amazing story here. We'd want to stand it up, whether or not it involved my sister.'

I hit the brake a bit too hard because I misjudged the turning of an amber light to red.

'Jesus, Gil!' She grips her seat. 'The first lesson you taught me was never to let any story become personal. You said the rubbish journalists are those who don't know when to drop an investigation. We're never going to get this in print. We should drop it.'

She may be right, but I won't debate it.

I drift absent-mindedly to the left, which elicits a long beep from a Ford Mondeo. As the Mondeo accelerates past, through the window I see the driver shouting something. I am not minded to work out what he's saying. Jess is holding the handle above the window with grim determination.

'It's Lorimer I'm most surprised by. People like Sands and Streatham are paid to be cunts. But I took Lorimer at his word when he said the paper's independence was worth more to him than his job.'

Jess shoots me a sideways look. 'There's something I've been wanting to tell you.'

I'm startled by a motor cyclist who shoots in front of me. 'Shit!' I shout. 'Sorry, go on.'

'I read something I shouldn't have done. And the moment I tell you, I am breaching confidentiality. I'm breaking company rules.'

'Yeah, but no one will know. Spit it out.'

We've crossed Pentonville Road and are on Islington High Street. Traffic has thinned out and I drive with fewer manoeuvres. Jess relaxes a little.

'You know the fax machine we use has almost the same number as the one in Lorimer's office?'

'Yup.' The fax numbers are identical, except that ours ends with an 8 and Lorimer's with a 9. On a few occasions, a fax has come through for Lorimer on our machine because someone pressed the wrong button. Generally we find out when Lorimer's PA comes racing to our office, red-faced and swearing.

'An intriguing fax turned up yesterday. Addressed to Lorimer and marked "confidential". I couldn't resist giving it a quick once-over.'

'Naturally.'

'The heading was "Media Corp Share Option Scheme 1997". There was a covering letter and several pages of technical detail.'

Another traffic light is on orange, but this time I accelerate rather than brake.

'It included his personal allocation of Media Corp options.' She reaches down to the rucksack in the footwell and pulls out a piece of paper. 'It's probably easier if I read you what it says.'

I take my eyes off the road and glance at her with a mix of pride and anticipation. 'Please tell me you didn't half-inch a private letter to the editor?'

'Of course not,' she says indignantly. 'I left it exactly where I found it. After I'd taken a photocopy.'

'That's my girl.'

'Don't patronise me, you sexist twat.'

'I was being postmodern and ironic.'

She unfolds the paper and reads, '"We are pleased to inform you that the remuneration committee has awarded you the option to buy shares at the agreed price, in the terms of the following schedule", blah blah blah. Basically, over the next two years he can buy a quarter of a million shares every three months at the current price. So if the shares go up in the meantime, it's free money.'

'And if they go down ...'

'... it's worth nothing.'

I let the implications of that sink in as we sit at a red light. 'So, just to be clear: Lorimer has a significant personal interest in not doing anything that will knock the share price?'

'That's about the size of it.'

The light turns green. 'Is that why he shut down my story?'

'Honestly, I think he has more integrity than that. But there is a conflict of interest.'

'To put it mildly,' I say. 'But if Media Corp is using US-style share options to bind in execs and editors, that's a big deal. If I stood to make tens of thousands of pounds from Media Corp's share price going up, I think that could affect my news judgement. Don't you reckon?'

'It's like some fucking mafia operation!' Jess bursts out. 'Just offer massive bribes to everyone who matters to big up the boss and his business.'

I've rarely seen her so fired up. 'Don't you remember when Breitner bought the *FC*, all that stuff he spouted about the imperative of cherishing our impartiality?' she continues. 'That people bought the paper because they trust what we say, and we'd be torching everything we've created over 150 years if we messed with that? His sermon was that we're all temporary stewards of the *FC*, and the paper has a life and importance beyond the interests of its shareholders. And so on and so on. Well, Lorimer's going to be tested now. Breitner wants to turn the *FC* into just another PR vehicle, with Lorimer as chief spin doctor.'

'Lorimer's not so bad.' I can't believe I'm defending him, after he shopped me to Streatham and killed my story. But he is decent – and Breitner and Streatham are thugs. 'The thing he doesn't have, that all great editors need, is the instinct to routinely tell the rich and powerful to fuck off. He's too nice. But I don't think he's bent. He'd be mortified by the suggestion that Breitner had bought him.'

'Because the truth hurts?'

'No. I don't think so. The problem is he hates conflict, and Breitner is a bully.'

'Possibly.'

Jess turns away and stares out the window, seething. We're approaching Harringay. Finsbury Park is on the left, door after door of seedy hotels that are probably knocking shops on the right. I clock that if we overshoot our destination, we'll arrive in another few minutes at White Hart Lane. I have an overwhelming urge to go there, or rather back to the magical Tottenham Hotspur team of the early 1980s, sharing with Clare our pride that the two magnificent Argentines, Ardiles and Villa, had chosen our Spurs as their home. And then, from nowhere again, I am overwhelmed by a black sadness that I'll never see her again.

'Boss?'

Jess is poring over the *A–Z* on her lap, checking it against the street signs. 'Next left. We're nearly there.'

It wasn't easy to track down Henryk Deyna, the builder who drove the van that hit Clare. He's not on the electoral register or listed on the land registry, presumably because he's renting. But his business is more substantial than I expected. He's not a bog-standard builder. He installs alarms and calls himself a 'security consultant', and he must be doing all right because he has set himself up with a limited company. That was how Jess found him, registered at Companies House as the sole director of HD Security, address given as 49 Hewitt Road, London N4.

Which turns out to be an avenue of small late-Victorian houses just off Green Lanes, where Turkish Cypriot restaurants rub up against IRA-supporting pubs. At number forty-nine, a low brick wall protects a tiny paved front garden, which is strewn with bits of wood and sodden cardboard boxes. As we walk up the path, there is a smell of mouldering food in bins.

Jess rings the bell on the frame of a shabby wooden door whose brown paint is bursting and peeling. Net curtains are drawn across a bay window and there are no lights on inside.

'Doesn't look promising.' The sky is overcast and heading for twilight, but perhaps he's still at work. 'Do you want to try again?'

We both stand there, feeling slightly idiotic and wondering what to do, when the neighbour's door opens. A middle-aged lady emerges.

'You're wastin' your time, darlings,' she says, in a luxuriant Jamaican accent. 'The chap who lived there, he's packed up and left.'

There's no privacy between the two front paths, just a three-foot high wall. I guess there's not much privacy between the occupants, either.

'When was that?'

'About three weeks ago.' *A few days after he hit Clare with his van.* 'I saw him leaving with two suitcases.' She looks us up and down, trying to work out whether a man in a blue suit and scuffed brown brogues and his colleague in a tweed skirt and kitten heels are here on official business of some sort. 'Did he owe you money?'

'No, nothing like that.' She seems to have taken us for the landlords. That's not the look I've been striving for. Jess jumps in.

'We've been rude. I'm Jess and this is Gil. Henryk is my uncle.'

The neighbour nods. She's unconvinced, though. Proper Londoners are naïve if they take at face value what a stranger on their doorstep tells them. 'Dolores,' she introduces herself. She's decided we don't need a surname. 'Everyone calls me Dolly.'

'Jess has been worried about Uncle Henryk because we haven't heard from him for weeks,' I say. 'It is odd he moved out. Did you have any reason to think something might be wrong?'

Dolly taps the dividing wall. 'He kept himself to himself. Mind you, he was never any trouble. Apart from his gardens, shocking mess they are. A jungle of weeds and rats. I asked him to tidy them up and he said he would. But look for yourself.'

'Sorry. That sounds like uncle. I think he was pretty lonely. Fed up. I've been worrying about him.' Jess is hitting her stride as the anxious niece. I'm impressed. 'I never understood why he wanted to live in a big house like this on his own. Did he have visitors?'

I can see Dolly's wariness is melting. Well done, Jess. 'I never saw anyone but him go in or out of that house, the whole two months he was there. And those hours he kept. Usually out at night and back in the morning, sometimes really early. Quite often he'd wake me at six by slamming the car door. I don't think he could have known how much noise he was making.'

'I'm sorry,' says Jess.

'It's not your fault, darling. I'm just saying his habits were not normal. Was he a night watchman or something like that?'

'He was in security,' I say.

'Ha,' she says. 'My brother was "in security". That would explain it.'

Jess picks up Dolly's hint. 'Explain what?' she asks.

'Them three men, parked outside the house. All night long, just sitting in the car. Something didn't feel right about them. I almost called the police.'

I share a glance with Jess. 'When was that?' I ask.

'Four nights ago.'

'You didn't happen to get the number plate, or anything?'

Dolly gives me a hard stare and purses her lips. Maybe I've pushed my luck too far.

'I think we've taken enough of your time,' says Jess quickly. 'But thank you so much. Can I give you my number?' She takes out her notebook and scribbles down her work, mobile and home numbers. She tears out the page and hands it to Dolly. 'If Henryk comes back, or if you hear anything about him, could you give me a call?'

Dolly takes the paper cautiously, as if it might be some kind of trap, and tucks it in the pocket of her apron. I assume that's the last we will hear from her, or from Henryk.

We head back to my unglamorous Peugeot. I notice that someone has traced a message in the dirt on its back window: 'Clean this fucking car.'

'In case you're wondering,' says Jess, before I can open my mouth, 'I still think you are in fantasy land, not deep state.'

'You don't think it's suspicious? Strange men hanging around in the dead of night? Deyna claiming to be a builder to the police but having a "security" business, and vanishing right after the accident?'

'Installing alarms is sort of building work. And loads of people move from rented home to rented home. You are seeing what your trauma wants you to see.'

'OK, Dr Jess.'

Just as I'm opening the car door, I hear the Nokia's plinkety ringtone.

'That's yours, not mine,' says Jess. I snatch a quick glance around me. Am I going to be mugged if I take it out here? Nah. All quiet.

The digit sequence on the small screen is unfamiliar, so I can't be sure if the person on the line is someone I would rather avoid.

'Hello,' I say, not revealing my name, in case the caller has misdialled.

'Mr Peck,' says a deep South African growl. 'My name is James Breitner.'

Oh fuck.

'You and I need to have a chat.'

Chapter 17

JAMES BREITNER THE SECOND. JIMMY Breitner. The name conjures up myth as much as man. It's odd how media tycoons seemingly want to be as monstrous as an Orson Welles' fiction. Darling of the political right, demon of the left. He grew up in the Cape, son of a local farmer and his wife, who were shot dead when they confronted armed robbers. Adopted by his dad's sister and uncle, he excelled at school, sold the farm at the first opportunity and went to work for a bank. The turning point in his life came when a school friend came to him for a loan for the family business, a local newspaper, the *Cape Town Courier*. Instead of a bank loan, Breitner used his small inheritance to become a part-owner. He got the news bug, squeezed out his friend, and then mortgaged the *Courier* to buy another newspaper, then another, then a television station, then network after network, across the world. Today Media Corp reflects and creates popular culture, it builds up and knocks down celebrities, it makes and breaks governments. The myths about Media Corp are extreme. The reality is worse.

Within his business, he has two incarnations. Sleeves rolled up, eating and joshing in the canteen with the hacks that work for his newspapers and television stations. And plotting the next phase of his ambition to own the whole world, shielded from prying eyes in an exquisite, absurdly over-priced Georgian townhouse, hidden in a traffic-free street in St James's.

Which is where I was instructed to present myself at 10 a.m. It's now eleven, and I have been here well over an hour, having – against the habits of a lifetime – bowled up fifteen minutes early. With every tick of the elegant grandfather clock in the corner, I become jumpier and more on edge. On the walls are eighteenth-century rustic scenes in gilt frames, originals, I presume. I've had more than enough time to study them in minute detail, to interrogate the symbolism of the milkmaids and shepherdesses and fauns, and also to scan every page of the *Tatler* and *Country Life* mags that are on the walnut Queen Anne table. It's meant to feel like the London home of the heir to a historic estate – except that everything is too perfect and coordinated to have been inherited. It all speaks of money, power and secrecy.

My nervous energy would send a Geiger counter into overdrive, the kind of feeling I had years ago before a make-or-break exam. Perhaps this *is* an exam. I've worked for Media Corp for the best part of a decade, but this is my first meeting with Breitner. He's the most powerful media owner in the UK, perhaps in the world. He controls the destiny of my industry. And arguably me along with it.

The inner door swings open. I'm already rising to my feet, springing up like a jack-in-the-box as a well-tailored man steps out. He's tall, thin, with ash-blond hair and blue eyes. In his narrow-lapelled suit and horn-rimmed glasses, he's like something out of a 1940s Carol Reed film noir. Not Breitner, nor a direct employee. He is the elusive Third Man I've been chasing.

'Robin.'

Muller halts and turns. He flashes a smile, as if it's the most natural thing in the world that I'd be here. It's a smile my female friends at college told me was irresistible, so it gave me pleasure to reveal that he was more interested in my sex than theirs. Yes, I know, 'I'm an arsehole', as Marilyn would say.

'Peck. It's been a while. How are you, old bean?' he says, as if blissfully ignorant of my frantic attempts to contact him. 'Nice suit, I must say. Inky-fingered hackery has worked out for you.'

'I get by,' I reply. 'I'm not sure if your office told you, but I've been trying to get hold of you.'

'Yes. I know. So sorry not to make myself available. Busy time. We will catch up, I promise.' I don't believe him. He gestures with his head towards the doorway he's just exited. 'First time with Jimmy?'

'Yuh. He summoned me. But –'

'Word to the wise. He'll play a game, always does with people he hasn't met before. Take it in your stride.'

'Right.' Muller hasn't changed. Charming. Clever. Selfish. And I'm not going to let him go now that I have him. I've left the waiting room and am blocking his path to the stairs. He is beginning to feel uncomfortable. 'We need to speak, Robin. Seriously.'

His eyes dart over my shoulder, calculating how far I will go to obstruct his departure. Perhaps he remembers the time in the Chicheley junior common room when I very loudly and publicly called him a 'Tory cunt' after an argument about Thatcher's privatisations. Discreetly, he removes a business card from a silver holder and scribbles on the back.

'This is my private mobile number. Call me.' No trace of a smile now, as I pocket his card. 'Toodle pip,' he mouths. Just in time. As the card slips into my pocket, the inner door opens and a great hulking bear of a man strides out. Instantly, the atmosphere changes. It is as if someone's thrown a switch and four million volts of electricity are fizzing.

Jimmy Breitner is a presence. Only about five foot ten, but seemingly as wide as he is tall. Although fat, he carries a good deal of muscle with it, like a retired boxing champ. He wears black trousers, a crisp white shirt, tight around the biceps, and – disconcertingly – leather mule slippers.

He's showing someone out, who was presumably in the meeting with Muller. I hear a jocular voice I know only too well. It's Mephistopheles Ringer. *Of course* he's here. Again, I puzzle over which side Ringer is on, what's motivating him. After all, it was he who nudged me into thinking that it was Breitner putting the squeeze on Kendall to drop the pensions tax.

No time to solve the mystery. Hands so vast that they seem more suited to the building site than the boardroom engulf my right one and shake it so hard that I fear my arm will be wrenched from its socket. 'Gilbert Peck,' says Breitner, booming, as if I am a long-lost friend. It's one of those voices so deep it could make glassware tremble. 'How the hell are you? Thank you for coming. I gather you know *Sir* Bob.' He lingers on the title, teasing Ringer with it.

'Everyone knows Gil' says Ringer. 'Or at least, everyone who counts.' And he directs a hint of a smile at me. Ringer's Hermès tie is immaculately knotted, his hair flawlessly blow-dried, nothing to suggest he's not in control – but I see just the faintest shadow of anxiety behind his grey eyes. 'You'll deliver that message to our mutual friend,' Breitner says to Ringer. It's an order, not a question. 'If he wants our backing, he can bloody well work for it. We're not being taken for granted.'

'Righty ho, Jimmy.' Bob Ringer nods his head, pays obeisance to the baron. He's dismissed. I turn to nod goodbye to him and when he's out of Breitner's line of sight he winks at me.

I follow Breitner through the inner door. If the waiting room was Jane Austen Georgian, his office is Versailles. Huge, ornately-framed mirrors and oil paintings cover the walls, while the furniture is fussily carved and gilded. It is overwhelming. There is nothing subtle about the message Breitner wishes to convey: the Sun King had nothing on him.

'Sit down, Mr Peck.' He waves me to a Louis Quatorze sofa and I sit on it, straight-backed and terrified to move. The paintings in my eyeline are all nudes: big-breasted women, small-breasted women, women crouching in their baths or reclining invitingly on chaises longues. They look nineteenth-century French – Gérôme, Ingres, Degas, Manet. Presumably they are real.

Breitner enjoys my discomfort. *He'll play a game with you.* 'You like my collection?' he asks. 'I like to surround myself with beautiful women.'

'What's that?' I ask pointing to a modern painting of a heavyset Rottweiler with lachrymose eyes, pride of place behind Breitner's desk.

His amused expression doesn't change. 'Nelson was my best friend.' This monster of a man is sentimental. 'I miss him. Do you like dogs, Mr Peck?'

'I have a cat.'

211

That was definitely the wrong answer. 'A cat!' The contemptuous way he says it carries an unmistakeable if unspoken subtext. *Cats are for grannies. Are you a granny, Mr Peck?* 'I judge a man by how he relates to a hound. And vice versa.'

'We had a dog when we were growing up,' I say, and then feel this sounds lame. It's not going well.

There's a knock at the door. Breitner says, 'That will be our mutual friend, Mr Streatham. Jock, my lad, come in.'

And then to me, 'I thought it would be helpful for Jock to join us. He's always accusing me of getting carried away, when he's not around.' He gives me a big wink, which has its desired menacing impact.

'So we're on the record,' I say, chancing my arm, and then I instantly regret it. The rule is everything is on the record till you're told otherwise. I am being an arsehole today.

'Don't be daft,' Jock growls. He doesn't take a seat, but folds his arms and leans against the wall, just out of my eyeline so that I can't look at him without craning my neck away from Breitner.

'Just three blokes having a chat.' Breitner reaches behind him, where a crystal decanter and a set of whisky tumblers sit, and pours three glasses.

'You're probably wondering why I wanted to meet you,' says Breitner. He takes an ugly gulp of whisky and leans forward, sizing me up.

In my hand the crystal is heavy enough to brain a man. I have a cartoonish thought that maybe I'll need the weapon to get out of here. *Kendall axed Clare's pension tax after his meeting with Muller. Muller represents Media Corp. Media Corp owns the FC, and when I tried to write my story I got Streatham breathing down my neck and Lorimer spiking it. Lorimer, who has millions of pounds of share options dangling in front of him, courtesy of Jimmy Breitner.*

In the back of my mind I hear Jess's voice cautioning me that it's all circumstantial: that Breitner had no motive to kill the tax if his pension fund's in rude health, and – the biggest flaw – that even if he did, once he'd nobbled the Chancellor, then why would he care what happened to Clare? A thought runs through my mind as I stare into Breitner's heavily lidded eyes: *did you snuff out Clare, you monstrous cunt?*

Stay calm, stay calm, stay calm. Whispering it inaudibly three times is good luck.

Breitner revolves the heavy watch on his wrist. 'There's only one thing on all our minds at the moment.' A pause, those eyes drilling into me. 'The fucking general election.'

It's not what I expected and my surprise must show because his lips open in an understated smile revealing flashy dentistry.

'Jock tells me that you know more than anyone else on my payroll about the socialists.' I feel flattered. 'Are they going to win?'

'Well, nothing is certain in politics . . .'

'You don't need to hedge with us, sonny,' Streatham barks from over my shoulder. I may be wrong, but I think he is trying to be friendly, even if it is in the way of a snarling dog whose tail is wagging. Have I misread the situation? 'Just give it to us straight. We're all on the same team, aren't we?'

The whisky smells of peat and smoke but I decide not to drink – which is hard, because it is without doubt well above my price range. 'The polls give Labour a healthy lead.'

'We can all read the polls.'

'Obviously they predicted a Labour victory last time, and that turned out to be rubbish, so you can't take the numbers for granted. But the lead is far bigger now, and it is considerably more solid.' I smell the whisky again. 'Two things. First, the pendulum always swings eventually and the Tories have been in office for a long time. Second, Johnny Todd has positioned himself as a Tory in Labour clothing, or maybe it's the other way round. Either way, he is about proving to swing voters that he's competent, not ideological.'

I realise that my delivery is nervous and very obviously halting. 'Thank God we put you in the papers and not on the fucking television,' says Streatham.

'Just for the avoidance of doubt,' I say, ignoring him, 'Labour will win, and win big.'

There's a barbed silence in the room. It's not what Breitner wants to hear. Finally, he says: 'What does that mean for us? I assume our taxes are going up, we'll be bowing and scraping to the Brussels Stasi, and God help the free press.'

I'm surprised by how much Breitner seems to rely on a caricature of Labour and how little he knows about Todd and his ambitions. 'On Brussels, yes, Todd would be less hostile to the EU. But he is different from his predecessors. When it comes to taxes, he wants to be seen to be on the side of business. And as for income tax, I broke the story that he's committed not to increase either the basic rate or the higher rate. But they will try to increase tax revenues in less conspicuous ways, by, for example, forcing pension funds to pay tax on the dividends they receive.'

I pause for a moment. Breitner briefly looks at Streatham. Streatham interjects, 'What about the media?'

'Well, it's true that Todd's press secretary, Cameron Fisher, detests what he sees as the right-wing tabloids, who he and Todd blame for Labour losing the last election. They will try and close the *Globe* down. Not literally of course. But they will try to marginalise it, to make it look out of step with the country, to deprive it of access to power. From memory, Fisher is an old friend of yours. So presumably none of this is a surprise.'

Again the chilly silence. This is my moment. I take a breath and look Breitner directly in the eye. 'I mentioned the pensions tax. What impact would it have on Media Corp?'

I hear Streatham cracking his knuckles. Breitner doesn't blink. 'That's an odd question. What makes you think it would have any kind of impact on us?' *On us.*

'Well, there's chatter in the City that *our* – your – pension fund is in trouble.' I'm improvising. Again. Jess tells me there's no evidence there's any kind of a hole in the Media Corp fund, but although I trust her, I've also learned to go with my intuitions because sometimes they turn out to be deductive leaps. 'If there's a big deficit, the tax on dividends would be a pain.'

Breitner is still. And then, very suddenly, he slams his fist on the desk. 'That is a crock of shit!' he says. 'If you value your career, you won't repeat it.' His South African accent is stronger in his rage; each syllable is stressed. 'Do you hear what I am saying? Do I look like a man on the brink of ruin?'

He's wearing a watch worth more than my salary in a room that cost more to furnish than I will earn in my life. *But I didn't say anything about him facing ruin. Why jump to that conclusion?*

Streatham intervenes, perhaps sensing that Breitner is revealing too much. 'Aren't we here to talk about politics?' he says. 'Shall we get back to that?' There is a brief silence. It takes all my willpower not to drink the whisky. I try not to tremble.

'The most important thing,' I say haltingly, 'is that Todd knows Labour can't win unless the party is seen to be in the centre of politics. I don't see that as a convenient pose, to be dropped when Johnny's in Number 10. It's his credo, his guiding star, such as he has one.'

'It's "Johnny", is it?' says Streatham. 'Nice and cosy.'

I redden. 'It's "Johnny" to everyone. That's his style.'

Streatham laughs. 'I'm just winding you up, sonny. I wasn't born yesterday. Todd is a phoney who needs everyone to be his friend.'

Breitner perks up. 'Wanting to make friends isn't such a bad thing, Jock. But is Mr Streatham right? Does Todd need to be loved?'

I am intrigued by Breitner's inquiry. 'Maybe. He's exceptionally charming. And he's not ideological in the old Labour sense of despising people because they went to Eton or own vast tracts of Hampshire, or because they happen to be the proprietor of right-leaning newspapers.'

'We own papers of all persuasions and none,' Breitner says disingenuously. 'That's our prerogative. But are you telling me he has no convictions?'

'I think he has one, or at least one that matters: he believes there is no point in being in politics unless you win power, unless you are in government. He sees opposition as fatuous, and he will do more or less anything to escape it.'

'Hmmm, more or less anything?' Breitner echoes. The room lightens as outside the sun emerges from behind a cloud. 'But when he wins, won't he be the puppet of the trade unions?'

I consider for a moment. 'That is a risk. But it's unlikely. Don't forget, they've been beaten up by Tory governments for almost two decades. If he wins big, they'll be so euphoric they'll let him do whatever he wants. At least for a while.'

'Maybe,' says Streatham. It's unnerving, having his interjections from over my shoulder. 'But as the man said, "gratitude has a short half-life".'

I turn to face him. 'Even if you are right, Johnny will use whatever time he has to reinforce his control of the party machine. Perhaps I should have mentioned: he is ruthless.'

Breitner smiles. He turns and looks at the Rottweiler. I'm reminded of Harry Truman's famous line: *If you want a friend in politics, get a dog.*

'What Mr Breitner wants to know is whether Mr Todd is someone we should be trying to do business with,' Streatham says. 'Ramsey has turned out to be a prize arsehole. Unfortunately, he's our arsehole, because if the *Globe* hadn't backed him in 1992 the socialists – and they *were* socialists then – would probably have won. It's hard for the *Globe* not to stick with Ramsey. But what if we didn't? What if we supported Todd?'

'Honestly, I'm not sure what you would have to lose.' It's not something I planned to say, but as I do, I realise quite how true it is. 'He's going to win anyway. So what would you gain from backing the losers?'

'And you think he has the balls to face down the unions?'

'He came into Parliament in 1987, just as the tide was turning against the hard left. And he has dedicated much of his career to lessening the party's financial dependence on the unions. But they're always going to have a big role. The clue's in the name, after all. But he's got big balls.'

217

Breitner looks at Streatham and both roar with laughter. What have I said that's so funny? Before I have time to consider, Breitner is standing and Streatham has wandered over to escort me out.

'It was a pleasure to meet you, Mr Peck,' says Breitner, looking at my full glass. 'My whisky doesn't meet your standards?'

I say something about not drinking before six.

'Drink up, laddie,' says Streatham. *Fuck you, Streatham.* I ostentatiously put down the tumbler, untouched.

'I value the work done by loyal colleagues,' Breitner says, with the stress on *loyal*. 'Loyalty is everything with me.' He turns again to look at Nelson's portrait. "Take care, young man". I am on warning.

Streatham walks with me back to the landing outside. 'That was very educational. Mr Breitner has taken a shine to you.'

All I can muster is, 'It was a privilege meeting him.' Streatham slaps me on the back and leaves me to make my own way out.

What on earth was that all about? I don't believe Breitner wanted my expert insight into the election. I didn't tell him anything he couldn't have read in one of my columns in the *FC*. He wants my measure.

I am feeling shaky. I need to call Jess and talk it through. I turn left down the narrow lane and on to the main road. Just as I'm about to take out my phone, I see Robin Muller across the street, walking in half circles as he barks animatedly into his mobile. I won't let him get away this time. I run towards him, almost getting hit by a black cab, and catch his eye. He frowns in not-very-well-disguised dismay, and mouths, 'Two minutes.' In fact, he takes ten, but I'm still there when he finishes.

'How did you get on with Jimmy?' he asks.

'Like being in a shark tank, wearing a suit made of raw meat.'

He laughs. 'How funny to see you like this, after all these years. Bit different from college.' *On the drugs relay.*

'At least then we were dealing with people we could trust.'

'So true.' He puts a hand on my arm. 'I heard about your sis. I hope you're OK.'

'Actually, that's what I wanted to talk to you about.' Out here on the street, I know I can't keep him long. I have to dive in. 'Clare had been working on a plan to tax the dividends going to pension funds. You were spotted in the Treasury meeting the Chancellor, and straight afterwards the Chancellor dropped the policy. Clare went ballistic, shouted at Kendall in front of his entire office.'

'Your sister came to see you a couple of times at Chicheley as I recall. I remember she seemed pretty determined. But on your precise question – you know I don't work on the asset management side of the house? Pensions are not my bag.'

'Don't be coy, Robin. You know what I do for a living. Your corporate clients *all* have a strong interest in whether the income going into their pension funds is taxed or not. The tax on the funds is an indirect cost to them. And sometimes a direct cost, if it forces them to increase their contributions to the funds.' I remember Breitner's unprompted protestation. 'There may be businesses ruined by the tax change.'

Muller looks past me, scanning the passing cars, and doesn't take the bait. I won't be distracted.

'Did you pressurise Kendall to drop the planned abolition of the dividend tax credit?' Again, silence. 'We can talk on whatever basis you like. Off the record if you prefer. If anyone ever asks, this conversation never happened. I just want to know why my sister was so upset, days before she died.'

That gets a snort. *'Talk on whatever basis.* You know I work for Schon. And we never talk to the press, on any basis. Don't be an idiot. Of course we're not going to talk, even for old times' sake.'

'Just tell me what you can and I promise I'll never attribute anything to you, even in private.'

He looks left and right. 'I know you've been through hell, Gil, but my advice is stay away from all of this. It's delicate stuff. And honestly, I don't think there's a story.'

'I know your PPE days were a while ago, but if there isn't a story, how can my digging around be a problem? Your two statements are not consistent.'

'Fuck you!' he snaps. 'I am doing my best to be nice. But you haven't changed. Just do yourself a favour and walk away before you do a lot of damage. Especially to yourself.'

A black Mercedes is crawling down the street towards us.

'What the fuck happened?' I ask him. 'You used to be cool. Now you're just a wanker.' Muller gives the car a curt wave and steps forward to the kerb.

There's nothing more to be had from him. I was naïve to think I'd get anything at all. But his warning has reminded me of Breitner's parting shot.

'What happened to the dog?'

He turns. 'What?'

'Breitner's Rottweiler.'

'You don't know?'

The Merc has stopped. The chauffeur has climbed out and is holding the back door open for Muller, but Muller doesn't get in. He wants to tell me this.

'Breitner was hosting a family dinner in South Africa, at his mansion on the Cape coast. The dog was sleeping in the corner.

Breitner called him over and fed him a scrap off his plate, then sent him away again. But the dog didn't go. He climbed up and took a piece of meat from Breitner's kid's plate. Everyone was laughing about it, but Breitner was furious.'

He pauses, making me ask the question. 'And?'

'Breitner took the dog outside and shot him. Dead.'

Traffic has started to build up. A white Ford Escort honks. With a smile, Muller slides into the back seat of the Mercedes. The door closes with that cushioned *thunk*. Muller winds down the window.

'I'd offer you a lift Gil. But you're not going my way.'

Chapter 18

THE ADRENALINE RUSH OF MEETING Breitner has been replaced by a sinking despondence. I'm standing outside the eighteenth-century hatters Lock and Co., on St James's Street. I've been sticking my nose up against this window for as long as I can remember, never quite summoning up the courage to go inside to be measured for a Regent or Chelsea Fedora.

'What do you think, Gil?' Jess's voice, down the phone, trying to draw me back. 'I'm not sure you're listening.'

'Would I look the part in a pork pie?'

Jess growls in frustration. 'For God's sake, Gil, you're becoming a caricature. You dragged me into this madness, at least do me the courtesy of listening.'

'Sorry.' I am. 'You have my attention.'

I hear her click her tongue. From the moment she joined my team she felt like a younger sister. Siblings forgive each other.

'Fire away.'

'Dolly rang this morning.' Dolly? Oh yes, the woman who was Henryk Deyna's neighbour in Wood Green. 'Apparently there were night-time visitors at Uncle Henryk's house last night.'

The trilby can wait. 'Interesting. Good old Dolly.'

'She doesn't miss a thing from behind that curtain. Around ten she heard a car stopping. A large, black saloon car parked, with two men and a woman inside. The woman and one of the men got out and went to Henryk's house.'

I switch the phone to my other ear. 'Go on.'

'Here's the funny thing: they rang the bell, and when no one answered they took out a key and went inside. Dolly said she heard the sound of furniture being moved. They were there for about an hour.'

'I don't suppose she made a note of what they looked like,' I say hopefully.

'She couldn't see the man in the car. But the other two were smartly dressed. The man was stout, big belly, bald head, dark suit and white shirt unbuttoned at the top. The woman – Dolly called her "the boss lady" – was wearing a brown wool trouser suit and had brown hair cut in a bob.'

'Dolly is bloody wonderful.'

'She keeps 'em peeled,' Jess agrees.

'And the car?'

'VW Passat. She even got the number plate.'

'Amazing. It would be useful to know who owns it. Don't you have a nark at the DVLA?'

'Bribing a public official is against the law and against *FC* policy,' Jess reminds me. 'Also, it will be pricey.'

'I'll have a think about that. In the meantime, we should find out who owns the property. We haven't done a Land Registry search on the house itself yet, have we?'

'I'll get on to it. Anything else?'

I've been walking while we talk, down St James's Street towards Pall Mall, where the confidence of Queen Victoria's imperial Britain is manifest in the serried row of overbearing gentlemen's clubs. It's where Sherlock met Mycroft. Which sparks a thought.

'Do you think they could have been spooks?'

An intake of breath. 'We've discussed this before, boss. Just because Kendall was Home Secretary, that is *not* evidence.'

'But he worked with them for years.'

The walk, and Jess's news, has focused my thoughts. I've let myself be sidetracked. I've been so busy trying to track down Muller, and been so bullied by Breitner and Streatham, I've neglected my prime suspect.

'Whatever Muller said to Kendall in their meeting, whoever he was acting for, it was still Kendall who made the decision to ditch the tax raid. He's at the centre. Everything comes back to him.'

I pause, waiting for Jess's inevitable objections, coolly ticking off the reasons I'm probably wrong. All I hear is breathing.

'I don't need Muller to tell me what he said to Kendall,' I continue. 'I just need to find out what he's got on him.'

'Why is Kendall any more likely to tell you than Muller? He's got more reason to hide it than anyone. And he's already told you to fuck off.'

'I'm not going to ask Kendall.'

'Who, then?'

'Who do you think?'

Jess and I have been working together so long, we instinctively know the other's next moves. 'That's risky, boss.'

'There's nowhere else to go.' A grumbling cranking engine is approaching from behind. I stick out my hand to flag down the black cab. 'I'll call you back in a bit.'

The taxi pulls up and the driver rolls down his window. 'Where to, young man?'

'Breitner House, please.'

Breitner House is a modern pyramid of gold-tinted glass rising out of south London docklands. It's one of those areas where all the ages of London are sandwiched together cheek by jowl: New York-style loft apartments in converted Dickensian warehouses; 1930s council estates that are the last fortresses of a white working class which has mostly fled north and east to suburbia; Tower Bridge looming in the background and the river flowing only fifty yards away. Four centuries ago, Shakespeare's Globe theatre stood a few hundred yards to the west and soon it will again: you can see scaffolding surrounding faux-Tudor half-timbering, where an American actor is building a replica.

I've always wondered if Breitner was aware of the proximity when he moved his tabloid from Fleet Street to its new home five years ago. The stock in trade of both Globes was – and is – sex, scandal, and the foibles of our rulers. Both play to a baying mob. As Shakespeare wrote, 'I have seen corruption boil and bubble till it o'er run the stew; laws for all faults, but faults so countenanced, that the strong statutes stand like the forfeits in a barber's shop, so much in mock as mark.' It might have been a *Globe* editorial.

Thatch and wattle have given way to steel and glass, but in other respects not much has changed. Sanctimonious politicians lecture us on how to behave, and then follow another code or none themselves: witness the Tory ministers and MPs in the last few years exposed for pimping themselves out to the highest bidder. In Breitner's *Globe*, no less than in Shakespeare's, anyone and everyone is a legitimate target for public humiliation.

When it comes to our rulers, no one kowtows before skewering quite like Kevin Wilkinson. The *Globe's* political editor can match wits with the Prime Minister's spokesman in the Lobby briefing, but he also has a bloodhound's nose for scandal. At the Palace of Westminster, he is feared, loathed and reluctantly admired, by prey and colleagues. His preferred route to a scoop is to play a round of golf with the government's deputy chief whip, who has a black book on the peccadilloes of every Tory MP (I say *a* black book, but I assume it runs to volumes). When the chief whip needs to bring a troublesome backbencher into line, or make an example *pour encourager les autres*, the deputy feeds Wilkinson a titbit: an MP's regular excursions to a pub favoured by rent boys in Clapham; another's secret third home, a flat in Kensal Rise, where he's installed a young Commons secretary and where he has a habit of 'working' into the small hours. All that Wilkinson has to do is put a snapper outside said pub or maisonette and Bob's your uncle: a salacious *Globe* page 2 scoop, divorce papers to follow. If Kendall is hiding something, the bloke most likely to have an inkling – apart from the whips themselves – will be Kevin Wilkinson.

Will he help? Our relationship is a wary one. Like me, he is a story-scenting predator. He's right at the top of the journalistic food chain. It's not his natural instinct to share red meat. But we have an accommodation of sorts. I've laid off salacious stories with him that weren't right for the *FC*, and when the deputy chief whip has told him some arcane detail of a change to rules for company boards – so vital to our readers, so irrelevant to his – he has pushed that intelligence in my direction. The *Globe* doesn't care all that much about the Cadbury Code on Corporate Governance, and the *FC* takes the patrician view that if an MP smears Cadbury's Dairy Milk over his toy boy lover that is his business and not ours. So in theory I should be able to offer him something to make it worth his while to tell me what I want to know about Kendall – but it will require a bit of improv.

I rang ahead from the cab to make sure Wilkinson would be there. I was pretty sure he'd have gone to the morning editorial conference and would not head to the House of Commons until after lunch. Even so, it takes me longer than anticipated to negotiate my way inside. A makeshift desk has been set up at the entrance, where plain-clothed security men are questioning everyone. Breitner's notoriety, and the *Globe*'s no-holds-barred British flag-waving, make it a target for terrorists and cranks. It's only last year that the IRA set off a three-thousand pound bomb in Canary Wharf, not so far from here.

'Kevin Wilkinson's expecting me,' I say, which gets me into the lobby, but it takes my *FC* photo pass to reassure the lady at the reception desk.

'One of us,' she says.

Wilkinson comes down in the lift and swipes me through the glass security gates. 'What brings you to the underworld? Shouldn't you be spinning for Todd and your Labour mates?'

I ignore the provocation as we step into the lift. Wilkinson worshipped Thatcher, regards Ramsey as a traitor, and sees Labour – even a Labour Party reupholstered by Todd – as agents of the devil. He is presumably going through a crisis of confidence and conscience, because if Todd wins as big as seems likely, a remade Downing Street will cast Wilkinson into the desert. He won't like going from oracle to the man who knows nothing. Can he bring himself to crawl to Todd and – hardest of all – to his old subordinate, Fisher? I choose not to touch this nerve. Instead I say, 'I've got a proposal for you.'

'Oh, darling, have you *really*?' he replies, laying on the Kenneth Williams innuendo. 'Come into my boudoir.'

The lift doors open and I follow him into the newsroom, half the size of a professional football pitch and filled with so much noise, activity, blinking screens, ashtrays and strewn paper that it makes the *FC*'s seem like an academic library. As we walk past the picture desk, it is difficult not to notice that pretty much every one of its larger display screens is displaying young, amply endowed topless women.

Wilkinson sees me looking. 'Better than a mug shot of the Governor of The Bank of England, no?'

'Doesn't this stuff bother you?' I say. 'It's 1997, for Christ's sake.'

'Too right it's 1997. Punters don't want lectures on the Equal Pay Act from prune-faced feminists. They want bouncy girls who know how to have a good time.'

I don't know if he's just saying that to wind me up, or if he genuinely believes it. Probably both.

In his glass cubicle, he plonks himself behind his desk. He offers me a plastic swivel chair on casters, which I take, and a fag from a packet of red Marlboros, which I don't.

'What can I do you for?' he says, lighting up.

'I'm working on a story about the Chancellor.'

'Course you are.'

'A little bird tells me he's been playing away from home.'

'That's doesn't sound like an *FC* story.'

'Maybe you're a bad influence on me. Anyway, that same little bird also told me that you might have chapter and verse on what Kendall does when he's off the range.'

He folds his hands and leans across the white laminated desk. 'It's an interesting idea. But if we had what you call "chapter and verse", we'd have run the story.'

He hasn't denied it. 'Maybe you've just got a sniff of it, not the whole thing. Or – just maybe – Kendall knows that you know, and you can just pull his strings, turn him into your nark. That might be more useful to you than publishing and cutting him loose.'

Wilkinson widens his eyes theatrically. 'My goodness, Peck, you posh broadsheet journalists have evil minds. Are you suggesting that a great British institution like the *Globe* would engage in common blackmail? Should I be consulting my lawyers?' Another touch of *Carry On*.

'I'm not insinuating anything, darling. I just want to know about the upstanding Tory member.'

'All in good time. What's in it for me?'

I got this meeting by suggesting I had a tip for him. Which I do. Kind of.

'Jackie Elstree. Sixties sex-kitten, now a national treasure.'

Wilkinson cups his hands in front of his chest and makes a heavy lifting gesture.

'Her latest squeeze is at least thirty years her junior. I assume a kiss-and-tell from him would be a decent property?'

I can see from Wilkinson's face he's tempted. 'Have you got his mobile number?'

'I can get it for you.'

'That would help.' Neither of us says it out loud, but we both know what he means. Even if the toy boy refuses to speak to the *Globe*, it's a fair bet he won't have changed the factory-set PIN for accessing his voicemail. Wilkinson, or one of his colleagues, will be able to dial in and listen to all the messages. The first the toy boy will know is when he gets a call from a *Globe* reporter, probably female, inevitably speaking in a flat, matter-of-fact way, warning him that his darkest secrets are about to be all over pages 1, 7, 8 and 9 of the *Globe* – though he can soften the blow by agreeing to an interview. An offer that can't be refused.

It is a hideous invasion of an innocent person's privacy, but right now I have bigger fish – and a dead sister – to honour. Wilkinson leans back in his chair.

'Your turn,' I say.

'Have you heard of the McTavish memorandum?' Bruce McTavish is deputy chairman of the Conservative Party. But this is the first I've heard of a so-called McTavish memo. I shake my head.

'That political genius, Peter Ramsey, asked Bruce to compile a dossier on all ministers and Tory MPs who have something in their private lives they would rather not read about in the *Globe* during a general election.'

Did I hear him right? 'The PM commissioned a document listing every potential scandal that might befall the Tory Party? Is that what you just said?'

Wilkinson gives a sarcastic smile. 'I know. It's extraordinary. But Ramsey's been so damaged these last few years by all the revelations about his misbehaving colleagues that he wanted forewarning just in case anyone's caught with their trousers down during the election campaign.'

My brain is going into overdrive with excitement, in much the way I imagine that a prospector would have become feverish at hearing of the Klondike. An official guide to all the venal sins and misdemeanours of Tory MPs? That would be my every Christmas captured in one handy booklet.

'Two questions. First, why in God's name would Ramsey not see that he was inviting disaster? And second, please tell me you have a copy.' Actually, I am praying he doesn't, because I want it as my scoop.

'You know why: he's a world-class tosspot. And no I don't. Tragically. There are only twenty copies in existence, all numbered. The reason I know about it is one copy *has* gone astray and Smith Square is panicking.'

Smith Square, an elegant Georgian quadrangle near the Palace of Westminster, is where the Conservative Party has its central office.

'Bloody hell!'

'Apparently the Home Secretary had a few too many beers in the Marquis of Granby and managed to get all the way home to Battersea before noticing that he didn't have his briefcase with him. And no one knows whether he left it in the pub, or in a cab, or whether someone nicked it. Ramsey's having kittens. It couldn't be funnier.'

Why has Wilkinson brought this up? I remember what Bob Ringer said, about Kendall not being able to keep his trousers on. I wonder what Ringer knows about the memo, whether he has a copy.

'Is there anything in it about Kendall?'

'That's my understanding.'

'Which is to say ...?'

'We're pretty sure that it says he is a pathological shagger. But absent the memorandum, we haven't got the detail. Yet.'

'*Yet?*'

'We've had one of our paps stake him out.' The *Globe* thrives on offerings from paparazzi. 'We've got a couple of pictures that aren't conclusive, but they are, how can I put this, suggestive.'

'Can I see them?'

By now, Wilkinson's face is half hidden in a haze of smoke. 'We're not in the business of giving stories away. Even if we are all on Breitner's team. Internal competition and all that.'

I don't like being reminded of our institutional link. 'I gave you Jackie Elstree's toy boy.'

'And I am grateful. But it's not in the same league as an exclusive about the bonking chancellor. If we can prove it. Just imagine what we'd do with it.'

I certainly can. CHANCELLOR OF THE SEX-CHEQUER. KENDALL'S MINT BABE. The cheeky girl on page 5 saying 'Keith Kendall's certainly raised *my* interest rate.' A classic in the making.

'What if we collaborate?' I venture, tentatively. 'If I can stand it up, I'll give you everything I have, and we can do the story at the same time.'

'Nah. We get first dibs. You'll report it as a *Globe* exclusive.'

He knows he has me over a barrel. Which is why he's remained top of his game for so long. 'OK. Deal.'

He stubs out his ciggie. 'Give me five minutes.'

Through the glass wall, I watch him go to the centre of the newsroom and start a conversation with a grey-haired man in pinstripe trousers and shirtsleeves. Together, they walk to the far side of the office where there is what looks like a safe. I watch, intrigued. That safe is famous on Fleet Street. Rumour has it that it's stuffed full of cash that *Globe* hacks can take out and deploy to buy stories. No fingerprints, no trail, no questions asked. Annoyingly, from where I am I can't see inside.

The safe door opens, closes, and Wilkinson saunters back holding a slim cardboard file. He locks eyes with me. 'If you write one word about this without telling me first …'

'You have my word.'

'And I know where you live.'

He opens the file and examines the contents for a moment, then passes it across the desk. I almost drop it in my excitement.

There are five pages of contact sheets, and half a dozen larger prints. Post-it notes are attached to the A4 copies giving date and time. Each of them shows the front of a substantial Georgian terraced house.

'That's Kendall's place in Chelsea,' says Wilkinson. 'Cheyne Walk. Rich bastard.'

The pictures have that grainy quality that comes from being taken through a long lens in the dark – between 2 and 3 a.m., according to the notes, on the third of February. Shortly after two, a man is seen leaving the house. There are three snaps of him, but I can't make him out: he has a scarf wrapped around his chin and mouth and the nearest street lamp is too far away to cast much light on his features. About the only distinguishing thing I can see is the logo on his anorak.

Nearer three, the door opens again. This is more promising. A woman appears. She steps out – *click* – turns back – *click* – and embraces Kendall on the doorstep. *Click click click*. Then they part and she walks down the steps.

Click.

The photographer must have been in a car just across the road. As the woman reaches the pavement, she glances slightly to her right and the camera catches her face properly. No scarf or hood, no attempt to disguise who she is. In the low-light picture, enlarged to A4, every grain of the film stock is blown up so large that the effect is like an impressionist painting. And like an impressionist image, you can see exactly who it is.

The folder drops from my hands. The photos scatter everywhere. 'Careful, you spastic!' Wilkinson shouts, but I hardly hear him. I'm still looking at the woman in the photo, on the floor, whose eyes are burning right through me.

Clare.

Chapter 19

I AM ON MY KNEES, SCRABBLING around, frantically picking up pictures. Wilkinson's on his feet, but he doesn't come round the desk. For a moment I'm hidden from him. I don't want to stand up. I want to curl into a ball and shelter under the white laminated desktop. I need to hide for just a few moments, to regain my equanimity. Even in my distraught state, I know that's impossible.

If I stay down any longer, Wilkinson's going to call the men in white coats. I tuck the pictures in the manilla folder – I can't bear to look at them – and get back on my chair. 'I'm a klutz.'

'See someone you recognised?' he joshes.

If he only knew. I don't meet his eye, but give what I hope is a passable imitation of a casual shrug. 'Bit jittery this morning; overdid it last night.'

'Only last night?' He's lighting another cigarette already and the smoke is making me nauseous, the revulsion of the recently reformed. 'So we understand each other, if I find you are holding out on me, you are dog meat. Understand?'

His swagger is what I need to displace the shock of the photo. I grit my teeth. 'Kevin, we have a deal. And if you knew anything about me, you would know I don't break contracts. If I find anything printable, I'll let you know. Now go fuck yourself.'

My aggression reassures him. He grins. It's funny how I can tell such a big lie with conviction. Not in a million years am I going to allow my sister's photo on the front page of the *Globe*, in what would presumably be a mocked-up embrace with the Chancellor of the Exchequer. My mission is to *prevent* the *Globe* from publishing.

Now I feel trapped in this glass box, Wilkinson's second-hand Marlboro smoke is poisoning me and I'm desperate to wash my hands after touching the floor. *Got to get out of here, got to get out of here, got to get out of here.* The silent chant, the reassuring troika, I calm a little.

'I'll keep you posted,' I tell Wilkinson.

'And the number,' he reminds me. 'Jackie Elstree's toy boy.'

'You'll get it.'

'I'll show you out then, squire.'

Before leaving, I head for the men's room. As I diligently wash my hands, every digit, under the nails, I stare at myself in the mirror. I am startled by how stretched and pale the skin seems, by how deep my eye sockets seem to have sunk. *Is that really me?*

I escape from the building in the grip of panic. It's not far to the river and that's where I want to be. Looking out across the brown water. I can see a couple of mudlarkers on the opposite bank with their metal detectors, scavenging for the detritus of our past. Over the centuries, everything from clay pipes to corpses has been tipped into this river. I feel envious of their carefree investigations. For a moment I imagine an escape to a different life where no one knows me and I can calmly potter in the mud.

'Then I come back to myself. *What did I just see?*

A photograph of Clare leaving the Chancellor's chi-chi house, alone, at 3 a.m. Is there an innocent explanation? I struggle to think of one. Even if they needed to work on a big policy announcement or speech in the early hours, it would have been at the Treasury.

The *Globe* didn't put a photographer on Kendall because they thought he was making plans for the budget. And that snap shows Clare as I've never seen her: looking up and down the deserted street, as if she could sense the danger; staring straight into the photographer's lens without realising. She didn't look frightened. She looked wary.

What did Bob Ringer tell me? *Keith Kendall is a naughty boy who can't keep his hands to himself.*

I remember what I asked Jeremy: *No telltale signs? Sudden departures from the office that aren't in the diary? A decision to walk somewhere rather than take the ministerial car?* I'd been asking about Kendall, but now I recall that was how Jeremy described Clare's erratic behaviour in recent weeks.

And Charles: *She was six weeks pregnant. We hadn't had sex since before Christmas.*

Me: *Which minister ran the security services until two years ago?*

Maybe I should have seen it sooner. Maybe I knew, but couldn't bear to articulate it – because even though I like to think of myself as a relentless bloodhound for a story, the scent of some trails is too poisonous. The photograph has shaken me badly: Clare's grainy eyes staring out, saying *you can't ignore this any longer.*

Clare was having an affair with Kendall. She was pregnant with his child. That was the leverage Robin Muller had when he went to see Kendall, tipped off by his client Breitner, who was alerted by Jock and the *Globe*. And that is why Kendall dropped the policy. Naturally Clare was incensed, livid. She'd been doubly betrayed. It all made total sense.

And maybe that wasn't the only favour they asked. As long as Breitner knew Kendall's secret, he had him in a headlock. The Chancellor of the Exchequer as their puppet. So Kendall did the only thing he could. He got rid of the problem.

This is the kind of idea or hunch I would dismiss as a lurid absurdity if I heard it from another hack. But I can't shake it off. My cock-up theory of history has been put through the crusher.

Every day the *Globe* is full of stories of crimes of passion: cheating spouses who murder wives, or lovers, so they can start a new life or reclaim an old one. Is the Chancellor of the Exchequer immune to those impulses? You could argue he has more at stake.

Not much more than twenty years ago, the leader of the Liberal party hired a hitman to murder his gay lover, to avoid exposure. And another half century further back, there was Victor Grayson, who knew too much about how the Prime Minister, David Lloyd George, sold honours: he vanished forever. We like to imagine there are certain proprieties in British politics, that our lot would never wield an ice pick or a poisoned umbrella. But it would be absurd to suggest we have fewer than our fair share of jealous or vengeful maniacs.

I think back to Kendall at Clare's funeral, his reaction when I mentioned Thomas Hardy having an affair with his cousin. No wonder. How callous must he be to come to the funeral after what he'd done? Was he there to cover his tracks, or did he enjoy humiliating us?

I need to talk this over with someone, anyone. Who can I call? I can't inflict this on Mum and Dad – Charles hasn't even told them Clare was pregnant. The person I trust most is Jess, but I worry this will compromise our professional relationship. I can't bring myself to confide in her, at least not yet.

I have only one option, even though it makes me uneasy – because our relationship is supposed to be 'light'. Marilyn, who already knows about the unborn child. It crosses my mind she will feel conflicted if I tell her all my fears about Kendall – and I am not sure I can trust her to keep them to herself, not to find a way to exploit them for the benefit of her boss. But my life is a study in conflicts of interest, of boundaries crossed, of decency trampled.

Marilyn answers straight away. 'The bad penny. I was about to call you.'

'I need to see you.'

She laughs. 'That's straight to the point. We're days from the election and all you can think about is sex in the afternoon?'

'It's not that.' I hesitate. 'I've got a problem.'

She seems to sense the hurt in my voice. 'Are you OK?'

'I need to talk.'

'About Clare?' She is never slow on the uptake.

'Yup. And Kendall.' Where to even begin? 'It's a mess.'

'You sound awful.' She pauses. 'Listen, I'm with Johnny right now, but I'll have a few minutes in about half an hour. Call me back then.'

'Is it possible to see you?' I push. It is way too risky to discuss this on the phone. Eavesdropping on a mobile phone conversation is not difficult with the right kit. And I assume whoever would feel threatened by my enquiries would have no problem hiring people with access to that kit.

'I haven't got time ...'

'It's just to talk. I'll keep my hands in my pockets. Promise. Please. It won't need more than a few minutes.'

She sighs.

'Can you be in Bermondsey at two?'

'What's in Bermondsey?'

'Me. At two o'clock.' She gives me the address. 'I'll see you there.'

From Southwark to Bermondsey is only a couple of miles, but it's a journey to another country. The address Marilyn gave me is the Beatrice Webb housing estate, a vast 1930s redbrick complex of low-rise council flats. It used to be largely white working class and, according to folklore, was one of the more crime-free parts of London because they had a rule that they never nicked from their own. After years of high unemployment, it is battered, rundown, depressed. Windows are barred or boarded-up, walls are covered in graffiti, and there is litter – Coke and beer cans, newspapers, dog shit, used condoms – everywhere.

The buildings are in a rectangle overlooking a scrubby patch of brown grass. It was originally a play area for kids, though judging by the small group of pallid teenagers on the far side, it's now only a haven for dealers and addicts.

This was Dickens' London. It was remade by a welfare state. And if it was ever the new Jerusalem, it's become Gomorrah. Dickens would not struggle to find stories of deprivation, and perhaps even less hope than when he was chronicling.

Marilyn stands on the periphery of the grass, wrapped in a long black-and-white houndstooth coat and keeping a wary distance from the teenagers. With her pageboy haircut and a cigarette dangling from her hand, she affects the 1960s chic of the Nouvelle Vague.

'Why are we here?' I discreetly nod towards the teenagers. 'It feels dodgy.'

'They're probably more frightened of us than we are of them.' She might be right. The teenagers have their backs turned and are all deliberately looking in the other direction. They must assume we're social workers about to ask them why they're not in school. Since I've arrived, the group has shrunk.

Then I realise the kids aren't bothered about Marilyn and me. By a doorway on the east side of the quadrangle there are three men with short haircuts and dark overcoats, earpieces connected to bulges in their jackets.

'What's going on?' She rolls her eyes at me. Which is fair enough: there can only be one reason why Marilyn and Special Branch would be here. 'Johnny?'

'He's inside number thirteen.'

There's something odd about this. Politicians doing walkabouts on housing estates is nothing new. It's all part of the 'man of the people' schtick. Even the Tories do it. But there should be dozens of people: TV vans and news crews, local party workers, central office flacks and minders. Not Marilyn, and a few disgruntled drug dealers whose work's been interrupted.

'We've only got a few minutes,' Marilyn warns me. 'He'll be out soon.' She peers at me closely. 'So what's so bloody important that you have to make a detour to Bermondsey to tell me? And before you ask, no, I'm not going to marry you.'

I smile briefly. 'Look, you probably think I'm mad but I have good reason to believe Clare was having an affair with Kendall. That it was *his* baby.'

Marilyn blows out a long stream of smoke. 'Fuck.'

'Yeah.' What else is there to say? For a moment, the two of us stand without speaking, to a soundtrack of London traffic, construction and birdsong that won't be drowned out.

'I can't decide whether this is massive and important, or whether you're just nuts,' she says. I can tell her mind is already calculating what it means for the election.

'For fuck's sake, Marilyn, I didn't tell you this so you could use it.'

'I get that. But I can't exactly un-know it.' Her face flushes. 'I wish you hadn't told me. Just to remind you, I'm advisor to the Leader of the Opposition, and the Tories have moved up two points in the polls in the last week. What do you expect me to think?'

'Well, you could show a bit of empathy? How do you think I feel?'

She reaches out and squeezes my hand, with a glance over her shoulder in case the Special Branch men are watching. She'll never be too careful. 'Imagine what would happen if it became public. Something like this would completely knock the props out from under the corrupt Tories. They'd go down to the biggest defeat in a hundred years. From what I know about your sister, she'd want that. Wouldn't she?'

'Maybe.' I don't know. Would she want the misery and humiliation that my parents would suffer? Would she want the playground teasing that would be inflicted on her boys? A wave of anger surges inside me. I kick one of the Coke cans. It flies through the air and lands with a rattle that draws surprised looks from the teenagers and the Special Branch. 'Just to be clear, this is my well-sourced surmise. But there's not enough undeniable evidence. Or at least not yet.'

'Do you want me to do some digging? See what I can find?'

'I don't think you're hearing me, Marilyn. I am talking to you because I need to talk to someone.' I stick my hands in my pockets, trying to make sense of my chaotic thoughts. 'But it must never get out. It would destroy my parents, Clare's family, me! Think about her reputation.'

What reputation is that? the angry part of my mind asks. Her reputation as the goody-two-shoes, high-flying golden girl? All those tributes at the funeral? Are they lies? What do I really know about Clare? Did I just buy my parents doting view of her? I feel sick.

Then, to Marilyn I say, 'How could she let herself be seduced by him?'

'Young woman, powerful man.' Marilyn shrugs. 'Happens all the time. Even to the good girls.'

'Not to Clare.'

'Except you have evidence to the contrary. Unless you believe in immaculate conception.'

Marilyn can see she's gone too far and tries to pull my hand from my pocket to make up for it, but I draw away like a sulky teen. Suddenly I'm hissing viciously at her, 'You don't know anything about her.'

Marilyn flinches but stands her ground. She won't be cowed by anyone, and she can't hide the disgust and pity in her expression. She can't see I need a fight, to release my anger, at Kendall, at my sister.

Her silence is the perfect rejoinder: *You don't know anything about her.* And nor did I.

'I'm not sure I'm the help you need,' she says at last. 'Maybe you should talk to a professional, a counsellor or something.' She puts her hands up in front of her chest, as if to protect herself. 'I care about you, Gil, I really do. But I am way out of my depth. What I do know is this: if you go charging around like a wounded dog, someone will get hurt.'

So long as it's Kendall, I think. And then there's the unmistakeable voice I hear everywhere these days. "Allo, 'allo. What's going on 'ere?'

Marilyn and I both spin around. Todd, grin switched on, is striding towards us from one of the flats. He walks with purpose, gaze fixed on the horizon, as though being filmed for a party political broadcast. His over-polished black Oxfords skirt the litter and poo as though protected by a force field.

'Hi, hi, hi. Wasn't expecting you here, Gil.' He gives Marilyn an irked look. 'This isn't really a press thing.'

'Gil wanted to talk to me about a sensitive story,' Marilyn butts in.

'Sorry,' Johnny says. 'I was being neurotic. Pressure of the election. Coming here is a thing I do, and I've managed to keep it out of the press for years.'

'You sound dodgy,' says Marilyn. 'Tell him.'

Johnny looks embarrassed, and uncomfortable. Not something I've observed before. 'I come here when I need to recharge. To look around, talk to a few people. *Real* people. Without the cameras and the soundbites and everyone second-guessing my motives.'

I can't decide if this is genuine or the ultimate in Todd blarney. Most MPs are more diligent in forging connections with their constituents than is popularly believed, but we're not in Todd's constituency and he's a busy man. So what is he up to?

'Look over there.' He raises his arm and points above the rooftops to the gleaming pointy-topped tower across the river: 1 Canada Square, fulcrum of London's new financial district at Canary Wharf. 'We have the money to build palaces for bankers and lawyers. Not that I'm knocking bankers and lawyers,' he adds hastily. 'We need them.' Even off the record, Todd does not want the *FC* to think he has anything but the greatest admiration for the wealth creators of the City and Canary Wharf. 'But with all the income they generate, all the taxes they pay, we should have the resources to make sure no one lives in conditions like these.'

He pauses, sweeping his gaze around the estate. For the people who live here, looking at the towers of Canary Wharf must feel like staring at the moon.

'Families where no parent has worked for a decade. Teenage addicts. Girls becoming mothers at fifteen, sometimes younger. Kids who grow up thinking that the only career choice is living on benefits and the route to a home of their own is falling pregnant so they can get a council house. It's everything that's wrong with Ramsey's Britain.'

Much of this is standard campaigning stuff. But not what comes next. 'It's what's wrong with the Labour Party, too. We say we are the guardians of a welfare state that we created. But *this* isn't what Beveridge and Atlee had in mind. It's not a safety net – it's a trap.'

Todd has the knack of the superstar politician – Clinton, Reagan, Thatcher – of making you feel you are the only person with whom he or she has ever shared such thoughts, that only you matter. I know I am being seduced, and it is hard to resist. But out of my mouth comes the voice of my dad. 'We've lived through almost twenty years of tax cuts for high earners and big business. Surely it is time to reverse that, at least in part, so we have the money to turn this wasteland back into a safe playground for kids?'

Todd pauses. The spell has been broken. 'Are we off the record, Gil?'

'Erm, I'm not sure. Probably. I didn't come here to write a story about you. But there is a story here, isn't there? If you want to tackle deprivation, but you won't put up taxes, then it's all just good intentions, isn't it?'

He shakes his head. 'Look, I don't want any of this written up. Or at least not now.' He looks at Marilyn for approval, and she nods. 'But I am happy to chat if for the time being this is all between us.'

I blow the air out between pursed lips. 'Sure.'

'What you've just said about taxes being too low,' Todd continues, 'is simplistic. Socialism worthy of the name isn't a commitment to soaking the rich, it's a commitment to lifting up the poor. My Labour – Modern Labour – believes in creating the conditions in which the economy can grow faster, expanding the size of the cake so that everyone can have more. That may even require some taxes to be cut.'

Again, Bernard Peck is in my head and I parrot him. 'If the cake is getting bigger, and there's no redistribution, no increase in taxes on the rich, then those who already have the most end up doing much better in pure cash terms than the poor. It's simple arithmetic. What is the point of a Labour government if the gap between rich and poor widens? Are you saying that worsening inequality is a price worth paying?'

He looks hurt. 'What you have to understand about me is that I am proud to be Labour. But some of my colleagues think that the only test of being a socialist is whether you want to put up taxes for the rich. I disagree. That's posturing, socialism as narrow and tribal, as a badge on a donkey jacket. I want wealthy, successful people, who believe in social justice, to have a home in Labour. Of course, there might be times when we have to put up taxes on one group or another, and of course it's fair to ask the rich to pay their fair share. But I don't believe in increasing equality by penalising success and levelling down. What I want is a country of aspiration.'

He hasn't answered.

'Capitalism can be tamed and constrained to be a force for good,' Marilyn supplies.

'Exactly.'

I turn my eyes to Canary Wharf, those enormous financial factories with their blinking electronic ticker tapes that continuously update the price of money. '"It is a category error to think capitalism can ever have a conscience".' I recite.

Todd's eyes narrow. '*The Future of the Left*, by Bernard Peck. That's the opening line. The book that changed my life.'

'Changed your life?' I am flabbergasted. *The Future of the Left* is Dad's most famous book. Written in 1972, it promotes a creed of democratic socialist state intervention that Todd has been working tirelessly to turn from articles of faith into heresy.

'Of course. It's the times that change, not the values we stand for. I only succeed if I acknowledge the debt to the great men who built our party.'

His charm works. I am off guard and say something I regret.

'Do you know, I've never actually read it.'

Now it's Todd who professes surprise. 'But it's a classic.'

'I've started it so many times. But I never got past the chapter on the Gorbals' tenements. In my defence,' I add feebly, 'I lived that book, every day, throughout childhood.'

Even breakfast with Dad – 'continental', of course, vast wedges of Edam squeezed between laterally sliced baguette – was a sermon on the perniciousness of the market economy and the wrongheadedness of monetary economists like Friedman. In a family of atheists, it was politics as religion. Being in the Peck family required adherence to a few simple tenets: all decent people are socialists; Tories are stupid or bad or both; belief in God is the superstition of the feeble-minded; and never (repeat *never*) smoke. Oh, and all true Pecks support Tottenham Hotspur. Most of my life has been the delicate business of bending, if not breaking, all these strictures. Apart from the one about supporting Spurs.

'Have you ever read *The Autobiography of John Stewart Mill*?' I ask. Todd gives me a quizzical look. I am oversharing. 'It's about how hard it is to have a father who wants you to follow in his intellectual footsteps.' Dad insisted both Clare and I read it, as a teenage rite of passage. It was one of his ways of telling us what he expected of us. This memory is a trigger. I understand how terrible Clare's death must be for Dad. But I kill the thought almost as soon as it enters my head. 'Dad wanted us to change the world. I ran away.' I look hard at Todd. 'Clare tried her best.'

I fall silent. Todd tries to put me at ease. 'As you know, Gil, I met Clare only recently. But I was bowled over by her. She would have been such an asset to a Labour government. She had given so much thought to the big question that we've just been discussing, how to increase resources for the state, without damaging the private sector's capacity to create employment and generate taxable revenues.'

A nerd's tribute to my nerdy sister. Despite himself, Dad would be proud. It is a struggle not to cry.

'I'm sorry,' Johnny says. 'It's still raw for you.'

I shrug, not trusting myself to speak.

'So young and so promising,' he adds. 'Do you understand any more about what happened?'

I shoot Marilyn a warning look. As much as Johnny Todd wants me to trust him, this is neither the time nor place. I feel compelled to tell him only that it wasn't her fault. 'Clare was a brilliant cyclist. But among the things that simply don't make sense is why she wasn't wearing her damn helmet.'

Todd puts on a tight smile, which is supposed to look solicitous. 'Sorry,' I say. 'That's of no interest to you.'

Todd lowers his eyes to show he understands. 'Clare had a lot on her mind,' he says. 'We all get a bit absent-minded when we are under pressure.'

It's banal but it nettles. *You didn't know my sister. The more she was under pressure, the more brilliantly she performed. Kendall obviously wanted her out of the way, got her drunk and then hid her helmet, before waving her off to her bicycle.*

I have to hide my anger. I need to know what Todd knows.

'When Clare briefed you on the plan to tax pensions, did she tell you anything about why Kendall dropped it?'

Todd looks at his shoes. Is he summoning up a memory or trying to hide something? 'Even when Clare was breaking the rules she was proper. She hinted someone had leaned on Kendall and that he is a pathetically weak man. But there were no names or pack drill.'

Clare, why did you sleep with that creep? Why?

Todd seems to read my mind. 'They're terrible people, some of these Tories,' he says. 'We have to get them out.'

I would gladly see Keith Kendall sent into oblivion. But I am unhappy about the 'we'. I'm not on Todd's team. I hate the way he assumes he can co-opt everyone he meets. Though perhaps my unease is with myself, for secretly hoping he isn't too good to be true, that it isn't all spin, that maybe he is someone in politics I can trust and respect. My cynicism – or, as I like to think of it, my impartiality – is what keeps me going.

A navy Rover saloon pulls up on the street behind us. Marilyn spots it and nods at Todd, who clasps my hand with both of his. 'Keep in touch, Gil. I've got to head back to the Commons. Shadow cabinet.'

The security officers have glided over. One gets in the front seat, while the other holds the door open. It's unusual for a Leader of the Opposition to have security, but Todd's brother Crispin was, of course, a controversial figure in the British army, posted to Northern Ireland during The Troubles.

'Are you heading that way?' says Todd. 'Can I offer you a lift?'

Marilyn pre-empts me. 'You're just two minutes' walk from your office, aren't you, Gil?'

It's actually around fifteen minutes, but I take the hint. 'That's kind, Johnny, but the walk will do me good.'

'That may be better,' he says. 'We wouldn't want rumours about how close we are, would we?'

Who is the 'we', this time? Me and him? Me and Marilyn?

As Todd gets in the saloon, Marilyn turns to me and mouths, 'I'll call you.' They drive off, and I'm left alone on a desolate patch of grass. The pasty teenagers are drifting back. Taking out my phone here might attract the wrong kind of attention. I walk briskly away and when I reach the river by London Bridge, I dial.

'Treasury press office,' says the harassed-sounding junior official.

'It's Gil Peck here, from the *FC*.' Traffic roars over the bridge, while a rusted barge rumbles underneath. 'With the election on, I'm trying to work out the best way of setting up an interview with the Chancellor. Who would I discuss that with?'

Chapter 20

Thursday, 17 April – 14 days until Election Day

OR TEN DAYS, I TRY to do the day job. There's a general
election on, and elections are supposed to be the high-
lights of a political editor's career. In normal times it
would be the centre of my life. But right now it's displacement
activity. I go to the party press conferences, I write assessments
of the statements and pledges that matter. I even go to the Lib
Dems one morning, which shows that I really am trying hard
to look committed and serious. They are polling a bit higher
than when the campaign started, and a serious Lib Dem surge
at Labour's expense is one of the few pathways to an outcome
that would leave the Tories with the largest number of seats.
Even in my confused state, I am not betting on it.

I feel like an actor playing the part of a political editor, and
assume that everyone can see that for me the job is a pointless
game, a memorised ritual, which starts when I leave the flat at
seven for the daily briefings. When they're done I loiter around
Burma Road until it's time to file, and then head for The Groucho.
I drink the best part of a bottle of Club Mâcon, quite often on
my own. Even when there's someone there from my circle, they

can tell I am in a funny mood, and do their best not to make eye contact. I stumble home at one or two in the morning, collapse on my bed, usually with my clothes still on, and am out like a light. But at 4 a.m. every single morning, an alarm goes off in my head and I wake up in a panic I can't name. Even as it subsides, the anxiety remains, so that a return to sleep is impossible. *Save me Clare, save me Clare, save me Clare.* Daytimes are fuelled by caffeine, cocaine, and the adrenaline of the deadline. At around two in the afternoon most days, I can't keep my eyes open, and I drift into unconsciousness for a fitful fifteen minutes, bolt upright at my desk. Usually, I am aroused by the phone, or by Jess asking if I need anything. I can tell she's worried about me, but I insist everything's fine.

I am a ghost floating through the neo-Gothic corridors of Parliament and the conference halls of Westminster. I observe the photo ops, the unveilings of giant posters, the rousing leaders' speeches to adoring crowds at rallies. I spend a day on a battle bus with Todd, touring the battleground constituencies, the swing seats. I do the same with Ramsey. The spin doctors spin me, my Lobby colleagues share private jokes with me. It's all a great game. But neither my heart nor mind are present. Mostly, I fixate on what they would all think if they knew that the Chancellor had an affair with a married aide who became pregnant and was killed days after he corruptly tore up the policy she had created. That would bring all residual doubt about this election to an end. He would resign on the spot, the Prime Minister would be tainted by the inevitable questions about what he knew about it all, there would be no chance of redemption for the Conservatives. At that point, the election might just as well be called off and victory awarded to Todd.

I know it's true. But there's no point even talking to the *FC* until I have unambiguous evidence, given how reluctant the editor will be to bring down a Chancellor of the Exchequer – after all, the *FC* has lived a hundred years embedded within the moneymaking machine that is the City of London. And what do I actually have? A blurred photograph of Clare leaving his house – suggestive, not conclusive. An autopsy that says she was pregnant, but all chance of a paternity test gone the moment the crematorium flames engulfed her. Witnesses – who may never go on the record – to Clare's blazing public row with Kendall. And as Ringer told me, it's an open secret in the higher echelons of the Conservative Party that Kendall struggles to keep his flies done up.

If I could only get my hands on the McTavish memorandum. Despite Wilkinson's confidence, I initially wondered if he was fantasising. Would the Prime Minister really create a dossier of the misdemeanours of his own colleagues, knowing the risk that it would fall into unfriendly mitts?

But yesterday I ran into Lord Malmsey, the Tory chief whip in the House of Lords, the Captain of the Honourable Corps of Gentlemen at Arms, who knows *everything*. I waylaid him in the courtyard that leads to Black Rod's Garden and, as we talked about what Ramsey would need to do in the couple of weeks left before polling day, I casually mentioned the McTavish memo.

'You know about that, do you?' Malmsey said.

'I don't suppose you would like to share your copy with me?'

'You've got to be fucking joking. I shredded mine as soon as I'd read it. It's beyond me what Ramsey was doing commissioning it. I'll never understand that man.' He shakes his head mournfully.

'What exactly did it say about the Chancellor?'

He burst out laughing. 'I've always admired your enterprise, Peck. Happy hunting.'

Not even a non-denial denial. There is no question the memo will prove everything I need. But I have run out of ideas about how to get it.

There is, however, something else I can do.

On Thursday morning I jump out of a black cab at Paddington and run to catch the 10.50 to Worcester. I am sweating buckets and I can see from the station clock that it's 10.52. Shit. I can hear my mum's voice in my ear telling me that my habitual lateness represents the height of disrespect for others. And then I hear over the loudspeaker: 'The delayed 10.50 to Worcester will now be departing from platform six at 11.05.' Thank goodness Ramsey's idiotic privatisation of the network has turned a poor service into a laughable one. There's even time to get a black Americano.

Calm down, Gil. Calm down. And then, despite myself, I feel the habitual wave of rising panic. *I want everyone to live except me, everyone to live except me, everyone to live except me.* I chant it three times. And then feel another two times might help bring about the opposite of what the words say. To be clear, I don't want everyone else to die. I just want to stay alive long enough to avenge Clare.

I walk to the train and find a seat in first class. Before sitting down, and for the tenth time, I check my bag and pockets. Two phones, one pager, a notebook, laptop and two cassette tape recorders. Nothing left to chance.

One of the phones rings.

'Why aren't you on the train?' says Jess. She must have heard the station announcer in the background. 'You haven't missed it, have you?'

'It's been delayed.'

'Oh, well. I wish you had missed it. This is a crazy idea.'

'Thanks.'

'I still can't believe Kendall agreed.'

'You know me. I can be pretty persuasive when I need to be.'

Truthfully, I am equally amazed Kendall is seeing me. I started by ringing the Treasury press office, who said that because there's an election, I had to speak to Tory central office. I then got hold of a speccy, spotty twenty-six year-old, Gavin, who's been appointed to be Kendall's press minder for the election. He's one of those fresh-out-of-Oxford Tory boys who is ludicrously impressed by anyone who works for the great *FC*.

'I'm working on a colour piece for the Saturday edition,' I lied. '*The Great Tory Fightback*.' And then I laid it on with a trowel. Kendall as the future of the Conservative Party. Most of the press so obsessed with Modern Labour and its dynamic new leader, the Tories struggling to win any coverage, let alone the softer sort that might humanise them. Blah blah blah. Gavin bought it immediately – and was even grateful.

'Would you mind if I'm not there with you?' he asked. 'We're a bit thin on the ground and I'm supposed to accompany the Home Secretary to Waterloo for a press thing about the Channel Tunnel and immigration.'

'It will be fine, Gavin. I've known the Chancellor for years. Trust me.'

So here I am, booked in for a day of shadowing Kendall: a chat on the train to his Cotswolds constituency and then a walk around a couple of well-appointed villages as he hits the campaign trail, culminating in tea with him and the fragrant Lady Mandy.

I scan the front page of the *FC* that I've brought with me. The splash is a story by Jess about Labour's plans to set up a new regulator for the City. I have a slight pang of conscience that she is bailing me out, doing my job. And then, to my genuine amazement, the door to the carriage wooshes open and there she is, grinning.

'Jess! What the hell are you doing here?'

'I couldn't let you jump out of the plane without a parachute all by yourself.'

'But you can't come to the interview!'

'I thought you might want company on the way.'

I don't say anything, except a mumbled thank you. If I open my mouth, I might blub. She sits down opposite me, leans across the table and squeezes my hand.

'No need to thank me. If you fuck up, and the *FC* sacks you, I'll be bored out of my skull. And we can't have that, can we? So when are you going to confront him?'

Gavin told me Kendall had a red box to get through – documents to read, letters to sign. Could I hang on forty-five minutes or so before wandering down the train to find him, he asked. I wait until the train is just outside Oxford before I get up to find the Chancellor.

Jess gives me an anxious look. I can see she is desperate to make a final attempt to change my mind, but she presumably guesses it's pointless.

'Don't lose your temper,' is all she says.

'I'll do my best.'

'Seriously. Don't lose your rag.'

I head to the back of the train. On a Thursday morning, it's almost empty. In the last carriage there's only one table occupied, at the far end. Kendall stands to greet me.

'Gil.'

'Chancellor.' He offers me his hand and, despite everything I shake it. 'Good of you to make time for me.'

'No photographer?' He sounds disappointed.

'He's meeting us at Evesham.' The lie trips smoothly off my tongue. I haven't told Mary Nichols or Lorimer I'm doing this interview, and I certainly didn't bother to book a snapper. By the time I've grilled him, I very much doubt he'll want to be posing for pictures.

I'd assumed that without Gavin, he'd be on his own. His special advisers have been seconded to Conservative Central Office to help with the campaign; and because it's election time, and this is supposed to be a political interview, there is no civil service minder from the Treasury. But there is a young woman, probably early twenties, sitting opposite him.

'Gil, Elaine. Elaine, Gil,' Kendall introduces us. 'Elaine is my constituency secretary.'

She slips out to make room for me, and it is impossible not to notice the length of her legs and shortness of her skirt. She takes a seat across the aisle. Given our recent history, I'm slightly surprised he didn't feel the need for a proper minder. But he sees the *FC* as the house paper and will presumably always feel safe in the company of an *FC* hack. He is so smug and entitled it's beyond his comprehension that I might know the truth about him. He smiles benignly at me.

'How do you think it's going for us?'

There's no point in flattering him. Labour started the campaign ahead in the polls and nothing suggests the Tories are closing the gap, or at least not in any meaningful way. 'Do you want the truth, or shall we just move on?'

'That bad, eh?'

I take out my mini-cassette recorders and put them on the table between us. 'You don't mind?'

'I'd worry if you didn't.' The red lights comes on. 'Where shall we begin?'

Across the aisle, the long-legged girl stands up. 'I'm going to the buffet car, if there is one,' she announces. 'Get you something?'

'Tea, thanks. Gil?'

'Coffee would be great.' The last thing I need is more caffeine: I'm buzzing with nervous energy. But what the hell, perhaps it will marginally slow her return. 'Black, no sugar.'

She sways down the corridor in heels. Kendall is relaxed, sprawled on the seat. *What right do you have to be happy?* As his assistant passes him, he pats her bottom. She turns and wags a finger. I feel sick. *Is he fucking her now? What a piece of work. I wonder what she would think if she knew what he did to my sister.*

I look at his fleshy face, all reddened cheeks and hanging jowls, and his corpulence. I fight off hideous images of him on top of Clare. It's a vision from Dante's Inferno.

'Gil?' The tape is running and he's still waiting for a question.

I've been agonising about this moment for days. Lull him into a false sense of security by asking some conventional political and economic questions first? Drop a few hints and see if his conscience makes him come clean? Or dive straight in? Even as

I boarded the train I hadn't made up my mind, but now I know exactly what I want to say.

'How long were you having an affair with my sister? Did she tell you she was carrying your baby?'

Kendall freezes. Our brains run ahead of us: in his head, he was probably already halfway through the answer he'd rehearsed about whether the Bank of England should be given autonomous control over interest rates, or some such. For a moment I see him playing the question again to himself, thinking: *did he actually just say what I think he said?*

Then his face turns from its leathery, pockmarked grey to crimson. His jaw clenches.

'Have you taken leave of your senses?'

'Quite the opposite.' Now that it's out there, all the energy inside me has focused to a knifepoint. I lean across the table. 'The only thing I can't work out is, did you have her killed? Or was it just convenient for you when she died? Without her helmet and pumped full of alcohol. Which you knew.'

Kendall shrinks back. He checks over his shoulder, but the lovely Elaine is nowhere to be seen. The rest of the carriage is empty. No one's going to rescue him.

'You were being followed by a long-lens photographer.' He flinches. Good. 'Did you know that? Clare was photographed leaving your flat at three in the morning. To be honest, I can't think what she saw in you.'

'We'd probably been working late. It happened, not often, but occasionally.'

'*Working late,*' I repeat sarcastically. 'Is that what they call it these days? All you "back to basics" Tories who can't keep your flies zipped? Working late?'

'You've gone mad!'

'That's why you dropped the pensions policy. Because Robin Muller and Jimmy Breitner put the screws on, threatening to expose your affair.'

'You haven't a clue, have you?'

'And then there's the McTavish memorandum.' I wasn't sure whether to mention it. There's a chance that Ramsey hasn't let Kendall see it, so he doesn't know for certain what's in it. But he'll assume the worst. 'I assume you've read it?'

'I'm aware of the claims in it.' Bingo! I've got him. 'Unsubstantiated, uncorroborated claims.' *Hurry up.* It can't be long before the girl gets back. I don't dare take my eyes off him. I need to decipher his face. 'If you read that I was having an affair with a Treasury official, you'll also know the official is not named. Your sister is not mentioned. Would you like to know why?' It is a rhetorical question. 'It is because if you knew anything about me, you would realise the suggestion that Clare and I were together is absurd.'

How can he still be denying it? I can feel a noise building in my brain and, though I swore to Jess I would try not to lose my temper, I didn't count on this level of provocation. 'I don't fucking believe you. My sister shouted at you in front of your whole office after you canned the tax rise for pension funds. She would not have done that if you were just any old boss. She never lost her cool.'

Kendall looks surprised. 'It's true she did take my decision on the tax personally. I was slightly amazed, not to mention a little embarrassed for her. It was just politics; I didn't understand why she was so emotional. I assumed it was her woman's wotsit.' He flutters his hand.

'She was pregnant, you arse! With your child!' I realise I am shouting.

He falls silent. I assume I have shamed him, finally, into a confession. But when he speaks, there's neither guilt nor repentance in his voice.

'Gil, I know you are upset. Anyone in your position would be. But I can categorically assure you that I was not having an affair with Clare. If she was pregnant – and this is the first I've heard of it, and I'm truly sorry if she was – I was not the father.' There is a momentary pause. 'If you were a better-informed journalist you would not have bothered me with any of this nonsense. And, frankly, if you were a better-informed brother, you would realise how wrong your theories about your sister are.'

Now it's my turn to freeze. If he'd slapped me in the face it wouldn't have brought me down as quickly, or hurt half as much. For all he may look like a genial and portly country squire, Keith Kendall has honed his rhetorical skills at the despatch box. He knows how to humiliate.

'I did know my sister.' The screaming in my head is so loud that the only way I can tell I'm shouting is the way Kendall flinches. 'I knew my sister.'

He shakes his head, and that hurts more than anything – because he is speaking the truth. With every day that's passed since her death, I've learned how much she and I had become strangers. I lost her long before she died.

Kendall gestures me away. 'I think our interview, as you laughably described it, is at an end. Please leave.'

From the end of the carriage I hear the sudden clatter of the tracks as the door opens. The assistant's coming back with the tea and coffee. I stagger down the swaying train, shouldering past Elaine, only just avoiding a collision. 'That was quick,' she says. 'Did you get everything you want?'

I grunt an affirmative and charge on.

What on earth have I done?

Charlbury station is a single platform in the middle of the Oxfordshire countryside. There's no ticket office, just an empty waiting room and a broken vending machine. Rumour has it that it only survived the Beeching cuts because the then prime minister had a house nearby. Otherwise, there's little to justify its existence.

This is where Jess and I escaped from the train. It was pointless travelling further. I sit on the hard wooden bench, clutching the tape recorders and staring into the bushes on the far side of the track. I am not about to throw myself on the rails. It would be pointless; the next train won't be through for an hour yet.

The platform is empty, apart from Jess, who has wandered down to the far end to make calls on a story. I told her what happened, pretty much everything. She said nothing. Gave me one of her 'you're an arsehole' looks. And we have barely exchanged a word since.

Obsessively, I listen to the tape of our interview, rewind and listen again. As if playing it over and over will reveal something I missed. Or lessen my acute humiliation.

Have you taken leave of your senses?

If you read that I was having an affair with a Treasury official, you'll also know the official is not named . . .

If you knew anything about me, you would realise that the idea Clare and I were together is absurd.

Wait a minute. I pause the tape and squelch back at high speed to play the sentence over.

If you read that I was having an affair . . .

Fuck. He's not denying an affair. He's saying it was not with *Clare*.

What an idiot I've been! I need to speak to McTavish. But it's never felt plausible that a pumped-up, stuffy Scots Tory like him had the contacts and knowledge to produce a compendium of Tory sins and misdemeanours. And certainly not on his own. He may have corrected the grammar and put his name on the jacket, but there is only one person capable of compiling such a dossier of Tory shame . . .

I put the tape recorder down on the bench and take out the Nokia. My hands are shaking. My confidence is so crocked I half expect the PA to put the phone down on me, as if news of my transgressions has already travelled back down the Cotswold line to London. But all she says is, 'I'll put you through.'

'Peck, old chap,' booms Bob Ringer's voice. 'To what do I owe the pleasure?'

'Kendall,' I say, without preamble. 'Who's he been shagging?'

'You know a gentleman never tells.'

'For fuck's sake, Bob!' For our entire acquaintance, I've stroked his ego and played his games; I've never spoken to him so abruptly. I've stunned him into silence. 'Was it Clare?'

'Clare?' He sounds puzzled.

'My sister. Who died.'

There's a pause while he takes that in. Then he snorts and starts roaring with laughter, so loud it almost bursts my eardrum.

'Bob?'

'I'm sorry, that was insensitive of me.' He's struggling to keep a straight face at the other end of the phone. 'I know this must be painful for you. But it's priceless.'

'Enlighten me.'

Another burst of laughter, that he finally chokes off. 'Do you really not know?'

'Apparently not.'

'Your naïveté is endearing, dear boy. The journalist who knows everything.' More chuckles. 'To coin a phrase, let's go back to basics. Kendall is married because he always wanted to be a Conservative MP – and local Conservative associations who choose the candidates tend to prefer married gentlemen. But our Mr Kendall swings both ways. And his preference, if he has to choose, is to take it up the chuff.'

I grimace at his language. 'Sorry?'

'How graphic do I need to be? Kendall's a shirt lifter. A woofter. He likes pretty young men. Always has.'

'You're saying ...' I feel moronic. I think back to the snaps Wilkinson showed me. I was so convinced I was looking for Kendall's girlfriend, I didn't look closely enough at the young man coming out of the flat.

I need to back up. 'Does Lady Mandy know about the Chancellor's extra-curricular activities?'

'Of course. That's how the other half live. Separate bedrooms. She'll be fucking the tennis coach, or her Italian teacher, or probably both at the same time. We live in an age where *Confessions of a Window Cleaner* is a political documentary.'

I feel a powerful sense of relief. Ringer has proved I wasn't completely wrong in what I thought I knew about Clare: she really wouldn't fuck a fat Tory. 'I take it this boyfriend works in the Treasury?'

'Spot on. Ramsey's having kittens about it. He thinks if it gets out that his chancellor is buggering a male employee it'll cause so much noise no voter will hear a word he says.'

I wince again at his crudeness. 'Thanks Bob. Anything else you know about the affair?'

'Apparently the young man is a bit sensitive. Thinks he's in love, can you believe it? With chunky Kendall. You couldn't make it up.'

'Does he have a name?'

'Aaaah. Well, that's for you to find out. Sorry, old bean.'

I can't work out whether he's pretending to know, or does know and wishes to withhold. Ringer never likes to hand over quite everything. No matter, an idea is forming. Young man, highly strung, works at the Treasury. And then I am back at Clare's funeral, in the colonnade, Kendall recoiling from an official, as if he was radioactive.

'Thanks again, Bob. You've been a great help.'

I have more than enough time to ruminate on the slow train back to London. Lambing can't have been long past and the fields are filled with gambolling young ones, unaware of the massacre to come.

I have a good idea who Kendall was sleeping with. But who was the father of Clare's baby? I was so convinced it was Kendall I am now out of ideas. How on earth to find out? Charles doesn't have a clue. I don't know any of Clare's friends well, certainly not well enough to phone them out of the blue and ask a question like that. Plus, if Clare was having an affair, she would have done it the way she did everything else: methodically and with discretion.

Do I really want to go around London asking all and sundry who my sister was shagging? London is a village: word gets out.

I haven't been thinking clearly. Clare was pregnant by someone other than her husband. Clare was killed. It's natural to leap to the conclusion that one caused the other. But that's correlation, not cause and effect. All I have is Charles's assertion, given moments after he found out about the pregnancy, that it wasn't his. Thinking about the state he was in when I spoke to him on the phone, is it plausible that he got his dates wrong, or forgot a night they'd had together, or was simply in denial that he'd lost a child as well as his wife? It's all possible. And I was dumb not to see that. Clare wasn't killed because of the baby. Far more likely that she was killed for something she knew. There might have been any number of secrets she kept that would be a motive for silencing her. And one of those lethal secrets would be the identity of the man Kendall was shagging.

Jess and I say our goodbyes on the concourse at Paddington.

'With luck, Kendall will be too much the repressed Englishman to make much of a fuss,' she says. But I can tell she is unconvinced. 'He can't really complain without repeating what you said and he has too much to hide to want to open that can of worms, I reckon.'

'I think I've got the story,' I tell her. 'The identity of his lover. And I can prove it.'

Her face clouds. 'Please give it up, Gil. It's not worth it. You're in danger of doing yourself irreparable damage. Get a bit of rest. Please.'

'Don't you want to know who it is?'

She shrugs. 'Probably better if I don't.'

As soon as I'm in a black cab, I call Wilkinson.

'I need to see the photos again.'

'OK.' He's non-committal, on his guard. 'Explain.'

'I've had a hunch I can identify the lover, but I need to see the pictures to be sure. Can I come over?'

'I'm heading over to Burma Road now. I'll be late for the Lobby if I wait. So will you,' he reminds me.

'Not going today. Could you fax the pictures over?' He hesitates. 'I promise, I'm not going to nick the story. A deal's a deal. If you send them now, we may even get the scoop tonight.'

'What's your number?'

I triple check the fax number as I read it off my business card. It is the very last thing I want going to Lorimer's machine by mistake. As soon as I reach the *FC*'s offices, I tear upstairs to my desk. The phone is winking at me, telling me there are messages. I ignore them. I stand by the fax machine, like a dog protecting a bone. I check the paper and make sure the line is working. I have to stop myself from ringing Wilkinson to double-check he has the right number. I haven't eaten all day and I'm feeling light-headed, not completely present. I think about nipping to the loo for a calming snort, but I don't dare leave the machine unattended. *Let it be him, let it be him, let it be him.* Prayer said, the machine talks in its alien squeak with the one half a mile away and the roller begins to crank. Three pieces of shiny grisaille spew from the machine. They are blurrier than the originals, but clear enough for my purpose.

271

I am too anxious and excited. I take them back to my desk and lay them out on the desk. There's Clare. There's the door opening. And finally, the one I had dismissed: the young man emerging from the front door. North Face jacket, hood pulled up over the head, and Adrian Mole-style spectacles. I would have registered him earlier if I hadn't been looking for someone else. He looks as he did when I met him in St James's Park, when he was jumpy about photographers behind every tree and I thought he was being ridiculous.

Jeremy.

Even though I'd guessed, it is still a shock. I sit still, brain frozen, for a few moments.

When I asked him, he flat out denied Kendall was having an affair. I've totally misread him, his motives and ambitions. What else has he been holding back?

I dig through my notebook and find his number. I'm about to dial it when my desk phone rings. I want to ignore it, but some habits are ingrained: as a journalist, I have to pick up, just in case it's a story.

'Gil? Its John.' Lorimer. The editor. Shit. I shouldn't have answered. His voice is crisp and sharp, in headmaster mode. 'We need to have a talk. Could you come to my office?'

'Just give me ten minutes to ...'

'No, I don't think so. It can't wait. Come down now.'

Despite the alleged urgency, he keeps me waiting outside his office. I sit on the steel-framed sofa, staring at the Thames and wondering whether I care that my glorious career at the *FC* is probably over. Lorimer's PA sits at her desk, zealously tapping her keyboard; she won't meet my eye, must have guessed I am about to get a bollocking. Or worse.

Through the glass wall I can see Lorimer on his phone, shirt untucked at the back, pacing, stretching the phone cord almost to snapping point. He is flushed and agitated; when he's finished, he slams it down so hard I can hear the clatter.

'Send in Peck!' he bellows.

I go in. 'That was the Chancellor on the phone.' Behind his half-moon glasses, his eyes are dark with rage, his cheeks flushed. 'I've had his people on at me all afternoon. They're threatening to withdraw all cordial relations with us, with the paper, if I don't fire you.'

'I understand. You should do what you have to do.'

'I know you've had a terrible time. But honestly! You can't use your *FC* calling card to conduct private vendettas. It drives a coach and horses through our code of conduct and is grotesquely unprofessional.' In Lorimer's world, there is nothing more shameful than being unprofessional. The men of the *FC*, and they are largely men, are nothing if not self-controlled and always courteous, especially in the presence of Chancellors of the Exchequer. 'I have a flavour of the lurid and crazy accusation you flung at Keith. For goodness' sake, Gil, what came over you?'

Keith. I am about to tell him who Kendall was really shagging, and check myself. 'I made a mistake. I was pursuing a story. I misjudged it.'

'Misjudged? That's a bit like calling the publication of the *Hitler Diaries* a misjudgement. It was a fucking car crash.'

Unlike me, Lorimer only swears when he's under intense pressure. It's a bad sign.

'John, I've loved working here. It has been a dream come true. I've crossed a line. I know that and I am profoundly sorry. If it makes it easier for you, I can resign.'

There's a pause. Lorimer takes a deep breath.

'Look, I probably *ought* to sack you. But Kendall is a cunt. Always has been. And there is no way I am taking orders from him – or any politician – about who I fire. Even if you do deserve it.'

'That's amazingly generous of you.'

'No it's not. The *FC* would be finished if we were seen to be taking orders from the Tories or any politicians. And you've had a terrible time. Maybe the paper should have supported you better. I don't know ...'

He tails off, then starts again. 'You're in a bad way. I've talked to your colleagues. Everyone respects you. *Most* people like you.' He attempts a weak grin. 'But they say you are out of control, drinking too much, maybe doing other things too; things that aren't good for you.'

Is that what people say? My fucking colleagues.

'Also, there's talk that your relationship with one of Todd's advisors is not just a professional one.'

Fuck. Marilyn and I have been discreet. I haven't told anyone. Has she talked? I'm about to protest, but Lorimer interjects. 'I actually don't want to know. But if it got out that you were making slanderous accusations against the Chancellor, while conducting a relationship with the one of the main advisors to the Leader of the Opposition ...'

There's nothing I can say.

'You need support. Expert support.'

'What do you mean?'

274

'I think therapy might be sensible. A formal evaluation at least.'

'What are you saying?' Having been relieved at not being sacked, I am now anxious again.

'I want you to go to the Minster for assessment. I imagine they will need to keep you there for a week at the very least. Probably longer.'

The Minster is the most famous drying-out clinic in the country for spoiled pampered rich people, soap stars, the children of multi-millionaires, who can't handle the coke or the booze. I am horrified. I am not one of *them*. I can give up alcohol and the drugs any time I like. I am *not* an addict.

'Boss, what are you thinking? The Minster? Seriously, I can sort myself out.'

'Gil, this is not a negotiation, it's an instruction. The Minster is a serious therapeutic institution. Your costs will be covered by the private health scheme we give you. You will get yourself there this evening.'

'But there's an election. And I'm the political editor.'

'You should have thought about that before you started raving at the Chancellor,' he says quickly. Then, more thoughtfully, 'I am sorry. We'll cope without you. You have a great team.' He peers at me again over the top of his specs, an eagle fixing my position with meticulous precision. 'OK?'

I feel like a despondent five-year-old. 'Yes, boss.'

I turn to go, but he's not finished. 'For the avoidance of any doubt, you are to do precisely no work until the docs say you are fit and healthy to come back. And when you return, you will go nowhere near Kendall, and you will do no reporting that has anything to do with Media Corp, or Jimmy Breitner, or anything else that is looming large in your feverish and distressed imagination. If you are working again before the first of May, you will concentrate exclusively on conventional politics.' He opens the door for me. 'Understood?'

Chapter 21

Monday, 21 April – 10 days until Election Day

'YOU'VE HAD A TOUGH TIME and we're here to help you get back on track. But in the end, only *you* can take control of your life. It is all about *your* choices.'

Penelope McGovern, the Minster's senior addiction specialist, has a voice that is calm and soothing. There's a faint trace of a Scottish accent, but the posh Edinburgh kind that soothes like freshly harvested honey. She's in her early fifties and immaculately groomed: no white coat, thank goodness, just a simple cashmere rollneck and greyish-blue plaid skirt whose lack of ostentation is seriously pricey. The combination of her knee-length black, soft leather boots, wide mouth and perfectly sheared shoulder-length grey hair is prompting an inappropriate fantasy. I fight it off. *Stop it, stop it, stop it.*

We are sitting in her airy office in the Minster's famous Edwardian manor house, somewhere in the greenbelt between London and the M25. Although the mock-Tudor ceiling mouldings remain intact, everything else about the décor is inoffensively modern. I am on a deep-cushioned, rectangular beige sofa. Dr McGovern sits opposite on the matching armchair. On the wall are the kind of primary colour expressionist screen prints that can be acquired by the dozen from Cork Street dealers. It's light, shirt-sleeves warm, and scrupulously inoffensive.

Through tall windows to our right I can see manicured lawns and sculpted hedges. There are a couple of tennis courts behind a walled garden. This therapeutic clinic masquerading as a country house is frequently featured in tabloid spreads as one tired and emotional celebrity after another checks in for a rest cure. I think I can see Baz from the 1980s thrash metal group Jizzelica taking a stroll; and a children's TV presenter, who recently starred in a double-page spread in the *Globe*, sniffing coke off the breasts of a glamorous escort. I wonder whether I'll be able to win his confidence and extract information I can use in future trades with Wilkinson.

My mind is wandering.

'Gil?' This is the third day we've met and Penelope seems increasingly frustrated that I am not wholly engaged. 'I wonder if we could chat about Clare again.'

I've done my best over the last two days. But I don't see why I should tell Dr McGovern, or anybody, what I feel about her, especially since I am struggling to tell myself what I feel. I loved Clare, but I am furious with her. Did I even know Clare? These are the thoughts that collide. They're mine. I don't want to share them, not even with the alluring Dr McGovern. But I need to get out of this place. I have to play the game.

'Sure.'

'Tell me again about how you feel she protected you in childhood?'

'Dunno. She just did.' I've reverted to being a monosyllabic, grumpy teenager.

'Can you explain what you mean?'

'We looked out for one another. Our parents had big ambitions for us, so big they were hard to bear. We supported each other.' Actually, I'm not capturing it properly. 'She was my big sister. She protected me. Just that.'

'Can I ask, do you dream about her?'

That's a new question and it makes me think. 'It's weird. I don't. Or at least if I do, I never remember when I wake up.'

'How do you feel when you wake up?'

Shall I tell the truth? 'I feel anxious. I normally wake at around four, gripped by panic about something I can't name or identify. And then I can't get back to sleep.'

There's a pause. She writes something down in her top-of-the-range, brown leather Filofax and then looks directly at me. 'Right now, you are certainly suffering from trauma, perhaps even post-traumatic stress disorder. That would hardly be surprising, since you were alone with her in the hospital as she was dying.'

'OK . . .'

'But there is an underlying problem, too. You've talked to me about how you've been using cocaine and alcohol and even casual sex for some years now.'

I give a shallow nod.

'So, it's my view, from talking to you, that you use these in an addictive pattern. Your issues and your addictions are intimately connected. We have to treat both.'

'With all due respect,' I say, 'you're over-analysing. I take the coke because it helps me focus, I drink because I enjoy it. But it's *my* choice. I'm in charge, I can give up any time. As for sex, I'm in a relationship of sorts; I'm just useless at commitment.'

279

I don't add that Marilyn couldn't be less interested in commitment either – unless it's to her boss.

'Do you believe that? I can see on the surface you are a great success, very much at the forefront of your profession. But that does not mean you don't have an addiction problem. Have you heard of the expression "high-functioning addict"?'

I like the idea of being high-functioning. I want to smirk, but I realise as I do that I must look like a fool to her.

'To address the underlying issues, you need to recognise your addiction. Or rather: addictions. For what it's worth, you may also be addicted to the adrenaline of your job.'

Of course I am addicted to the adrenaline of my job! It's why I love it. If you think I'm giving that up, you're the one that's insane.

'Can I ask: have you heard of a condition called ADHD, or Attention Deficit Hyperactivity Disorder?'

'Isn't it that condition where kids won't sit still and won't do as they're told – and are generally a pain in the arse?'

She sighs. 'That's a sort of over-simplified version, I suppose. As you say, a condition where someone is restless and impulsive, but can also be capable of intense concentration or hyper-focus? Does any of that resonate with you?'

'What do you mean?'

'You're an intelligent man, Gil. I am asking whether, if you look back at your childhood, or indeed now, if people remarked that you wouldn't sit still, wouldn't do what you were told, did things on the spur of the moment without thinking? But at the same time you were able to go into your own world and pursue projects or hobbies to the exclusion of everything else?'

This is annoying, probably because it is on the money. When I was at school I would drive the teachers mad by fidgeting. *Stop tilting back on your chair, Gil. It'll fall backwards. You've already needed stitches in your head this term.*

'Surely all bright kids are like that? There's nothing special about me.'

She smiles. 'I've been specialising in ADHD for years now. I believe that it's a condition that affects not only children but also adults. I can't be sure, but I suspect that you have ADHD and that you use the cocaine to control it. As you may know, Ritalin is the main pharmacological treatment for ADHD. Would it surprise you to know that for those with ADHD, cocaine can have a very similar effect in supressing the symptoms, and that you may be self-medicating?'

I don't know what to say. I say nothing.

'I'd ask you to think about all this. In particular, we should talk about whether it would be helpful to get you a formal ADHD diagnosis. You are taking huge professional and health risks with your cocaine habit. The risks of taking Ritalin are somewhat less.'

Shit. She thinks I am a mentalist. I am *not* fucking mentally ill.

'I have my own system for coping. It works.'

'Really? Do you really think it works? Would you be here if it was all fine?'

'I think I am doing OK.'

'So why do you think your employer wanted you to come here?'

'Because I suffered a temporary lapse of judgement.'

'Please explain.'

I shrug, still the surly teen. 'I asked the Chancellor of the Exchequer why he fucked my sister and got her pregnant. And I might have accused him of murdering her.'

For the first time, Dr McGovern seems lost for something to say; she looks concerned, as though she might have miscalculated. 'Did you really say that?'

'Not word for word, but yes, more or less.'

'And how does that seem to you now, what you did?'

I'm sorry about it. But probably not in the way Dr McGovern thinks I should be. I'm not sorry for Kendall: I'm sorry I took a punt on a story that turned out not to be true. It doesn't happen often, but when it does it stings my pride like hell. And worse than that, I'm angry with myself for thinking Clare would have been having an affair. The more I think about it, the more convinced I am that Charles got the wrong end of the stick. They must have slept together and he just doesn't remember. Maybe once when he landed from New York, still jet-lagged, half-asleep. There's no way Clare would have been having an affair.

Dr McGovern is waiting for my answer.

'Accusing the Chancellor was a misjudgement. But there was a lot of circumstantial evidence. I got carried away. I regret that.'

'I'm glad to hear it. But I need to ask you one or two other questions.'

'OK.'

'Have you been hearing voices at all?'

'What do you mean "hearing voices"?'

'Is there somebody talking to you, and just to you, in your head.'

'No, of course not. I'm not crazy.'

'Gil, it's my responsibility to ask these things. You have had a very serious shock and you are a user of hard drugs. A psychosis is not out of the question, especially after what you just told me.'

282

'Look. Given that I assume you are totally bound by rules of confidentiality, the Hippocratic Oath or whatever, I am very happy to tell you why I reached that conclusion about the Chancellor. I may have been wrong about his relationship with Clare, but I was not wrong that he's seriously dodgy.'

'I think we should leave the Chancellor out of this,' she says hastily. 'One other thing: do you sometimes hear noises that no one else can hear.'

'I don't think so. Unless you're referring to that incessant screaming.' She looks alarmed. 'I'm joking! No, I don't hear strange sounds.'

She tugs the hem of her skirt down and scribbles something in the Filofax.

'I know this is very hard for you to absorb. What you are going through is complex. Clare's death must feel like an earthquake. Grief is an incredibly powerful force and you are still very early in the process, probably somewhere between denial and anger.'

Now she sounds like bloody Patrick Munis.

'You had the trauma of being with her when she was dying, on top of the shock of her loss, on top of all the unresolved issues between you. And you've possibly got ADHD.'

At this point I wonder whether to tell her about my OCD, but calculate I'll never get out of here if I get on to that. Another time.

'There is something else I need to ask. Why do you feel so compelled to prove that your sister's death was not a random accident? Why is it your personal mission to show the world that she was killed?'

I am quiet for maybe thirty seconds. 'Look, Dr McGovern –'

'Call me Penny.'

'Look, Penny, there is considerable circumstantial evidence of foul play.'

'Is that what the police think?'

'The police don't know everything I know.'

She looks troubled again, presumably reverting to her initial diagnosis that I am a fantasist.

'Do you think it is possible you are pursuing this conspiracy theory because in some way you feel guilty that you didn't protect her? Are you trying to make up for the rupture in your relationship with her by proving only you can save her now?'

No, I think she was murdered because she somehow threatened the most powerful people in the country who, it turns out, are psychopaths. And I am a fucking good reporter who is going to destroy those who destroyed her.

I say nothing. For a couple of minutes.

'Look, I know you think I'm imagining things, but I swear that I still have my marbles. I was a bit overwrought the other day, when I saw the Chancellor. I accept that. But there is a lot about the last few weeks of Clare's life that doesn't add up. And yes, I do feel it is my responsibility to make sense of what happened. Is that really so wrong or crazy? I am her brother, for God's sake.'

Penelope clearly doesn't want to answer. She makes another note, then glances at the clock.

'We're almost out of time for today, so can I ask you to do one last thing for me? Can you tell me a story about Clare that would give me a sense of her, from your point of view?'

'Any story?' I am playing for time. This is hard.

'Just something that shows to me what she means to you.'

'Something from our childhoods, or more recent?'

'Literally anything.'

'OK.' I cast my mind back, and take a deep breath. 'Although she's a couple of years older than me, we were always close when we were kids. Mum says that when I was born she wasn't jealous. She would sit and watch the cot for hours, just sit there and watch, and shout for Mum whenever I woke up or cried. It became one of those myths that Mum would always trot out at family occasions, pesach or Christmas lunch. But I think it was mostly true.'

She nods. 'Tell me more.'

'On the way to school once, I was mugged by some boys from the fifth form. I had an LP with me, David Bowie's *Ziggy Stardust and the Spiders from Mars*; I was taking it in to play during a music lesson. The older kids didn't actually want the record. They took it from me, took it out of the cover and threw it like a frisbee across the park. It was ruined.'

Telling this story is dangerous. I can feel that tingle between my eyes and cheeks, the tremor in my jaw. *Keep it together*.

'After school, I told Clare. And two days later she frogmarched the two boys across the playground and they presented me with a brand new copy of the LP. They were bigger than her, but they were terrified of her. That's my sister.'

Penelope leans forward. She seems moved, though I remind myself that in her profession sincerity is a tool. 'Your sister seems to have been a very impressive person.'

'She hated injustice.'

The carriage clock on the mantelpiece gently chimes the hour. Penelope shuts the Filofax. 'I'm afraid that's time. We'll pick up tomorrow.'

'Any thoughts on when I can go home?' I ask hopefully.

'You aren't being held captive Gil. You can leave at any time. But my sense is that we can help you, if you'll just be a bit more patient, a bit less afraid, a bit more open. If you expose the wound to sunlight it will heal.'

Apart from the psychotherapy and the prescription meds, the Minster feels like a super-luxe, middle-class holiday camp, almost a spa hotel. Along with the tennis courts, there's a lap pool, a gym, an art studio, potters' wheels, a music room, and instructors for everything. For physical well-being, there's a choice of aerobics classes, Tai Chi, two types of Yoga, and meditation. There are also assorted talking therapy sessions for groups of us. At ten there's the alcoholism group, 11.30 till lunch is cocaine and Class A drugs, and around teatime is love and sex addiction. Yesterday I tried the booze session. 'My name is Gil, and I am a recovering alcoholic.' But even as I said it, I felt phoney. Although I drink too much, I don't wake up gagging for a drink. I am sober most of the time. During the day, anyway.

I tried my 'I'm in control' line on the authentic alcoholics. They weren't impressed.

'Do you think you might be in denial?' a fifty-something lady in sweatpants and a grey T-shirt asked, gently.

Probably. But denial is a better way of life than hanging out with losers like you.

I haven't returned to the session today. Maybe I'll give sex addiction a go later, just for a laugh. The sun's out and I wouldn't mind knocking up on the tennis court. I wonder if the coke-addled kids' TV presenter is up for it. I imagine I'll be able to track him down in the sex addicts session this afternoon. The good news is that – although I am still having terrible trouble sleeping – I haven't missed the drink or the coke as much as I expected. There was some sweating last night and a very weird dream. I was in Clare's office and I saw her bike helmet on the shelf behind her. I picked it up and threw it out the window.

Maybe I should have mentioned it to Dr McGovern, but I've only just remembered.

There is one addiction, however, that is causing me intense pain for its forced absence: hackery. I can't bear to be away from the action. Not knowing what's going on, who's talking to who, who's up and who's down. I'll go mad if I can't escape this prison soon. *I want my phones.*

There's a knock at the door, though that's a courtesy rather than a necessity. This is a hospital, after all, and it would be a mistake to allow the guests to lock themselves in. No mobile phones are permitted and there is no bedside landline, just a panic button.

'Coming,' I grunt. When I open the door there's a receptionist there.

'Mr Peck? There's a call for you.'

For a moment, I'm almost tempted to believe there's a god who answers my prayers. Perhaps it's Lorimer saying all is forgiven, that the paper can't cope without me. Or Jess, with some info that will at last reveal the truth about what happened to Clare. I am struck by how excited I am. Any contact with the outside world is water in the desert.

'Would you like to take it in one of the booths downstairs?'

That's a rhetorical question: there's nowhere else I *can* take the call. 'I'll be right down.'

Off the main entrance, there are dark wood cubbyholes with phones, where you can sit on a white armchair and turn your back for the pretence of privacy. It's like a hotel from the 1930s.

I pick up the receiver, half in dread, just in case it's another bollocking from the office. 'Hello?'

'Just putting you through,' says the receptionist. A click, and then a silence.

'Hello?'

'Gilbert?'

'Dad? Why are you calling?'

'Does there have to be a reason?'

'Sorry. Just ... unexpected. It is nice to hear your voice.' To my surprise, I am telling the truth. 'How on earth did you track me down?'

'Your mobile seemed to be switched off and no one was picking up at your flat. I rang your Commons phone and spoke to one of your colleagues. Nice young lady. When I explained who I was, she told me you hadn't been feeling 100 per cent. Which was a bit of a shock to your mother and me. You might have told us.'

An excruciating pause. Of all the people in the world who I'd want to know what I've done, Dad is the last on the list. I squirm.

'I'm sorry, Dad. It was thoughtless of me. I just didn't want to worry you.' That's a fib. It's not about them, it's me: I couldn't face the humiliation. 'I've been overwrought. The impact of Clare.' Despite myself, there's a catch in my voice. 'And, well, I behaved a little unprofessionally. I was a bit over the top in an interview.'

Silence. 'What did you do?'

I hadn't expected such a direct question. It isn't typical of our relationship, where we talk about safe things – such as whether Spurs should be ecstatic or worried that arch rivals Arsenal have appointed an eccentric French economist as their new manager – but never explicitly about the important stuff, let alone anything that might involve *feelings*.

I cast about in my mind for a sanitised version that's convincing, even one that might cast me as the brave lefty journo putting the corrupt Tory minister on the spot. But even as I start formulating the white lie, it dies inside me. I can't do it. I don't *want* to do it. For reasons I can't explain, I need my dad to know how badly I fucked up.

'I accused the Chancellor of having an affair with Clare.'

There's a long silence. *What have I done?* I begin to panic. Dad's well into his sixties. He's fit, but his blood pressure is too high. Has the shock caused a thrombosis? I should have dissimulated, not broken the habit of a lifetime.

And then I hear something that takes me by surprise. It starts out gently but is soon full throttle. Dad is laughing. Not in a mean or nasty way. But deep from the belly, as though someone has told him the most hilarious joke. It's the kind of laugh I haven't heard since the two of us – well, the four of us watched Morecombe and Wise together in the 1970s. In between the roars, he manages, 'Why on earth would you think that? Keith Kendall's rather more likely to have an affair with you than with your sister.'

What?

All I can manage is, 'You knew?'

'I was at university with him, remember?' Dad says. 'He wasn't *out*, to use today's term. But you know what it's like at college. No one had secrets. He had a fling with a lad from my corridor, who also eventually got married and went on to be a professor

289

of history at Harvard. I shouldn't tell you this, but when I was very drunk one night I actually necked with him at a party.'

Dad! Too much information!

'It's all right,' Dad assures me. 'It was before I met your mother and she knows all about it. She thinks it's terribly funny. But what on earth made you think there was anything between him and Clare?'

The moment of levity has passed. The oppressive sadness is back.

'It's complicated. I was told Clare had a fearful public row with Kendall, and then I heard he was having an affair with one of his staff. I added two and two, and got five.'

I consider telling him about Clare's pregnancy. That would really smash down the barriers between us, but it would be devastating for him and Mum. I decide against.

'There was a tax policy Clare had been working on, something she really believed in, that she thought would help raise important sums to invest in public services. Kendall was championing it, but then he reversed and axed it. Clare was furious, and did something I would never have expected of her: she called him "fucking corrupt" in front of his officials.'

Another pause. When he's thinking, the wait is nerve-wracking. And it's normally a precursor to proving I'm a fool.

'This policy you're talking about, I assume you mean her idea that the Treasury could raise billions of pounds by abolishing the exemption of pension funds from paying tax on the dividends they receive?'

I've wrapped the phone cord around my index finger so tight it's left a welt. 'You knew about that?'

'When your sister was working on something thorny, she would often chew it over with me.' Immediately I feel another emotion, jealousy – though I am not sure whether I am jealous of Clare, for having Dad's attention, or Dad, for having such a mutually trusting relationship with Clare. I'm left feeling an outsider in my own family again.

'Did she give you any clues as to why Kendall canned it?'

'She said he'd capitulated to pressure. I think the expression she used was "nobbled". As far as I could gather, a business that's very important to the government would have been in dire straits if its pension fund had lost all those tax credits. In some way or other, billions of pounds were at stake. This business somehow twisted the Chancellor's arm.'

'Billions of pounds were at stake? For one business? She said that?'

'Yes.'

That doesn't make sense. No pension fund on its own stood to lose that much. 'Did she tell you which business felt so threatened?'

'I did ask. But you know Clare. She followed the rules and she didn't want to tell me. Do you have any idea who it was?'

I don't hesitate. 'Media Corp.'

I hear a rubbing sound. I know exactly what's happening. Dad is scratching his chin with the middle fingers of his right hand. It's his 'tell' when he's thinking hard about something difficult.

'That makes sense. She loathed Breitner and the hateful values of his papers. She would have reacted very badly to Kendall surrendering to his pressure. Can you prove it?'

Now it's my turn to pause for thought. Dad has asked the only question that matters. It's time to learn humility. I thought I knew beyond reasonable doubt that Kendall had fathered

Clare's unborn child, and that was an almost career-ending misjudgement.

'I have circumstantial evidence. But everyone's denying it. I can't write it – yet.'

And I can't give up. If Breitner stood to lose billions – which clearly Clare believed – he had a motive to want her silenced and out of the way. And he would have had less of a troubled conscience ordering an accident for her than he would shooting his own dog. Though it still doesn't explain why it would suit him to have her disappear, when he'd already forced Kendall to pull the tax.

'I've got to get to the bottom of this.'

I brace myself for the inevitable rebuke. I assume he will now tell me not to stir things up. To leave well alone, that I will only make a mess of things.

Something has changed.

'Son, your mother and I think you are doing the right thing. We want you to find out what happened. But please take care. Don't put yourself at risk.'

Wow. It has been years since I haven't felt a failure in the eyes of the legendary, much-loved Bernard and Ginger. I am certain Clare knew Breitner's secret. She wanted to blow the whistle on him. For her, and for Mum and Dad, I will be *her* whistleblower.

I have a sense Dad wants to say something else. I pre-empt him by saying unfamiliar words. 'I love you, Dad. Give my love to Mum.'

Even down the phone I can hear Dad is embarrassed. This is hard for him.

'I'm proud of you, Gil. Mum sends her love.'

That's as close as he can get to reciprocating and it's all I can do not to burst into tears.

'And Gil?'

'Yes?'

'Don't do anything stupid.'

I actually laugh. 'What, me?'

Fifteen minutes later I stuff my shirts, pants and toothbrush into my holdall, smile at the lady on reception, and walk out to my battered Peugeot in the car park. There is an election on. And there is a debt to be repaid. To Clare.

Chapter 22

'You're embarrassing yourself,' I tell Cat. 'Do you think if Clint Eastwood had been on his own for three days, he'd make himself ridiculous by lying on his back and begging to have his tummy rubbed?'

First Dad, and now Cat. It's funny how those who for years prided themselves on being able to take me or leave me suggest they would actually care if I disappeared. Despite myself, I am pleased. The purity of a no-strings existence can be wearing. Cat rubs himself against my leg and runs ahead of me, directing me to the emptiness of his bowl. 'Don't kid a kidder, Cat. I paid Tracey to feed you.' Tracey is the sixteen-year-old daughter of my upstairs neighbour. 'OK, OK. As a treat you can eat again.'

The cleaner has been today and the flat has that welcome-home smell of Flash, bleach and newly vacuumed carpets. 'Did you make any progress on the case while I was away?' I ask Cat. 'Any breakthroughs I need to know about?' Cat is concentrating too hard on his second supper to pay me much attention. 'No? OK, well I need to crack on, before my bosses notice I've busted out.'

The *FC* made me hand over my work phone and pager before heading to the Minster. 'We'll just look after them for a bit, so that you get a proper rest,' said the disingenuously solicitous bloke in Personnel, who didn't seem to know that the *FC* pays for a second phone. I go over to the mahogany chest of drawers in the bedroom. Top drawer: pants and socks, as per the law. Under the socks – phew – silver Nokia, the Bat Phone.

I dial 121. 'You have sixty-one messages.'

Oh shit. I can't be arsed to listen to them. And there are another twenty-three recorded on my landline's Ansafone, as many as it could hold before the tape ran out. They'll be my bedtime lullaby later. Right now, I need to make a call.

'Her Majesty's Treasury,' says a cheery operator in a sing-song voice.

'Jeremy MacDonald, please.'

Tuesday, 22 April – 9 days until Election Day

The Pizzeria Elefantessa is on the north side of the three-lane roundabout at Elephant and Castle, in a 1960s shopping centre redolent of Eastern-bloc brutalism. All the money and power of the City of London is just a fifteen-minute walk north over London Bridge: it's as though the Thames is a barrier between unfettered capitalism and remorseless state planning. The Berlin Wall has been dismantled but as Todd implied to me, there might just as well be our very own Berlin Wall right here, separating the wealth and ambition of the capital's financial centre from the dilapidation, failing schools and poverty of hope in estates that sprawl around the Elephant and the Old Kent Road.

Not that the ebullient owners and waiters of the noisy, bustling pizzeria give a stuff about any of that. They've rented a vast warehouse of a space for next to nothing, to serve cheap but delicious pizza and pasta to locals and tourists from across the river like me. It's packed to the rafters every night, which is wholly unsurprising given that it's hard to spend more than twenty quid for two or three robust courses and a carafe of vino.

There are posters and corny pictures of elephants on every wall, pirouetting in tutus, bespectacled and reading *The Times*, singing at the opera. The noise of the massive, exposed air-conditioning system is drowned out by the almost deafening chatter of lubricated punters. I'm already sitting down, nursing a glass of basic Chianti from one of those bulbous bottles encased in straw, when Jeremy arrives. He puts his black North Face anorak on the back of his chair, revealing a navy-blue jumper in fine wool with a collar and zipper at the neck. I assume it's John Smedley, and approve.

'Wine?'

Jeremy puts his hand over the glass. 'I'll stick to water.'

'Have a slice of garlic pizza bread. Unbelievably delicious.'

'My tummy doesn't do well with garlic.'

Jesus. He is hard work. Even getting him here was an effort. 'Work is busy,' he told me when I rang him. Which I did not believe for a moment. During an election campaign, pretty much everything in Whitehall shuts down. It was only when I mentioned the photographs that he agreed to meet.

'What'll you have?'

He peers at the menu. 'I'm not very hungry. Maybe a salad?'

I get the waiter's attention. 'One insalata Caprese, an insalata mista, and a quattro stagioni pizza. All to come at the same time.'

My mood lightens as soon as the order is in. I love coming here, even when the conversation with my guest is bound to be gruelling. Poor Jeremy is in purgatory and would rather be anywhere else.

'So it turns out you were spot on the other day in St James's Park,' I say, between mouthfuls of garlic bread. 'There *was* a snapper following us. He'd been watching you for some time. I assume you know why.'

I pull out my rucksack from under the table and extract the thin folder with the photographs Wilkinson faxed me. Jeremy takes it gingerly and opens it with conspicuous trepidation. He grinds his teeth as he examines each one.

'That's you, isn't it?'

He nods.

'At the Chancellor's home?' Another guilty nod, like a schoolboy found with a copy of *Knave* in the boys' loos. 'Why were you at Kendall's house in the early hours of the morning?' He stares into his glass of water, blushing furiously. 'My sources tell me you were shagging him.'

He stands up abruptly and I think he's going to walk out. 'Calm down, Jeremy. I am not here to embarrass you. I know how loyal you were to Clare so I would never do anything to hurt you. I just want to understand. Whatever happens, I don't think your secret is going to stay secret. It's much better if we talk and make a plan.'

Jeremy plonks himself down.

'Gil, I'm not fucking the Chancellor.'

'You were though, weren't you?'

He avoids eye contact and starts absent-mindedly tapping the blade of his knife on the table.

'For goodness' sake, Jeremy. You're not the only person to wake up the morning after and realise you made a stupid mistake. Tell me what happened.'

He bows his head. 'I had to take important papers to his home. He invited me in for a drink. He flattered me and, well, one thing led to another.' It's like talking with a convent girl from the 1950s.

'Were you OK with that?'

'He's the Chancellor. I admired him. At first I was excited. Now I think he took advantage.'

'You're probably right. Why was Clare at the house with you?'

'I needed to tell someone. She was the only person I could trust. I wanted to break it off but he kept inventing reasons for me to go back to his home. I didn't know what to do.'

'So when did you talk to her about it?'

'I think it was in January. It was the afternoon and I was in her office. She said I was looking a bit down and asked why and I burst into tears. It must have been the pressure of bottling everything up. I hadn't been sleeping for days. She put an arm around me and everything came spilling out.'

'What did she say?'

'You know Clare. She hated bullies. And she thought Kendall had crossed a line. She was harsher on him than I was, to be honest. She was livid and said she would sort it.'

'That sounds like Clare.'

'He was horrified when he saw both of us on the doorstep. We went in and she read him the riot act. Told him he was abusing his position and if he didn't stop she would inform both the Cabinet Secretary and Lady Amanda.'

I am smiling. My sister. 'How did Kendall react?'

'He tried to bluff it out. Insisted we were both consenting adults, that he'd done nothing wrong, that his private life was nobody's business. Then Clare dropped your name into the conversation, reminded him that you work for a newspaper that takes a close interest in what goes on at the Treasury. That settled it.'

Me? She mentioned *me*? For the first time in I don't know how long, I feel good about myself. 'I wish we'd had that conversation.' Jeremy gives me a puzzled look. 'Clare left a message for me not long before she died and I didn't see it till it was too late to call her back.'

He shakes his head. 'It must have been about something else. This was a bluff and Clare knew it. I would never have confirmed any of what happened to anyone in the media, even you. My mum would die if it came out. And maybe I would have had to leave the Treasury.'

I glance at the photos again. 'Going back to that evening: you left, and then she left?'

'She made Kendall apologise to me. Which he did. He was pathetic, actually. Grovelling. Said he would leave me alone. And then I went home. She stayed longer, to sort a few other things out, she told me, though she didn't say what.'

I take a swig of wine and allow myself to feel pride in my sister's courage. I wonder if I'll ever forgive myself for not seeing her message in time. *Why didn't you speak to me sooner? Why didn't you just call me and together we'd have worked it out?*

Kendall must have been horrified that she knew about his affair with Jeremy. It was knowledge that gave her the power to bring him down. Again, I can't kill the thought that it would have been so easy for him to remove and hide the bike helmet.

'Jeremy, you and I both loved Clare. I need to know why she died. I've never needed anything so much. Are you sure you've told me everything that is relevant?' I take another gulp of the red. 'Who knew about you and Kendall?'

'No one, I think. Except Clare.'

300

'Are you sure. Remember, the *Globe* was stalking you. They clearly had an idea. Did anyone from the paper contact you?'

'No, but ...' Jeremy trails off. 'A couple of days later, Kendall called the two of us into his office. Someone tipped him off the *Globe* had pictures of us leaving his house.'

'Who tipped him off?'

'That's just what Clare asked. Kendall wouldn't say, but he was obviously nervous, anxious. He begged us to swear that if any reporter contacted us, we would just say we went to his home to deliver policy papers.'

'Did Clare agree to that?'

He nods. 'Her priority was to protect me. If Kendall wasn't bothering me, she saw no reason to blow things up.'

My mind is racing with possibilities. Who was trying to put the squeeze on the Chancellor?

Time to try a different angle. 'When we met in the park, you said Robin Muller from Schon Partners had been to see the Chancellor. Was that meeting before or after Kendall told you about the paps outside his home?'

'Oh gosh.' He rubs his glasses. 'Before. I think about three days before. Definitely before. Why does that matter?'

'I think Robin Muller was there representing Media Corp, which owns the *Globe* – and, as you know, my paper too. Media Corp would have been in serious trouble if the Chancellor had pressed ahead with Clare's plan to impose the tax on pension funds. My hunch is that Clare was aware of that.'

My pizza arrives. It looks delicious, but I ignore it. 'Did she ever mention Media Corp to you?'

'No. But I knew she was refusing to just let the pensions thing die. I told you she kept vanishing to meetings outside the office that weren't in the diary. I wonder if she was trying to find out who had got to Kendall? She must have been doing something she thought was important because when she returned she was usually on an up.'

'Any idea where she was going, who she was meeting?'

'She never said. Though she used an odd turn of phrase after one of her disappearances.'

'What do you mean?'

'I asked her where she'd been and she said she'd been put through the wringer and laughed, as if it was some kind of joke.'

The wringer? The Ringer! It's not possible.

Jeremy gawps at me. 'Are you all right? You're looking a bit flushed.'

Chapter 23

'**D**EAR BOY, HAVE THEY LET you out of the funny farm?'

How does he know? I'm outside the pizzeria, freezing my nuts off, wondering what savage stacked these concrete blocks here to create this hideous shopping centre, and marvelling at Bob Ringer's omniscience.

'Who told you?'

'I think you know.'

I'm not going to play his tedious game. 'It's about Jimmy Breitner that I'm ringing you, actually.'

He bursts into laughter. 'I've remembered why I like you. How can I help?'

'Why didn't you tell me that my sister had been in touch with you?'

He takes a moment. Has a trace of conscience survived all those years of scheming for whoever pays him best.

'Gil. Forgive me.' That's a first. 'But I tried to tell you the bit that mattered. I told you to think about your own pension?'

I remember that – although at the time I was distracted by the lobster. So he *was* confiding that the Media Corp pension fund is in trouble. Which is what Clare had worked out. Clever Clare.

'Can you tell me precisely what you said to Clare?'

'I thought I just did.'

'So you gave her the lowdown on Media Corp?'

A pained sigh. 'Sometimes I despair at your obtuseness. Now listen carefully. Media Corp is an occasional client. It would be a gross breach of confidentiality for me to reveal anything they had not explicitly authorised me to say. So for the avoidance of doubt, at no point did the words Media Corp pass my lips. And I don't think I said anything to you about Media Corp, either.'

God, I hate this game. Being lectured on confidentiality by Bob Ringer is like getting lessons in marital fidelity from almost any member of the cabinet. I suck it up.

'Yes, Bob,' I say wearily, 'the idea that you would say anything disloyal about a client is absurd. But to be clear, Clare did speak with you?'

'Yes.'

'And?'

'And she asked me about a client, and I told her *I* was unable to tell her anything.'

I clock his stress on the 'I'.

'You're not someone who likes to be unhelpful, are you, Bob?'

'You know me so well.'

'So if you were bound by confidentiality, is it possible you might have directed her to someone less constrained, someone who could talk to her more freely?'

'As you say, I try to be helpful.'

'You've always done your best for me. And as you know, I very much appreciate that.'

'Think nothing of it.'

'This person who would have been able to give Clare the information she needed: is this someone who I can contact?' I am trying to keep it light, though this feels like life and death.

'That's not how it works,' he says. 'This is someone you don't contact. But I will pass on your message and we'll see what happens.'

An articulated lorry swings past me and round the great Elephant roundabout. Brake lights and tail lights streak the darkness. *Turning and turning in the widening gyre*. I feel a little dizzy.

'Thanks, Bob. When can I expect ...?'

'Leave it with me.'

I'm outside my front door, trying to put the key in the new lock, when Bob rings back.

'Tomorrow night. Be at the Eldon Street entrance of Broadgate at eleven o'clock.'

In a career not short on strange meetings, these are eccentric instructions. But I am not going to argue. 'Should I carry a copy of the paper tucked under my left arm?' I ask, as a joke.

'That might be a good idea.' And before I can ask if he's serious, he rings off.

Wednesday, 23 April – 8 days until Election Day

Just occasionally, my job feels like a scene from a movie. I'd like to think it was a high quality 1950s film noir, though at times it's more like the sort of spoof thriller you'd get from the creators of *Airplane!* I'm standing on the corner where Eldon Street becomes Broad Street Place, where the old City of London tries its hardest to look like techno-modern Wall Street. In spite of my voluminous dark navy Yamamoto overcoat, I am hugging myself to keep out the chill, while waiting for a man I've never met, who may only be able to identify me by the rolled-up copy of today's *FC* that is tucked under my left arm. The stakes feel high. *I mustn't fuck this up, mustn't fuck this up, mustn't fuck this up.*

I've been waiting for fifteen minutes. It's Wednesday night and the City is a ghost town. Apart from a few trainees and juniors at the assorted law and banking firms, who've been coerced into proofreading prospectuses and offer documents into the small hours, most workers have gone home. Any minute now, London Underground staff will draw the iron grille across the entrance to the station. I feel exposed, vulnerable.

Am I being played? Is Bob chortling at his prank, while wallowing on a fat sofa with a single malt and a Cohiba Esplendido?

A black cab comes rattling down the street and I decide that's a sign for me to give up. It noses to the kerb only a few yards away and, although its light is off, I wander over to see if he'll drive me home.

A slim man in an immaculately cut black overcoat with a chocolate velvet collar opens the door and carefully dismounts. He has boxy black spectacles, hair that is Brylcreemed back with short back and sides, and – like me – a copy of the *FC* under his arm.

'Gilbert.' He shakes my hand. 'Hugo.'

We've never met, but I know who he is. Hugo Rep, dealing partner of Palatine and Co., the Queen's stockbrokers. Palatine is the only one of the City's eminent and ancient stockbrokers that has remained a partnership and has not sold itself for a fabulous sum to an American or Swiss bank. That's not because their partners are uninterested in wealth. It's because for two hundred years Palatine partners have made so much money from doing things in their own supremely arrogant style, they won't lightly give it up. What these days would be called their 'franchise' – what they would call their inheritance – must always be preserved and passed on to the next generation of partners.

Rep is a legend, the Macavity of the City. He has a mystical understanding of the London market. If you're the finance director of almost any big British company looking to buy up a slice of a rival, you will tap him up for advice. He'll know where to find the stock, what price to pay, and how to execute the deal before anyone notices.

'Forgive the eccentricity of this meeting,' he says, in clipped vowels, 'all this cloak and dagger stuff. We're going to walk for about ten minutes and we can talk when we reach our destination. If you could stay a few yards behind me, just so that it's not too obvious we're together?'

This is even odder than I expected. Are these precautions because of what happened to Clare? Is he in some way the *cause* of what happened to her? I'm on hyper alert, repeatedly checking over my shoulder and glancing in every shadowy doorway as I follow Rep east through Liverpool Street station. He goes at a brisk clip, taking the stairs two at a time. I almost break into a jog to keep up.

He crosses the vast cavern of the station and bounces up the stairs to Bishopsgate. Even at this time of night, we have to dodge cars and vans to cross, walking a diagonal to veer north. We pass the new pseudo-Palladian buildings that have been erected as a classical veneer for the Wall Street barbarians who've taken up residence. Then we speed-walk around the rundown perimeter of Spitalfields market till the white spire of Hawksmoor's magnificent Christ Church looms. We are now on Fournier Street as we enter seventeenth century Huguenot London. I can smell the faintest aroma of Bangladeshi curry drifting down from the cafés of Brick Lane.

Rep stops outside number thirty-three, a flat-fronted, red-brick Georgian terrace, with stucco pilasters framing the door. He unlocks it and goes inside, leaving the door open. Feeling more than ever as if I've walked into a John Buchan novel, I check left and right to be sure I haven't been followed, then enter.

It's dark and freezing. I can hear movement on the floor upstairs, which I assume is Rep, though just at this moment anything seems possible. My heart beats faster as I climb the bare wooden stairs. From what I can see, the house is derelict. There appears to be no electricity and the panelled walls are patchy and peeling.

'Wait there,' Rep says, as I reach the landing. He's in a sparsely-furnished sitting room, lighting candles in dull brass sconces attached to the walls. They cast a flickering, yellowish glow over the room. We've stepped back two or three centuries.

He goes to the windows and draws heavy blue jacquard curtains. Only when he's confident we cannot be seen does he gesture me to come into the room and take a seat on a varnished hard-backed chair – probably Georgian, definitely uncomfortable. He pulls up one that looks marginally more forgiving, inasmuch as it has a bit of upholstery on the base.

'Sorry it's so basic. A project of mine. It is a duty to preserve our heritage.'

'Which means no central heating?' I say flippantly. Rep ignores me. He has not removed his coat and I don't even think about taking off mine.

'I would like to have a conversation that never happened, if you understand me.' I contemplate switching on the cassette tape hidden in my pocket, but think better of it.

'That would be fine.'

'Bob Ringer tells me you are trying to join up some dots. As indeed was your sister.'

'You spoke to Clare?' For a moment, the bizarreness of our surroundings melts away.

'I was very sorry to hear what happened to her. I hope it had nothing to do with our discussion.'

'That's what I'm trying to find out.'

'All I can do is tell you what I told her.'

'Media Corp,' I guess. 'The pension fund.'

There is a trace of a frown; he doesn't much care for anyone breaking his flow.

'I take it you are a member of that scheme, as an employee of the *FC*?'

'That's right.'

'Then I have difficult news for you. It's bust.'

Bloody hell. I couldn't care less about my own pension. Retirement feels a lifetime away. But it is gratifying that my instincts were right. 'How and why?'

'Breitner used the scheme to fund his adventures. Rather ill-advisedly, he used it to purchase shares in a fashionable technology venture that went spectacularly bankrupt in January.'

A memory is jogged. 'Albion Super Highway. It was a car crash. But I didn't know he put cash from the pension scheme into that deal.'

'It wasn't the first time he's used the fund to hide his less successful punts. The problem for Jimmy this time is that the

Albion loss is too big to cover up for more than a few months, a year at most. And then he got wind of what Kendall was planning. Or I should say, what your sister had devised.'

'The dividend tax credit.' I suddenly feel a chill. 'Less money for pension funds would have made it harder for him to cover up the Albion loss.'

'It would have been impossible. If the tax credit was removed, the trustees of all pension funds would have been under a fiduciary duty to review whether their funds could absorb the cut in income. Just a box-ticking exercise, for most, but for Breitner it would have been a disaster. The black hole would have been exposed and there would be no way he could keep the news from getting out, because the actuaries would have insisted he increase contributions to the fund. And that would have been a significant credit event. In fact, his bankers would have probably seen it as material adverse change in his circumstances, allowing them to call in their loans.'

I think I know what that means. But I want Rep to spell it out.

'The hole in the pension fund, exacerbated by the abolition of the tax rebate on dividends, would in effect increase Media Corp's debts – and very substantially. That would breach the covenants on six billion dollars of loans to Media Corp, because Breitner's ability to repay the six billion dollars would be seriously diminished. Ergo, every single creditor could demand immediate repayment.'

'Breitner would be bust!'

'Correct.'

I think back to Breitner's office, him leaning back in his chair with that smug smile on his face. *Do I look like a man on the brink of ruin?* Pants on fire.

'So, for Breitner, it was a matter of life or death to stop the abolition of the tax credit.'

'Also correct.'

'And the Chancellor duly obliged.'

'After your friend Mr Muller paid him a visit.'

'Why do you think he's my friend?'

He flashes a fake smile.

Why is Rep revealing so much? I have enough experience of the *echt* posh to know I can't take a single thing he says at face value. And I am struck by what he *hasn't* mentioned.

'Breitner's in the middle of buying Capital Television,' I observe.

The flickering candle is reflected in his lenses. 'So I have heard.'

I recall what Jess told me. 'Capital is a cash cow. If Breitner seizes control of it, he will deploy its huge free cash flow to repair the pension fund.'

'And to pay back his American bankers.'

'American' almost sounds like a term of abuse.

I hold my nose and press on. He has shown me the breathtaking audacity of Breitner's rescue plan. By hiding his pension-fund hole, Breitner is keeping his share price artificially high, and he is using those overvalued shares as currency to buy Capital. Once Capital is under his thumb, he'll direct all the cash generated by television advertising into the pension scheme. As if by magic, the hole in the pension fund will vanish, the bankers will be reassured, and Breitner's remorseless growth will resume.

It's a confidence trick: exchanging his funny money, his worthless shares, for Capital's real cash. It's ingenious, but risky. If all the little ducks aren't in a row, his house will come tumbling down. If word leaked to the City and investors that the pension fund is rotten, official watchdogs would weigh in, Media Corp's shares would crater and the takeover of Capital would be scuppered.

And once the watchdogs were sniffing around, the politicians would at last feel emboldened to ask questions and intervene. Would the enlarged Media Corp make Breitner too powerful? Would there be too little competition in the television and newspaper industry, undermining democracy with a reduction of media voices and views? The deal could – probably should – fail the public interest test. Any government with a backbone would say no to Breitner.

'Is it relevant that Schon Partners are underwriting the bid for Capital?' I ask, recalling Jess's forensic analysis. 'Aren't they on the hook for a billion pounds if it goes wrong.'

'A lot more than that. The reason they are backing the Capital takeover is because they are already up to their eyeballs in Media Corp debt. They've loaned Breitner so much money, the only hope they have of getting it back is to prop him up by throwing good money after bad.' He sniffs. 'As they say, if you owe the bank a few million pounds, it's your problem. If you owe them a few billion, it's theirs. Breitner has Schon by the goolies.'

No wonder Muller was doing Breitner's dirty work for him. But I am uneasy; why is Rep spilling? What is his angle?

'Are you involved in the Capital takeover?'

'I'm afraid that's straying beyond your mandate.'

That's an affirmative, then. 'I thought you acted for Breitner.'

'Not on this occasion.'

That's interesting. Has Breitner sacked Palatine? Is this Rep's retaliation? For Palatine, loyalty is determined by what will maximise the partnership share, the millions of pounds of profit trousered by the partners at the end of each year.

'And you disclosed all this to my sister?'

'The material facts, yes.'

'Why did you help Clare?'

'Let's say that I am not a fan of James Breitner. I am not convinced that his ownership of important British institutions is necessarily a good thing.'

'I suppose, as an *FC* journalist, I should leap to his defence.'

'Breitner hates Britain. Or rather, he hates everything that makes this country great. He is here from the colonies to prove he's better than us. If he gets control of Capital, he'll be unstoppable.'

'That's a bit over the top, isn't it? Capital's only a commercial TV company.'

'Media Corp will be Capital plus all those newspapers and everything else he owns. With Capital as the jewel in his crown, who will dare to stand up to him? Which prime minister would have the guts to challenge him?'

I'm puzzled. 'I'd always thought that on the big political questions, you and your firm and Breitner would be aligned. You share his contempt for the European Union, for example.'

Rep tips his head to one side. 'Don't believe everything you hear. You must know that Palatine has long-standing relationships with some of Europe's oldest investment houses. It's what keeps the show on the road.'

He's flirting, pulling back the veil on one of the City's last great secrets: the connections between Palatine and the older financial firms of Paris and Milan, some of which date back to the Middle Ages. These are networks that sustain the wealth

313

and influence of a tiny number of elite European families, through cross-shareholdings in insurance, finance and industry. They are the networks that rebuilt Europe after the Nazi predations.

It's beginning to make sense. Whatever patriotic ideals he may spout, the reason Rep wants to blow up Breitner is presumably because he's working for another foreign media business or conglomerate that wants to acquire Capital, probably one from the Continent. There's no point asking who: he'll only tell me I've *strayed beyond my mandate* again. But it's in his interests to whip up a public stink about Breitner, to create an opening for his mystery client to steal in and snatch the prize.

Now that I think I understand his motivation, I am calmer. Everything is business. 'I don't suppose you have documentary proof of any of this?'

'Are you doubting that my word is my bond?' There's a twinkle in those dark eyes. 'I am sure a clever boy like you will be able to secure the proof you need. Now, if you will forgive me, that's our business done, except to remind you that this conversation never happened, we've never met and we never will.'

If I can corroborate what he's said, it's more than enough to burn down Breitner's entire empire. Not just make him bankrupt, but have him handcuffed and marched from his lavishly furnished townhouse to a spartan cell.

As I step outside and look both ways down the empty street, I'm on edge. If Clare's death was not an accident, because she knew too much, that has implications for my safety. If Rep told Clare what he's told me, she was a double threat to Breitner. She was in a position to trigger an audit of his pension scheme and expose the black hole. And she could urge ministers to block his takeover of Capital. My big sister, and she alone, had the power to decide whether Breitner, Streatham, Muller, Media Corp and Schon would be cast into oblivion.

That must have been why she paged me, the day she died. She knew I could help. I ball my fists. *Why didn't you call me sooner? I could have told you how dangerous these people are. I could have helped!*

The lights of Commercial Street seem far away. I check over my shoulder again and take out the phone. I'm not going to make Clare's mistake. I am going to share all I know now.

It's well after midnight, but Jess answers at once. 'Gil?' She sounds wide awake. 'I was just about to ring you.'

'I've got the story,' I start to say, but she's already talking over me.

'I've found out something you need to hear.'

I pause. 'You go first.'

'You remember Dolly? Deyna's neighbour, in Wood Green?'

'Yes.'

There's a cab coming with its light on. I flag it down, relieved to be getting out of here.

'The Passat that came in the dead of night with the three execs who went through Deyna's house? She gave me the registration. I ran it by my snout at the DVLA and he's just come back with the details.' Her voice is taut. She sounds almost as anxious as me. 'You'll never guess who it's registered to.'

I get in the back seat of the cab and slam the door.

'Actually, I think I can.'

Chapter 24

THIS IS THE ULTIMATE DENIABLE story. I have all the answers, but no documents or on-the-record testimony that would allow me to write it. And time is running out. Once Breitner completes the Capital takeover, it will be as though the pensions black hole never existed. I doubt any prime minister will feel inclined to launch a retrospective investigation into the most powerful media magnate in the country. I have to get enough evidence to publish it before the deal goes through. Even if Lorimer won't run it, I can place the story elsewhere. If no newspaper has the balls, there's always *Private Eye*. And if I get fired in the process, so what? There are other employers and other jobs. If I had dependents, I suppose I would be a bit more circumspect. But it's just me and Cat with No Name.

And Jess. After she'd confirmed what I'd suspected – that the car at Deyna's flat was registered to Media Corp – I spewed out everything that Rep told me. 'You should probably steer clear of this toxic mess,' I warned her. 'I've got enough credit in the bank that I can afford to piss a few powerful people off so I'll be all right whatever happens. You're starting out. The career risks are not the same ...'

She was characteristically withering. 'Don't patronise me. I can look after myself. This story is going to be massive – and when it goes out, my name's going to be all over it.'

'Then you'll be escorted from the building with me, too.'

'I wouldn't have it any other way.'

We need to tap up every contact we have in the City to verify what Rep told me. A multi-billion pound deal like this doesn't happen unless many tens of bankers, brokers and lawyers are working on pages and pages of contracts and legal documents. If we can just find someone who's got a few relevant pages they can slip us, or who's willing to speak on the record, we're off to the races.

'I've been on this story for weeks,' Jess reminded me. 'No one wanted to spill even on deepest background, let alone for publication.'

'But now we know more precisely what we're looking for.'

We were still talking after midnight, as Wednesday slipped into Thursday. 'There's no point ringing anyone at work,' Jess said. 'No one is going to talk about this from their office.'

'Right. I always find that people are a bit more forthcoming on a Sunday. There are fewer distractions, and they need a reason to ignore their children.'

'So what shall we do today?'

'Follow up your DVLA lead. Find out what those Media Corp flunkies were looking for in Deyna's house.'

That is why, at 7 p.m. on Thursday evening, I am in my scarred and filthy Peugeot, going to pick up Jess from outside Carriage

Gates in Parliament Square. One hand is on the wheel, the other clutching the Nokia to my ear.

'What the flip is Hugo Rep up to?'

Bob Ringer chuckles down the line. 'You spoke to him, did you?'

'All that "Breitner is a bad person, bad for Britain" bollocks.'

'I'm sure Palatine is only doing its patriotic duty.'

'If I know my City history, at Palatine it's always been partners' profits first, Queen and country a long way second.'

'Dear boy, you've become dreadfully cynical. And so young.'

'Come on, Bob. What's this really about?'

'Surely you can guess.'

'I imagine there's some European client of Palatine that has its eye on Capital, but doesn't want to get into a bidding war.'

'Bright boy.'

'But what about you, Bob? Why did you put me on to Hugo? I saw you coming out of Breitner's office the other day. You shouldn't be helping Rep apply the coup de grâce.'

'Between us?'

'Of course.'

'Jimmy is a tight-fisted "see-you-next-Tuesday". He still owes me for some work I did for him last year and he's trying to Jew me again on the Capital deal. So fuck him.'

'Bob, you're talking to a Jew.'

'Ah. Yes. Sorry. As you know, most of my best friends are Jews.'

'You don't have any friends, you disgusting anti-Semite.'

'True enough.'

There is an awkward pause.

'Look, I'm embarrassed. Forgive me. I'm sure you know that I am a paid adviser to the Israeli government.'

Nothing would surprise me.

The phone drops from my hand as I frantically grab the steering wheel. A towering lorry – the kind that does removals, a pantechnicon – is swinging left into my lane. Apparently the driver can't see me.

I pound my fist on the steering wheel, blaring the horn. High up in his cab, the driver is so close he probably wouldn't notice me unless he stuck his head out of the window and looked straight down. But how can he not hear me?

Now I know what it feels like to be a beetle in the shadow of a looming human foot. Slowly, very slowly but relentlessly, the lorry squeezes against the right side of the car. The Peugeot shudders. I jerk the steering wheel, trying to turn away, but it's locked tight. My wheels are hard up against the kerb and there are iron railings lining the pavement to stop silly tourists from meandering into the road. They are a deathtrap for me. There's nowhere to go. *Oh fuck! Is this it? Am I going to die?*

The lorry is still coming. The right side of the car, my door and the roof, bends menacingly towards me. Against the lorry's weight, the frame feels as flimsy as tinfoil.

I'm not going to make it. I scramble to undo my seatbelt, but the catch is dodgy and there's a trick to releasing it. In my panic, I can't. Even if I could, I'm not sure how I would get out. The door is bowing in towards my knee. In a moment, my femur is going to be snapped against the steering column. *I'm dead, I'm dead, I'm dead.*

I'm not. With a screech and the sound of crunching metal, both vehicles lurch to a stop. I'm thrown forward – and suddenly I'm grateful I didn't manage to undo my seatbelt, because I'd have been thrown head first against the windscreen. Instead of which I'm just winded.

The roof of the car has been bent down so far it's touching the headrest and there's a sharp crease in the metal that would rip my skull open if I moved my head the wrong way. The driver's door has been crushed like a Coke can. It will never open again and is about a millimetre from my thigh. I'm shaking uncontrollably, but seemingly uninjured. Miraculously.

I release the seatbelt and wriggle over to the passenger seat. The left-hand side of the car is almost unscathed, like a house attached to one that's burned down. The lorry's momentum dragged me past the railings and I open the street-side door. On the pavement, my legs give way and I reach for the street lamp to keep myself from collapsing.

A group of passers-by have gathered to gawp. They give a small round of applause, as if I'm one of the entertainers – magicians, jugglers and clowns – who perform a few yards from here in the piazza at Covent Garden. My car is blocking one lane. A white VW Golf has pulled up behind me and a lady gets out. White blouse, blue jeans, cross-cropped hair. She runs towards me shouting, 'Are you OK?'

I am still quivering and struggle to form words. All I can think is: *how am I alive?* I glance up at the cab of the lorry, expecting to see a contrite driver jumping down to see if I'm all right. But the door is shut. The setting sun glares off the window. All I can see is a dark silhouette behind the golden glass.

Why doesn't he get out?

There is the beep beep of a large vehicle reversing. The lorry is grinding backwards.

'Hey, arsehole!' the lady shouts. 'Where are you going?'

Too late. He puts the lorry into gear and starts driving south towards Whitehall.

'Get his number plate,' says the outraged VW lady. 'Have you got a pen?'

I fumble in my jacket pocket, but by the time I extract my pen and notebook the lorry is vanishing around the corner.

'That was weird,' says Golf Lady. She takes the notebook, frowns, and starts writing uncertainly, trying to remember what she saw. 'Almost as if he wanted to crush your car.'

A Vauxhall Astra estate in Met Police livery pulls up. This part of London, so close to Downing Street, is crawling with police.

Two officers, a woman and a man, leave the vehicle and walk to me.

'Is this your car, sir?' says the female officer, while her colleague walks around the other side to inspect the damage. I am beginning to feel calmer. The shakes are subsiding.

'Yes.'

The male officer whistles through his teeth and gives me a look that says I've had a lucky escape. 'Do you want an ambulance?'

'I don't think so. I don't even think I'm bruised.'

While the female officer directs traffic around us, I go to look at how bad it is. The frame looks as though it's been crushed between the thumb and forefinger of some kind of Gogmagog. My car is a write-off. It's a miracle I got out. *Thank you Clare, thank you Clare, thank you Clare*, I whisper.

'What's that?' the policeman asks. I shake my head.

'Tell me what happened,' he pursues.

I describe 'the accident' but in the telling I cannot escape the terrifying idea that this was intended; that someone was trying to squash me. I look towards Whitehall, as if the driver might feel remorse and come back to apologise. 'He drove off. Do you think there's any chance you'll find him?'

The female says, 'Leaving the scene after a collision is a crime under the Road Traffic Act. We'll do our best. Did you get his number plate?'

'I was in no state to write it down. But the lady in the Volkswagen might have done.'

'Which lady in the Volkswagen?'

I look around, expecting her to be parked behind me. But she and her car are gone. While I've been speaking to the police, she drove away. And she's taken my notebook and pen. 'That's odd. She was the only proper witness.'

The woman officer gives me what feels like a pitying look.

'I'm afraid you can't leave the car here, sir,' she says. Traffic is backing up behind me, to the National Portrait Gallery.

I tell her about my grace-and-favour parking space, just a few yards away, down the Mall. 'Do you think it's driveable?' I ask.

The policeman prods the tyre doubtfully with the toe of his boot. 'Not sure you should start the engine. But if you release the handbrake we can try to push it.'

I nod and climb in to the passenger seat. I am going to have to steer from here. The police have asked a couple of bystanders to help. The male officer asks me to release the handbrake and I lean to the right and take hold of the steering wheel. I can just about control the direction of travel. And with the woman officer guiding the traffic around us, we roll slowly down Trafalgar Square.

She gets into her car and turns on the warning lights, to follow us and protect us. With my police escort, I am travelling exactly the route that either Todd or Ramsey will take, also flanked by outriders, after the election in just a few days, when they'll journey to the Palace to ask the Queen for permission to form a government. Our more eccentric cortège trundles under Admiralty Arch and down the majestic Mall. The roped-off car park, just by the dazzling white of the Institute of Contemporary Arts, is in view.

Once the car is parked, I wriggle out again – ignoring the bemused looks of pedestrians – and give the police a formal statement. There isn't much to say and they're not desperately interested. A traffic accident with no one hurt is not a priority.

I try to impress on them the strangeness of what happened. 'I've never seen anything like it,' I keep saying. I repeat what the vanished VW lady said. 'Almost as if he was trying to crush my car.' I am babbling.

'You've had a shock,' the policewoman says. 'Get some food and a hot drink inside you. Perhaps have a doctor take a look at you. In case of whiplash.'

'I will,' I lie.

As soon as they've gone, I find my phone in the passenger footwell, where I dropped it, and call Jess.

'Where are you? I've been hanging around for the best part of an hour.'

'I've had an accident.'

I explain what happened. 'Jesus, Gil! I don't know what to think.'

It's obvious we are both having the same thought: was someone trying to silence me, eliminate me, kill me? My heart is thumping and there's a slight pain in my chest; I know that if I don't take a few slow, steady breaths I will hyperventilate.

'Are you OK, Gil?' Jess asks.

'Give me a minute,' I gasp. I squat, breathe in through the nose, out through the mouth, ten times. Gradually my equanimity is restored. 'Gil?' I hear, as a tinny squawk because I am holding the phone by my side. I put it back to my ear. 'Hi, Jess. I'm OK now.' She talks deliberately and calmly. 'You had a lucky escape. We should call it a night and take stock.'

'Absolutely not.'

'Gil!' She's using her stern voice. Experience has taught me it's wise to listen to her. But ...

'Don't you see?' I say. 'If they're coming after me, it proves we're on the right track. They feel threatened. We're getting close.'

If Clare refused to be intimidated, nor will I be. I pump myself up. It will be tomorrow or the next day when the wide-awake panic will start.

'Look,' I say to Jess, 'this is my fight. You really don't have to come if you don't want to.'

'Of course I don't want to! I'm fucking *terrified*.'

I have no right to put her in harm's way. But it's hard to hide my disappointment.

'I understand,' I say.

'No you don't.' Fear makes her voice sharp. 'I'm shit-scared but obviously I'm coming. This is *our* fight.'

The relief I feel is a physical sensation. 'Oh my God, Jess. Thank you!'

'Shut up. Pathetic gratitude doesn't suit you. What's the plan?'

The adrenaline is flowing again. I am determined to bulldoze forward.

'Meet me at the barriers of Charing Cross Underground station in fifteen minutes.'

The great thing about the London Underground is that lorries aren't allowed down there. Even so, I stand well back from the edge of the platform and scan both directions, looking for anyone who might want to nudge me on to the lines. Jess can tell I'm on heightened alert, I think, but is too polite to mention it. After the train clatters in on the northbound Northern Line, Charing Cross branch, we take it to Leicester Square, and then change to the Piccadilly Line. Thirty minutes later, we exit at Turnpike Lane.

By now it's nearly nine o'clock: the bars and Turkish restaurants are packed as we traipse down Green Lanes. The smell of coriander, garlic, grilling meat and warm flatbread fill the air. I promise myself that when this is over I will come back and stuff my face with hummus, Turkish salad and kebab.

Soon we are outside number forty-nine Hewitt Road. I've managed to put the accident out of my mind – my superpower of compartmentalising difficult emotional issues, packing them into a sealed box. But approaching Deyna's front door, there's a flick of fear. I think of the silhouette in the driver's cab, behind the glass, and again hear the VW lady's comment: *Almost as if he wanted to crush your car.* Has Deyna been out this evening driving a pantechnicon? I want it to be a mad, paranoid idea. But I was inches away from being turned into mincemeat.

An old Saab is parked by the kerb outside the house. The front garden is even more of a tip than before, filled with newspaper pages and carrier bags that have blown in. The noxious smell of rotting food rises out of two grubby black plastic bins. Nothing to suggest anyone's been living here for weeks. The front rooms are dark, though through the window I can see the living-room door has been left ajar and there's a light on behind it.

We ring the bell, but all it does is summon a tabby cat who appears at our feet, miaowing. We try Dolly's door, too, but she's not home.

'Wasted trip,' Jess says. 'There was a pub back there ...'

'... the Salisbury. Famous IRA hangout. Just the ticket.'

'Let's head over there and I'll buy you a Guinness.'

'Disgusting stuff. And I'm not sure the white wine will be quite up to standard.'

'You really are a pretentious twat.'

I'm not listening. 'What about that?' I say. A few doors down, there's a gap between the houses that looks like the opening of an alleyway. I follow it between two garden walls, then turn left along the backs of the houses until I'm behind Deyna's house. The fence here is rickety boards, with a door in the middle buckling from its hinges.

I try the handle.

'What are you doing?' hisses Jess.

The door opens an inch, then stops. There's some kind of cabin hook serving as a basic lock on the other side. I take out my pen, push it through the crack and flick up the hook.

'You can't do this!' says Jess. But I can. I step through, and she follows, closing the gate behind us.

We're in a derelict yard: tufts of brown grass, pots filled with lifeless plants, piles of old bricks, a broken fridge. Treading carefully, I make my way to the kitchen door. The dim glow I saw through the front room seems to be a hallway light that's been left on. I can see the outlines of cabinets and a table through the latticed panes of glass in the door.

The door's locked but, peering through the glass, I can see a key in the lock on the inside. I check the neighbouring houses.

Dolly's on the left looks empty, but there are lights on in the property to our right. I can't let them hear me.

I wander over to the pile of bricks and pick up one that's been broken in half. 'Please don't do what I think you're about to do,' Jess hisses.

Returning to the door, I take off my Gore-Tex cycling jacket and place it over one of the glass panes.

Jess grabs my arm. 'For Christ's sake, Gil! First you nearly die in a traffic accident, now you're breaking and entering. Stop now. If we're caught, it's the end of our careers.'

I think of what Lorimer would say if he knew I was here and not sobbing into a handkerchief on Penelope McGovern's sofa. 'I'm on borrowed time.'

'You're mental.'

'I've seen this so many times on the telly, but I wonder if it actually works?'

As I raise the brick, I remember my brother-in-law Charles on the day of Clare's funeral. *Someone broke in while we were out. Put a brick or something through the glass back door. Her office looked ransacked.*

I know who they were working for, and what they wanted.

'Fuck you, Breitner,' I mutter to myself, as I smash the brick into the window.

Despite my precautions with the coat, the sound of shattering glass is unmistakeable. In my guilty ears, it sounds as loud as a bomb going off. Surely the neighbours must have heard it?

I freeze in fright and stand still for a few minutes. I'm ready to run for the back gate at any sign we've been noticed, but – amazingly – we don't seem to have attracted anyone's attention.

I shake a few splinters of glass off my coat, brush it down and put it on again. Then I carefully reach my hand through the jagged hole.

'Shit!' I haven't been careful enough. I nicked the base of my palm on a piece of broken glass that's still in the frame. A trickle of blood appears and runs onto the cuff of my Commes des Garcons shirt – that's going to be a bugger to get out.

'For fuck's sake,' whispers Jess, 'you could have severed an artery.'

Too late, it occurs to me that if there are bolts at the top or bottom of the door, we're fucked. Blood drips off my wrist onto the kitchen floor as I turn the key in the lock, then withdraw my hand. Moment of truth. I turn the handle and push.

The door opens.

The kitchen is tiny, only large enough for a two-person table. The cupboards are classic 1980s MFI, the countertops grubby white Formica. All I can take in initially is the overpowering stink: putrid food left in the bin, turning to compost.

I don't dare turn on the light. I step forward cautiously and immediately clatter into a kitchen chair. Please let Dolly still be out ...

Jess has come in behind me. 'I can't believe I'm doing this,' she whispers to herself.

Edging around the furniture, I head towards the front of the house. The light that I glimpsed from the street is coming from upstairs. Looking up, I can see a bare bulb hanging over the landing.

It was probably left on by the last person who was here. It must have been on for days. Mustn't it?

I pause for a moment, seized by indecision. To retreat now, to have done all this for nothing, doesn't bear thinking about.

But what if the light wasn't left on by mistake? What if there's someone upstairs?

I catch another whiff of the smell from the kitchen and that decides me. No one could stay in this house with that smell. And surely they'd have heard the smashing glass and come to look.

Unless they locked themselves in a bedroom and have called the police?

I remember the lorry towering over me, the screech of bending steel. I think of Clare, who had nothing to protect her. Not even a helmet.

I'll take my chances.

I can't see a switch to turn off the light from down here, and I don't dare turn it off in case someone clocks it. But if I go into the front room upright, I'll be silhouetted to any passing pedestrian who happens to turn their head. Feeling ridiculous, I get down on my hands and knees, curse that my trousers will be coated in dust, and crawl across the bare floorboards. Most of the furniture has been removed, if there ever was any, but there's an old brown wooden desk standing by the window. I get to it and paw around the surface, then pull out each of the drawers and check inside.

The desk is empty, apart from a few pencil shavings and an empty biscuit packet. If there was something here, the people Dolly saw must have cleared it out.

I scrabble back to the kitchen. Jess is crouched in the middle of the room, surrounded by stinking rubbish. By the light filtering in from the hallway, I can see takeaway boxes, napkins stained with the fat of doner kebabs and burgers, empty beer cans and mouldy bread. She's emptied the whole kitchen bin onto the floor. The stench is so strong it makes me gag.

I have dragged Jess here in the dead of night, made her an accomplice in a crime, and here she is up to her elbows in this shit. 'I don't deserve a friend like you,' I mutter.

I've embarrassed her. 'You are so right. And you are definitely going to want to see what I've found.'

With a look of triumph, her hand comes up holding a filthy envelope, which she hands to me. I take it between finger and thumb, curiosity outweighing the stab of revulsion at the thought of all the bacteria I am touching.

For a moment I can't think what she's on about. There's no writing on the envelope, no address or postmark. Nothing that would tell us anything.

Then I see the logo in the bottom left corner, just under my thumb. A globe spinning on its axis, with the continents picked out in spidery lines, stained and blurry through contact with a teabag.

It takes me a minute to clock what I'm seeing. It's not in its natural habitat; usually, you'd find it bigger and bolder at the top left of a newspaper front page, next to a thick red stripe behind bold white print.

Flipping fuck!

'That's a *Globe* envelope.'

Jess and I stare at each other in silence. I think of the people Dolly saw who came to this house, the couple who spent an hour inside, presumably emptying the desk and erasing any trace of Deyna, the threesome who came in the car registered to Media Corp. They must have overlooked the kitchen bin, either because they were put off by the smell or saw it filled with dead takeaways.

It's the missing piece. At last I can prove a direct line from Breitner to the man who killed Clare, via one of his newspapers and a dingy house off Green Lanes. And maybe because we've at last made a breakthrough, and are so close to finishing Clare's work, I become frightened. Properly scared.

A siren breaks the silence in the house. Not near, but it sounds as if it's coming towards us.

'We should get out of here,' I say.

'I never wanted to be here in the first place.'

We run for the alley. I'm terrified and out of breath, but the rhythm of my pounding legs focuses my thoughts. The image in my mind is not of Deyna, or the lorry, or even Breitner. It's of a big steel safe sitting in a glass-walled newsroom.

If you are Breitner and you want to pay off a man like Deyna, you don't just have the accounts department raise a purchase order. That would create a paper trail. Auditors might ask questions. But as luck would have it, he has within his empire a tried-and-tested system for paying out large sums of cash, with no record of where the money ends up. His journalists employ it every day to pay off snitches, celebrities, bent cops and PR people. It's not money laundering, it's just *ex gratia* payment for services and information rendered, so routine that the accountants classify it as generic journalistic expenses. When a nark needs a reward, the cash is withdrawn from the newsroom safe, placed neatly into an envelope and handed over, with thanks. There is a single control over what happens to the money. The journalist making the withdrawal has to write their name and the amount in an innocent-looking ledger. I need that book – and there is a man who can get it for me.

Chapter 25

THE PICCADILLY LINE TRAIN RATTLES along the tracks, swaying and juddering, sporadically illuminated by the blue light of electricity sparking on the fourth rail and bouncing off the black tunnel wall. The carriage we're in is almost empty: it is that mid-point between the rush to go out and the plod home. I'm relieved: it means I can spot anyone whose intentions might not be friendly.

Jess is sitting on the worn multicoloured fabric of the bench opposite. She's taken a ballpoint out of her handbag and is clicking it repeatedly and nervously.

'If you're not going to say it, I will,' she says at last. 'We're out of our depth.'

There's no reassurance I can offer. Whatever false comfort I took from telling myself that I was in the grip of irrational paranoia vanished when I saw the envelope.

'What are you going to do?' she asks.

'Not completely sure. We haven't quite got all we need to file that undeniable story. Yet.'

Click click click. She hates my 'yet'. 'Gil, I'm not sure this is just a story any longer. Shouldn't we alert the police? We are talking about serious criminality, possibly murder.'

'We could talk to them. But what we have is a lot of surmise and maybe some circumstantial evidence. I am not sure how seriously they would take us – especially when they hear who we are accusing. How does it sound to you: "The most powerful media baron on planet Earth murdered my sister and then tried to bump me off too"? They're going to think my grief has driven me mad. Remember that's what I thought – and I'm me!'

'We've got motive. We've got the beginnings of a paper trail.'

'Do we really have that? Let's take stock. First, that dynamite briefing from Rep was so off the record that if the police approach him he'll deny all knowledge of me. Jeremy will never co-operate with an enquiry because he's worried his mum will find out he's gay. The Polish security contractor has vanished – and to all intents and purposes never existed. And the one bit of incriminating evidence we have is something we stole while breaking and entering into a private house. If we go to the police now, the most likely outcome is that we'll be charged with burglary and that will be that.'

There is an old lady four seats away on Jess's side of the train who gives me a funny look and I realise I have been talking too loudly. Lowering my voice, I say, 'We can't go to the police, or write anything, until we have demonstrable evidence of the hole in the pension fund and that it was Breitner who paid off Deyna.'

Jess has stopped clicking the pen and is giving me a sceptical look. 'We're going to struggle to obtain any of that.'

'No one said this job was easy. But I do have a sort of plan.' I explain about the safe in the *Globe*'s newsroom. 'I have to get inside it.'

'That's not the craziest idea you've ever had,' she says. 'But it's close. And how exactly does it actually help us prove anything?'

'There will be a record of someone removing a large sum of money around the time that Clare was killed. I need to see who took the cash.'

'I get that. But how on earth are you going to get into the safe?'

'Our friend Kevin's going to open it for me.'

'Kevin Wilkinson? Why would he do that?'

'Because he thinks I'm working with him on a story he's desperate to publish.'

'Namely?'

'Namely that Kendall is rogering Jeremy.'

'You're going to hang that poor boy out to dry?'

'Nah. Probably not. But there's no harm in Kevin thinking I am.'

Out of instinct, I pull out my phone. No signal down here, but we'll be back at street level soon.

'No need to call Kevin.'

'Why not?'

'I've got a better idea.'

She retrieves her Palm PDA from her coat pocket and taps it with the stylus. 'Yup, I was right. It's Frankie Crowther's leaving party. I presume you've been invited?'

I'd forgotten that Crowther was quitting journalism, like so many of my fellow foot soldiers, for the putative gold of public relations. 'I imagine my invitation is on my desk in the Burma Road.'

'Kevin will be at the party, won't he?'

Wilkinson was on the *Telegraph* for years, so it's likely he and Crowther are mates. 'Probably.'

The train screeches into Finsbury Park station and the doors rattle open. 'This is your stop,' Jess reminds me.

I don't move. Neither does Jess.

'You really don't have to come with me,' I tell her. 'You went well beyond the call of duty tonight. Why don't you head home?'

'Fuck off, Gil. I'm coming.'

'Thank you.'

''S'all right.'

'I'm grateful.'

'So you should be,' she says. 'The wine will be shit.'

With a beep, rattle and swoosh, the tube doors slide shut, and the train starts to crank forward again.

Fifteen minutes later we are in front of a low-rise, 1960s modernist block that is an island between the brutalist concrete of the Barbican housing development and London Wall's multi-lane highway. The building belongs to the Woodcutters' livery company, one of the medieval guilds that has survived wars, fires, famines and plagues to become a sort of Boy Scouts' pack for City executives who can't bear to go home after work. There aren't many foresters and lumberjacks active in the City these days, but there are plenty of bankers, brokers and solicitors who join the livery for the rich dinners – normally a heavy slab of beef and cauliflower cheese – the cellared claret, the ritual of passing the loving cup, and the opportunity to share confidential information away from the ears of regulators.

Crowther's leaving do is on the top floor, the fifth. Stepping out of the lift, I'm confronted with a blast of noise and colour. The carpet is blinding orange and there's a hubbub of voices (mostly male) and clinking glasses coming from the tapestried livery hall at the end of the corridor. The party's been going for some time.

I walk past portraits of the aldermen and Lord Mayors who represented the guild, and queue at the booth which functions as a cloakroom. There's only one, overworked attendant, who barely looks at me as she takes my Gore-Tex jacket and hands me a raffle ticket in exchange.

We're about to enter the main room when Jess tugs me back.

'What if Lorimer's here?'

'He never comes to these dos. Don't worry.' Slightly belatedly, however, I realise that there will be *FC* journalists here. Word will get to Lorimer that I am back in circulation, days earlier than he expected or wanted.

'I'll try to keep a low profile.'

'Gill' roars a familiar voice. So much for that. Frankie Crowther is standing by the double doors that lead into the main function room, clutching a glass of white wine so full it spills on his every syllable. 'So glad you could come. And you've brought Robin the Girl Wonder with you, too. What an honour.'

'Fuck off and die, Frankie,' says Jess. Frankie roars with laughter, as if it's just banter. Jess purses her lips and doesn't disabuse him. This would not be the moment to nuke him, given that we have a job to do.

'When do you start your new life?' I ask. My mouth is on autopilot as I scan the room for Wilkinson.

'I'll take a couple of weeks to decompress,' says Crowther. I assume his rest cure will be a fortnight spent pissed out of his bonce. 'Then it's all systems go.'

'You'll be missed, Frankie.'

He taps his heart. 'At last, you reveal your true feelings.'

'Nothing personal. I just hate it when hacks go to the other side.'

'Journalism is finished,' he says, draining his glass and looking for a waitress to refill it. 'The future is communications. That's where the power is now. And the money.'

He's goading me. I choose not to respond. Guests are still coming in and Frankie's graced us with enough of his time. He turns to greet other latecomers.

'Let's split up,' I say to Jess. 'I'll look for Wilkinson, you keep an eye out for anyone else who might be useful.'

'Useful how?'

'Anyone who might be able to confirm what Rep told me about Media Corp's pension fund.'

It's the money trail that matters. If Breitner was involved in Clare's death, he'll have employed enough random intermediaries to keep his hands seemingly spotless. But when pension funds are actuarially valued and takeover prospectuses drafted, there are thousands of pages of published and unpublished supporting documents. And as the financial and legal advisers do their investigations and due diligence, all it needs is just one with a conscience, who sees a deficit where there should be a surplus and whose silence can't be bought. Just one honest banker. That's all it takes. To lay Breitner low.

Jess and I start circulating. It's a large room, and Frankie Crowther seems to have more than two hundred best friends, or at least two hundred thirsty contacts. They're all here in their Hugo Boss suits and Hermès ties. Robots all. I am slightly – only very slightly – self-conscious that I haven't shaved for four days. But in my Comme shirt and black Dries jacket, it's a look. My *parfum du jour* however is not so hot: *eau de Deyna trash can*.

A waitress walks past with a tray of white wine, red wine, and sticky orange juice. Of the three, I assume the white is least toxic. It's warm, of course, and too sweet, but I drain it and take another. Then I suddenly remember that I haven't eaten all day. I'd better slow down.

I'm starting to feel light-headed, dangerously disconnected from reality. It's not just the alcohol. This room, too warm and bright and loud, is not ideal after the stress of the past twenty-four hours. Most of the faces are familiar, but they aren't friendly: they're either wary contacts or competitors.

'Hello, mister.'

Someone familiar breathes in my ear. Her smell is unmistakeable and always seductive. I turn. Marilyn is exquisite in a blue silk blouse, brown leather trousers and heels.

'You've been ignoring my calls,' she scolds.

'It's been a difficult few days. Sorry.' I steer her towards a quieter corner near the door. 'How come you're here? A week to the election, shouldn't you be poring over polling data from swing seats or bollocking one of my rivals?'

'I needed a night off. It's all getting too intense. Johnny's convinced we're going to lose and he's driving me nuts.'

'You're ten points up in the polls.'

'Yes,' she sighs, 'Johnny won't believe it'. She tilts her head. 'That thing we talked about, in Bermondsey. Your sister, the baby. Did you ever get to the bottom of it?'

I reflexively screw up my eyes, in pain. 'It wasn't Kendall's, if that's what you're asking.'

'Then whose was it?' She's too eager. I am uncomfortable.

'I never found out. Maybe Charles got his dates wrong, maybe it was his.' I jut my jaw forward. 'If you hoped Kendall's love child would be the sensation that settled the election, you're out of luck.'

'You know we wouldn't have used it. I would never do that to you.'

I *think* I believe her. 'You don't need it. Johnny would have to appear live on TV buggering a donkey for you to lose. And even then it might just be a hung Parliament and a coalition with the Lib Dems.'

That wins me a laugh, before her face goes serious again. 'He's wanted this all his life and is terrified of jinxing it. His control freakery is off the scale.' She puts her hand firmly on my bum and pulls me towards her. 'I could use some de-stressing, actually.'

'Careful. I thought we were supposed to be discreet.' She looks up at me with kohl-lined eyes, lips slightly parted. All I want to do is leave and fall into bed with her. It's torture. This is not what I came here for.

And then, over her shoulder, someone saunters into my field of vision. He's coming out of the lift: Alex Elliott, Media Corp's communications director. He heads for the cloakroom and hands the lady a large red and white Head sports bag.

Frankie Crowther's words echo in my brain. *PRs, they're the real power brokers.* Elliott will be up to his eyes in the Capital takeover. He'll have the answers.

Marilyn can sense she no longer has my attention. 'You've seen someone more interesting than me?'

'Sorry, Marilyn. Give me a few minutes.'

'For fuck's sake, Gil. Let's just get out of here.' She runs a finger down my cheek. 'It will be the release we need.'

I'm torn. But I have to stick to the plan. 'I can't. I'll explain later.'

I've upset her, but she hides it. She gives me a coy smile and spies a Tory special adviser she's known since university.

Elliott has joined the party and is chatting with Crowther. I can see Jess has had the same thought as me. She's hovering, waiting to pounce. I sidle over.

'Wilkinson's over there,' she says, pointing towards the back of the room. 'Drinking with his mates.'

'I'll nab him in a minute.'

She gives me a sideways look. She can tell when I'm up to something. 'What's up?'

'I have an idea.'

'I don't like the sound of that. What about Wilkinson?'

'He's not going to leave while there's wine flowing. You go and distract Elliott. Make sure he doesn't look in my direction.'

I go out to the lobby and join the queue for the cloakroom again. Through the double doors I can see Jess is now deep in conversation with Elliott, making a heroic effort to disguise her contempt for him. If I know him, he probably thinks she'll go home with him, and will only become more convinced with every insult she throws.

'Do you have your ticket, dearie?' says the grey-haired lady in front of the desk. She doesn't look at me. She'll have been paid twenty quid for the night, plus tips, and is now desperate for us all to leave so she can get the last bus home.

I hand her the ticket she gave me earlier. 'It's a coat and a bag.'

'You should have two tickets then, my love. One for the coat, one for the bag.'

'Oh.' As if this has not occurred to me. 'Sorry.' I go through my pockets theatrically, turning them all out. 'Are you sure you gave me two? I only seem to have the one.'

She gives me a shrewd look. But she decides I look all right. All she says is, 'You probably dropped it. Happens all the time with these flimsy tickets.'

'They should invest in a proper tagging system,' I sympathise.

'What kind of bag is it?'

'A Head sports bag. Red and white.'

She scans the steel shelves behind her. 'This one?'

'That's it.'

I take the bag and my Gore-Tex jacket and put a pound coin in the saucer on the desk. My heart is pounding. This is the second time in my adult life I've stolen, and both crimes have been executed in the space of just a few hours. I scan left to check that Elliott isn't looking in my direction. Jess still has him prisoner. I hurry for the stairs.

I'm one flight down when I hear the clack of heels coming down behind me. I turn, shielding the bag against the wall with my body. It's Jess.

'I saw what you just did. You're insane!'

I say nothing. I don't want to say anything incriminating where there is a risk of being overheard.

'How was Alex?'

'Absolute mega twat. He was trying to pull me. Can you believe it?'

'Funnily enough, I can.'

'He loves you, by the way. Said he'd heard you'd been locked in a padded cell, and hoped you would be permanently sectioned. Stared at my tits a bit while I pressed him about the Capital story. When he finally realised there was no way I'd ever suck his cock, he made his excuses.' She pauses. 'Where are we going, by the way?'

'Somewhere private.'

At the next landing, I try one of the doors leading off the stairwell. It opens onto a corridor lined with offices and more portraits of pompous men in dark suits wearing heavy gilt chains round their necks.

Jess looks up at the ceiling. 'What if there are cameras? What if someone finds us?'

I don't see any cameras. 'If anyone comes, we'll pretend we snuck away for a quick shag.'

'Oh yes, that would definitely rehabilitate us in the eyes of Lorimer.'

'It's preferable to the truth.'

At the end of the corridor, we find a small boardroom, unlocked. Orange light from the street lamps streams through the windows, giving us just enough illumination that we don't have to turn on the overhead lights.

'You do know we are breaking the law, again?' she says. And then firmly takes the bag from me, before I can protest, places it on the table and unzips it.

At the top, in a plastic Waitrose carrier, are sweat-stained workout clothes. Jess removes the bag delicately, holding it away from herself as though it's radioactive. Then there's a Toshiba laptop, which is promising, until I turn it on and am asked for a password. Underneath, three pink cardboard files. And right at the bottom, tucked in a corner, one of those small plastic bags used by banks for storing coins that contains a small silver foil parcel.

Jess looks at me and smirks. Neither of us makes any comment.

'Let's go through the files.'

We take one each. By the orange-sulphur glow, with a low hum of the party as the soundtrack, we read.

For fifteen minutes, there's silence: just the sound of rustling paper, and the scratch of Jess's biro as she makes the occasional note. Then, like divers surfacing for air, we both look up at the same time and gaze at each other.

'Got him.' I murmur.

'Looks like it.'

'What have you found?'

'You go first.'

I hold up a sheet of paper. It's a memo to Breitner and the Media Corp board, headed *Albion Super Highway*. It describes the financial impact of the particularly disastrous acquisition of a British internet start-up that Breitner made two years previously. The company had talked up its share price with ambitious plans to lay fibre-optic cables all over the country: Breitner bought into the hype and paid a huge premium. But Albion couldn't get regulatory permission and so the only hole that got dug was the one the company collapsed into. The business went bust, wiping out the two billion pounds that Breitner had invested.

'Listen to this. *We bought Albion Super Highway through Mastiff Inc., a Cayman Islands associate of Media Corp, the Breitner family trust and Media Corp Pension Scheme 1. On 26 February, all shares in Albion were transferred to Scheme 1. There is therefore no need to take the loss of £2.12 billion through the company's profit and loss account or its balance sheet. Our auditors have confirmed the transaction, and that there has been no breach of our banking covenants or any credit event. On a non-actuarial valuation, Scheme 1 has moved from a surplus of £210 million to a deficit of circa £1.9 billion.*'

344

An accompanying flow chart shows the movement of the liability from a secret corporate vehicle in the Caymans to Media Corp's main pension fund. At the bottom of the chart, preceded by a tiny asterisk, is this statement: *Our lawyers confirm there is no legal obligation on Media Corp to make good the deficit in the fund. The board may wish to consider whether there is a moral obligation.*

No legal obligation. Only a possible moral obligation not to deprive printers and secretaries and subeditors and writers, many of whom had worked for Media Corp and its predecessor companies all their lives, of the pensions for which they had been saving, and which they had been counting on for when they retire. I wonder quite how long the board spent evaluating whether to allow Breitner to dump the loss from his failed investment, his reckless gamble, on thousands of his present and past employees. Maybe a couple of minutes?

Jess looks stunned. 'Bloody hell. Any director worth his salt would have blown the whistle rather than go along with this cover-up.'

'I think Clare was their conscience,' I say. 'Which is why she had to be silenced. What did you find?'

'A paper about the impact of Clare's pension tax reform on Media Corp. It says cash going into the fund would be reduced by around thirty million pounds every year, which on a discounted cash-flow basis increases the liability by about another half a billion.' That would be serious in itself – but it's not the biggest problem for Breitner. 'There's confirmation the tax reform would be a trigger for shareholders to demand an up-to-date pension valuation, to assess the impact of the reform on the solvency of the fund.' Jess gives me a meaningful look. A formal valuation of the Media Corp fund would be a catastrophe for Breitner.

'The massive Albion-size loss would be exposed,' I say. 'Questions would be asked about why pensioners are taking the loss, and not the holding company, or Breitner himself. That is not a debate Breitner would want to have in public.'

'Now listen to this.' Jess reads: '*Neither Media Corp or the Breitner family trust have the funds to make good a deficit of circa £1.9 billion. The triennial valuation of Scheme 1 is due to be published in September 1998. At that juncture it would not be possible to withhold knowledge of the deficit from pensioners and creditors, and there would be a risk of insolvency. We therefore have a limited window to find a solution.*'

I look at the last file. It is headed 'Operation Lazarus', and though all the names are in code, the disguise is gossamer thin. It describes the business case for a takeover of a company called 'Bow Bells' by another called 'Top Dog'. 'Bow Bells' has the one thing that 'Top Dog' needs: cash, hundreds of millions of pounds of it, spewing in every year from advertisers. If Bow Bells' shareholders can be persuaded to exchange their shares for Top Dog's shares, before Top Dog's creditors cotton on to what's gone wrong, Jimmy Breitner will rise from the dead. Exactly as Rep told me.

The Capital acquisition *is* the difference between life and death for Breitner. And Clare came within a whisker of ruining it all for him. *But how did Breitner know?*

My eyes hurt from reading in the dim light. There are far too many thoughts in my head; I'm desperate to nick the contents of Elliott's silver foil package.

'We should put it all back,' says Jess. 'Before Elliott realises.'

'No.' I put my hand protectively on the files. 'We need the evidence. For a while Elliott will think someone took the bag

346

by accident and that it'll be returned. In the meantime we'll write the story.'

'For the *FC*?' She snorts. 'You're joking. Lorimer's share options will be toast if this comes out.'

I'd forgotten about Lorimer and his conflict of interest.

'I'll think about where we place it. But don't take the files anywhere near the office,' I say. 'Just get them home. Photocopy the lot and draft a potential news story and an inside-page explainer.'

'But we've stolen the documents. How can we use them?'

'There's a clear public interest defence. And any complaint by Breitner or Media Corp would be confirmation of their authenticity. Breitner is toast.'

For the first time in weeks, I feel less like prey and more like the hunter. Jess wouldn't mind settling the odd score either.

'What was it Elliott said to me when I asked him in The Groucho if Breitner was planning a bid for Capital? "Crock of shit", or something like that? I'd so love to see his face when we run this.'

'At least now we know why it was so important for him to lie about it.' There's so much to talk through. 'If it's OK with you, I'll swing by later and we can take stock.'

She looks bemused. 'What on earth are you going to do before that?'

'Wilkinson.' The files can seriously damage Breitner, perhaps even bring him down, but they don't prove the link between him and Clare. Outside I can hear the sounds of loud drunk people hailing cabs. The party's thinning out: if Wilkinson hasn't left already, he will soon. I have to get back.

'I'll come with you,' Jess offers.

'He's less likely to open up in front of witnesses. But there is something you can do for me.' My mind is racing ahead, formulating wild plans. 'If you get a call from me in the next couple of hours, don't speak. Hang up and ring Kevin's direct line at the *Globe*. I may need you to distract him.' I scribble his number on a page of my notebook and hand it to her. 'As for all this stuff, take the documents with you but leave the bag behind and everything else in it. Well, maybe take the baggie. If you can find a way to hide his holdall before you leave, so much the better.'

I leave her and run back upstairs.

Chapter 26

THE MOB IN THE LIVERY hall has thinned out. The guests have reconstituted themselves into small intimate groups, like gaggles of geese around an artificial lake. I can't spot Marilyn and I wonder, with a pang of jealousy, if she's found someone else to de-stress with. As someone whose formative years were the free-love 1970s, I shouldn't begrudge Marilyn disappearing to shag someone else. But I do.

Frankie Crowther is lecturing Patrick Munis, who looks bored. Elliott is at the bar, chatting up the *Globe*'s glamorous showbiz editor. I catch his eye, to prove to him that I can't be the tea leaf who pinched his sports bag, as and when he discovers it's gone walkies. But where's Kevin? For an anxious moment I think I've missed him. Then that familiar throaty laugh assails me. He is in a corner, holding court to awestruck young hacks who seemingly view him as some kind of Solomon of the Lobby.

The waitresses are tidying up, but there are still a few glasses of the mediocre white clustered pathetically on the long table at the side of the room. I scoop one up and meander towards Wilkinson. As I approach, I can hear the laughter of men who have had too much to drink, and who excuse their sexism as ironic.

'Did you see Miss Whiplash giving dictation to Peck earlier this evening?' roars Wilkinson, who presumably hasn't spotted me. 'Seems to me she's got him where she wants him.'

A porky young reporter from the *Globe*, whose name I can't remember, roars as though he's never heard anything quite so witty. Public school pillock.

Wilkinson spies me. 'Speak of the devil. How are you, old fruit? I understand you've been a bit tired and emotional.'

I grit my teeth. This is a moment to turn the other cheek. 'Could I pry you away for a moment or two for a quiet word?'

'I'm off duty, old son. You look like you've been sleeping rough. Not a great look for a representative of Her Majesty's Lobby.'

'I've been busy. Assumed you'd want to know I've made progress on that story we were discussing at your shop.'

I have his attention. The one thing Wilkinson and I have in common is that when there is the possibility of reeling in a front-page scoop, we are never off duty, whatever he claims. He apologises to his disciples and we move out of the hall and into the deserted corridor.

'I hope you aren't wasting my time, Peck. What have you found? I'm assuming it's about the sexual habits of our friend Mr Kendall.'

'I've tracked down his boyfriend.' I instantly feel a pang of guilt. Am I really offering up Jeremy as bait? I have no choice. I'll find a way to protect him.

'Tell me more.'

'He works in the Treasury. And I think he is ready to tell all. Kendall shafted him, literally and metaphorically. And he wants revenge.'

'Ah. The noble emotion, the lust for vengeance. What's he got?'

'Apparently Kendall likes to wear a giant man-size nappy and to be spanked.'

'Really? The Chancellor of the Exchequer?' Wilkinson's eyes are on stalks.

'I'm messing with you. I don't really know precisely what they did in bed, apart from the obvious. What I do know is that Kendall took advantage of my contact's junior position and pressurised him to have sex. It was an abuse of his ministerial position. And my contact feels it is his public duty to expose his misconduct, to protect others.'

'Oh, I'm sure your source has a high moral purpose. But let's get serious for a moment. How much does he want?'

'Ah yes. He does need cash. His career will be kaput once he's gone public. And as you know, my paper will only pay journalists, we never pay sources.'

'Thankfully we don't have those absurd scruples. How much?'

'Twenty grand.'

Wilkinson puffs out his cheeks in disbelief. 'Twenty grand! I am not sure we'd pay twenty grand for snaps of Prince Charles bumming a lady-in-waiting. He's going to have to adjust his expectations.'

'I told him that. I said ten grand would be nearer the mark. But we've got a bigger potential problem. Before I got to him, he'd reached out to a school friend who works at the *News of the World*. His friend's on the sports desk, but has already told him that the paper will pay for his story. So if you want it, you're going to have to move fast. I think we should do the deal tonight, or you risk losing it.'

351

'Tonight? Really?'

'My source is desperate. We need to lock him in or he'll go elsewhere.'

I can see Wilkinson smells something's not right. But equally, he knows my reputation for delivering top quality scoops. He's torn, but his most basic instinct is not to see the story go to a rival. He's pumped up by the opportunity to humiliate his competitors, and if he was the worse for a bottle or so of mediocre wine a few minutes ago, he is now sober. 'Ten grand is a lot of money.'

'Yes. But think of the splash headline: "My gay love romp with Chancellor". "Kendall's mint beefcake". Ten grand is cheap at the price.'

'Don't ever apply for a job as a splash sub.' I think I've landed him. Almost. 'One more thing, Peck. What's in it for you? This isn't an *FC* story.'

'Kendall was a shit to my sister. I want him brought down.'

That's close enough to the truth. The words come out raw and bitter. Wilkinson can't doubt my sincerity.

'I'll need to take advice. Give me a minute.' He takes out his phone and walks into a corner in the hall. Left on my own, I ring Jess. 'I think I've won his confidence,' I whisper. 'The plan is to go with him now to Breitner House.'

'Are you sure that's a good idea on your own? Shouldn't I meet you there?'

'It'll be fine. But keep your phone on.'

There's stale cigarette smoke in the air. Right now I'd kill for a fag. *I don't need to smoke, I don't need to smoke, I don't need to smoke.* Wilkinson strides purposefully back, grinning ear to ear at the prospect of tonight's hunt. 'We're on.'

We say goodnight and good luck to Crowther. 'I fear we'll all be joining you on the dark side before too long,' Wilkinson says to him.

I grimace. 'We'll grab lunch once your feet are under the table,' I say, just to be polite. Then I wave at Alex Elliott, whose hand is around the waist of the showbiz editor, and we leave. We are a decidedly odd couple, and I wonder what speculation we've prompted about what we're up to.

The ratio of black-cab supply and demand on a Thursday night on London Wall is decidedly in favour of the customer. Within a couple of minutes, we are ploughing down Moorgate and towards London Bridge. I'm on the foldaway seat, back to the driver, facing Wilkinson. Exhaustion is knocking on my door and I am struggling to keep it at bay.

Wilkinson is relaxed, in his element. 'For a posh broadsheet journo, you've got a nose for a story. You should come and work for a proper newspaper.'

'Very funny.'

'Truthfully, I think Crowther has taken leave of his senses,' he says. 'PRs are the enemy. I can't stand the younger generation coming into our trade who think we're all on the same side. We can't ever be on the same side as PRs. It's a constant war against the forces of darkness.'

I don't say what I am thinking, that he's always doing seedy deals with dark forces to land the stories he wants. As am I. But at least his heart is in the right place. We're all fucking hypocrites, but it's better to be a hypocrite than to aspire to PR.

'You know I am part of that younger generation,' I say.

'Yeah, but you seem to have come into the trade for the right reasons.'

'And what would they be?'

'To cause trouble. Not to stick your tongue up the backsides of the rich and famous.'

'I'll take that as a compliment.' And I do, because for all that I loathe Wilkinson's politics and ethics, he is a pro who has broken more stories over the past thirty years than many newspapers achieve in their history. If the *Globe* ever stopped selling itself on its daily menu of tits and bums and bile, its journalism might be noticed.

The glass on the front of Breitner House is a forbidding jet black. Even seeing the owner's name above the door gives me a shiver. The security guard checks Wilkinson's pass, types my name into his computer and waves us through the bank of turnstiles.

Upstairs, the newsroom is not quite empty. A brace of night editors will stay almost until dawn, until it's too late to slip a late-breaking story into a very last edition. One, to my surprise, is doing *The Times* crossword. The other is reading Proust, the Scott Moncrieff translation in its famous sky-blue jacket. Really.

Wilkinson greets them. 'I need to have a quiet word with young fellow-me-lad here. Can you toddle off for ten minutes and take a fag break?'

They don't need telling twice and walk to the river side of the office into a communal room containing a coffee machine.

'Right,' says Wilkinson, taking two large keys from a desk drawer. I follow him over to the safe I saw before, where he kept the photographs of Clare and Jeremy. His hands show a slight tremor and it takes him a moment of fiddling with the keys and cursing under his breath to open the heavy steel door.

While he's distracted, I reach into my pocket. I don't dare take out the phone in case he notices, but I redial the last number I called. Jess's. I place my finger over the small speaker, so that when she says hello, KT can't hear.

Before he opens the door, I say in a very loud voice – which I hope Jess can hear – 'I'm dying for a cigarette. Could I bum one?'

Wilkinson chucks the packet at me, and his Bic lighter, and then returns to the safe. While his back is turned, I take the phone out of my pocket, note that Jess seems to be on the line and hang up.

The safe swings open.

'The crown jewels,' says Wilkinson with a flourish. 'You can look, but no touching.'

The safe has two shelves. On the top are a series of manilla folders, some bulging with documents and photos, others so slim I wonder if there's anything inside. Wilkinson can see me gawping. 'Sadly if I told you what's in these, I'd have to kill you. But take it from me, if most of this stuff became public, some of the most famous and revered people in the country would struggle to find work on the buses.'

On the bottom shelf is a scruffy wooden box made out of plywood. Wilkinson pulls it out and lifts the lid. There are piles of banknotes inside it: tens, twenties and fifties, some crisp and new, others dirty and creased, rubber-banded into bundles. Thousands of pounds. And wedged down the side is an old-fashioned, slightly worn red ledger, the sort you can buy for a couple of quid in WH Smith.

Wilkinson takes out the box. 'I'm not going to give you the full ten grand tonight. Tell your source he can have two grand up front and the rest on delivery.'

I nod. Almost instantaneously there is the faint but unmistakeable sound of a landline ringing. To Wilkinson, it is as distinct as a dog whistle. 'That's funny,' he says. 'That's the phone in my office. I'd better take it. Might be the boss.' He looks rattled. The chain of authority in this place is clear.

He closes the safe door, but doesn't lock it, and almost jogs the twenty yards to his room. Over his shoulder he shouts, 'Keep your hands off the money! I know how much is there.'

As soon as he's looking the other way, I reach across to the box and take out the ledger. It's thick with entries. What I have in my hands is the *Boys' Book of Bungs*. In normal circumstances I would be orgasming at the thought of it, scanning every entry to see who the *Globe* paid for what story. But I have no time. Goodness alone knows what fiction Jess has concocted to keep Wilkinson on the phone, but at some point he'll smell a rat and rush back.

The ledger is in my lap and I have my back to Wilkinson's office so he can't see what I'm doing. Even so, I have to be quick. Heart in mouth, I go to the last page of entries and skim. There are withdrawals most days, typically for two hundred quid or less. For each entry, there's a date, an amount, a codeword or number, and then the initials of the employee making the withdrawal. This is double-entry bookkeeping that shows the cost of outing cocaine-snorting soap stars and two-timing celebrities.

There's no date on the envelope we found in Deyna's house, but I can guess when the money would have changed hands. Clare's 'accident' was on the third of March: and there, on the

356

very same day, I find what I'm looking for, the only entry for which there's no description, just a blank space. Five thousand pounds. No code number, but two angular initials scored in blue biro for the authorisation. 'KW.'

'Kevin Wilkinson,' I mutter under my breath.

'For fuck's sake, Peck, I told you not to touch anything.'

Wilkinson looms over me. I was too engrossed to hear his return over the hum of air-conditioning. I stand up, refusing to be intimidated.

'Why did you take out five grand on the third of March?' I ask. 'What was it for? Who did you give the money to?'

'That's none of your business.'

'You're wrong. That money was for the man who killed my sister. I have every right to know your role in this.'

Wilkinson is rattled. Breitner is a monster, but Wilkinson is just a hack on the payroll who surely has a conscience.

'I seem to remember that only a few minutes ago you were heaping scorn on journalists who stick their tongues up the arses of the rich and powerful,' I remind him. 'Who are you protecting by not telling me?'

I've struck a nerve.

'I never knew why the money needed to be handed over.'

'Well, that's convenient for you. I'm telling you now, you were paying off a thug. A hitman.' I have to summon all my self-control. 'You realise you are an accessory to the killing of my sister?'

'I don't believe you! I was just doing what I was told.'

'That's your defence? Pathetic. Who gave you your orders?' I am so wound up that my early warning system fails.

'I did, of course.'

The menacing Glasgow Gorbals accent. *Shit.*

I turn to face Jock Streatham. He's wearing a grey suit with a faint lilac check in it, a Tory-blue knitted silk tie, and black Gucci slip-ons, polished so bright they reflect the overhead lights. His sharp-edged cheekbones, normally a pallid white, are pinkish, as though he's recently done vigorous exercise.

And he's brought company. A little way back – but not too far – stand two sharp-suited minders who, like Streatham, have skinhead haircuts. They are the kind of security guards who've recently retired from those parts of the armed forces that specialise in hurting people with close, unarmed combat. I'm trapped.

'I suppose you rang him while you were in your office,' I say to Wilkinson. But that can't be right. There's no way Streatham could have got here so quickly.

'Don't be stupid,' says Streatham. 'He rang me as soon as you said you needed ten grand. Do you think Kevin has the authority to hand over that kind of money to any Tom, Dick or flying woofta?'

Wilkinson suddenly looks grey and old. 'What was all that about you and I being the same kind of trouble-making journalists?' I say to him. 'You're just another company man. You might as well be in PR.'

'Don't be an arsehole, Gil,' says Streatham. The minders move a couple of steps closer. 'Let's go somewhere we can have a chat.'

'Fine,' I mutter.

We leave Wilkinson standing by the open safe. If there's honour among thieves like me, he should feel ashamed. But I'm not banking on it. Streatham leads me across the newsroom, with his two minders in lockstep behind. The night editors are nowhere to be seen; I presume they've been ordered to make themselves scarce. There are no witnesses.

'Mr Breitner had high hopes for you, Gilbert,' says Streatham, calling the elevator. 'He still does. He thinks you're a fine journalist, maybe even editor material. But he is worried you are not seeing things properly.'

'I think I'm seeing things with great clarity.' I consider telling him how much I know, and the evidence I collected from Elliott's holdall, but I think better of it. I don't want to endanger Jess. And, right now, my assumption is that professions of ignorance are more likely to keep me safe.

The elevator doors open. The minders are immediately behind me, leaving me no option but to get in.

'Mr Breitner sent you to the Minster so you could get the support you need,' Streatham continues. Ah. That was Breitner's idea, not Lorimer's – I should have guessed. 'Clearly, your psychological condition is more fragile than we realised. Since you chose to reject the voluntary approach, he thinks you need treatment in a more secure, bespoke facility.'

'You're kidnapping me?' The elevator creaks as we descend. There is an unreal, nightmarish quality to what's happening.

'Don't be ridiculous. We're not doing anything of the kind. You've had something of a traumatic time and, in your distressed condition, you forced poor Mr Wilkinson to bring you to our offices and then made fantastical allegations against him and us. As your employer, with a duty of care, we are simply checking you into a facility that will make sure that you have the rest you need.

'We're going to drive you there now. Steve and Ali here will take it in turns to stay with you, for your own good, until we're sure you're fit and healthy again.'

The elevator pings and the doors slide open. The minders, get out first and the one I think is Steve walks to the glass turnstiles in the middle of the ground floor reception, while the other matches me pace for pace at my side.

'I suppose I should be grateful Breitner didn't just have me knocked off my bicycle,' I say.

'Mr Peck, as I said, you are suffering from wild imaginings. You just need a bit of time away from all the noise. Mr Breitner only wants the best for you.'

I'm beginning to identify with Mr Breitner's dog. I see a stretch Mercedes with tinted windows waiting for us on the kerb outside. I am more certain that I mustn't get in that car than I have been of anything in my life. But my options are limited.

Suddenly, there's an electric click. The main doors are locked, but there's a night door to the left and the guard has just buzzed it open. A woman with a blonde ponytail and a figure-hugging white top skips in, the rubber of her tennis shoes squeaking on the granite floor. She walks past the security guard behind his desk, scans her pass, and comes through the revolving turnstile. She's got her Walkman headphones on and is oblivious to me. It's only when she's through that she spots us. And – thank goodness – smiles warmly at me.

She takes off the headphones. 'Gil?' She is surprised to see me, as well she might be.

'Ange, darling.'

She's Ange Levinson, the *Globe*'s royal editor. More relevantly, she was on the same journalism course as me at Cardiff, after I left Oxford. I've never been happier to see anyone.

The two minders edge away. If they are escorting me on my last ever journey, they are smart enough not to want anyone to remember them being here with me.

'What are you doing here?' she asks.

'I might just as well ask you the same question.'

'Princess Di story. Just got some new snaps of her leaving that Chelsea gym with someone we don't recognise. The editor wants me to find out everything I can before conference tomorrow. And you know me, I was never one for sleep.'

I move closer to her. Closer to the barriers. I think she may be flirting with me, and I've never been so grateful. The thing about Ange is she was always a brilliant, instinctive journalist, the best in our year. She gives me a quizzical look and I am pretty sure she knows something is up. She's taken in the minders and can see Streatham loitering in the shadows near the lifts. I assume she recognises him. Everyone in our trade does.

'What did you say you were doing here?'

'I've been working on a project with Kevin Wilkinson. It's an interesting story. I'd love to tell you about it.' I've noticed that the guard on the reception desk – not a young man from the special services, but a paunchy bloke in his fifties, probably an ex-copper gone to seed – has moved and is standing by the night door. He's left it open, having clocked that we are leaving.

I have just one chance. *Now.* Without warning, I lunge forward and vault over the glass swing door that's next to the turnstiles, right hand on the stanchion. Ange gapes as one of the heavies lunges at me and I almost fall. But he misses, and I charge for the exit. I can't afford to look back: I just run, faster than I've ever run before. I hear Streatham shout, 'Shut the fucking door!' but too late. The night watchman clearly does not want to be bashed by a mad hack and actually gets out of the way as I career through the exit, head down, like a wounded rhino.

There's a nip in the night air of this late April, which only spurs me on. No time to think. Just run. As fast as I can. North on to Tooley Street – where, *thank you, God*, a night bus is clanking and clunking along. I get ahead of it and frantically wave at the driver, but we're nowhere near a stop and it's obviously more than the driver's job is worth to do me a favour and save my life. Fuck him! As for black cabs, not a single one has its light on.

My lungs hurt with the effort of sprinting. Ahead, I spy the towering cylindrical vats of the Sarson's Vinegar factory. The acidic cloud blowing from it permeates my skin and makes my eyes water. I'm now on a narrow Victorian side street, all alone, as far as I can tell. Somewhere behind me I can hear the clatter of the leather soles of Streatham's minders as they try to find me. Are they armed? It doesn't really matter. I don't stand a chance if they get themselves close enough to make contact. I never took the hands-as-lethal-weapons option at Oxford. All I can do is keep running and not look back.

I go through the darkness of a wide railway bridge. Why is there no one around? I fumble in my pocket for the Nokia. I need to call Jess, warn her, get help, but I can't stop long enough. I try to work out where I might find people I could plead with to call the police, or act as potential witnesses to whatever Streatham's men have in mind for me. The railway lines mean London Bridge station can't be far. But where?

I'm suddenly boxed in. On one side of the street, the railway arches make an unbroken rampart, gleaming with the rusting metal signs nailed above them. HAND CAR WASH. SERVICE AND MOT. Opposite, there's just a long wall of builder's hoardings, plywood boards covered in graffiti, topped with razor wire.

Light strobes the broken ground from a train passing overhead. I glance back and feel a brief moment of hope. My pursuers haven't rounded the corner yet. Do they know I'm here?

And then I spy it. A hole in a fence. Where two of the boards meet, someone has pried them apart to make a narrow, V-shaped gap. No time to think. I charge across the street, crouch down and squeeze myself in, praying that Breitner's minders don't see my shadow inching through.

I've come out into an open stretch of broken ground. Some kind of undeveloped wasteland, probably new desolation caused by developers, possibly one of the very last untouched bombsites from the war. I can't afford to run too fast here: there are too many broken bricks, old prams, bags of rubbish, pieces of smashed glass. I make my way gingerly across it, breathing hard. I've got a stitch in my side and the blood is pounding hard in my ears.

I hear the syncopation of another throbbing beat, a resonant bass sound. For a moment I can't locate it, but then I realise it's coming from ahead, from a huge brick warehouse that rises up where the rubble ends. Lights flash and dance in filthy windows on the first floor. It must be a rave. And that means a sea of people. If I can only get inside, I'll be surrounded. Safe.

I hear a shout behind me. Breitner's thugs. I curse myself for not closing the gap in the fence. They must have seen it and followed me in.

'Stop being an arsehole!' one shouts. 'We just want to talk. No need to run.'

He must be fucking joking. There's some kind of door to the warehouse. If I can get to it, maybe it will be open, a passage to freedom. It's only twenty yards. I try to sprint again, but the ground is treacherous and uneven. With every step I risk tumbling on a loose brick or gashing myself on the metal of an old bed or chair and I daren't look back.

I'm closing in on the shed. Fifteen yards ... Ten ... I can see light through the door frame, hear the soaring of a synthesiser riff. I am desperate to be in there, in a state of MDMA induced bliss, oblivious to the existence of Breitner, or Streatham, or Ali, or Steve.

With a crunch, my foot lands heavily and my ankle bends. Pain knifes through it, so acutely I drop to my knee. *I won't surrender.* I stand and struggle on, but every step sends agony shooting up through my leg. Broken? Sprained? It doesn't matter. I can't run any more. I'm hobbled, barely able to hop forward. And then my shoe bangs against a piece of rusted iron, catches, and pitches me onto the ground again. This time I bang my knee on a lump of concrete.

Footsteps crunch remorselessly on the rubble right behind me. I can hear laboured breathing, and the *whip-whap* of legs in suit trousers rubbing together.

In the sky above, the gantries of cranes are silhouetted against the city glow. The flashing light of a solitary plane high in the sky. What I would give to be in it, flying literally anywhere. But I'm stuck. And a fleshy face breathes on mine.

'Looks like you've hurt yourself, young man,' he says. 'Steve and I will help you up.'

All the fight in me drains away. One on each side, they hoick me under my arms and more-or-less carry me back across the desolate plot. At the gap in the fence, they take no chances. Steve goes first, Ali pushes me through next, and I'm back by the railway arches, a prisoner.

Suddenly the cocktail of pain, cold and fear has me shivering uncontrollably. The black stretch Mercedes I saw earlier is parked on the other side of the street. Ali and Steve guide me across. One opens the rear door, the other ushers me inside, one hand on the top of my head so I don't hit it on the door frame. It's all very Met Police. If only they were the Met.

A blast of warm air hits me as I enter the limousine. I sit on the bench facing the back. Staring at me from the opposite seat is a man who looks as broad as he is tall. I've met him once before. There's no mistaking the deep and brutal contours of that face under the yellow light of the ceiling lamp.

James Breitner.

on the other side of the street. 48 and Steve guide me across. Once more the road along the other makes me inside, one hand on the top of our head and don't trip on the door frame. It's OK? Blue Pages, If only they were the Mrs.

At last, stronger at lift me as I carry the limousine I sit on the bed sitting the back changing from the opposite seat is a man who looks up, head. I let it sit. I've seen him once as there's no mistaking the deep and broad outline of that face under the yellow light of the sitting room.

James Brother.

Chapter 27

ALMOST SOUNDLESSLY, THE CAR PULLS out. I notice that the original chauffeur is left on the pavement: one of the security men must have replaced him. The soundproofing is so complete that the lights of London are like a movie with the sound turned down. I hear the click of the doors being locked from the control panel in the front. No escape.

I face the back window, opposite Breitner. Jock Streatham sits beside me. Ali and Steve are behind a glass barrier in the front seats. I don't know where they're taking me, and I don't ask. In my head I am telling myself, over and over, as an internalised chant, *they're going to kill me, they're going to kill me, they're going to kill me*. It is my way of protecting myself against the worst that could happen. As usual, it is very important to chant it the 'right' number of times. Nine should do it.

Now. Jump.

'Why did you murder Clare Peck, my sister?'

Breitner does not miss a beat or bat an eyelid. He is harder than a steel girder. I understand how he's absorbed the stress of constructing an enormous worldwide business while being such a bogeyman for so many.

'I like my journalists to ask challenging questions. It's why my newspapers are so successful. But I don't expect my people to make fools of themselves by talking rubbish.'

'Mr Breitner never met your sister,' says Streatham.

'You hired a hitman named Henryk Deyna to knock her off her bike. You paid him five thousand pounds in cash, from the *Globe*'s newsroom safe.'

'I have never heard of anyone called Henryk Deyna.'

There's the hint of a grin as he says it – because he doesn't have to demean himself by issuing an explicit order to get what he wants. His *modus operandi* would be to talk out loud about his ambitions, needs and frustrations with his courtiers and retainers. Like a pharaoh, he would simply assume that his revealed will would become deed, without the bother of issuing an instruction. When the *Globe* remorselessly destroyed the credibility of the previous leader of the Labour Party, Roy Parker, everyone knew it was following Breitner's agenda, though he never told the editor how to execute the devastating character assassination. In an agenda-setting pre-election speech, Parker broached the social imperative of breaking up press giants, like Media Corp. This was the warrant for his execution. Within days the *Globe* was digging up and publishing story after story about Parker's student links with the IRA and the PLO, anything that showed him unfit to be prime minister and have his finger on the nuclear button. He never recovered.

Clare was more deft. But Breitner knew she posed more of a threat to him than Parker had ever done. She had to be silenced. His lieutenants knew their duty. An accident was arranged. Nothing could ever be traced back to Breitner. Not even a nod or a wink. But I don't have to pin the murder on him to hurt him.

'You've heard of Clare. She devised the plan, adopted by Kendall, to raise substantial sums, billions a year, from pension funds. It would have allowed desperately needed money to go to schools and hospitals. It would have helped most of us, especially those with the least, while hurting almost no one. Except for a billionaire whose fortune turns out to be a fraud, a lie. You. So Robin Muller was despatched to put the squeeze on the Chancellor of the Exchequer. And you armed Muller with what the Globe had found out about Kendall's preference for young men. You blackmailed Kendall.'

Breitner says nothing.

'Clare guessed what Muller had on Kendall because she was counselling Kendall's lover. What she couldn't understand was why Schon cared. So she went digging. And she was smart, smarter than me. And just as persistent.'

My voice starts to rasp. I am not going to give Breitner the satisfaction of seeing me cry. I swallow and blink to fight the tears.

'Thanks to a banker who takes your money but holds you in contempt, she located the black hole in your pension fund.' Breitner winces. 'She knew all about your disastrous investment in Albion and how you sicked it on your pensioners. She was going to shame you in public, hang you out to dry. She threatened to ruin you.' I am starting to speculate, to busk. But I know Clare would never have kept quiet about any of this. She would always confront the villain, the bad guy. Like Dad, her hatred of injustice would have made her blind to the personal risks.

'She humiliated you, even more than your fucking dog humiliated you.'

369

The car glides over Westminster Bridge. Through the tinted windows I see the Houses of Parliament and Big Ben lit up. Normally I feel pride at what the Palace of Westminster represents, a bulwark of democracy and freedom against the autocrats and tyrants. Tonight all I feel is how the thug opposite me has captured and corrupted so many of its occupants.

Breitner has his gaze clamped on me. Unblinking, unsmiling, a predatory beast biding his time before tearing me limb from limb. He leans forward and speaks with the precision of a barrister.

'To be clear, neither I nor anyone in this motor vehicle ever met your sister or spoke with her.'

No emotion.

'I didn't say she spoke with *you*. But she spoke to people close to you, including Kendall. Word got back. You knew she was going to destroy you.'

'Supposition. Hearsay. You are a better journalist than that.'

Streatham breaks his silence. 'If you ever tried to run that story, Mr Breitner would take steps to ensure that you wouldn't even get a job on a freesheet in the Hebrides.'

There is malice in his eyes, anger pulsing off him. He thinks he can intimidate me. He's misjudged. When I am confronted with another man's rage, my habitual response is to lash out. It's not a good look.

'Shut the fuck up, Streatham. I can sink all of you. You committed criminal fraud.'

'You don't have proof because it's not true.'

'Albion Super Highway and its colossal losses was transferred from your Cayman's vehicle to the Media Corp pension fund, the two-billion-pound loss on your crappy bet shunted to your employees. That in itself would be of interest to the Serious Fraud Office. And then there is the little matter of Operation Lazarus, the takeover of Capital TV, on a false prospectus. Is there any mention of Scheme 1's black hole in your offer document for Capital? No. There. Isn't. When I publish, you are toast.'

I am glaring at Streatham as I say this, my jaw clenched. I have enough self-awareness to know that I look like a maniac. Streatham doesn't like it. 'Calm down, laddie. Calm down.'

Breitner is more composed. 'These are unsubstantiated allegations.'

'I'm afraid not. I have documented proof. If you doubt me, perhaps you should telephone your colleague Mr Elliott.'

Breitner's eyes dart to Streatham. I've got him.

'Mr Lorimer would never print it. You're finished.'

'Are you threatening me with losing my job?' I actually laugh out loud. 'Do you honestly think I care about that? Or that I'll have any trouble getting it into print?'

Truthfully, I am not convinced any paper would print it. There is a weird and unhealthy understanding among rival newspaper proprietors and editors that they almost never write about each other. But Breitner is less clubbable than most newspaper owners. And as I mentioned to Jess, there's always *Private Eye.*

'Except that you're in my car,' Breitner hisses, leaning in slightly. 'And unless I am mistaken, I don't see any kind of keyboard in here.'

The Merc has navigated Hyde Park Corner and is gathering pace down Park Lane and towards Knightsbridge. Past Harvey Nichols, and the Versailles of department stores, Harrods, on towards the great Victorian museums.

371

'Are you trying to frighten me?' In my head, I say – three times – *you cunt, you cunt, you cunt.* It's fortunate I'm so wound up, otherwise my body might remember to be paralysed by fear.

'Gil, my friend, you've been under intolerable strain,' says Streatham. 'You were devastated by the death of your sister, your career has not been going in the direction you wanted, your love life is a mess, you have an unfortunate drug habit. The tragic truth is that if you decided this was the moment to end it all, perhaps with an overdose, everyone – even your nearest and dearest – would understand. Though of course we'd all be terribly sad.'

Streatham is telling me this is my last chance to save myself. Thank God for my hyper-focus.

'How naïve do you think I am? Do you believe there would be no consequences if I were to disappear? Am I the sort of person who comes into a gang fight with a water pistol?'

This is not going how Breitner expected. His knee has gone into spasm. It looks like a tic, a recognition that *he* is not in control of events. I am.

'I have copies of all the relevant files.' I can't do anything to put Jess in danger, so I improvise. 'They are in four separate secure locations. And I have given clear instructions that if I do not make contact for forty-eight hours, those documents are to be released to *Private Eye*, the BBC, the *Sentinel* and the Metropolitan Police. Oh, and just in case you don't know, Kim Jansen at the Met is an old friend. I've already provided her with the relevant background.'

I am a creative genius. Yes, I spoke to Kim weeks ago, and she told me I was wasting my time. Yes, Jess has Elliott's files. Beyond that, it's grade A nonsense. I make a mental note to create those copies if I am ever out of this hell-bound limousine.

'You might want to consider whether writing my obituary is worth all the bother it will cause you.'

For a moment, all I can hear is the hiss of the air conditioning. Breitner is staring hard at me. I read no meaning in his eyes. Has he bought my bluff? Or am I still a fly to be swatted, an untrainable dog to be shot.

He breathes out. 'Mr Peck, I am sorry we got off on the wrong foot. As I have told you before, I admire your journalistic persistence and insights.' He sounds as if he's reading a statement his lawyers advised him to make. 'But I must advise you, for the sake of your own reputation, that if you were ever to print, or even hint, at any of what you have just suggested, we would sue you through the British courts for every penny attached to your name. And then we would sue you for every penny you might earn for the rest of your life.'

He presses a button and the glass dividing screen comes down. 'Stephen, there's been a change of plan. We'll drop Mr Peck here.'

I feel relief, mixed with disappointment. I wanted to see him in pain. He won't give me that satisfaction. Breitner's gaze flicks back to me, as if surprised to see me still there.

'I think, Mr Peck, you may exaggerate your importance.'

Before I can work out what that means, or where we are, the car pulls over. Ali opens the door. 'Mr Breitner would like you to leave the car now, sir.' I step out, wincing at having weight on my ankle again. Disconcertingly, Streatham follows. Why? The door closes behind me, and Breitner is driven away. I'm in the middle of an empty street with Streatham. And Ali.

We're outside a pub, the Old City Arms. In front of us is the monstrous entrance to a bridge, two great green blocks on either side of the road, ornamented with scrollwork and acanthus leaves like a pair of Victorian mausoleums. They're the anchors of a suspension bridge: a chain of iron slats swoops up from them towards a pair of turrets. To the sides, I can see the black gleam of the river flowing fast underneath. This is not my part of town, but I am pretty sure we're on the north side of Hammersmith Bridge.

'We're going for a walk, sonny,' says Streatham.

My instinct is to run, but my crocked leg won't let me. The bridge has been closed to road traffic, except buses, for the past three months. At this time of night, it's empty. Streatham leads the way. Ali stays uncomfortably close behind me. We're on a narrow pedestrian path that runs along the edge of the bridge, separated from the road by a low rail of girders. My only escape would be to jump into the Thames, which is no escape. All I can do is hobble along, our footsteps ringing loud on the iron bridge.

Streatham decides it's time for a parable. 'You know the IRA tried to blow this up last year?' I did know. I'm a fucking journalist. The biggest bomb ever placed on the British mainland – forty pounds of Semtex – but the detonators failed to ignite it. 'Joke is, when the council examined the bridge to check the Provos hadn't left anything behind, they found the whole thing was falling apart. The murdering bastards actually saved the bridge.' He snorts. 'You know the moral of the story? What doesn't kill you makes you stronger. And you are nowhere near scratching us.'

While he's been talking, we've walked to the centre of the bridge. The central portion is covered in scaffolding which they've put up for the repairs, shrouded in plastic sheeting like a Christo installation. Below me, I can hear the gush of the Thames between the piers.

Streatham stops where the water is deepest and the current strongest. I am suddenly aware of the chill of the night air. The fear that I've been suppressing all night is pulsing in my every nerve.

'What are you doing? Breitner instructed you to let me go.'

'What Mr Breitner says, and what he means, are not the same thing.'

For a moment I am paralysed. But only for a moment. *Kill the cunts. Kill the cunts. Kill the cunts.*

'How the mighty are fallen. The great Jock Streatham, once the most feared editor on Fleet Street, courted by princes and prime ministers, now just a two-bit thug. You're pathetic.' I am freezing and my teeth are chattering. I'm not going quietly. 'Did you enjoy organising the killing of my sister? After you ordered Wilkinson to bung five grand to Deyna, did Jimmy pat you on the head and say well done. Do you take pride in your servile duties?'

Tonight is different for Streatham. He is having to get his own hands dirty, actually do the deed himself. Does he have any qualms? I will needle him.

'You must really worship Breitner to demean yourself like this to save *his* skin. How does it feel, Jock, having to look me in the eye rather than issuing an instruction to a lackey from miles away? Are you feeling excited? Have you got a hard on? Will you go home and fuck your wife, filled with the satisfaction of doing a job for the boss? Or perhaps you will stop off first at the office in the hope that Jimmy will let you suck him off?'

'Fuck off!'

I need to keep him talking just long enough for a night bus or cyclist to come past, so that I can scream for help. Streatham takes the bait.

'Do you think anyone is going to miss you, Mr Peck? It's smarmy cunts like you, who think you are better than the rest of us, who are ruining this country. You put on airs as a great crusading reporter, but you wouldn't know a proper story if you were standing in the middle of the M1 and it came steaming towards you.'

'Actually, Jock, when I started out you were one of my heroes. I used to think you were a journalist. But you were always a nonce, weren't you?'

Wind off the river makes the plastic sheeting snap and rattle. To my ears, it is as loud as gunshots. To my right, I hear the rustle of Ali reaching into his jacket. I don't dare take my eyes off Streatham, but I have a bad feeling about Ali.

'Are you planning on shooting me? A bullet wound is harder to explain than a girl getting knocked off her bike?'

'I don't think that's the scoop. No. You were out on the razzle, as usual, and became maudlin about your sister in your cups. You came here to end it all. When you jumped, you bashed your head on the side of the bridge as you fell and were knocked unconscious. It's a spring tide. Strong current, lots of water. You had no chance. Such a sad story. The *FC*'s tribute won't leave a dry eye in the house.'

It is an odd experience, hearing the report of one's own demise. He presumably thinks I will surrender to the inevitable. But I've never believed in determinism, always in free will. As a journalist, what I do is change the course of history, never give in to it. I am not going to let this desiccated husk of a once-great hack tell me how my story ends. Fuck him. It's personal between him and me. For Breitner and Deyna, silencing Clare was just business. But I've been dancing around Streatham since I was a cub reporter. He's always known who I am, yet he had no compunction in arranging the murder of my sister, no matter what the collateral harm to me and my family. I won't stand for it.

'We've known each other a long time. Don't make it harder than it has to be,' he says. God, the narcissism: as if I care whether he's finding it difficult.

Ali pads nearer, behind me. My neck tenses; in my chest it feels as if a hand is squeezing my heart. I assume oblivion is at hand and I brace myself for the impact of a cosh on my skull. I move near the fence, the guard rail, so I can keep an eye on them both.

I look around in desperation. Surely someone must be coming? But the bridge is empty. I pat my pockets, wondering if there's anything I can use as a weapon. Maybe I could use my pen to gouge out Streatham's eye? I don't have a pen – VW lady drove off with it – but there is something. A slim, oblong piece of plastic. My Sony tape recorder. I pull it out and wave it above my head, a warrior brandishing his spear.

'What the fuck?' says Streatham.

'Do you remember these things, Jock? They make a record of what people say?'

Streatham goes still. 'Is it on?'

No need to answer. He can see the red light blinking in the darkness.

'How long has it been going?'

'Long enough.' Somehow, I manage to force out an approximation of a defiant laugh. 'How thick do you think I am?

Everything you and Breitner said in the car, everything you've said just now, it's on tape.'

This is not true. I pressed the 'record' button seconds ago when I took it out of my pocket.

'Go ahead, throw me in the river or whatever you have planned. I can't stop you. But it'll make interesting listening for the police.'

'There's nothing incriminating on there.'

'Really? You really think that the police won't want to speak to Jimmy Breitner and Jock Streatham and their security guard Ali, the last people who saw me alive, about why they killed my sister, Clare Peck, and me?' I am shouting deliberately, so that Streatham knows the recorder will pick up everything and he can't escape being implicated in my death. I take a step away, and my legs are now touching the guardrail. 'You know the great thing about magnetic tape? It can survive exposure to water. So when the police fish my body and the recorder out of the river, what will they do when they hear the great Jock Streatham telling me he's already written my obituary and how I'm going to have an accident and fall in the Thames?'

He puts out his hand. 'Give it to me!'

'I don't think so.'

I can see he's about to make a grab for it. Between him and Ali, they could easily wrestle it off me. Awkwardly, I put my free hand on the wooden handrail behind me and push myself up and on to it. It's a near-suicidal gambit. I'm tottering on a nine-inch wide strip of bleached wood. There's nothing to hold. In front are Streatham and Ali; behind me nothing but a 35-foot drop into the black, icy Thames. My body sways with the effort of keeping balanced, trying to take as much weight as possible off my injured ankle. I can feel myself tipping backwards, as if the river wants to pull me down, but if I try to fight it I'll fall face first into Streatham's arms.

If Streatham or Ali lunge for me, they'll knock me over the edge, tape recorder and all.

'Give it up, Gil,' Streatham says. 'Maybe we can talk about this.'

I glance over my shoulder. Should I jump? The dark water gleams like a mirror; where the current puckers around the piers, I can see how rapidly it's flowing. Could I get to the bank, or would it carry me away and under?

A gust of wind hits me. Not much more than a breeze, but it doesn't take much. I wobble back, throw my weight forward for balance. Pain stabs through my ankle and I almost lose my footing completely. I windmill my arms wildly, teetering on the brink.

'You can't stay like that forever,' says Streatham. I notice Ali is edging forwards again. Perhaps he reckons he can grab me and haul me in.

The handrail starts to rumble, vibrate, making it harder still to keep my balance. A bright yellow beam banishes the darkness, picking out our stand-off like a scene on stage. A night bus is coming over the bridge.

Streatham and Ali turn uncertainly towards the light. Will the driver see them? Will he spot me, standing on the bridge rail looking for all the world like a man about to end it all? They are looking at the bus and it's my only chance. I leap – not back into the river, but across to the girder on the other side of the path. Fear and adrenaline, desperation, has turned me into a circus acrobat. I grab a suspension cable to prevent myself falling and then jump onto the road. My ankle is agony but desperation has turned me into a sprinter. The noise of the bus's engine is too close: I can smell the diesel fumes, almost feel the heat of the engine. And behind me Streatham is shouting obscenities. I daren't look back but I can hear his leather shoes land with a snap on the road, then a terrified 'oh fuck', a thud, the squeal of brakes.

I look back. Streatham must have fallen flat on his face when he tried to follow me over the girders, the shiny leather soles of his immaculate loafers providing no grip. It was impossible for the double-decker to avoid him though the driver tried to swerve. The bus has come to an abrupt halt, with its front now blocking the lane for oncoming traffic.

There is a bloody heap of clothes under the chassis. Streatham. Or what *was* Jock Streatham.

The driver jumps out. 'Oy, mate! Come and help me please. Help!' I look across the bridge for Ali, but he's scarpered. His loyalty is to Breitner and the last thing he needs is to be at the scene when the police arrive.

Passengers have got off the bus and started to gather around the body. No one is bothering to attempt CPR. I can hear the bus driver talking to base on his radio. Soon there will be police and ambulances, a thousand questions. I know I should stay. There are plenty of witnesses, so I should be safe. But I don't feel it. Not after everything that's happened. There will be a time for me to talk to the police. Not now. I need to run – hobble – as far away from here as is humanly possible.

In the confusion around Streatham's corpse, I limp north. The hoardings around the scaffolding hide me from view. I'm shaking so hard that if I don't keep moving I'll collapse and never get up. It's only when I'm on the far side of the bridge that I realise I'm still clutching the tape recorder. I try to remember those last exchanges with Streatham. Was there anything he said after I pressed 'record' that might incriminate him, or Breitner?

I rewind for a few seconds, then press play. No sound comes out. I press the 'eject' button. There's no tape. I hurl it away. Plop. It's engulfed by the river.

Another wasted opportunity to secure justice for Clare. And then, against my expectations, a quiet satisfaction creeps over me. Tonight has been a living nightmare. Breitner may be miles away enjoying a glass of vintage Armagnac. But Clare's assassin is strawberry jam. The Pecks, sister and brother, have stopped Streatham getting away with it. This is justice. Rough. Partial. But justice all the same.

I start to take in my surroundings. This area, the no man's land between Hammersmith and Shepherd's Bush, is my least favourite part of London. I've never understood the point of it. Pretty much everywhere else has some kind of history and personality, but this borough seems bereft of everything. Not even the sheer ugliness of south London's brutalism.

I take out my phone as I limp past the rows of anonymous houses and shops. Jess answers before the ringtone can start.

'Where are you?'

'Long story.' Gabbling, I unload everything that's happened since I left the party. I probably sound hysterical, particularly when I get to the part on the bridge. Jess goes so quiet I can't tell if she believes me. I'm not sure whether I'd believe me.

'Streatham is dead.'

'Jesus,' she breathes. 'How are you feeling?'

'I'm fine.' I will be fine.

'You're not. I'll come and get you.'

'Listen to me.' I'm almost shouting in my impatience. 'I told Breitner that I had copies of all the incriminating documents. I didn't mention you, but it won't take them long to cotton on. They know we work as a team and someone will have seen us at Frankie's party.' Suddenly, I'm terrified for Jess. 'Don't go out. Stay where you are and get that story written as quick as you can.'

'You think the story's what matters right now?' She sounds almost as hysterical as I do.

'It's the only thing that can save us.' Most of my thoughts are swirling chaos, but this I can see as clear as day. 'As long as they think they can suppress what happened, we're in danger. As soon as the story is out, they've nothing to gain by coming after us, and a lot to lose.'

She pauses. She can't fault the logic. 'Lorimer will never run this.'

'You're right. But I have an idea.'

I explain my plan. She doesn't like it, and nor do I, much, but we don't have a choice.

'Do you need me to come and get you, boss?'

'I'll be fine. Write the story, get some sleep, and keep the door locked.'

We ring off. I've been so engrossed, I hadn't noticed I've come all the way up Shepherd's Bush Road and have reached the corner of Shepherd's Bush Green. It's a quaint, rural-idyll of a name for what is actually a triangle of exhaust-poisoned grass in the middle of a traffic gyratory. Streatham's death is a result, but I have to settle accounts with Breitner too. As a minimum, I want him bust, forced back to South Africa in ignominy, no longer the maker and breaker of governments, just a forgotten failed businessman. Clare would approve.

It's 2 a.m. I'm on my own, hurt, in a part of London I can't stand. It's time I went home, though the only one waiting for me is a cat who is even more of a sociopath than me. I feel an uncontrollable desire to make a telephone call to someone I never feel the urge to call.

Dad answers surprisingly quickly, given the time of the night. He's alert. Why wasn't he asleep?

'Gil. Is everything all right?' There's concern in his voice, and too late I clock how insensitive I am. This is how he heard about Clare; now every unexpected phone call could be a harbinger of disaster.

'Everything's fine, Dad,' I try to reassure. 'Nothing to worry about.'

A silence. He's probably waiting for me to explain why I'm calling at this ungodly time of night.

'Are you up? Can I come over?'

'Of course.' Whatever he was expecting, it wasn't that. 'I'll put the kettle on.' Another pause. Then, tentatively, as if he's feeling his way carefully, 'It'll be nice to see you.'

'You too.'

'Are you sure everything is all right?'

'Yes. I promise, Dad.' I've been angry for so long, with my family, my work, myself, that I forgot something that matters more than everything else. Dad had a daughter. I had a sister. She's gone. And that means Dad and I have something big and important in common, to share. We can help each other. And there is something else, too. One very bad man is dead. Breitner is going down. Gil and Clare, we were always a great team. We always will be.

'Actually, I'm pretty good.'

Chapter 28

E LECTION DAY IS THE EMPTIEST news day of the year. For a political editor, there's mileage in ringing candidates for on-the-ground colour; or chatting with those running the national campaigns, to get a sense of how they think citizens are exercising their democratic right. But until the polls close at 10 p.m., it's all surmise and speculation. The best thing to do is pretty much nothing, to preserve energy for the overnight marathon. This is the first day I am willingly following Lorimer's instruction, and taking a day off.

It's a proper English spring, warm, blossomy. I'm on the upper deck of the number 24 bus, travelling up Camden High Street towards Primrose Hill. I'm acting on an impulse and I'm not sure it's a good one. I woke up thinking that, on this of all days, I wanted to hang out with my nephews, Clare's children. Perhaps as unexpected is that when I rang Charles, he was pleased.

'You can meet them at the school gates and walk them home if you like,' he said. 'It would be nice if the au pair could have the afternoon off.'

'Sure. But do you think they'll recognise me?'

'You'd be surprised. Since the funeral they've been asking when Uncle Gil would come over. Kids are smart.'

'Yours seem to be.' *Clare's.*

The bus's engine rumbles as it sits at idle. There are roadworks ahead and we're having to wait while an apparently endless queue of traffic comes through the other way. I pick up the paper in my lap and gaze again at the front page.

It's the *Globe*, from my daily delivered pile. I brought it with me as a cherished prize, the spoils of war. It shows that I've won. That Clare won. In some ways, it's a *Globe* classic. There's a huge picture of the PM's head peeping out of the top of a dustbin, under the massive headline TIME TO BIN RAMSEY. And in only marginally smaller letters underneath, it says TODD WILL CLEAN UP BRITAIN. The accompanying editorial is, if anything, less subtle. Its conversion to Todd's Labour is breathlessly excitable. And, if I am frank, a bit embarrassing. Breitner knows that the world in which he is all powerful is being swept away, partly because of his own arrogant excesses, partly because the British people have had enough of his political patsies. This is his last throw of the dice, a humiliating attempt to ingratiate himself with tomorrow's Prime Minister. It won't save him.

There have been a number of counter-intuitive headlines on the front pages of Her Majesty's press over the last few days. First a market-shaking scoop in the *Sentinel* published last Saturday. MEDIA CORP IS 'INSOLVENT', said the headline, while the strap added 'MPs say Breitner must answer questions about pension fund'. On page five there is a linked column that carries the photo byline of a pasty-faced man in steel-rimmed rectangular spectacles. Alan Scott, the wanker Clare seemingly trusted. There's not a lot of conspicuous humility in his account of why *his* revelations are so important to the future of British democracy and the media. It's a bit of a contrast to his look of sheer disbelief after Jess handed him *our* story on a garlanded plate.

'This is painful, boss,' she said, when I told her we had to give pretty much the whole thing to him.

For Jess and I, seeing *our* story under a rival's byline is as galling as it gets. 'It's shit. But what choice do we have? We can't write it, can we?'

'He'll win Journalist of the Year for this.'

I grind my teeth and say nothing. It fucking hurts.

When Jess went to see him, on my instructions, he kept asking, 'Why aren't *you* running this?'

I'd given Jess the line. 'Just tell him it's because Breitner owns the *FC*, and there is an obvious conflict of interest. And also that Clare would have wanted him to have the scoop.' I had to ask Jess to deliver the gift though. I couldn't face doing it myself. Pathetic, I know.

To be fair, Scott did a proper job on Breitner with how he wrote it up. Almost everything was there: the Albion Super Highway losses, the black hole in the pension fund, Breitner's desperate attempt to get his hands on Capital TV's cash. Clare's tax on pension funds was only mentioned in passing, but that didn't matter. There was enough in his copy to keep the Serious Fraud Office, the Securities and Investment Board, and the Monopolies and Mergers Commission investigating for months.

Gratifyingly, Media Corp's share price tanked on the morning the story dropped. The shares were down more than 30 per cent by 10 a.m. But in the hours and days afterwards it crept gradually up again. As yet no bank has called in its loans and the statements from the authorities – the SFO, the SIB, the MMC – are all of the stalling variety: versions of 'we don't comment on possible or pending investigations'.

'What's going on?' I asked Jess, after the share price had regained two-thirds of its losses, and there had still been no police raid on Media Corp's offices.

'Everyone's waiting for the election. They want confirmation the Tories are out and that Breitner no longer has powerful allies in high office.'

She is probably right. And I don't have a scintilla of doubt Todd will not only win, but win huge. I am so confident that on Sunday I bet two hundred pounds at fifty to one that the Tories won't win a single seat in Scotland or Wales. Bye bye, Breitner.

On Monday night I was kicking myself for not wagering more. Because that's when the *Globe* ran another story I know something about. At 10 p.m., while in The Groucho having a quiet drink with Jess, the *FC* night news editor rang me. I moved to the foyer. 'Gilbert, sorry to trouble you, but I wanted to make you aware of the splash in the *Globe*.'

He read me the screaming headline: MY GAY DAYS WITH CHEATING CHANCELLOR. Fucking hell. Jeremy has coughed. And to Kevin Wilkinson. For which he too will win a fucking press award. I hope he chokes on it.

I rang Jeremy immediately. 'Sorry I couldn't tip you off,' he said. 'The paper swore me to secrecy. And they've squirreled me away to a lavish hotel in Hampshire, to protect me from the media storm.'

'But . . .' I was so shocked, I couldn't get my thoughts in order at all. 'What about your mum?'

'Here's the funny thing. I told you I was worried about what she would feel about me being gay, that she would be mortified. But she said she always knew.' He laughed. 'Quite a way to come out, really. But I'm glad.'

'Why do it now?'

'I couldn't sleep knowing Kendall had got away with it. Don't judge me, but I wanted to get my own back. For myself. But also for your sister.'

'You know this will cost you your career in the Treasury?'

'You're probably right, although don't forget *I'm* the victim.'

'I'm afraid the mandarins won't see it that way.' Surely he knows that the British establishment way is not to make a fuss in public? If a Chancellor has misbehaved, better to deal with it discreetly, out of the gaze of the hoi polloi. Even if Jeremy keeps his job, all routes to promotion would be blocked, for the duration.

'Well, I made sure the *Globe* would cushion my fall, if it comes to that.' He sounded almost happy. 'They've given me quite a decent safety net.'

'How much?'

'Fifty thousand.'

'*Jesus.*'

There was a pause. Then he said, 'Do you think she would have approved of what I did? Clare, I mean?'

He has touched a nerve. Recent events have shown me how much she changed during our estrangement, so I may be the worst person to ask. But I am certain of one thing. I'm not sure she would have approved of your choice of publication, but she always stood up to bullies. And Kendall is a bully.'

This seemed to reassure Jeremy. And I assume he was grat-ified when, the following morning, Downing Street issued an exchange of terse letters between the Prime Minister and Chancellor, in which the Chancellor's resignation offer was accepted. The absence of the normal pleasantries from the Prime Minister – the habitual and clichéd thanks for service to queen and country – was conspicuous.

'Why do you think Breitner decided to destroy Kendall?' I asked Jess when I returned to fill her in. 'Obviously he sanctioned the payment to Jeremy. No one else would have had the authority to pay fifty grand.'

'He's clearing the decks,' she replied. 'As we know better than anyone, his empire is close to collapse. Anything could tip it over the edge.' She explained that if I had found a way to publicise my knowledge that he'd been blackmailing Kendall, that might have been the last straw for his bankers and been curtains for his business. 'By bringing down Kendall in the pages of the *Globe*, any suggestion of blackmail would seem ridiculous. Breitner strung up Kendall to save himself.'

I poured myself another glass of Sancerre. 'It won't be enough to save him.'

At that moment, the Nokia rang again. It was Marilyn. I went back to the foyer. 'This is un-fucking-believable.'

'You've seen the news, then?'

'Your fingerprints are on this, aren't they?'

'Are you suggesting I derive any satisfaction from the fall of Keith Kendall?'

'They're finished, those lying, cheating Tories. We're going to do it. Even Johnny might relax now. Maybe.' She was so excited, her sentences fired out in staccato fragments. 'We're going to thump them, bury them. It's a new start for Britain.'

*

The traffic lights turn green and the bus lumbers on. Unusually, I've allowed plenty of time and I arrive at the school five minutes early. Maybe the shame of keeping my dead sister's children hanging around by the school gates on their own was too much even for me. There's a mob of mostly women gathered by the wrought-iron railings, surrounded by a mess of prams, toddlers and dogs on leads. They all seem to know each other. I am the stranger from another planet.

There's a lot of election chatter. Most have already voted and there is a buzz of change in the air. This is prosperous, university-educated North London, a land of broadcasters, advertising executives and celebrity academics. Which means they hate the Tories and are what would once have been called class traitors. I am picking up a lot of 'We're really going to get them out this time'; 'I'm not sure I completely trust Todd, he is a bit too slick, don't you think?'; 'But he's so much better than Ramsey and the Tories'; 'Absolutely!'

The end-of-the-day bell rings and suddenly there's a cacophony of shouting kids swarming towards the exit. I scan for Sam and Luke, but Luke spies me first and – nice surprise – runs towards me and gives me a hug. 'Uncle Gil, Uncle Gil,' he shouts, beaming and bouncing around like a puppy on two legs. Sam, as the elder brother, is more restrained. 'Hello, Uncle Gil,' he says formally, though he smiles too.

'Uncle Gil, Uncle Gil, can we go to Imran's?' asks Luke, as the lollipop man ushers us across the pedestrian crossing.

'What's Imran's?'

'That shop over there. Can we buy sweets?'

'Does Daddy let you buy sweets?'

There's a moment's silence. 'Well, sometimes,' says Sam.

I am not so thick as to miss a child's disguised fib. But I embrace the role of indulgent uncle, and we load up with Haribo Starmix and fizzy cola bottles, to squeals of excitement from Luke.

Just as we're leaving, the Nokia rings. It's Charles. 'All fine?'

'All good. I've got the boys, just on our way home.'

'I hope they haven't conned you into buying them sweets.'

I theatrically cover the mouthpiece with my hand and turn to the boys. 'Your dad says he hopes you haven't tricked me into buying you sweets. What do I say?'

They collapse in fits of giggles. 'Tell Dad he's a big banana,' says Luke.

'I heard that,' says Charles. 'I'll be home around six. Bernard and Ginger are coming round too. They'll probably stay the night and watch the results with me.'

'That sounds nice.'

I ring off and we walk past Victorian villas that speak of a past age of confidence and optimism. 'Race you home,' Luke announces suddenly. 'Last one back is a silly ninny!'

And we're off. Obviously, I'm the ninny, and always would be, even without a sore ankle.

I retrieve the key from a neighbour forewarned by Charles and let us in. The next ninety minutes are a frenzy of times tables – I am stunned that Luke already knows eight times seven – scales on the piano and a Power Rangers video that I sense has been watched several hundred times: Luke, in a Mighty Morphin mask, acts out every scene in real time.

Charles has left a Bolognese sauce in the fridge, which I heat up. The boys are halfway through supper when the doorbell rings. It's Mum and Dad: Mum clutching a large Tupperware box full

392

of latkes wrapped in kitchen paper, and Dad holding a bottle of champagne.

Dad hesitates. I hesitate. I try to put my arm around his shoulder, a sort of half-hug. We are both a bit embarrassed. But it's a start. It's easier with my mum, who I peck on the cheek. 'You're not working today, dear?'

'There's nothing to do till later.'

'I hope those naughty boys have been good for you? Luke, Sam, have you been kind to Uncle Gil?'

'Course not,' says Luke. 'He's a silly ninny. Didn't you know that, Grandma?'

'I've always had my suspicions. Now come here and give your grandma a hug.'

Dad, always wary of conspicuous displays of emotion, waves the bottle of champagne. 'Better get this in the fridge.'

Seconds later the key turns in the lock and Charles comes in. 'You're back early, Charles,' says Mum. She beams. 'That's nice.'

'Couldn't stand it in the office any longer. Don't forget most of my shop are true-blue Tories. They think the election of a Labour government will see their bonuses taxed at 99 per cent.'

'If only that were true,' says Dad.

'Shoosh, Bernard. Charles, your father-in-law is only having his little joke. He doesn't really mean that.'

'Yes he does, Grandma, you know he does,' says worldly-wise Sam. 'Everyone knows that Grandpa hates bankers.'

There's a moment's painful silence and then Charles roars with laughter: 'You little tyke. I hate bankers too. But if I wasn't one, how would we pay for your Nintendo games?'

We move to the sitting room. When I get a moment, I am compelled to ask Charles, 'How's my old friend Robin Muller?'

Charles shrugs. 'Hyperactive as ever. There is a big deal in process.'

'The Media Corp takeover of Capital?'

He shoots me a stern look. 'Give it a rest Gil. This is a family night, right?'

'Yeah. Sorry. Force of habit.'

'The bed is made up,' Charles says to Mum and Dad who haven't brought much with them, presumably because this is home from home. I feel jealous.

'I don't know how late I'll want to stay up,' says Dad.

'Don't lie, Bernard,' says Mum. 'You know you'll be the last one to go to bed.'

'Can we stay up? Please!' says Luke.

'It's school tomorrow, darling,' Mum reminds him.

'Let's see how tired you are,' says Charles.

Dad looks at Sam. 'The last time Labour won an election was in 1974. Can you believe that? Your Uncle Gil and I stayed up to watch it. Gil, I think you were only about twelve or thirteen at the time. You were desperate to watch the results. And you struggled so hard to keep your eyes open, but eventually I had to carry you into your bed. Do you remember any of that?'

I sort of do. What I mostly remember, though, are the preceding days, when as a pipsqueak young teenager – I was a Young Socialist – I would knock on doors canvassing for Labour. I'd learned the patter from Dad. 'Can we count on your vote, madam?' I would say. What the middle-class ladies of Belsize Park made of the descant sing-song pleadings of a Jewish campaigner, in a purple suedette jacket and red loons, goodness only knows.

394

Dad jolts me back. 'I began to wonder whether I'd live long enough to see another Labour government. Though I'm not sure Johnny Todd is really one of us.'

'He's not as bad as you think Dad. Honestly.' I tell him about my encounter with Todd at the Bermondsey housing estate and what drives him. 'For what it's worth, he worships you. He quoted your book.'

For a moment Dad looks flattered. And then, 'He may have read it, but if he understood it – which I doubt – he's rejected it. All he's interested in is what I believe you people call "spin".'

'Is that "spin" so terrible if it actually allows Labour to oust the Conservatives you hate so much, after almost twenty years?' I'm not sure why I'm defending Todd. I don't owe him anything. I'm supposed to be an impartial observer, the referee, not a player. But there are times when it's impossible to deny my convictions, inherited from Dad and shaped by my own experiences. Also, Todd has adopted Clare's pensions tax. For that I owe him.

'Clare would be on my side,' I say, instantly regretting it. It's been two months, no time at all. None of us can really believe that she's not about to walk in from the kitchen with five mugs of strong builders' tea.

'I'm not sure you're right, Gil,' says Charles. 'She was scathing about Todd.'

'Really?' I look to Dad for support. 'I thought she rated him.'

He looks uncertain. 'Sometimes she did. I'm not sure.'

'Absolutely not.' Charles is adamant. 'When he came on the telly, she switched him off. Said he was a phony.'

I share a look with Dad. We're confused.

'That reminds me ...' says Charles. 'Can I have a word, Gil?'

Leaving Mum to act out an impromptu glove puppet show with Luke, and Sam and Dad talking about their favourite Spurs players, I follow Charles back into the hall, up the stairs to a small study at the back of the house. It overlooks a garden teeming with apple blossom. Framed pictures of the boys and the family cover all the walls and stand propped on every surface.

'Clare's study,' says Charles. 'I've left it as it was. I don't come in here.'

'I understand.'

He gestures to a cardboard box sitting in the middle of the floor. 'A chap from the Treasury brought this round a few days ago. Her PA, the one who was in the papers.'

'Jeremy?'

'It's Clare's things from the office. He'd been holding onto them all this time – very apologetic. I can't really bear to go through it all, and it would be too much for Bernard and Ginger. Do you think you could have a look, see if there's anything important? Sorry to ask.'

For the first time today, I feel on the edge of disaster, again. Anxious. I don't know why. 'Of course. Leave it with me.'

Rather than picking up the box, I sit down cross-legged on the floor and open it. I am a child once more, looking at big sister's things. Unsure of what I will find.

At the top are more framed photographs of Charles and the children: first day at school, in a playground, in the school play. There's a professional picture of Clare and Charles on their wedding day; one of Mum and Dad in the French Residence, when Dad was given the *Légion d'honneur* for his work reinterpreting Marxism for the post-industrialised world.

And then I freeze. It's me and Clare, similar ages to Sam and Luke now, holding hands outside London Zoo. Clare is cradling a small monkey that's wearing a spangled waistcoat and Arabian pantaloons. There was some kind of organ-grinding traveller who owned the monkey, I remember. He charged maybe ten shillings for children to excitedly clutch the exotic animal and have their picture taken. It would be banned today. Too cruel. But the picture is a window and I lose control. I weep, as quietly as I can, trying not to drip tears on the photo.

There's more, and I need to speed up, because I want to have a few more minutes with the boys before I have to leave for work. Under the photos is the bike helmet, which I can barely bring myself to touch. Then a mug adorned with the Spurs' cockerel, and another with the Beatles' Apple logo. One for pens and one for tea, by the looks of them.

Finally, right at the bottom, is a black leather Filofax. My hands tremble slightly as I open it. Turning through a few pages, I see Clare's familiar, geometrically precise handwriting: her appointments and meetings, but also notes and scribbled thoughts. I can't really concentrate enough to take them in properly, though I can see she jots down times of meetings and brief notes to remind her of what was said or agreed. There is a reference to her telling the Chancellor to stop bothering 'JM'. Which prompts me to wonder why Jeremy didn't return her stuff earlier. Maybe he didn't want us to see the clues to his affair. I feel let down by him, but not for long. I hear cackles and splashes and Charles's plaintive voice trying to get the boys into their bath.

After the calendar, there's a section of ruled pages for notes. Clare seems to have used this as a sort of mental dumping ground. Lines from poems and song lyrics; shopping lists and meal plans;

books that people have recommended; funny things the boys have said. Scribbled sums – mortgage payments next to the public sector borrowing requirement. There are longer chunks of text too, where she's had something on her mind she wanted to remember.

And, right at the end, there is something that is almost a short essay. She's noted the date at the top of the page: 2 March, 1997. The day before her accident.

I read.

J is a dangerous man. He can charm people into thinking that he alone is the answer to our prayers, but all he wants is control and power. He does not really care about making lives better. He is seducing the country and he will become PM.

Socialism was forged for another age. It has to be rethought for an age of information, an age of services, an age where the forge, the mill, the mine and the lathe are no longer the foundations of our way of life. But this is not J's mission. He has neither the intellect nor the ambition. What he wants is adoration, little else.

He will win because people believe in him. They believe he can restore faith in politics and public service. When he doesn't – because he doesn't have the imagination and because he is too selfish – there will be a heavy toll. All he will leave is cynicism, disenchantment and chaos. And after he has taken what he wants, he will walk away, protesting his innocence, blameless in his own mind, and leave the country holding the baby.

Just like me.

I blink. 'J' is clearly not 'Jeremy' here. 'He will become PM' – it can only be Johnny Todd. But why such bitterness? As if he's a sociopath, who Clare alone can see.

She took a huge risk and met him in secret. He was her hope. He promised to enact the policy that Kendall had dropped and he has kept his promise. The abolition of the dividend tax credit is in his manifesto. From tomorrow, assuming Labour win, it will be officially part of the government's programme. Did she assume he would renege on this pledge to her? Or was there something else?

I return to the diary section. It starts on the first of January. I'd scanned it before, but now I read each day's entries meticulously. Meetings, phone calls, parents' evenings, dinners with Mum and Dad, a doctor's appointment. But interrupting all of them, a single letter, attached to varying times of the day or night: 'J'.

Johnny Todd, chatting with me in his kitchen, in shirtsleeves: *I met her in a few transition meetings.* He is a lying bastard. Clare was meeting him every week, sometimes several times a week. At lunchtimes, early afternoons, a couple of Thursday nights when she was supposed to be at a book group, and once on a Saturday morning when (according to the journal) Charles had taken the boys to football practice.

The shadow of a conversation I had in my parents' house comes back to me, the first time Jeremy voiced his concerns about Clare. *She'd been a bit different lately. She kept popping out of the office, nothing in the diary. She even missed scheduled meetings. I had to cover up for her. It was out of character.*

Oh God. Charles on the phone, after the post-mortem results came through: *She was six weeks pregnant. We hadn't had sex since before Christmas.*

I am fantasising. Making this up. None of this is true.

But here it is, in her handwriting: *He will walk away, protesting his innocence, blameless in his own mind, and leave the country holding the baby.*

Just like me.

I feel sick. The blow is physical. I have to get out of here. I run downstairs, into the sitting room where Luke and Sam are flapping around in their bath towels, shouting and screaming 'Return of the Mack, return of the Mack', as though it's the funniest song ever.

'Are you OK?' Charles asks. He frowns, seeing the Filofax I'm clutching. 'You look pale.'

'I'm all right. It was hard, but I'm fine. But I've just noticed the time. I have to shoot. Sorry Charles. I must get to the Commons to start our coverage.'

Charles looks anxious and sad. I hope he doesn't think that yet again I am putting my career and work before family. I want to tell him everything. But I can't. Instead I do something I should have done a long time ago. I go up to him and hug him, hard. I don't look back because I don't want to see his reaction, or for him to see that my eyes are full of tears.

'Thanks for having me,' I shout at Luke and Sam. 'It was such fun hanging out. Whatever you do, don't tell Dad about the sweets.'

And then I run.

Chapter 29

'WHAT TIME DO YOU THINK Todd will be back in London?' I've rung Jess while walking down Fellows Road towards Chalk Farm, where I'll get on the Northern Line. The pain in my ankle is a blessing. It distracts from the screaming in my head. As I approach the junction, there's a black-on-white placard announcing POLLING STATION outside a church hall. There's a stream of people back from work to vote, and I want to shout, 'Don't do it, don't vote for Todd!'

'It's hard to say for sure,' Jess says. 'I asked Fisher. They've laid on a Jag to bring him from Birmingham to the South Bank just as soon as the returning officer has announced. He reckons he should arrive around two in the morning.'

Labour has booked the terrace outside the National Theatre by the Thames for its post-election party. Choosing a location with such cultural significance is the first time Todd has flirted with hubris, though I assume he banned all references to a 'victory' party. I have an invitation, from Marilyn. She said she assumed I wouldn't be able to make it, because I'd be beavering away filing and revising copy all night long, as we hit a rolling series of edition deadlines. She's wrong. I will be there.

I can't suppress the hideous idea that Marilyn must have known all along, that her boss was fucking and deceiving my sister while she was fucking me. The betrayal inflames me. 'Where are you now, Jess?'

'Burma Road.'

'I'll be with you in half an hour or so.'

At the station I show my travel card and take the lift down to the platform. Or rather two Gils will take the train. There's Gil on his way to put in an all-night stint covering one of the most important stories of the year, maybe of the decade: the end of one party's long reign and the start of another's. With him is the Gil who has just entered his dead sister's nightmare. I know that my reporting will be exemplary tonight, because my hyper-focus is switched on in a crisis. Unless you have my kind of addiction to work, unless work is your drug of choice, you won't understand how I can carry on having just fallen into Clare's hell. The thought of asking for time out doesn't occur.

By 9.30 p.m., the Burma Road is buzzing. We're like the crowd at Wembley before the Cup Final. Or maybe a better analogy is with the teams in their respective dressing rooms. Because in just half an hour we'll all be frantically bashing away on our keyboards, playing what for us is the match of the year, trying to interpret first the exit poll just after ten – the preliminary estimate of the outcome – and then from midnight onwards the steady stream of constituency results. Every room is full, every television turned to BBC1, or ITV or Sky News. From the *Globe*'s room I hear Wilkinson barking instructions to his junior colleagues, to start preparing portraits of the winners and losers. *Cunt*. Before I reach our desks, I see Scott in the corridor.

We look at each other, I mutter hello, he nods, and we walk past each other. We have a shared secret, not a bond.

At 10 p.m., Big Ben tolls sonorously. Not via the television, but right here, outside my window. A fraction of an instant later, David Dimbleby is on screen, announcing that interviews with voters outside polling stations all over the country have led analysts to predict with a high degree of confidence that Labour will form the next government – and that it has probably won by a near-record landslide. This should not be a surprise, given what opinion polls have been showing for some time, but somehow it is. The story is as big as it gets and has electrified the press gallery. We've all been writing that the British people wanted a change. The overwhelming majority of them have now voted for one, they've executed it. But what does it mean? It has been so long since Labour has been in power, memories are dim about what follows from a transfer of power. And as for Labour's leader, he's not a chip off any kind of block. Who is he? What will he start to do in just a few hours' time when he moves with his young family from Tufnell Park to 10 Downing Street?

He will win because people believe in him. Clare was spot on, though that wasn't a remarkable or unconventional view. *They believe he can restore faith in politics and public service.* Also correct. *When he doesn't – because he doesn't have the imagination and because he is too selfish – there will be a heavy toll. All he will leave is cynicism, disenchantment and chaos.* I trust my sister's judgement. I always have. She had personal reasons for denigrating him. But those personal reasons go to the heart of who he is.

On my screen, I call up the profile of Todd I prepared long in advance. I amend it, adding – in reported speech – that a senior official who was close to him fears he is more interested in power for power's sake than for what he would do to rehabilitate the country. I close by writing, 'Socialism may be out of time. It may need rethinking for an age of information, an age of services, an age where the forge, the mill, the mine and the lathe are no longer the foundations of our economy. But this may be a secondary consideration for Mr Todd. According to the well-placed official, Britain's new prime minister will struggle to restore faith in politics and public service, and if he fails his legacy may be cynicism, disenchantment and chaos. ENDS.' I press the 'send' button, and wonder whether any of the assorted editors back at base will query my new conclusion. It somewhat jars with the mood of the country. But I am sure Clare was right. She always was.

If only we'd talked.

Peter Snow is excitable on the television and gesticulating at his maddening Swingometer. If the swing to Labour turns out to be as strong as the exit poll predicts, then all these blue seats are going to turn red, he says. It's a remaking of the electoral map.

'Boss, can you hear me?' I realise Jess has been speaking to me, but I've been distracted. 'That revised Todd profile you've just filed ...' she says. 'Slightly harsh ending, isn't it?' I shrug.

The broadcasters are now going to constituency counts all around the country and results are starting to be announced – first in a trickle, then a flood. And it becomes increasingly clear that the sharp swing to Labour of the exit poll is an understatement. I turn to Jess. 'Get back the splash copy, would you, and insert a few more superlatives? You know the sort of thing. "The biggest swing to Labour in history". "May presage the start of a long period in opposition for the Tories". That kind of thing.'

'I'm already on it.'

Just after 1 a.m., all the TV channels go to their live feeds from Todd's Birmingham count. On the podium is the mayor, wearing his chain of office. Next to him are the candidates and their spouses. The Raving Loony Candidate, who is next to Todd, is dressed as a giant smiling phallus. Jess and I burst out laughing. 'I think he agrees with your judgement, boss.'

Mrs Todd, Rona, is wearing a beautifully cut navy-blue suit, either Dior or top-notch knock-off. Her face looks like thunder. She's not happy for some reason, though it can't be because of the result. Todd has scooped 70 per cent of votes cast, an overwhelming margin of victory. His speech is short and self-deprecating, saying that so far the night has gone well and he hopes that he'll be able to live up to the trust placed in him by the British people. Although he knows that he's done it, he is not being presumptuous. He'll wait for the TV channels to call the result and for Ramsey to formally concede. His eyes keep darting stage left, as if there's someone in the wings and he wants to get away. The parochial rituals of constituency politics are a chore, and he is about to make his debut on a much bigger stage. Shortly afterwards we watch him climbing into the dark blue Jag. A TV reporter shouts, 'On your way to Downing Street, Mr Todd?' He smiles at the camera, winks, and gets in the back seat.

By 2 a.m., the Burma Road has thinned out. The last deadlines for the late editions are approaching, and some of the hacks have left to catch a few hours' sleep. Tomorrow will be a long and packed day, with pages of analysis and reaction to prepare for Saturday's papers. But all the political editors are still here, the chroniclers of history in the making. Ramsey retains his seat by a whisker. Even Mrs Thatcher's former constituency in North London is seized by Labour. It is a rout.

'Flipping fuck,' says Jess for the umpteenth time, as another familiar Conservative MP is obliged to rethink his career plans.

I've done all I can here. 'Jess, I need a favour.'

'Another one?'

'I want to wander over to the Labour do at the National. It'll help with the copy for Saturday. Good colour. Also, I might pick up some gossip about who in the shadow cabinet will make it into government and who will be knifed by Todd.'

'OK. But what are we going to do about the splash for the final edition and the potential slip?' A 'slip' is a last opportunity to change copy, for the final paper that will hit the streets.

'The story isn't going to change in any fundamental way. And if there are any other sensational constituency results, or new quotes, just shove them in. I trust you totally. And if anything happens where you want a second opinion, just ring me.'

'And what makes you think I won't delete your byline and substitute mine?'

'I would be disappointed if you didn't.'

The seasons have turned. The night air is warm and London is alive with car horns being tooted to celebrate Labour's success. Todd's triumph. As I hurry over Westminster Bridge, lights shimmer off the Thames. Behind me on the right are the Houses of Parliament, about to be seized in a bloodless coup by a new generation of MPs and a party that has at last escaped the wilderness. Immediately opposite is St Thomas's Hospital, and I can now put a face to that voice I heard asking after Clare when I was there. But why did he go to the hospital?

I stop in the middle of the bridge and look east. Carried on the wind a few hundred yards from downriver are the chants of ecstatic Labour activists, singing along to the anthem of the age, Blur's 'Song 2'. 'Woo-hoo,' they shout. 'Woo-hoo.'

Woo-fucking-hoo. Maybe Todd really cared about Clare. Maybe. Was he planning to make it up to her in some way after the election? But if so, why was she so bitter? It doesn't make sense.

I walk on. As I leave the bridge I skirt disused County Hall, a municipal palace before Thatcher abolished the Greater London Council, now vacant and searching for a new purpose in Todd's Britain. I turn left and walk towards the noise. On my right now is a symbol of the renewal of Britain planned by an earlier Labour government, the Royal Festival Hall, with its revolutionary mixture of concrete and glass. And there in front of me is the ecstatic mob, hundreds of shouting, laughing and singing Labour supporters. On the electronic screen at the top of the National Theatre's Duplo-Box buildings, it reads 'Modern Labour, a new start for Britain.' Music is pumping from loudspeakers, segueing from Blur, to Oasis, to Suede. Huge swivelling spotlights are making patterns in the night sky. This is not the traditional British politics of men in badly cut suits shaking each other's hands and offering congratulations over a glass of warm beer. Something has changed. It is a euphoric rave.

A sea of happy people is between me and the National Theatre. I ring Marilyn. She's shrieking above a din of drunk colleagues. 'I can't believe it, Gil! It's better than I dared to hope. We've done it. We've done it!'

'Where are you?' I also have to shout to be heard.

'I'm inside the National. Are you still in the Commons?'

'I'm just by the Royal Festival Hall. How do I find you?'

'Go to the left side of the National, stage door. I'll tell security to let you in.'

By the time I've managed to push my way through the crowds and shown my press card to security, Marilyn is waiting on the other side of the glass door. She throws her arms around me and I inhale her intoxicating smell of cigarettes and perfume. She whispers in my ear, 'We did it Gil! We fucked the Tories.' The warmth of her body and her unalloyed joy at having vanquished her opponents are an irresistible aphrodisiac. But I can't be distracted. Not now.

'It all feels a bit unreal,' I say. 'In just a few hours, you'll be choosing your desk in 10 Downing Street.'

She grabs my arm and pulls me through the crowd. The foyer of the National Theatre is MC Escher made real: paradoxical staircases, connecting halls, mezzanines and balconies that seem impossible to reach. Today, all of them are rammed with aides and party workers, candidates and tomorrow's ministers. Actually, *today's* ministers.

Marilyn turns back to me. 'Come and work with us, Gil.'

Is she joking? For a moment I feel excited by the idea, and then guilty, a little ashamed, soiled. This is how my sister was seduced.

'I am not sure that would be good, for either of us.'

Either she can't hear me properly over the din, or she's too drunk to notice my frostiness. 'Johnny is impressed with you, really likes you. He wants you to join the team.'

Really? Johnny actually said that? It feels abusive. I react. 'That's flattering, Marilyn. But Johnny would have to be the world's most extreme narcissist to fuck one Peck and then think it's a good idea to fuck the other one. But then, he is an utter narcissist, isn't he?'

Marilyn comes to a sudden halt and I bash into her side. She turns and stares at me. 'What the fuck are you saying?'

'You lied to me, Marilyn. You knew Clare was my sister, probably from the beginning. And you knew how often they were meeting, and that theirs was not a normal professional relationship. You knew they were having an affair.'

She looks around, flustered, anxious we'll be overheard. Everyone is delirious at the victory. No one is paying us attention. 'You've gone mad. Stop it.'

'Now I understand why Johnny was the only person in the country who thought he could lose the election. If it came out that he was fucking a Treasury official who was breaking the Official Secrets Act, if it became known she was pregnant, that would have been impossible for him to survive. The scandal would have finished him, and Labour. Perhaps forever'. I have a blinding realisation of quite how stupid I've been. 'I trusted you, Marilyn. I told you everything about Clare. Even that she was pregnant. You knew more than anyone else. And you reported it all back to your boss, didn't you? You manipulated me.'

Marilyn is about to reply when a commanding female voice pre-empts her. 'Marilyn!'

My jaw clenches. It's Rona, Todd's wife, forcing her way determinedly through the mob. She has changed out of the Dior and into jeans, cowboy boots and a tight-fitting T-shirt embroidered in red sequins with the slogan 'Modern Labour' on the front, and 'Modern Britain' on the back.

'Found you,' she says triumphantly to Marilyn. 'Johnny needs you. *Now*, darling! He's having a last-minute wobble about his words to the adoring nation.'

'How long have you been here?' I ask. Rona couldn't be arsed even to look at me and I am not in the mood to be ignored. 'Where is your husband?'

Rona clocks me. She tilts her head to one side and narrows her eyes. 'I know you.'

'Gilbert Peck from the *FC*. I came to your house to interview your husband. You thought I was the new help.'

She laughs, coldly. 'That's right. We still haven't got a fucking nanny, actually. And no one with any sense will move with us to Downing Street. Are you good with children? Perhaps you'd like the job.'

'Not sure that's my area of expertise.'

'As it happens,' Marilyn intervenes, 'Johnny wanted Gil to join the Downing Street team, but he just flunked the interview.'

'What a shame.' Rona turns to Marilyn. 'Honestly, darling, please go and sort Johnny out. You know he can't function without you.'

Marilyn nods. 'We'll finish this later,' she says to me. 'But you are wrong.'

'She was pregnant,' I say, as though that means anything.

'What are you two gossiping about?' asks Rona, finally interested. 'It sounds riveting.'

'Gil's got the wrong end of the stick,' says Marilyn. 'He's taken two and two and decided the answer adds up to something worse than the Profumo scandal.'

'Gosh. I assume we're talking about people we all know?' says Rona. 'The thing about men in politics is that most have the emotional age of a thirteen-year-old – especially around sex.'

I gawp like an idiot. Is this Rona's bog standard routine, or is she sending me a message, that she knows Johnny screws the help and couldn't care less?

'You'll have to excuse us,' Rona says brightly. 'Come on, Marilyn. The new Prime Minister is in need of your services.' She rolls her eyes. 'The "new Prime Minister". Heaven help us.'

She gives me another warmthless smile and they push their way back towards an area cordoned off by plush ropes. I head for one of the bars, which are handing out Sol Mexican beer in the untinted bottle, and New Zealand Chardonnay in plastic cups. I'm desperate for a drink.

As I jostle through the densely packed crowd, I almost knock a bottle out of someone's hand. When I swivel to apologise, I see it's the Shadow – soon to be actual – Chancellor, Neville Tudor.

'Sorry.' I pause, and shake my head in disbelief. Tudor is with Alex Elliott, Media Corp's PR chief. Surely he should be less welcome than Pinochet?

'Alex,' I say with a display of mock solicitude. 'How brave of you to be here. But shouldn't you be on the other side of the river, in Smith Square, commiserating with your Tory pals? Such a terrible night for you.'

He forces a riotous laugh. 'Gil. Always the joker. The *Globe* backed Todd! As you know. We've won it again, for our readers. Modern Labour, Modern Britain. It's what we stand for.'

'Spoken like a t*rrrr*ue man of the people,' Tudor bellows. He's had a few drinks, and his Welsh accent is off the leash. 'There's always more joy in the Labour party over one sinner who repents, than ninety-nine righteous men.'

'Makes you wonder what's the point of being righteous,' I mutter. Everyone seems to have gone mad. 'Not got your sports bag with you tonight, Alex?'

Elliott winces. Fleet Street is awash with speculation about the source of Scott's scoop, helped along by Jess gossiping quietly in the Member's Lobby with a gang of young Tory MPs who hate Ramsey. According to Jess's version, Elliott was so pissed at

Crowther's party he left his bag in the back of a cab, and then somehow its contents were delivered to the *Sentinel*. Everyone now believes that's what happened: it even made its way into *Private Eye*. Elliott can't correct the record because he dare not admit the documents exist or that he was carrying them around.

'Very funny.'

'Seriously, shouldn't you be back at base? Going down with the ship.'

'And I thought you had your finger on the pulse. The shares are up 20 per cent today. Wall Street has gone mad for them.'

I'd been so busy focusing on my nephews, I've ignored what's been happening in the market – though I am surprised Jess didn't mention anything. It makes no sense. A Labour victory should be curtains for Media Corp. The stock should be wiped out.

'We're having a bit of a celebration, actually.' Elliott is very clearly talking to Tudor, not me. 'Annabel's. Jimmy's already there, if you'd care to join us later.'

Tudor famously has the stamina of an ox and he loves champagne. 'It would be good to raise a glass to Mr Breitner for his magnificent front page,' he says.

I feel sick. Before I can make a crack about champagne socialism, I hear a voice from behind shouting, 'Chancellor!' Marilyn's back, and it's no longer 'Shadow Chancellor'. They are the masters now. Ramsey hasn't conceded, but the conditionals and caveats are history, swept away. 'Johnny's getting ready to come out and do his thing. He needs you with him.'

'Of course.' Tudor drains his bottle of lager, looks for somewhere to put it down, and when he can't he just hands it to Marilyn, who – to my surprise – accepts it without a word of protest. I raise my eyebrows. He heads to the velvet rope. Elliott winces a smile at us and turns around to find someone more important and less hostile.

I'm left alone with Marilyn. Is she going to say sorry? Is she going to somehow make it right? I don't want to hate her. There's too much noise in my head. We haven't scratched the surface of what I want to say, about Clare, Johnny, us, everything. I don't know where to start. So I choose displacement.

'Why the fuck is Elliott here? I thought he was the enemy.'

'Not for Johnny. We're the party of entrepreneurs and wealth creation, Modern Britain, remember?'

'But the *Globe* destroyed your party at the last election. Breitner's going down in flames, having stolen from his employees and pensioners – stolen from your people. How can he suddenly be part of the family?'

I'm struggling to keep my voice down. In fact, I'm close to raving. Marilyn puts a hand on my arm. 'Calm down. We can't talk if you're like this. The *Globe* is onside. Johnny and Jimmy have an understanding.'

Jimmy? Jimmy and Johnny. The pairing feels like an assault, a one-two of punches to my head. 'They know each other?'

'They've had a couple of meetings. Constructive, helpful meetings.'

I get it. Elliott being here. The rise in Media Corp's share price. The bankers holding fire. It's a stitch-up. I've been stitched up. The country has been stitched up.

There's been a historic meeting. It won't be recorded anywhere. No one took a note, no one will ever talk about it. But it was a meeting that diverted the big river of Britain's destiny. Todd and Breitner struck a bargain. Media Corp would back Todd and Labour, full throttle, in the *Globe* – and a Labour government would repay Breitner by not stopping his takeover of Capital. Todd would suppress any initiatives to investigate the theft from pensioners, so long as the hole in the pension fund was filled – which it will be, now.

'What has he done? What have *you* done?' It's a howl, from somewhere deep inside me. 'Breitner has been a blight on this country all our lives. He's bust. You have the power to finish him off. Why would you rescue him?'

Even in our most intimate moments, I've always sensed there's armour, perhaps ice, around Marilyn's core. There's a part of her I could never reach. Now the armour is covering her entirely. 'You mean that crap in the *Sentinel*?' she says, witheringly. 'Typical old-left sour grapes. They resent success.'

'Breitner doesn't represent success. More than anyone else he backed a Tory party, a Tory government, that forced hardship and poverty on millions.' Why is she being so stubborn and unthinking? How can I make her understand? 'Breitner stole, Marilyn. He stole the savings of ordinary people, money they put aside money for their retirements. How can you brush all that under the carpet?'

'Breitner's not the enemy. Look at his story. He had the ambition, the drive, to create a world-leading business and thousands of top-quality jobs. It's that spirit we want to encourage. We need *more* Breitners, not to destroy them.'

The flawed argument is so fluently put that I can't tell if she believes it or if there is some other purpose I can't identify. I am betrayed, used.

'You're being naïve. Breitner may be on your side now, but he'll turn on you. Look at how he's dumped Ramsey. When you're no longer useful, he'll destroy you. And if you let him buy Capital, he'll be so powerful that no one will be able to control him. Not Johnny, not anyone.'

'We don't think so.' She says it slowly and deliberately, as an ending. The meeting is over. Her eye scans the crowd for other chores that need doing. 'Jimmy will owe us too much. And you've always underestimated Johnny.'

I recall a line of JFK's that Dad loved to quote – and even put right at the front of one of his books. 'Those who foolishly seek power by riding the back of the tiger end up inside it,' I say.

'We're not riding the tiger. We've put it on a leash.'

'Do you really believe that?'

I don't know whether she hears. A man with a walkie-talkie is waving at her from behind the velvet rope. 'I think we're done, Gil. It was fun.' She strokes my face with her forefinger and leaves.

She's right. We're done. I'm done. I don't try to stop her. I walk up the wide stairs and on to a terrace that overlooks the promenade. On the embankment outside are huge screens alternating between the BBC, ITV and Sky, piping the results to a mob whose energy is still rising. A stage has been erected on the right. The engineers are on it, making a final test of the equipment. It looks like the preparation for a rock concert, and a chant of 'Johnny, Johnny, Johnny' is building. At the back of the podium is another screen replaying Labour's party political broadcasts. The crowd roars every time Todd's face appears. His eyes seem to be taunting me.

And as that enormous, smug face grins out at me, I see what's happened.

Clare is lying in bed with Todd in a hotel room. She's already given him the pensions tax policy, but now she needs to blow the whistle on Breitner's theft from the pension fund. *Kendall has become Breitner's pawn. He'll help Breitner cover it up. But when you win, you'll be able to break free of Breitner's grip. You can destroy him.*

I see Todd's humouring smile. Clare is clever, brilliant, beautiful. But she's just a woman. Todd has met Breitner. They've spoken man to man. Breitner is an entrepreneur first and foremost. He just wants confidence that a Labour government will leave him to do what he does best, which is build businesses. And Johnny wants to give him that assurance, because it will symbolise everything about how Labour is changing. *Do you know how many Labour governments have served two full consecutive terms? None. Not a single one. But with Breitner as our ally, with Breitner onside, we can be in office long enough to really change this country.*

Clare wants to believe in Todd but she is disoriented. There is no taming Breitner; no being Breitner's friend. If Labour believes in making the changes the country needs, then Media Corp can never be an ally – because its values are antithetical to everything decent and good. *Johnny, look at the page 5 Globes, the topless women.* He laughs indulgently. *Oh come on. That's just a bit of fun.* She is becoming frustrated, upset. She has to tell him other important news. Maybe it will make a difference.

I'm pregnant, Johnny. It's yours.

He looks serious. The grin has gone. *That's wonderful, darling.* There's a pause. *What do you want to do?* And in that moment, all her illusions about him fall away. *I'm not sure. Probably keep the baby.* She becomes cold, businesslike. *I am assuming from your reaction that you're not keen.*

416

He smiles again. *Oh, Clare, I'm so fond of you. But you always knew about my family situation. My wife, my children – and of course the election. We've had fun though, haven't we?*

Clare feels lost. But only for a moment. Pecks are stubborn, resilient. *Johnny. I will keep the baby. And before you offer, I don't want your fucking money. And I will never tell anyone you are the father – unless, that is, you fail to do the right thing and deliver justice to Breitner's victims. In fact, if you choose to prop him up, I will take my story, our story, to the press. I think even the* Globe *would find it hard not to print what I have to say.*

And that was when Clare Peck became a lethal threat to the man whose only ambition was to be Prime Minister and remain in 10 Downing Street for a generation.

Later, Johnny Todd and Jimmy Breitner are in Breitner's Sun King drawing room. Their pact is sealed. A mutual support agreement. A mogul rescued, the price of a pretender's ascent to the highest office. Todd stands. He adjusts the knot of his turquoise tie, fixes his green eyes on Breitner's. *There is one other thing. There is a Treasury official who can make life uncomfortable, for both of us. Maybe you've heard of her? Clare Peck.* And that was that.

Clare had to act fast. I was the only person she could have trusted, because only I would have understood and forgiven everything. That's why she rang. But I was fucking Marilyn and missed the call. I failed her, and there is no point in trying to forgive myself.

'I would have saved you, Clare,' I whisper to myself. 'As you always saved me.'

Standing on the balcony, I look down on smiling, happy faces waiting for Todd to appear. I no longer want to be inside: I want to be out there. Just another face in the crowd.

On the stage, a well-known comedian has stepped up to the microphone and begins the familiar call and response.

'Modern Labour,' he shouts.

'Modern Britain,' the crowd bellows back.

'Modern Labour.'

'Modern Britain.'

I look back through the windows to the theatre lobby. Marilyn is trying to lead Todd out to the podium, but it's hard going. The crowd don't want to let him through. Todd is promiscuously shaking hands and hugging everyone. There's Alex Elliott beaming; Cameron Fisher in rapt conversation with Nigel Sands, no long spoon anywhere in sight. For a moment I think I even glimpse Robin Muller.

I try to lock eyes with Marilyn, hoping she'll register me, feel my despair, rescue me and rescue herself. I look for a sign that she harbours doubts. She doesn't. She is a believer.

With every cell of my being I want to complete Clare's mission, to bring Todd's world crashing down. But what can I prove? What do I have that cannot be denied? Clare's Filofax confession is in code. There's no proof that the child was Todd's, and after the cremation there never can be. If I somehow manage to get a newspaper to print my insinuations, all that will happen is that there will be a war of innuendo, probably for years. Breitner and Todd will unite to paint Clare as a fantasist, a hysteric, a Treasury official driven by left-wing ideological hate to breach the Official Secrets Act. Kendall will probably roll in behind them. They will besmirch her reputation, humiliate her husband, destroy my parents, turn her innocent boys into a laughing stock. Is that a price Clare would want paid? Is that justice, when Todd and Breitner will most likely never face justice themselves?

Clare, what should I do? This is not an OCD chant for comfort. I need her to guide me, as she always did when we were children. *Just do the right thing, Gil. You know what that is.*

I do. For once in my life, publishing the story is not the priority.

Johnny Todd has finally made it out of the theatre and on to the stage. The DJ has timed the music to perfection. 'Song 2' by Blur, Labour's campaign anthem. The chorus kicks in as Todd steps forward, arms flapping in a disingenuous 'calm down' gesture. The crowd gets the joke and continues to roar: 'WOO-HOO.'

He will make the country feel good about itself, for a while. But what happens when we find out that it was never about what we need, that it was always about him? What then? Where will voters turn when they learn that they've been gulled?

Rona is on the podium to the left of Johnny, but just behind him. Neville Tudor is on her right, parallel with her. To the back of the stage, eyes lit with joy and excitement, is Marilyn. I am at the front, just yards from her, and I try to connect with her. I shout and wave, but she's blinded by the television lights, and my voice is lost in the rapturous roar. I have lost her, but I've found Clare.

It's time to go back to my desk and check the splash copy for the last edition. My sister has told me everything that happened. I'm not going to write it. Today.

Acknowledgments

This book is presumptuous. I love thrillers and crime stories. Dorothy L. Sayers and John Buchan are heroes of mine. But I would never have dared write one without the encouragement of Ben Willis of Bonnier Books UK. But where to set it? Which time, which place?

Today's politics are dizzyingly complex and emotional. I don't yet understand them well enough. But I am clear that the fraught politics of personal and national identity, their triumph over the politics of class, have their poisonous roots in what felt like a brave new dawn twenty-five years ago. Which is why Gil Peck is riding his bicycle in the spring of 1997.

I discussed the project with my agent Jonny Geller and my partner Charlotte Edwardes. I expected both to chuckle indulgently and suggest I return to the so-called 'real world'. But they surprised me by encouraging me to have a go (and in Charlotte's case to edit the almost-finished draft with her normal panache and suggest judicious excisions of my clunkier metaphors).

Ben put me in touch with a brilliant thriller writer, Tom Harper, who could not have been more generous with his guidance, especially on structure and pacing. As a very mature student,

I hope I haven't let Tom down too badly. Biggest thanks go to him, Charlotte, Jonny and Ben.

This fiction is my fault alone. But Phil Webster, a distinguished former political editor of the *Times*, responded with characteristic generosity when I couldn't remember some technical details about the era. And the brilliant former editor of the *Financial Times*, Richard Lambert, is to blame for whatever knowledge I possess about how the blessed system of running this place worked and works. Richard gave me my biggest break in journalism by recruiting me and providing me with a licence to make trouble, at a paper that historically was always a goody-two-shoes.

I wouldn't have had the guts to write this without the love and support of my boys Max and Simon, who came into my life in the mid 1990s, of the inspirational Charlotte, and of the wonderful Margot, Douglas and Audrey, who have so generously given me a home. The soundtrack to my writing was Margot on the bass, Douglas shouting profanities over the internet at his gaming friends and Audrey learning her BM portion.

The Whistleblower is of course entirely made up. But in writing it, memories of my sometimes complicated – and never boring – family were triggered, and made me realise quite how much I owe to the Pestons: my mum, Helen, my sister Juliet and my brother Edmund. I love them very much.

Robert Peston, London, June 2021

If you enjoyed *The Whistleblower*, why not join the

ROBERT PESTON READERS' CLUB?

When you sign up, you'll receive news about *The Whistleblower*, giveaways, events, and exclusive material from Robert Peston straight to your inbox.

To join, simply visit:
www.thewhistleblowerbook.com

Hello!

Thank you for picking up *The Whistleblower*.

I never thought that the four non-fiction books I have written were in any way an apprenticeship for the much harder challenge of novel-writing. Those books were collectively an attempt to chronicle the political and economic forces that have created today's world – a world that often feels stranger than fiction. And because the events we are living through are so extraordinary, I decided that just possibly, fiction would provide an alternative way of explaining how we got here.

So I decided to set my thriller in the 1990s. It is when today's generation of political and business leaders came of age. It is when the traditional dividing lines between political parties became confusingly blurred.

The title, *The Whistleblower*, is deliberately ambiguous. At the core of the book is a woman of deep principle who pays the biggest possible price for doing the right thing, and it explores how the powerful and rich make the decisions that affect our lives. Protagonist Gil, a political journalist, always believed the British way of catastrophe was born of cockup, not conspiracy. But that's all about to change.

If you would like to hear more about my books, you can visit **www.thewhistleblowerbook.com** where you can become part of the Robert Peston Readers' Club. It only takes a few moments to sign up, there are no catches or costs. Bonnier Books UK will keep your data private and confidential, and it will never be passed on to a third party. We won't spam you with loads of emails, just get in touch now and again with news about my books, and you can unsubscribe any time you want.

And if you would like to get involved in a wider conversation about my books, please do review *The Whistleblower* on Amazon, on GoodReads, on any other e-store, on your own blog and social media accounts, or talk about it with friends, family or reader groups! Sharing your thoughts helps other readers, and I always enjoy hearing about what people experience from my writing.

Thank you again for reading *The Whistleblower*.

All the best,

Robert Peston

Keep reading for a Q&A with Robert Peston,
exclusive to this edition of

THE WHISTLEBLOWER

Q&A with Robert Peston

What made you decide to turn to thriller writing?

Lockdown was to blame. Many of us thought, during the pandemic year, 'Well if I don't try something different now, then when?' So for better or worse, *The Whistleblower* is the fruit. That said, I've always wanted to write fiction, and had a first go when I was twenty-six (about every ten years I look at that original manuscript and wonder whether it can be rehabilitated).

Gil is a fascinating, driven and flawed protagonist. What was the inspiration for his character?

Gil is an amalgam of many people I've known. There are bits of me in there, such as his obsessive-compulsive disorder and drive to find out something that will be the splash (the big story of the day). But there are also slugs of other people. I wonder whether friends will ask me, 'Is that me?' The answer is no, because Gil is not someone I've ever met, though there are things about him that are recognisable and familiar.

Why did you decide to set the novel in the nineties? What drew you to that decade in particular?

I chose the nineties for three main reasons. First, it was the decade that was probably most important to me in my career as a journalist. It was when my skills as an investigative reporter had come to maturity, and I found a voice.

It was also an incredibly exciting decade. The country was regaining its confidence. And the shift from Thatcher to Blair was about more than politics. It was about culture, and our sense of who we are as a people.

The final reason I chose the nineties was because I don't yet want to write fiction about today, because I am still trying to understand the complex world we inhabit. But I am convinced that the big characteristics of today's politics and culture have their origins in the big shifts of the 1990s.

The London of *The Whistleblower* features political figures similar to, but different from, our own. How did you find the process of fictionalising real life? Were there any challenges?
It was very important to me that the setting for the book should be authentic and compelling, but I did not want this to be a *roman-á-clef*, with the reader trying to guess who is who. I felt that if anyone was too much like a real politician or business leader of the time, that would be a distraction from the story and the ideas. That said, it was important to me that everything said or done in the book should be plausible in the UK of the 1990s.

Throughout the novel, we are always keenly aware of the count-down to Election Day. What is the period before an election like for a political journalist in real life?
As I say in the book, it is the World Cup for political journalists. That's because politics is a competition. There is only one winner. And that winner is even more important than the victor in an international football tournament. Journalists are the commentators. But unlike football commentators, we can influence the outcome of the match, of the tournament. So the stakes

are high for us. It is the most exciting continuous five or six weeks of our jobs.

In *The Whistleblower* we learn that even the most 'strait-laced' characters are harbouring secrets. As a journalist, what do you think are the most important skills needed to uncover secrets and hidden truths?

I was an investigative journalist for many years. The most important skill you need is the ability to build a relationship with a source, win their trust, reassure them that you won't drop them in it, and persuade them it is in their interest to share their secrets with you. You see Gil using some of these techniques in *The Whistleblower*. I may write more about this in my next Gil Peck book!

What was your favourite part of the novel-writing process, and what did you find most challenging?

I greatly enjoyed going back to the 1990s, reimagining the times, trying to paint the scenes. It was like rediscovering an old friend. What I found hardest was pacing the book – what happens when – so that it creates the right amount of tension at the right time.

Which writers did you look to for inspiration? Were there any particular books or authors who influenced you?

I've always loved the classics of thriller and detective fiction: Dorothy L. Sayers, John Buchan, Conan Doyle, John le Carré. I am sure they influenced me, though not in a conscious way. Years ago, I was addicted to Sara Paretsky's V I Warshawsky series and Robert B. Parker's collection of wry detective stories about Spenser. I think I may have wanted to be Spenser.

What are you reading at the moment? Do you have any recommendations?

I read a lot of non-fiction, especially about cultural and political ideas. In the thriller genre, I recently discovered the Irish writer John Connolly. His Charlie Parker books, a melange of classic private dick conceits and slightly nutty magical realism, are terrific escapism.